ONE DEADLY SHOT

Wilkins laughed. "You ain't gettin' out of it. Pull your iron."

"I don't need the advantage," Wes said. "When you're ready, make your play."

"Draw, damn you!" Wilkins shouted. His trembling hands hovered near the butts of his twin Colts.

Wes Stone said nothing, waiting. Suddenly Wilkins moved with blinding speed, drawing both Colts. He fired, the roar of his first shot blending into the thunder of the other. But he was about to learn—as so many had learned before him—speed without accuracy only got a man killed. Both Wilkins' shots were wide, and he stood there unbelieving, his eyes on Wes Stone.

Wes drew his right-hand Colt. He fired only once, with deadly accuracy.

TRAIN
TO
DURANGO

Ralph Compton

A SIGNET BOOK

SIGNET
Published by the Penguin Group
Penguin Group (USA) LLC, 375 Hudson Street,
New York, New York 10014

USA | Canada | UK | Ireland | Australia | New Zealand | India | South Africa | China
penguin.com
A Penguin Random House Company

First published by Signet, an imprint of New American Library,
a division of Penguin Group (USA) LLC

First Printing, September 1998

Ⓟ REGISTERED TRADEMARK — MARCA REGISTRADA

ISBN 978-0-451-19237-0

Printed in the United States of America
20 19

This work is respectfully dedicated to the towns of Silverton and Durango, Colorado. I am indebted to the chambers of commerce for their promptness and generosity in supplying me with printed records of their fascinating history.

The Durango and Silverton Narrow Gauge Railroad—once known as the Denver and Rio Grande—is still in operation today, making daily runs from Durango to Silverton. These days, instead of hauling supplies and ore for the miners, these coal-fired, steam-powered locomotives carry curious passengers back through time, to the glory days of the Old West.

This little narrow-gauge railroad, and a few others like it, truly deserve to be remembered in the pages of American history.

Prologue

"It's hard to believe Nathan Stone's dead," said Bryan Silver, as he and Molly Horrel stood before the grassed-over grave. "I've been reluctant to question Wes, since he didn't know Nathan was his father until after the shoot-out and Nathan was gone. If it isn't too painful, perhaps you can fill in the missing parts."

"I've accepted it," Molly said, "but I still miss him. I'll tell you as much as I can."

"If it isn't too personal," said Silver. "I have the feeling that you and Nathan were more than just friends."

"We were," Molly said, "and I could never talk about him to just anyone. But I feel comfortable with you, because you knew him so well. Perhaps you can understand when I tell you that Nathan was sick of killing, of having to prove himself with his guns."

"I understand only too well," said Silver. "He came west after the war. He was riding a vengeance trail, seeking the seven deserters who had murdered his family in Virginia. But when he had found and held them accountable, he had the reputation of a fast gun. He had become a killer, and it grieved him."

"I thought—hoped—he had put the past behind

him," Molly said. "He had rescued me from a bad situation in south Texas. When he brought me here to Granny Boudleaux's boardinghouse, we became close. When Nathan returned to El Paso for the last time, he put away his guns. I believed there was a chance for me—us—until . . ."

"Until Nathan learned Wes was his son," said Silver.

"Yes," Molly said, swallowing hard. "Wes was so much like him—lightning quick with a gun and always ready to take a stand for what he believed was right—it was scary. Wes made enemies on both sides of the border, and when they came for him, Nathan had to choose between me and the son he had known only a few days."[1]

"You still have a grudge against Wes," said Silver. "It's in your eyes, when you look at him."

"Yes," Molly said, "and I'm sorry. But he's Nathan all over again, and when I look at him, I'm reminded of all that I lost. I . . . I almost . . . hate him."

Her voice broke, and silent tears crept down her cheeks. She seemed so very young, so vulnerable, that Silver put his arms around her. But she soon got control of herself, drawing away from him.

"What about Renita, the girl Wes left here when he rode into Mexico after the outlaws who gunned down Nathan?"

"I resented her, at first," said Molly. "It seemed like . . . she had everything that I'd lost. I was almost glad when outlaws stole her away and took her across the border. I suppose I was hoping they'd use and abuse her, and that Wes would no longer want her."

"They did use and abuse her," Silver said. "Wes found her in a Mexican whorehouse."

[1] *The Dawn of Fury, The Killing Season, The Autumn of the Gun*

Molly laughed. "He is just so damned much like Nathan. I was living with King Fisher in south Texas, and Nathan knew it. Yet, when King turned nasty and I ran away, I came to El Paso and Nathan took me in. Ma always told me to behave myself, because no decent man wanted used goods."[2]

"All men are not alike," said Silver. "Palo Elfego—better known as El Lobo—found a girl south of the border, as well. She had been sold to a whorehouse, and her own father had disowned her."

"I . . . I didn't know about either of them," Molly said. "They never spoke of those days in Mexico, after Was and El Lobo brought them here. Now they've been taken away again, and they may be dead. I feel just terrible. I'm a dreadful woman, for not having been more understanding. Wes and El Lobo didn't deserve losing them again."

"They haven't lost them yet," said Silver. "If they're alive, we'll find them."

"You're actually going with them?"

"I am," Silver said. "This same bunch of outlaws they fought in Mexico is now north of the border, and stronger than ever. They're engaged in activities that could bankrupt the United States. Wes and El Lobo agreed to go after them, and through their efforts the gang was defeated in California. Renita and Tamara have been taken in an attempt to lure Wes and El Lobo into a trap."[3]

"And you're riding into it with them," said Molly.

"If I have to," Silver replied. "I'd never send any man on a mission that I don't have the guts to tackle myself."

"Small wonder that you and Nathan were

[2] *The Autumn of the Gun* and *The Border Empire*
[3] *Sixguns and Double Eagles*

friends," said Molly. "You think and talk just like him."

"I'll take that as a compliment, ma'am," Silver said.

"When will . . . or will you ever be coming back here? Will I see you again?"

"Well, now," said Silver, "do you *want* to see me again?"

Blushing furiously, she turned away. Placing his hands on her shoulders, Silver turned her around until she faced him.

"Yes," she said, her eyes not meeting his. "Now you know me for the shameless, forward woman that I am."

"You want to see me again because I remind you of Nathan," Silver teased.

"No," said Molly. "You think and talk like Nathan, but you're not like him. I . . . mean . . . you . . . oh, I don't know *what* I mean."

Silver's hands were still on her shoulders, and when he drew her to him, she didn't resist.

"You're an honest woman, Molly Horrel," Silver said, "and if you're willing, I'd like to know you better."

"Promise me you won't ride off and get yourself killed," said Molly.

"This is still the frontier, and I can't make such a promise," Silver said, "but I promise to do my best. Having a pretty girl wantin' to see me again makes a difference."

The sun had set, its crimson rays beginning to fade, as the first gray fingers of twilight painted the western sky. Molly's eyes met Silver's in silent understanding. He kissed her long and hard, and she didn't resist.

*   *   *

"Eat," Granny Boudleaux urged, when Wes, El Lobo, Silver, and Molly were seated at the table.

"I'm not all that hungry," said Wes Stone. "I have the feeling Renita and Tamara are in great danger."

"You not eating won't change that," Molly said.

"She's right," said Silver. "We'll get an early start in the morning. It's the best we can do. Somebody pass me the biscuits."

The meal was eaten in silence. Granny Boudleaux cleared away the dishes, leaving the coffee cups. Wes and El Lobo sipped their coffee, but Silver drained his cup. Sliding back his chair, he got to his feet and started down the hall to the front porch. Without a word, Molly got up and followed. Pausing with the coffeepot, Granny Boudleaux laughed.

"Tarnation," Wes said, "she don't waste time, does she?"

"Hush," said Granny Boudleaux. "Time is not a woman's friend."

Silver had taken a seat on the front porch steps, and Molly sat down beside him.

"They're goin' to wonder about us," Silver said.

"I don't care," said Molly. "I've been alone too long."

"I don't know when I'll see you again," Silver said. "I must destroy this conspiracy, and when we've rescued Renita and Tamara, I'll be forced to return to Washington to tie up the loose ends. If I send you the money, will you join me there for a few days?"

"Yes," said Molly. "I'd go with you now if you'd let me."

"Too dangerous," Silver said. "Frankly, I can't be sure I'm not endangering you, just sitting here talking. These outlaws we're after have a habit of hitting a man where it hurts him the most."

"How long have you been . . . doing this?"

"Twenty-five years," said Silver. "I'm forty-five

years old, and there are times when I feel that I've about played out my hand. When this case is behind me, I might just hang it up, quit Washington, and return to Texas."

"Oh, I wish you would," Molly said. "I'll lie awake nights, worrying about you."

"I'm flattered," said Silver, "and I promise I'll devote some serious thought to it."

The night wore on, and when they returned to the house, Silver retired to the room Granny Boudleaux had prepared for him. As was their custom, Wes and El Lobo shared a room. When El Lobo got to his feet, Wes spoke.

"Go ahead and turn in for the night, *amigo*. I aim to go outside for a while."

El Lobo nodded. Granny Boudleaux and Molly said nothing. They all knew what Wes had in mind. He went out through the kitchen, across the back porch, into the yard. Stars twinkled from afar, and a pale half-moon had begun to rise. Wes stood before the grave of his father, his head bowed, swallowing hard. Suddenly, almost imperceptibly, he moved, and the twin Colts that had been Nathan Stone's leaped into his hands. Deftly he spun them, and they dropped neatly back into their tied-down holsters. The grass rustled and Empty, Nathan's blue tick hound was beside him. His hand on Empty's head and his eyes on the distant stars, he spoke in a hoarse whisper.

"I wanted you to be proud of me, and if you had some way of knowin', I believe you would be. I took your guns, your horse, and your name. I swear before God that I'll never dishonor you, and that I'll never forget you."

There was a low rumble from Empty's throat that wasn't quite a growl, for he hadn't forgotten this lonely grave or the man with whom he had shared

so many trails. When Wes turned away, his sense of
loss was stronger than ever, and within him was a
feeling he had never before experienced. He believed
he was seeing his father's grave for the last time.

El Paso, Texas, March 20, 1885

"You're sure the four men who took Renita and
Tamara rode north?" Wes asked.

"When they leave here, they ride north," said
Granny Boudleaux.

"Thank God they didn't cross the border into old
Mexico," Silver said. "That's a sign that the bunch
we're after will be holed up somewhere in the south-
western United States."

Wes, El Lobo, and Silver were traveling light, carrying only what would fit into their saddlebags. They
had mounted their horses, but before they could ride
away, Molly ran to Silver. He leaned from the saddle,
and not caring what anybody thought, she threw her
arms around him. Granny Boudleaux smiled approv-
ingly while Wes looked away. El Lobo watched with
interest, a rare half grin on his rugged face. Anticipating their direction, Empty had bounded on ahead.
The trio rode north, not looking back.

Santa Fe, New Mexico, March 20, 1885

A few miles south of town, on the west bank of
the Rio Grande, four men hunkered around a fire,
drinking coffee from tin cups. A nearby cabin, built
of logs, had a single door, no windows, and a shake
roof. Smoke curled from a stick-and-mud chimney.

"I'm almighty tired settin' here watchin' this damn

cabin," Bolivar said. "Them females ain't goin' nowhere."

"Two of us could stay here, while the other two rides into town," said Reeves.

"*Sí*," Chavez said, "but that is not what the Señor Stringfield pay us to do. He say the two *hombres* that we must kill are *diablos* with the *pistola*. He say they be a match for us all."

"I'm with Chavez," said Hamilton. "We don't know these hell-raisers, and I can't see payin' the four of us, unless we're all needed. I reckon we'd better foller orders and stay here until we earn our money."

"At least he could have let us have our way with the women," Bolivar growled. "When we've gunned down the *hombres* that's comin' after 'em, who's gonna complain?"

Reeves laughed. "Stringfield didn't say we could strip 'em, either, but we did."

"We may regret that," said Hamilton. "Killin' a man is one thing, but mistreatin' his woman is somethin' else. Many an *hombre*'s had his neck stretched, just for insultin' some whore. These have the look of decent women."

Reeves laughed again. "When a woman's naked as a skint coyote, how do you tell the decent one from a whore?"

"For one who has known nothing but whores, it would not be easy," Chavez observed.

"Why, you damn Mex," said Reeves with a snarl, "don't you talk down to me."

He started to draw, but thought better of it, for Chavez already had him covered. The ugly muzzle of the Mexican's Colt was steady.

"When this job is done, I don't care if you kill each other," Hamilton said, "but I'll not have you messin' things up now. Put the gun away, Chavez."

Easing the weapon's hammer down, Chavez holstered it.

"This is the start of the second week since we took them women from El Paso," said Bolivar. "Suppose them *hombres* Stringfield's paid us to gun down don't show up? We'll be out of grub in another week."

"They'll be here," Hamilton said, "and we got to be ready for 'em. Remember what we was told about there bein' more work for us in Denver? If we botch this, Stringfield's likely to have us paid off in lead."

Within the cabin, Renita and Tamara sat near the fire, trying to keep warm.

"All outlaws are of a single mind," said Renita bitterly. "Can't they capture a woman without taking her clothes and leaving her stark naked?"

"It is better than it was in Mexico," Tamara said. "They have not sold us to a whorehouse."

"Only because they have something else in mind," said Renita. "We're bait for a trap."

"They want Wes and Palo," Tamara said, "but how will Wes and Palo know we have been taken away, and how will they find us?"

"The outlaws must know Wes and Palo are returning to El Paso," said Renita, "and I'm sure the men who took us left a trail for them to follow."

"We must not let them ride into a trap," Tamara said.

"We're stuck here in this cabin, with a locked door, no windows, four armed men outside, and not a stitch of clothes between us," said Renita. "What can we do?"

"We used our bodies to kill two guards in Mexico City," Tamara said. "Do all men not lust for the same thing?"[4]

"You just answered that question," said Renita. "In

[4] *The Border Empire*

the prison in Mexico City, we had only the two men. Here, we have four. They come in only two at a time when they bring us food, and they don't come near us. I think they will control their lust until they have killed Wes and Palo."

"I do not believe they will kill Wes and Palo," Tamara said. "They will know it is but a trap, and they will find a way to save us."

"Oh, I hope you're right," said Renita.

"I am right," Tamara said. "There is but one door, and the outlaws watch it, but this cabin is on the river bank, its back next to the river. Wes and Palo will not come through the door."

"But the walls are built of heavy logs," said Renita.

"The spaces between the logs are chinked with mud," Tamara said. "Some of the sticks they've given us for kindling can be used to dig the mud out. We cannot escape, but when Wes and Palo come, there will be enough of a hole for them to learn we are in here. I am ashamed of myself for not having thought of it sooner. Time grows short."

"You're right," Renita said. "Let's start digging now."

"One of us will dig at the chinking while the other listens at the door," said Tamara. "They must not discover what we are doing. You listen at the door, and I will begin."

Wes, El Lobo, and Silver followed the Rio Grande north, for it had been a dry year and the river was a ready source of water.

"We can follow the river right on into Santa Fe," Silver said. "Riding north from El Paso, it's the most logical destination. If they aimed to leave a trail for us, we'll be findin' tracks."

"Six horses will leave quite a trail," said Wes, "but we can't be sure they're the right tracks. Could be some *hombres* from south of the border, riding north on a raid."

"Not likely," Silver said. "You and El Lobo raised so much hell in Mexico last year, the powers in Mexico City are having to make a show of patroling the border."[5]

After a few miles, the riverbank turned sandy, with little vegetation. There were tracks of deer, coyotes, and shod horses. El Lobo dismounted and began studying the horse tracks.

"How old are those tracks?" Silver asked.

"Week, per'ap," said El Lobo.

But all the tracks were not visible all the time, and El Lobo studied the ground for almost a mile before he had accounted for all the horses. Nodding to Wes and Silver, he mounted his horse, and the trio continued along the river. Eventually there were open stretches of sand where Wes and Silver could see tracks of six horses.

"We'd better start thinking in terms of an ambush," Silver said. "We know they're riding north, so we don't have to follow the actual tracks. We can parallel the river, riding back to it occasionally to be sure they haven't changed directions."

It was sound thinking, and after riding a mile west, they again rode north.

"How far it be from El Paso to Santa Fe?" El Lobo asked.

"About three hundred miles, as I recall," said Silver. "I can't imagine six riders undertaking such a ride, unless they're lawmen or outlaws. Texas Rangers would be somewhat out of their jurisdiction."

Empty was well ahead of them, and they rode the rest of the day without sighting the riders they pursued.

[5] *The Border Empire*

"If we aim to have a supper fire," Wes said, "we'd better eat before dark."

Near sundown, they reined up, dismounted, and unsaddled their horses. Wes lit a small fire, putting it out when the coffee was ready and their bacon had been broiled. It was still early, so instead of turning in for the night, they talked.

"Silver," said Wes, "we're obliged to you for joining us in our search for Renita and Tamara, but what do you aim to do after we've found them?"

"Washington allowed me a month to rest and recuperate," Silver said, "and if we end this chase near Santa Fe, I'll still have two weeks that I don't have to account for. I aim to use that to learn as much as I can about the Golden Dragon. Since they've pulled out of California, I won't be surprised if they've left New Orleans and Carson City as well. That'll mean they've dug in somewhere else. If I can get some idea as to where they are—some kind of lead—then I'll telegraph Washington for permission to remain in the West for as long as it takes. Until I've broken this counterfeiting ring for all time, or until they have finished me."

"That's about what I expected," said Wes, "and I'm of a mind to throw in with you to the finish. I think El Lobo and me owe them a lot more than we've been allowed to repay. How do you feel, Palo?"

"Feel same," El Lobo said, "but what we do with Renita and Tamara?"

"I appreciate your willingness to join me in pursuit of the Dragon," said Silver, "but El Lobo has a point. This will be a fight to the finish, and entirely too dangerous for women, however courageous they may be. And you certainly can't risk returning them to El Paso, to Granny Boudleaux's."

"No," Wes said. "I'm not even considering that.

Remember, I once worked for the railroad, and I have friends in Dodge City. We can put Renita and Tamara up at the Dodge House. I'll ask Harley Stafford and Foster Hagerman to look out for them."[6]

"That might work," said Silver. "In fact, I could set up headquarters there, myself. At least until we have some sense of direction in this infernal situation."

"My arms grow tired," Tamara said. "It is your turn, while I listen at the door."

Taking up the stick Tamara had been using, Renita began digging at the hardened mud between the logs. Using only a stick, it was tiring, difficult work, but Tamara had made some progress. After only a few minutes, Renita could feel cool outside air.

"I've broken through," said Renita excitedly.

"Keep digging," Tamara said. "We must widen the hole."

"It's a little easier now," said Renita.

Soon there was an inch-wide gap between two of the logs, and by the time Tamara was ready to take a turn, there was an open crack almost two feet long.

"I will begin digging between the next two logs," Tamara said.

Wes, El Lobo, and Silver waited until daylight before lighting their breakfast fire. The meal was eaten quickly, and with Empty bounding ahead, the trio again rode north.

"We're covering at least a hundred miles a day," said Silver. "Unless these *hombres* are holed up somewhere beyond Santa Fe, we ought to be catching up to them sometime late tomorrow."

"They be in town, it be hell," El Lobo said.

[6] *The Autumn of the Gun*

"It's unlikely they'll be in Santa Fe," said Silver. "If they're planning to ambush you and Wes, they won't try it where the law's close enough to get involved. I think they'll be laying for us long before we reach town."

Their third day on the trail, an hour before sundown, Silver, Wes, and El Lobo reined up to rest the horses. Empty came trotting back, and when he was a few yards away, the hound turned back the way he had come. He paused, and looking back, growled softly.

"He's found something or somebody," Wes said. "I'll follow him. Maybe this is the camp we're looking for."

Wes followed on foot, and Empty led him back toward the distant Rio Grande. Before they reached the river, within a tangle of brush, Empty waited for Wes. There was a faint odor of wood smoke, and three hundred yards away Wes could see the gable end of the log cabin. Smoke curled from the stick-and-mud chimney. Suddenly the cabin door opened, and two men emerged, laughing. One of them dropped a heavy bar in place across the door. There was no wind, and Wes was unable to hear their words, for they were walking away from him, toward the opposite end of the cabin. But he had seen enough. Quickly he returned to his companions.

"I saw only two men," said Wes, "but there's a bar across the door of the cabin. Its back is facing the river. After dark, maybe we can approach it from the river and find out if Renita and Tamara are in there."

"I go," El Lobo said.

Wes and Silver said nothing, for they were well aware of the Indian's ability to move soundlessly through the night. Not daring to risk a fire, they ate jerked beef and drank river water. Two hours after darkness had fallen, El Lobo prepared to visit the cabin. The moon had not risen, and when the Indian faded into the shadows beneath the trees, Empty went with him.

"I'd be interested in knowing how he intends to find out if Renita and Tamara are in that cabin," Silver said.

"So would I," said Wes. "If there's a way, he'll find it."

Reaching the river well below the cabin, El Lobo climbed carefully down the bank. The water ran shallow, and he avoided it when he could. When he could not, he lifted each foot carefully. Empty had crossed the river and had become a silent moving shadow on the opposite bank. The riverbank on which the cabin stood was high enough to conceal a man, and El Lobo was careful to remain in its shadow. Nearing the cabin, he could hear men's voices somewhere beyond it. He soon stood looking at the barren log wall that was the back of the cabin. There was no sign of a window. Suddenly his alert ears caught a sound that was foreign to the night. A rasping, scraping noise, it seemed to come from the cabin itself. Quietly, carefully, El Lobo crept up the riverbank until he was near the back wall of the cabin. He waited, listening, and the strange noise started again. He dropped to his knees, and between two of the logs there was a flicker of light. The fire inside the cabin!

"Tamara," El Lobo whispered. "*Querido.*"

"Palo," came the response, "this is Renita. Tamara is here."

In an instant, Tamara was beside the wall.

"There are four *hombres*, Palo," said Renita, "and they have taken our clothes. What would you have us do?"

"You have wood and you have fire," El Lobo said. "Pile the wood next to the door and set fire to it. The fire will draw the *hombres* who take you prisoner. When they come, we will be waiting for them."

"We will do as you say," said Tamara softly. "*Vaya con Dios.*"

Silently, El Lobo crept away. When he was far enough downriver, he climbed the bank and made his way hurriedly to where Wes and Silver waited. Quickly he related to them what he had learned, and what he had instructed Tamara and Renita to do.

"That's a stroke of genius," Silver said. "We don't know where those varmints are, and we'd be prime targets, goin' near that cabin. But when that fire becomes big enough for them to see it, they'll come running. Then they'll become our targets."

Quickly they took their Winchesters from their saddle boots, and leaving their horses where they were, started for the cabin on foot. They approached the cabin from the front, concealing themselves within rifle range, where they had a good view of the door. They didn't have long to wait. Flames were soon climbing the door and licking hungrily at the shake roof.

"By God, they've set the cabin afire," Bolivar shouted. "Come on."

Once the four men were plainly visible in the starlight and in the light from the cabin's flaming door, Silver shouted a challenge.

"You're covered. Stand where you are and drop your guns."

But the challenge went unheeded. The four men went for their guns, firing at the sound of Silver's voice. But Silver and his companions were bellied-down with Winchesters, and the slugs sang harmlessly over their heads. Their return fire was deadly, and the four outlaws were cut down.

"Let's go," Wes shouted. "There's still time to put out that fire."

He reached the cabin first, tearing away the bar that secured the door. When it swung open, Silver and El Lobo ripped the flaming door loose. Wes kicked away the embers that had started the fire. In an instant, Renita was out the door, Tamara right behind her.

"Tarnation," said Wes, "every time I rescue you, you're jaybird naked."

"*Sí*," El Lobo said. "Tamara too."

The response from Renita and Tamara was very unladylike. Bryan Silver laughed.

Chapter 1

"I'll find the outlaws' camp," Silver said. "We'll need at least two of their horses."

"See if you can find clothes and boots for Tamara and me," said Renita. "We're just not getting much sympathy from these two coyotes."

Silver laughed. "I'll see what I can find."

When Silver departed, Empty followed him.

"*Perro* 'fraid," El Lobo said.

"He didn't like the stormy reception we just got," said Wes.

"It was no worse than the reception *we got*," Renita snapped. "We've been penned up here a week, afraid for our lives, and neither of you seemed concerned about how we might feel. Instead, you brought a strange man with you, and pointed out that both of us are naked."

"Hell, both of you *are* naked," said Wes, "and you've been among strange men for a week. The *hombre* with us is no stranger. He's Bryan Silver, and I'm fair-to-middlin' sure he's seen naked females before."

Tamara laughed. "We are not strangers to strange men, having been held captive in Mexican whorehouses. The Señor Silver is welcome."

"Thank you," Wes said. "He was a friend of my father's, and he's a good friend to El Lobo and me."

"Oh," said Renita, "it was him who took you away for so long, leaving us in El Paso."

"He didn't take us away," Wes said angrily. "He asked for our help, and we went willingly."

"We soon go again," El Lobo added.

"Then I'm going with you," said Renita. "You're not leaving me in El Paso, at the mercy of outlaws."

"*Sí*," Tamara said, "I don't stay in El Paso again."

"We don't intend to leave you in El Paso again," said Wes. "We'll talk about it later. For now, for Silver's sake, try to keep a civil tongue. Keep clawin' at us like a pair of harpies, and Silver will be wonderin' why we bothered trackin' down either of you."

Renita and Tamara said nothing, and Wes didn't know if they had accepted what he'd had to say, or if they had merely taken refuge in angry silence. Finally there was the thump of horses' hooves. Silver was returning.

"I kept two of the horses and turned the others loose," Silver said. "There was a pile of clothes and boots, so I brought them all. Now we'll make ourselves scare, so you ladies can sort them out and get dressed."

"You are *caballeroso*," said Tamara, "but you need not go. You are a *copanero*."

"*Gracias*," Silver said. "You are a *dama*, and I have heard much about you."

"*Bueno*," said El Lobo, obviously pleased.

Renita said nothing, and Wes thought she seemed a little put out because of Silver's gracious attention to Tamara.

"I'm goin' to search those *hombres* we gunned down," Wes said. "We just might find something useful."

"I help," said El Lobo.

Wes was somewhat amused, because Silver remained with Renita and Tamara, helping them untangle their clothing and to untie the knots for which the vengeful outlaws had been responsible.

"Squaw have sharp tongue," El Lobo said, when they were far enough away that Renita couldn't hear.

"One more word from her, and I'll take a quirt to her behind," said Wes. "Damn it, I had nothin' to do with her bein' penned up here, naked."

El Lobo laughed. "You leave her in El Paso, and the Dragon use her to set trap for you, *amigo*."

"Don't you dare say that where she can hear you," Wes said, "or I'll take the quirt to you."

Quickly they went about the gruesome task of searching the four dead men. Using a hat that had belonged to one of them, they collected the contents of their pockets. By the time they had finished, Renita and Tamara were dressed and tugging on their boots.

"We're not more than a few miles from Santa Fe," said Silver. "Tamara and Renita are half starved. I think we should ride on into town."

"I could use some grub, myself," Wes said. "That jerked beef and river water is about used up."

"We find much *oro* on dead outlaws," said El Lobo. "Talking paper, too."

"The gold's likely counterfeit," Silver said, "but the paper could be interesting. We'll take a look at it by lamplight, when we reach town."

Within an hour, they could see the lights of Santa Fe.

"Unless somebody has a better idea, I recommend the Santa Fe Hotel," said Silver. "An all-night cafe is close by."

"Empty knows the cook," Wes said. "El Lobo and me have eaten at the cafe and spent some time at the hotel before."

They went to the hotel first.

"How many rooms?" the clerk asked.

"One for me," said Silver.

"Two for the rest of us," Wes said.

"I hope you're not expecting Tamara and me to share a room," said Renita, when they had taken their keys and started down the hall. "She's as tired sleeping with me as I am of sleeping with her."

"*Sí*," Tamara agreed.

"The furthest thing from my mind," said Wes. "In fact, I was thinkin' we could forget about the grub and go straight to bed."

"Go on, then," Renita said, "but Tamara and me are going with Mr. Silver. He's agreed to feed us, and we haven't had a decent meal since we were taken from Granny's place, in El Paso."

"Oh, I reckon El Lobo and me can force down a few bites," said Wes. "Besides, we got to keep an eye on Silver. He's promised to Molly Horrel."

"Oh?" said Renita. "There must be something going on that Tamara and me don't know about."

"Considerable," Wes said, "and if you don't stop chewin' on my tail feathers, I won't ever tell you."

"Just keep one thing in mind, ladies," said Silver. "You can't believe everything this pair of coyotes tell you."

Reaching the cafe, they found it virtually deserted, for the hour was late. There was no problem getting the cook to feed Empty, for he remembered the dog from the last time El Lobo and Wes had been in Santa Fe.

"I got steak, ham, eggs, biscuits, spuds, onions, coffee, and apple pie," the cook said.

"Bring us some of all that," Silver said. "Scramble the eggs and put on a second pot of coffee."

"*Bueno*," said Tamara. "I follow the Señor Silver anywhere."

El Lobo laughed, and Wes regarded him with some envy. Renita said nothing. There was almost no conversation, and when the food was brought, they all dug in. Nobody had anything to say until they were down to last cups of coffee.

"After lying around on the dirt floor of that cabin for a week, I'm terribly in need of a bath," Renita said.

"*Sí*," said Tamara, "as am I."

"A tub and hot water can be brought up to your rooms," Silver said, "and while the two of you are taking your baths, Wes, El Lobo, and me can get together in my room. We still have to examine what was taken from the pockets of those outlaws."

"Then we won't know what you discover," said Renita.

"Wes and El Lobo can tell you as much as they feel it's safe for you to know," Silver replied. "The outfit that took you and Tamara from Granny Boudleaux's has reorganized, and is probably more powerful than ever."

"So you're going after them, taking Wes and Palo with you," said Renita.

"Renita," Wes said angrily, "it's not your place to interfere in Silver's business."

"It's my place to interfere in anything that could get you shot dead," said Renita, her eyes on Silver.

"She's right, Wes," Silver said. "Once you commit yourself to a woman, you have to put her first. Just as I valued Nathan Stone's friendship, I value that of you and El Lobo, and I won't rope you into anything that might damage your relationship with these young ladies."

Silver's gray eyes rested for only a second on Wes and El Lobo. He then looked at Renita and Tamara, and something about him had a profound effect on the two women.

"If it is something Palo feels he must do, I will

never stand in his way," said Tamara. "Not even if it costs him his life."

"I feel the same way about Wes," Renita said, "and I'm sorry that I have allowed my selfishness to take control of me."

"This has been difficult for both of you," said Silver, "and I in no way regard either of you as selfish. Wes and El Lobo have never faltered in the face of danger, and I have every confidence in their ability to accomplish what they set out to do. There's a diabolical conspiracy that could destroy this nation, and I'll fight it alone, if I must. Wes and El Lobo are almost solely responsible for the recent success in California, and if I have any choice, there's no other two men alive that I'd rather have siding me."

"Bryan Silver," said Tamara, "you are an inspiration. I do not know of this conspiracy, but I will urge Palo to join you. I would go myself if you would have me."

"So would I," Renita said.

Silver laughed, his eyes twinkling. "I am flattered, ladies. While the danger is such we can't allow you into the thick of the battle, you'll be considerably closer than El Paso, and I will be here until we have won. Wes and El Lobo will tell you more about what they have in mind. For now, I think we'd better be getting back to the hotel if you're to have your baths tonight."

With Renita and Tamara safely in their rooms, Wes and El Lobo knocked on Silver's door. Not wishing to remain in the room with Renita, Empty had gone with Wes. Silver opened the door, closing and locking it when Wes, El Lobo, and Empty had entered. Wes held the hat in which he had collected the belongings of the four dead outlaws, and upending the hat, he spread the items out on the bed.

"Four thousand in double eagles," said Silver,

"and I'm betting every last one of them is counterfeit."

"Let's see," Wes said.

Removing a knife from inside his right boot, he scraped the surface of one of the gold coins. Beneath a thin coating of gold, there was base metal. Quickly he scraped a dozen more, with the same result.

"Enough," said Silver. "Let's look at the rest of it."

There were two of the Dragon coins, with a dragon head on one side and a numeral one on the other.

"Proof enough that we're closing in on the Dragon," Wes said. "The coins they used in old Mexico had a numeral three, while those in California had a numeral two. Now these have a numeral one."

There were two scraps of paper, and Silver was studying them.

"Not much to go on," said Wes. "Just three words: *Grand Hotel, Denver.*"

"It could be a meeting place, a rendezvous," Silver said. "Had these *hombres* successfully bushwhacked you and El Lobo, they would have gotten more money."

"What about this piece of paper?" Wes said. "There's just one word: *Stringfield.*"

"Might be the name of a town," said Silver, "or the name of a man. Maybe these two pieces of paper go together. Stringfield may be the name of the contact, and the place the Grand Hotel in Denver."

"Should be easy enough to find out if there's anybody named Stringfield at the Grand Hotel," Wes said. "In fact, if we're going on to Dodge, we'll be able to take the train from Boulder. To get there, we'll have to ride almost through Denver. If this Stringfield is still there, expecting to hear from his four killers, we don't have any time to spare. If we go on to Dodge and *then* return to Denver, too much time will have passed, and he'll know the bush-whacking failed."

"You're dead right," said Silver. "We'd better ride out in the morning. I'd say it's at least three hundred miles to Boulder. If Stringfield *is* a contact, and he's at the Grand in Denver, it could be the start of something big time. We'll eat early in the morning and be ready to ride at first light. You'd better break the news to Renita and Tamara tonight."

"We will," Wes said.

El Lobo knocked on the door, identified himself, and was let in. Wes knocked on his own door, and when he had identified himself, Renita let him in. The lamp was turned low. The tub was still there, towels draped over its edge. Renita wore nothing but a smile.

"I reckon that water's cold," said Wes. "I could use some washing, myself."

"It's not all that cold," Renita said. "Wash, and I will watch."

"You'd better get in bed," said Wes. "We ride out at first light tomorrow, on our way to Boulder, Colorado."

"I don't care," Renita said. "We're going to have tonight, if we never have anything else."

Wes didn't get into the tub, but soaked one of the towels, using it to wash away some of the trail dust.

"Why are we going to Boulder, Colorado?" Renita asked.

"From there, we'll be taking the train to Dodge City," said Wes. "I once worked for the railroad, and was headquartered in Dodge. I have friends there. You and Tamara will be staying at the Dodge House. Silver will be there too, until this case is closed."

"I believe Tamara and me have the right to know what this conspiracy is all about," Renita said. "Silver seemed to think so too."

"I reckon you're right," said Wes. "In the left front pocket of my Levi's there are some double eagles with their faces mutilated. Get them."

The half dozen coins were counterfeit, taken from the slain outlaws. Renita spread them out on the bed, and Wes told her as much as he felt she needed to know.

"You and Palo are involved in something truly grand," Renita said. "But there are so many of them, and they're so powerful, how do you know where to start?"

"We found something on one of the dead men that might be a lead," said Wes. "We'll find out when we reach Denver."

"You've satisfied my curiosity about that," Renita said. "Now tell me about Silver and Molly Horrel."

"I've been away for months," said Wes. "Now we have a room all to ourselves, with a soft bed, and all you want to do is talk."

"I have plans for more than that," Renita said, "but first, I want to hear about Silver and Molly."

Wes sighed. Stretching out on the bed, he told her of the mutual interest that Silver and Molly seemed to share.

"I'm glad for her," said Renita. "Bryan Silver is the kind of man who would make any woman proud."

"I reckon," Wes said. "If he wasn't interested in Molly, I wouldn't want him spendin' too much time with you."

Renita laughed. "You're jealous of him."

"Some," said Wes. "There's just something about him. If I could figure out what it is and sell it, I'd be rich. I just had the feeling that if El Lobo and I hadn't been around, Silver would have had you and Tamara in bed with him. One at a time, or both at once."

"You won't have to worry about that," Renita said.

"If Molly has her claws in him, he won't have the time or strength for anybody else."

"You don't like Molly, do you?"

"No," said Renita. "After your father was killed, she'd have gone after you, if you had not ridden off to Mexico, hunting the Sandlin gang."[1]

"Tarnation, she's ten years older than me," Wes said.

"Nathan was ten years older than Molly," said Renita. "King Fisher was as old or older than Nathan, and Molly lived with him until they had a falling out. Any difference in age won't matter to a woman, as long as everything works out under the sheet."

"You can be *so* damn crude, and without cause," Wes said. "Molly doesn't even like me. She blamed me for my father's death."

"Perhaps at first," said Renita, "but you don't understand women, Wes Stone."

"Then I reckon it's time I was figurin' them out, startin' with you," Wes said.

Quickly he blew out the lamp and piled under the covers with her, while in the next room, El Lobo and Tamara still talked.

"I am proud of you, Palo," said Tamara. "It is an honor to have won the friendship and confidence of such a man as Bryan Silver."

"*Sí*," El Lobo said, pleased. "He *bueno hombre*."

In his room Bryan Silver lay across the bed, having removed only his hat and gunbelt. He did not know how long he might remain in Dodge, or what danger he must face in the days ahead. Leaning over, he turned up the lamp's flame. There was a bedside table with a drawer, and within it a few sheets of writing paper and some envelopes with the hotel's name and address. Sitting on the bed, using the bed-

[1] *The Border Empire*

side table, he quickly wrote a one-page letter. He folded the letter, placing it in an envelope, which he then addressed to Molly Horrel in El Paso. Removing his wallet from his coat pocket, he counted out five hundred dollars in currency. Tomorrow, before leaving El Paso, he would purchase a bank draft.

Across the street from the hotel, two men had concealed themselves in the shadows, as Silver, Wes, El Lobo, Tamara, and Renita had left the cafe.

"By God, it's them," said Olson. "We could gun them down from here."

"And have the law after us," Baker said. "We'll wait for a better time and place."

"Him and that damn Indian has got to die," said Olson. "I ain't forgettin' how they took our horses in the mountains, leavin' us to hoof it two hundred miles back to Santa Fe."

"I ain't forgot," Baker said, "but I ain't forgot they can shoot like hell wouldn't have it. They ain't shorthorns, either. We was all set to bushwhack them, when they got ahead of us, got the drop, and took our horses. We got to be careful."[2]

Silver was dressed, shaved, and ready to go when Wes knocked on his door.

"I know we aimed to leave at first light," said Silver, "but I have some business with a bank, and I must post a letter. We'll be maybe two hours later than planned."

"Might be just as well," Wes said. "I'm ready, and so is El Lobo, but not so with our women. After near two weeks of sleeping on the ground, they were ready for a bed."

Silver laughed. "I don't reckon you and El Lobo

[2] *Sixguns and Double Eagles*

keeping them awake late had anything to do with 'em not being up this morning?"

"Maybe," said Wes. "It took considerable time, telling them about the Golden Dragon. That, and we had to bullyrag them some. We told 'em you'd never seen a naked female before, and you was totally mortified."

He said it with a straight face, but he couldn't maintain it. Silver paled, and Wes had to laugh at his shocked expression.

"Damn you," Silver said, "you have your daddy's poker face. He could and would bluff with a pair of deuces."

"You should have brought Molly with you," said Wes. "Then you'd have somebody to talk to you."

"You could be in for some surprises," Silver said. "Even Nathan didn't understand my every move, and neither do you."

El Lobo came in, accompanied by Empty, who had been waiting in the hall.

"Tamara don't be awake," said El Lobo.

"I'm not surprised," Silver said. "You likely kept her awake all night."

"*Sangre de Cristo,*" said El Lobo, "she keep *me* awake."

"Let her rest a while," Silver said. "I have some business to attend to, and the banks won't open for another two hours."

"Since we're gettin' a late start," said Wes, "Renita and Tamara can eat when they're ready. I'm hungry now."

"So am I," Silver said. "I can eat now, and again before we leave town."

"*Bueno,*" said El Lobo.

With Empty following, they headed for the cafe. They were on the boardwalk, away from the protection of the hotel, when the roar of a Winchester shattered the early morning stillness. Wes stumbled as a slug ripped through his upper left arm, while a second one sent El Lobo's hat flying. Silver had his Colt out, but instead of firing, he had started across the street in a zigzag run. El Lobo was right behind him. Wes remained where he was, for there were no more shots from the bushwhacker. Men hurried from the cafe, and several from the hotel lobby, including the desk clerk.

"Charlie, fetch Doc Padgett," the desk clerk ordered.

One of the men from the hotel hurried away, as Silver and El Lobo returned.

"The varmint lit out when he saw us comin' after him," said Silver. "There's an alley with rat holes everywhere."

"I'm not hard hit," Wes said. "It missed the bone."

"Come on back into the lobby," said the hotel desk clerk. "I'm sure the sheriff will be wanting to talk to you."

Several blocks away, Baker and Olson crouched in the shadow of a vacant building.

"Damn it," Olson said, "you missed the Indian. Now they'll be on their guard, and we may not get another chance."

"You didn't do no better," said Baker. "You just nicked Stone in the arm."

"We'd better get back to our roomin' house and stay there for a while," Olson said. "I look for the sheriff to be nosin' around, asking questions."

"Yeah," said Baker. "That old woman we're rentin' from has been askin' around, tryin' to find out where our money comes from. I'm tempted to tell the old bat we're robbing banks and stages."

When Dr. Padgett arrived, he quickly cleansed and dressed the wound. There was no sign of the sheriff.

"I'm goin' back to my room for a clean shirt," Wes said. "Then we'll go eat."

Leaving Silver and El Lobo in the lobby, Wes returned to the room, where he expected to find Renita still asleep. But she sat on the edge of the bed, leaping to her feet when she saw the bloodied sleeve of his shirt.

"You're hurt," she cried. "What happened?"

"Bushwhacker fired at us," said Wes. "Silver and El Lobo went after him, but he lost them in an alley."

Wes hadn't locked the door, and Tamara rushed in.

"I heard Renita cry out," she said.

"Silver, El Lobo, and I were ambushed," said Wes. "Nobody was hit except me. I'm needin' a clean shirt."

"Oh, let's leave here as soon as we can," Renita said.

"Silver, El Lobo, and me were goin' to the cafe," said Wes, "and I'm still hungry. Both of you are awake now. Come on and go with us."

"I must go for my boots," Tamara said, "and I will be ready."

Renita wore not a stitch, and she blushed. Tamara laughed.

"I think it take her some longer," said Tamara, as she closed the door behind her.

"I think so too," Wes said. "Cover yourself with something, Lady Godiva. I'm half starved."

"You're making fun of me," said Renita. "I was about to get up, when you came in, all bloody. You shocked me."

"I've been bloodier than that," Wes said. "I don't understand how the Dragon's forces learned we were here."

"How do you know it was them?"

"I don't *know* it for a fact," said Wes, "but who else could it be? I have the name of a fast draw, and while there are some who would like to test me, they wouldn't shoot at me from cover. This varmint just narrowly missed shootin' El Lobo in the head. There's no gun glory, killing from ambush."

"If they're Golden Dragon killers, they'll follow us when we leave here, won't they?"

"I don't know," Wes said, "but we dare not overlook the possibility."

Tamara returned just as Renita was brushing her hair. Wes had already donned a clean shirt, and there was no evidence of his wound. When Renita was ready, the three of them met Silver and El Lobo in the lobby.

"The two of you don't look all that used up," Silver said, looking at the women. "Wes and El Lobo said you kept them awake all night."

"We did," said Renita, "and we'll do it again tonight."

"Don't get too noisy with it," Silver said. "We'll all be on the ground, and I'm a light sleeper."

With Empty following, they again started for the cafe. When they entered, several men nodded to them, having witnessed the shooting. They ordered their food, and when they had eaten, Silver slid back his chair and stood up.

"I have some business to attend to," said Silver. "All of you can stay here and drink coffee, or return to the hotel. I shouldn't be more than half an hour."

"That bushwhacker may be looking for you, as well as for El Lobo and me," Wes said. "Maybe one of us should go with you."

"No," said Silver. "I can take care of myself."

He left the cafe, walking along the street toward the busier part of town.

Chapter 2

Rance Stringfield was distinctly uncomfortable as he knocked on Drade Hogan's door. He was bid enter, and when Hogan nodded toward a chair, Stringfield sat down. He didn't waste any time.

"The men I hired in El Paso were to telegraph me upon the successful completion of their mission. I have heard nothing."

"You are sure they've had sufficient time?"

"Yes," said Stringfield. "They've had more than enough time."

"They've failed, then," Hogan said. "I can forgive anything except failure."

"I paid them with Dragon double eagles," said Stringfield desperately. "I am returning all the expense money you advanced me."

"I don't care a damn about the money," Hogan snapped. "Abducting the women and using them to bait a trap was your idea. Must I remind you that I don't pay for failure?"

"Damn it. I did the best I could," said Stringfield angrily.

"I don't buy excuses, either," Hogan said. "You are dismissed."

"But I—"

"*I said you are dismissed,*" Hogan shouted.

Without looking at Hogan, Stringfield got up and

left the office, closing the door behind him. The girl at the desk in the outer office regarded him with what might have been pity. Stringfield left the building, returning to his room at the Grand Hotel.

"You wanted to see me?" Gandy Franks asked, as he entered Drade Hogan's office.

"Yes," said Hogan. "You know we lost nearly four million in gold in San Francisco, I suppose."

Franks whistled. "I knew we was hurt some, but I didn't know it was that bad."

"Well, it was," Hogan said. "Not only have those responsible for our loss survived, I have every reason to believe they may be headed here."

"Damn," said Franks, "how did they get on our trail so quick? We ain't even settled in good, ourselves."

"Stone and Elfego each had a woman in El Paso," Hogan said, "and they were abducted for use as bait in setting a trap. Now it appears that Stone and Elfego have sprung the trap, taken the women, and may be on their way north. I have every reason to believe that Bryan Silver may be with them, for our contact in Washington informs me that he has not returned there."

"The lot of them lead charmed lives," said Franks. "What do you want me to do?"

"I want them destroyed," Hogan shouted, pounding the desk, "if it takes every damned gun-thrower west of the Mississippi."

"I don't even know what they look like," said Franks.

"I have a drawing of Silver, taken from a newspaper," Hogan said, "but nothing on Stone or Elfego. Stone has a hound that travels with him, and Elfego is an Indian. Both of them pack two guns and generally dress like saloon gamblers."

"I'll need some money," said Franks. "I'll have to grease the palms of some barkeeps and hotel desk clerks."

"You'll have it," Hogan said. "I pay for results."

Santa Fe, New Mexico, March 26, 1885

Wes, El Lobo, Renita, and Tamara waited at the cafe until Silver returned. Their bill at the hotel had already been paid, so they had only to take their horses from the livery and ride out.

"We're a good three-day ride from Boulder," said Wes.

"Not if we take the train from Durango to Denver," Silver said. "We're a little more than a hundred miles from Durango. The Denver and Rio Grande is a narrow gauge line, and the tracks reached Denver three years ago."

"That might be an interesting ride, if we can take our horses with us," said Wes. "The narrow gauge is a stranger to me."

"No reason why we can't take our horses," Silver said. "We'll need them to ride from Denver to Boulder. Narrow gauge tracks are only three feet apart, compared to four feet, eight and a half inches for standard tracks. Narrow gauge tracks allow the locomotive to take sharp curves with ease. Mighty handy in the mountains of Colorado."

"I'm not sure Wes should be going anywhere, until his wound's had time to heal," said Renita.

"Sorry," Silver said. "I kind of forgot about that. What do you think, Wes?"

"I think we need to get this town behind us, *pronto*," said Wes. "If that bushwhacker wants another shot at us, let him follow. He won't find it so easy to hide when he's on our back trail."

"Take whiskey with us," El Lobo said.

"Good idea," said Silver. "Then if Wes gets some fever, the red-eye should take care of it until we reach Durango."

"Durango sounds familiar," Wes said. "When we busted into the Dragon's headquarters in San Francisco, that was one of the words we found written on a scrap of paper. That and the names Elias Hawk and Hobie Denbow."[1]

"There must be more than one western town named Durango," said Silver, "but when we get there, we'll look around. Can't be more than a hundred souls livin' there, and I can't imagine how the Dragon would fit in."

"Why there be railroad?" El Lobo asked.

"There's some silver and gold in the area," said Silver, "and without the rails, the ore would have to be taken out on pack mules. Wouldn't be worth it."

Before leaving town, they reined up at a mercantile. Silver bought a quart of whiskey, which he placed in his saddlebag.

"What do you aim to do with that, if I don't get sick enough to need it?" Wes asked.

"If we don't soon destroy the Golden Dragon, I'll pick up three more bottles just like it and get roaring drunk," said Silver. "Then I'll go back to Texas, get me a hundred and sixty acres, ten cows, and a bull."

"Starvation wouldn't look good on you," Wes said.

"Hell, a man has to put down roots somewhere," said Silver, "unless he wants to end up like . . ."

"Me," Wes said.

"I wasn't about to say that," said Silver, "but now that you mention it, I reckon it's pretty much the truth. What *do* you intend to do? A few more years— less than ten, I'd say—and the frontier will become downright civilized. You can't drift from pillar to post, shooting and being shot at forever."

"*Por Dios,*" El Lobo said, "what else *hombre* to do? Dig in ground like squaw?"

---

[1] *Sixguns and Double Eagles*

"I am no squaw, and I do not dig in the ground," said Tamara.

"Nor do I," Renita said. "There must be *something* honorable a man can do, other than shooting outlaws and being shot by them. It's hell on a woman, being left behind and not knowing if her man is alive or dead."

"I reckon a man that's fiddle-footed and quick with a gun don't need a woman," said Wes.

"*Sí*," El Lobo agreed.

Silver had slowed his horse, falling a few paces behind. Renita and Tamara were silent, but their stormy eyes regarded Wes and El Lobo coldly. Wes felt the need to break the uncomfortable silence, and as so many men have before him, said exactly the wrong thing.

"Once we've whipped the Golden Dragon, I'm thinking of goin' to Washington. What about it, Silver? Could I hire on with the federals, doin' kind of what you do?"

"I'm sure you can," said Silver. "With your background, I can get you hired to replace me."

So total was their surprise, Silver's four companions reined up, staring at him. But he didn't laugh or smile, as they expected.

"Hell, I didn't mean I was after your job," Wes said.

"You wouldn't be," said Silver. "Once I destroy this conspiracy or it destroys me, I'm hanging it all up and going home to Texas."

"*Bueno hombre*," Tamara said.

"He is that, and more," said Renita.

"Dig in ground, like squaw?" El Lobo said, his dubious eyes on Silver.

Silver laughed. "Only to plant fence posts, Palo. I keep rememberin' those days when King Fisher was alive, when him and Nathan hired a bunch of wranglers and went huntin' wild horses, south of the border. I'm bettin' those horses are still there. With some seed stock, I could have me a horse ranch that would be the envy of all of Texas."[2]

"Last year," said Wes, "you told me the United States has a treaty with Mexico, and that it's illegal for Americans to cross the border."

"We do, and it is," Silver said, "but it didn't stop you."

"Damn it," said Wes angrily, "I had cause, and you know it."

"Yes," Silver said, "and I'll have cause too. I want me a herd of those mustangs."

"All these years you've preached the law," said Wes, "and now you aim to violate it yourself."

"But in no way that it will harm anyone," Silver said. "Mexican people are starving, and you think their politicians give a damn? Nobody owns those wild mustangs. Can you say it's wrong for me to take them, when for the first time since Nathan and King Fisher were there, some of those wranglers will have food in their bellies and a little gold in their pockets?"

"*Por Dios*," said Tamara.

There were tears on her cheeks, and the look she bestowed upon Silver was unlike any that El Lobo had ever seen. Renita was regarding Wes as though he had done something terrible, and he stopped just short of speaking to Silver in a manner that he would have regretted. Instead, he bit his tongue, forcing himself to speak calmly.

"You're right," said Wes. "When I crossed the border, I met some of those men who had roped wild horses for King Fisher and my father. They remembered, for they were as poor then as they are now. I can't fault you for crossing the river. If that's the best law Washington can come up with, I reckon I

[2] *The Autumn of the Gun*

wouldn't be satisfied there. Your idea of pullin' out just comes as a surprise."

"I reckon," Silver said, "but I started considering it, right after that bushwhacker cut down on us in San Francisco. The appeal of it grew stronger as I stood over Tom Rigger's grave."[3]

"A lot must have happened in San Francisco that you never told us," said Renita, her eyes on Wes.

"Some of it you don't want to know," Wes said.

"While we've been discussing the pros and cons of roping wild mustangs in Mexico, our own horses have had a chance to rest," said Silver. "Now we'd better ride if we aim to reach Durango today."

Olson and Baker watched as Silver, Wes, El Lobo, Renita, and Tamara left Santa Fe, riding northwest.

"There goes our chance, unless we follow them," Olson said.

"I ain't forgettin' what happened the last time we followed them," said Baker. "We had to walk all the way from the San Juans, without grub."

"There was a price on their heads," Olson said. "Twenty-five thousand dollars."

"We know why that is," said Baker. "They're hard as hell to kill, and I don't aim for them to have another shot at me."

Olson shrugged his shoulders. Bounty hunting had lost its appeal.

Durango, Colorado, March 26, 1885

Empty generally ran on ahead of the horses, but he paused when he heard a distant whistle. He disliked

---

[3] *Sixguns and Double Eagles*

railroad locomotives as much as he disliked steamboats.

"We're still quite a ways from town," said Silver. "The wind's from that direction."

"That train's arriving or leaving," Wes said, "and if it's leaving, it'll be gone before we can get there."

"No matter," said Silver. "I reckon we should spend a night there and see if there's a reason why the name of the town—if it *was* this town—was written on a scrap of paper in San Francisco."

"More important," Wes said, "I'd like to know if Elias Hawk and Hobie Denbow are here, and if they are, why."

"*Sí*," said El Lobo. "Kill."

"I reckon you and El Lobo had some trouble with them before," Silver said.

"We did," said Wes. "They chained us, along with some other *hombres* in a worked-out mine, digging low-grade ore. When we escaped, we should have gut-shot 'em both."[4]

"*Sí*," El Lobo said.

The sun had long since disappeared behind western peaks when they were at last able to see the distant town. The first stars had already blossomed in the purple of the sky, and a few pinpoints of light winked at them from various windows.

"We'd better check with the railroad before we do anything else," Silver said. "We'll be needing a boxcar for our horses."

There was no depot as such. A refurbished boxcar sat on a side track, and just above the DENVER AND RIO GRANDE logo, someone had hand-lettered BUSINESS OFFICE. Farther down the side track was a line of boxcars and ore cars.

---

[4] *Sixguns and Double Eagles*

"This is not end-of-track," said Wes. "The main line goes farther south."

"It will eventually reach Santa Fe," Silver said, "if the mines continue to prosper. Let's go ahead and pay for our passage to Denver."

A conventional door had been cut into the side of the boxcar office, and beside the door a bracket lamp burned. Wes nodded to El Lobo. He would remain with Tamara, Renita, and the horses. Wes and Silver entered the office.

"Use of a boxcar to Denver will cost you fifty dollars," said the agent in charge. "First-class passenger coach fare is forty-two dollars. Train leaves in the morning at ten. Have your horses here not later than half-past nine."

Wes dropped thirteen double eagles on the counter. Only when they had returned to their horses did Silver speak.

"I owe you for my fare and for half the boxcar fee."

"No," Wes said.

Silver said nothing. Mounting their horses, they rode on to what appeared to be the town's only hotel. It was a strung-out, one-story building of peeled logs. Instead of an office, there was only a window that opened to the outside.

"Three rooms, I reckon," said Silver.

Wes and El Lobo nodded. Silver dismounted and knocked on the window.

"Rooms are five dollars," said a voice from within. "Grub at the cafe."

"Three rooms for tonight," Silver said.

He paid and was given the room keys. He passed one to Wes and one to El Lobo. He mounted and they rode alongside the stretched-out building until they found doors with their key numbers painted on them. Beside each door was a lighted bracket lamp.

"I like the lamps outside the doors," Renita said.

"They are a nice touch, and considerably more than you'd expect in a mining town as new as this," said Silver. "Having railroad service to and from Denver makes a difference."

"We'd better find that cafe and eat," Wes said. "It may close early."

The entire town, such as it was, had been built alongside the railroad tracks. The cafe shared a building with a saloon, and there was no dividing wall. The saloon, it seemed, was doing a thriving business, while there was nobody but a bored cook on the cafe side.

"It's not the kind of place for ladies, under better conditions," Silver said.

"You are considerate to think of that," said Renita, "but we've been in worse."

"*Sí*," Tamara said, "and we were not there to eat."

"I may have to bring Empty some food," said Wes. "He hates saloons."

Silver laughed. "Just like his daddy before him."

They dismounted, and as Wes had expected, Empty chose to remain with the horses. The cook nodded to them as they entered, and having their choice of tables, they took one nearest the door and farthest from the saloon. There was shouting, cursing, laughter, and the clink of glasses.

"Can't you muzzle that bunch of coyotes for a while?" Silver asked, when the cook came to take their order.

"Sorry," said the cook. "The *hombre* that runs the saloon owns the cafe."

After they had ordered their meals, Wes arranged for some food for Empty. When the cook brought it, Wes took it outside and fed the hound. When he returned, El Lobo was on his feet, his hands on the butts of his Colts, and his hard eyes on a pair of men in the saloon. Taking a closer look, Wes understood.

"What's going on?" Silver asked, about to rise. "Palo, are you seein' a ghost?"

"*Sí*," said El Lobo through clenched teeth. "*Bastardos*. Kill."

"No," Wes said. "Sit down, before they see you."

For a moment El Lobo seemed not to have heard. Finally he sank down in his chair, his face still a mask of fury.

"It's Elias Hawk and Hobie Denbow," said Wes. "I'd give a lot to know what that pair of varmints is doin' here."

"No care," El Lobo said bitterly. "Kill."

"I understand your feelings, Palo," said Silver, "but Wes is right. Remember, we saw their names and the name of this town written on a scrap of paper in San Francisco, after we broke into that building that was Golden Dragon headquarters. Somehow, they figure into this conspiracy, and when all the dust settles, we'll be coming back to them."

El Lobo, listening to Silver, had begun to relax, but there were still beads of sweat on his rugged face.

"We know where they are, Palo," Wes said, "and before we can nail the Dragon's hide to the wall, we'll be comin' after them. You'll get your chance."

"If they're part of this terrible organization," said Renita, "why are we on our way to Dodge City, by way of Boulder, Colorado? Why don't you simply arrest these two and make them tell you where the others are?"

Silver laughed. "You are a lady with a head on your shoulders. It looks as though the two *hombres* over there in the saloon are headquartered here, so we can likely come after them any time. We're on our way to Dodge for several reasons. First, we aim to hide you and Tamara out among friends. Second, before leaving Denver, we must follow up a lead there. We believe we have the name of the man who hired the four killers who were planning to bushwhack Wes and Palo near Santa Fe."

"This varmint in Denver, if he's still there, will be much more important to us than Hawk or Denbow," said Wes.

"Right," Silver said, "and while Hawk and Denbow may recognize you and Palo as having escaped their mine, is there any reason why they should suspect you're fighting the Golden Dragon?"

"None that I know of," said Wes. "Why?"

"They may figure into this much stronger than we suspect, and in some ways that may become obvious as we get deeper into it," Silver said. "Let's eat and get out of here just as quickly as we can, and with any luck, we can avoid them until train time tomorrow."

"No like to hide," said El Lobo grimly.

"I realize that," Silver said, "but this is neither the time nor the place for a showdown with them. They may be more useful to us later on."

Concluding their meal, they left the cafe as quietly as possible, without arousing any curiosity among the patrons of the adjoining saloon.

"So far, I haven't seen a livery," said Wes.

"Neither have I," Silver said.

When they reached the lodging house, Silver again knocked on the lighted window.

"Where can we leave our horses overnight?" Silver asked.

"Picket or hobble 'em behind the building," said a voice. "There's graze a plenty."

Despite their doubts, they unsaddled their horses, allowed them to roll, and then cross-hobbled them. Their saddles and bedrolls they took to their rooms.

"I hope we can board the train tomorrow and get

away from here without trouble," Renita said, when she and Wes were alone in their room.

"So do I," said Wes. "Like El Lobo, I feel that we owe Hawk and Denbow something, but I can see Silver's side of it. If we made any such move now, it would draw attention to us without helping our cause. We'll have the Dragon gunning for us soon enough."

"Now I *am* afraid," Renita said.

"I'm sorry," said Wes. "I shouldn't have said that."

"Yes, you should," Renita said. "I'm afraid for you, but I don't want you keeping the truth from me. Me not knowing won't make it any less dangerous for you."

"Someday all this will be behind us," said Wes.

"Will it? Silver didn't seem to think so. That's why he's giving up his post and going back to Texas. Will we ever have a place of our own, where I don't have to worry about you having to shoot someone, or having someone shoot you?"

"I don't know," Wes said. "I won't believe Silver's giving up and returning to Texas, until he's done it."

"If he does," said Renita, "will that change your way of thinking?"

"Maybe," Wes said.

"I keep remembering something Molly Horrel said, after your father was killed, when you had ridden away to avenge his death. She said you would ride the same lonely trails that Nathan had, and that you would die with a gun in your hand, in the street of some dirty little border town."

"Damn her," Wes shouted, "she's never liked me. She had no business telling you such as that."

"She didn't tell me," said Renita. "I overheard her talking to Granny Boudleaux. But can you face me and say she didn't tell the truth?"

"I reckon I can't," Wes said. "Maybe you'd better think on that some more, before we stand before a preacher and have him read from the book."

"I have thought about it," said Renita. "You came for me, after I'd been sold into a Mexican whorehouse, when I wanted only to die. You took me for what I was, without question. Can I do any less for you?"

Wes went to her, placed his hands on her shoulders, and looked into her eyes. Then he spoke. "Before I leave Dodge, we'll stand before a preacher."

Silver, Wes, and El Lobo were awake before first light, and to their surprise, so were Renita and Tamara. Their horses still grazed peacefully. When they reached the cafe, several men were already there, but the saloon side had not opened for business. There was no sign of Hawk or Denbow.

"We should reach Denver late this afternoon," Silver said. "Maybe we can conclude our business there and ride on to Boulder the next day."

The locomotive steamed in from the south, right on time. The horses had already been taken aboard a boxcar on the siding, and it was coupled on behind the second passenger coach. The interior of the coaches was especially attractive, while the plush seats were the most comfortable Wes had ever experienced. But it was all wasted on Empty, for he found it no different from the other trains he had ridden. With a lurch of the coaches and a loud shriek of the whistle, they were off.

"I have never seen such beautiful country," said Tamara, as the train crept along a shelf that had been blasted out of the side of a mountain. "See the river so far below."[5]

---

[5] The Spanish called it *El Rio de las Animas Perdidas*—the River of Lost Souls. Now it is simply the Animas. This shelf, along which narrow gauge locomotives still run today, was blasted from solid rock, and is twenty-seven miles long.

"I rode the rails a lot when I worked security for the AT & SF," Wes said, "but most of it was across the Kansas plains, except for the stretch from eastern Colorado west to Boulder."

Conversation lagged, for there was much to see and little to say. The locomotive took on water at Silverton, along with several passengers, and the train continued on its way. It reached Denver in the late afternoon. Train men opened the boxcar so that Silver, Wes, and El Lobo could lead out their horses.

"We might as well find us a place to stay the night," said Silver. "Any ideas?"

"Let's avoid the Grand Hotel," Wes said. "If our suspicions mean anything, somebody there might recognize us. There's generally a hotel and a livery close to the railroad depot. There's a hotel near the depot in Boulder, where Harley and me always laid over."

"A friend of yours?" Renita asked.

"He was a friend of my father, and he's as good a friend as I ever had," said Wes. "He's in charge of security for the railroad, as I once was. He's one reason we're taking you and Tamara to Dodge. Another good friend in Dodge is Foster Hagerman, the division chief."

"I'm glad you have friends there," Renita said. "I thought the world of Granny Boudleaux, but I'd be scared to death, staying in El Paso."

"We wouldn't think of taking you back there," said Wes. "Not after you were taken by killers hired by the Golden Dragon. Don't worry; they won't know where you are."

After leaving their horses at a nearby stable, they walked to the Depot Hotel. Nobody seemed to notice them, but when they had taken their keys and had gone to their rooms, the desk clerk asked to be excused for supper. Instead, he hurried to the Grand Hotel, for he had information to sell.

Chapter 3

El Paso, Texas, March 27, 1885

"Silver is fine man," Granny Boudleax said. "You do right thing."

"But I hate to leave you, Granny," said Molly Horrel. "You'll be all alone."

"No," Granny said. "I sell this place and go to New Orleans. Live with my sister. But Nathan Stone staked me when I broke. He own half this place, which now belong to Wes."

"I don't think Wes would take the money if you offered it to him," said Molly. "Why don't you just consider it room and board, and wipe the slate clean?"

Parting with Granny Boudleaux was difficult, but Molly packed her few belongings in a travel case and took the next stage bound for Santa Fe. There she would take the Kansas City stage as far as Dodge. Silver had instructed her to go to the Dodge House and wait.

Denver, Colorado, March 27, 1885

The morning after their arrival in Denver, Silver, Wes, El Lobo, Renita, and Tamara had breakfast in a nearby cafe.

"The rest of you go back to the hotel and take Empty with you," Wes said. "I'll find the Grand Hotel and ask about Stringfield. We might as well leave the horses where they are, until we're ready to head for Boulder.''

Wes had no trouble finding the Grand Hotel, for it was all that the name implied. The winding stairway was seldom used, for there were newly installed elevators.

"I'm looking for a friend of mine, name of Stringfield," said Wes. "Is he still here?"

"I'll have to look it up," the clerk said.

Wes waited while he fanned through various files. Finally he found what he was seeking and turned back to Wes.

"Would that be Rance Stringfield?"

"It would," Wes said.

"Sorry," said the clerk. "He checked out early this morning."

"He left no forwarding address?"

"No," the clerk said. "That isn't customary. When checking in, he gave an address in St. Louis, but we're not allowed to reveal such information, unless it's to the law. You're not a lawman, are you?"

"No," said Wes. "I'm obliged, anyway."

Leaving the Grand, he started back toward the Depot Hotel. It was still early, and the saloons hadn't yet opened. Wes stepped quickly into a cafe and took a table close to the window. The man who had been following him passed without looking his way. The waiter hadn't yet reached the table, and Wes got up, slipping out through a back entrance. Behind a fence, Wes waited. His pursuer would take only the time it took him to discover that his quarry was no longer in the cafe. As the sound of hurried footsteps came within a few yards of where Wes was concealed, he stepped out into the alley, a Colt steady in his hand.

"Are you looking for me?"

The stranger was a big man, and if he was armed, he made no play. Startled though he was, his reaction was swift. He ducked through the cafe's back door, and Wes resisted the temptation to fire. Renita and Tamara were just a few blocks away, and he had little doubt that the Golden Dragon was well aware of it. He knew now that some of the conspirators were in Denver, and there was little possibility he and his friends could reach Boulder and take the train to Dodge without being followed. Reaching the hotel, he knocked on Silver's door.

"Come on to my room," he told Silver. "We have some planning to do."

El Lobo had heard him in the hall and stood in the open door.

"Come on to my room, Palo, and bring Tamara with you," said Wes.

When they were all together and the door closed, Wes told them the little he had been able to learn about Stringfield. Then, as much as he hated to, he told them of the stranger he had encountered behind the cafe.

"They follow us to Dodge," said El Lobo.

"It looks that way," Silver said.

"Then we'll be no safer there than we were in El Paso," said Renita.

"But you will," Wes said angrily. "It'll be up to Palo and me to see that you are, even if we have to pull out of this Dragon hunt and stay there with you."

"I would not have you do that for my sake," said Tamara. "You have promised Señor Silver."

"Tamara's right," Renita said. "Your father always kept his word. Can you do any less without being less a man than he was?"

"Damn it," said Wes desperately, "when a man has a woman to look out for, things change. Silver doesn't have that problem."

Silver laughed. "Oh, but Silver does. By the time we reach Dodge, Molly Horrel will be there at the Dodge House."

"May God have mercy on you," Wes said. "She lost one man to this bunch of outlaws in El Paso, and when she learns they're on our trail, she'll see it all coming together again. Only this time, she'll think of you lying dead with a gun in your hand, instead of Nathan Stone."

"Do not judge her unfairly," said Tamara. "The Señor Silver does not lie to her. She is aware of the risk, is she not?"

"She is," Silver said, "but I also told her I believed she would be safe in Dodge."

"They've taken Renita and Tamara," said Wes, "and that didn't work. There's a chance they won't try that again."

"We do not know that," El Lobo said.

"But we can't rule out the possibility," said Silver. "I think we'll have to do as we've planned, and go on to Dodge. Maybe I still have enough clout in Washington to enlist the help of the law."

"I don't have much confidence in the law, where the Dragon's concerned," Wes said. "I just don't believe the law will take you seriously when you suggest that these outlaws might harm our women to get back at us."

"You say you have friends in Dodge," said Silver. "Will they believe *you*, if you tell them Renita, Tamara, and Molly are in danger?"

"I expect they will," Wes said. "When Palo and me were on our way to Carson City, a dozen gunmen stopped the train a hundred miles east of Dodge. We came out on the short end of a gun fight, and we were laid up for two weeks. I doubt my friends have forgotten that. Trouble is, Hagerman's the division chief for the railroad, and Harley's ridin' the rails and gone more than he's there."

"There's nobody else you can count on?" Silver asked. "What about the sheriff?"

"Unless there's a different one, we can't depend on him," said Wes. "He seemed mighty relieved when Palo and me were well enough to leave Dodge."

"I don't want to go to a strange town and immediately become a burden," Renita said.

"Nor do I," said Tamara. "Get us guns and we will defend ourselves."

"Like hell," Wes said. "You wouldn't stand a chance against these varmints who are on our trail."

"Not so fast," said Silver. "The first thing I aim to do is find Molly a .31-caliber Colt pocket pistol and teach her to use it. I'm in favor of a woman defending herself, when she can, and we're up against a situation that demands it."

"Wes," Renita said, "I want one of those Colts."

"*Sí*," said Tamara, "and so do I. If Renita and me had been armed in El Paso, those brutes would never have taken us."

"*Bueno*," El Lobo said.

They were all of the same mind, and Wes gave in. "Then let's buy three of those .31-caliber Colts and some ammunition before we leave Denver. I doubt we can find either in Dodge."

"Since the Dragon knows we're here," said Silver, "the rest of you wait while I go for the weapons. When I return, we'll all ride out for Boulder."

"They follow you," El Lobo said.

"Let them," said Silver. "While I'm gone, go to the livery where the horses are. Saddle them and be ready to ride. I'll meet you there."

When Gandy Franks had received word from the hotel desk clerk that their quarry was in town, Drade Hogan had left his office for the day. But Franks was already there when Hogan arrived the next morning.

"I am not surprised they're here," said Hogan, when Franks had told what he knew, "nor am I surprised that Stone's already been to the Grand Hotel. I am disappointed, however, that you didn't assign a more reliable man to follow Stone. Now they know we are after them."

"Clancy's as good a man as we've got," Franks said. "He didn't know how Stone found he was bein' trailed."

"Clancy's been seen," said Hogan, "and he won't be worth a damn, following them. I trust you don't have him watching their hotel."

Franks laughed nervously. "I know better than that. I had Clancy and Drake watching the place, and when Stone left, Clancy followed. Drake's still there."

"Where are the rest of the men?"

"At our place on Cherry Creek," Franks said. "I told 'em to stay out of town. Last thing we want is to attract the attention of the law."

"Have them ready to ride," said Hogan. "I don't look for Stone and Elfego to leave their women here, and it's anybody's guess as to what we may expect from Silver."

"He hasn't been in touch with Washington?"

"According to our contacts, not since he left California," Hogan said, "and that worries me. Silver's the kind who's always one jump ahead."

"Every man has some kind of weakness," said Franks.

"When you discover Silver's, let me know," Hogan replied. "Now stay on top of this, and don't let them get away from us."

Cheyenne, Wyoming, March 27, 1885

It was near dark when Rance Stringfield rode into town. He went immediately to the Plains Hotel, as Drade Hogan had instructed him. Hogan had told him only that he was to meet a new man, and that when the meeting took place, Stringfield would understand the reason for it. Stringfield had been anxious, after the failure of the ambush he had arranged south of Santa Fe, but Hogan had seemed cheerful enough.

"Room for the night?" the hotel desk clerk inquired.

"Maybe later," said Stringfield. "First, I must talk to a man name of Jason Hawkins. Is he here?"

"Second floor, third room on the right," the clerk said.

Stringfield knocked on the door, and it was opened almost immediately. The lamp had not been lighted, and Stringfield's host was no more than a shadow.

"I'm Stringfield. You're Hawkins?"

"Yeah," said the shadow. "We'll go down the hall and use the back stairs. I know of a quiet place where we can have a beer and get some grub. Then we'll talk."

"I haven't taken a room," Stringfield said.

"Time enough after we eat," said Hawkins. "This place is never full."

They left by the hotel's back entrance, and instead of a street, there was an alley that led to a cross street that was as dark as the alley itself. There were a few points of light ahead, but Hawkins turned in the opposite direction. Uneasily, Stringfield followed, staying a pace or two behind. Suddenly Hawkins stumbled and went to his knees.

"What's wrong?" Stringfield inquired.

"Turned my ankle," said Hawkins. "Give me a hand."

Stringfield reached for the extended hand, and when starlight glinted off the blade of the knife, it was already too late. Hawkins lunged forward, driving the deadly blade into Stringfield's belly. Stringfield collapsed to his knees, only to have the

blade driven in again and again. Hawkins withdrew
the blade a final time, and Stringfield fell facedown.
As the blood and the life drained out of him, he fully
understood the purpose of his meeting with this
stranger.

Drake, watching the Depot Hotel, quickly recognized Silver. He had been told that if Silver and his
companions left, they were to be followed. Now he
was in a quandary, for only Silver was leaving. Swallowing hard, making a decision, he followed. Silver
seemed in no hurry, pausing occasionally to look into
a shop window. Reflection in the glass offered him
a perfect opportunity to observe activity across the
street. Silver was virtually certain he was being followed, but he went on. He would find a mercantile
or gunsmith, purchase the guns, and then confront
his pursuer. The business district was farther away
than he had expected, and he was tiring when he
eventually found a mercantile. It wasn't yet open for
business, so he sat down on a bench to wait. Drake,
his pursuer, could do nothing except continue the
way he was headed. Silver laughed.

"Damn him," Drake grunted. Somehow he would
have to double back, and he couldn't allow himself
to be seen again, for he would be recognized.

Silver waited half an hour for the store to open,
and he saw nothing more of the man he believed
was following him.

"Sorry," said the storekeeper, when Silver had
made known his needs. "Not much call for them
pocket guns. I don't carry them or the shells. But
there's a gunsmith just a few blocks north of here.
Right across the street from the Pretty Girl Saloon."

"Thanks," Silver said.

There was a back door, and Silver stepped out into
an alley. Seeing nobody, he crossed the alley, making

his way between buildings until he reached the next cross street. Taking a roundabout way, he kept to a parallel street until he believed he had thoroughly confused the man following him. When he again crossed to the street he wanted, he could see the towering sign of the Pretty Girl Saloon. Quickly he entered the nearby gunsmith's shop.

"I can fix you up," said the gunsmith. "I got four pocket Colts. Sure you can't use the fourth one?"

"No," Silver said. "Just the three, and a box of shells for each of them."

"You want holsters and belts?"

"Yes," said Silver.

"You bought more of these little guns than I've sold since I opened for business," the gunsmith said. "Good luck with whatever you have planned."

Just in case his pursuer had caught up to him, Silver again went out the back way. A side street took him in the direction he wished to go, and not until he was within a block of the Depot Hotel did he cross over. Only then did he see the stranger who had followed him. The man was across the street from the hotel, under an awning, leaning against the wall of a store building. He appeared not to notice Silver.

"Now you're about to get a run for your money," said Silver under his breath.

Reaching the livery, Silver found his companions waiting. His horse was saddled, and he mounted.

"Let's ride," Silver said. "That varmint across from the hotel's been following me, until I managed to lose him."

"He wasn't there when we left the hotel," said Wes.

"That's why I led him on a wild-goose chase," Silver said. "When he returned, he had no way of knowing the rest of you weren't still in the hotel, waiting for me. I doubt that he has a horse nearby, and before he can get his hands on one, we'll be long gone."

Wheezing for breath, Drake reached the Grand Hotel. When he pounded frantically on the door, Gandy Franks let him in, waiting impatiently until Drake had recovered his wind and was able to speak.

"They're . . . gone," Drake said.

"You were to follow them," said Franks. "Why didn't you?"

"Silver left the hotel, and I trailed him," Drake said. "When he returned, he didn't go to the hotel, but to the livery. The others had saddled the horses, and when Silver joined 'em, they all rode out. You didn't leave me no horse. You said it would draw attention to me."

"You were within sight of a livery," said Franks. "I made the mistake of thinking you were smart enough to go there for a horse if you needed one."

"But they was all saddled and ready to ride," Drake argued. "Time I got there and got a horse saddled, I'd have lost 'em. I didn't think—"

"That's your trouble," said Franks. "You *never* think. Get out."

"You want me to—"

"I want you to get out and stay out," Franks snarled.

"But you owe me—"

"I owe you nothing but a slug in the gut," said Franks, "and if we was anywhere else, you'd collect it now."

"I'll go," Drake said, "but you ain't seen the last of me."

"If you're in town this time tomorrow," said Franks, "you'll be gettin' yourself measured for a pine box."

Drake backed out the door, his hard eyes on

Gandy Franks. When the door closed and Franks was sure Drake was gone, he belted on his Colt and reached for his hat. He must not allow the unwelcome news to reach Drade Hogan. He swallowed hard, recalling the disappearance of Rance Stringfield. When it came to failure, Hogan had his own grisly rewards.

"We'll be in Boulder in less than an hour," Silver said. "If we're fortunate enough to board an eastbound train today, there's a chance we can be on our way before the Dragon knows which way we've gone."

"There's always the telegraph," said Wes. "That's got to be the way they headed off El Lobo and me, when we left Kansas City. While I hate to give them that much credit, I'd be willing to bet they have contacts in every town of any size."[1]

"Even Dodge?" Renita asked.

"Even Dodge," said Wes. "There's nothin' to be gained by playing down the danger. As you and Tamara know, we left you unprotected in El Paso."

"That was my fault," Silver said. "I cautioned you and Palo not to reveal anything that I had told you of the conspiracy."

"Now we have been told everything," said Renita, "and whatever lies ahead of us, I am not afraid. I have a weapon to protect myself, and even if that bunch tracks us down and comes after us again, Tamara and me will be ready for them."

"*Sí*," Tamara said.

"*Bueno*," said El Lobo.

"Both of you are more than worthy of being called Texans," Silver said. "I'm hoping that when I lay a

---

[1] *Sixguns and Double Eagles*

pistol in Molly Horrel's hands, she feels the same way."

Being familiar with Boulder, Wes led the way to the railroad terminal.

"Let me arrange for the tickets and a boxcar for the horses," said Wes. "There may be some trouble getting a boxcar on short notice, unless there's some folks here who may remember me from my days with the railroad."

Before Wes reached the ticket office, he heard a shout. He turned, his hand near one of his Colts, and to his delight, there was Harley Stafford.

"I couldn't believe it was you, hoss," said Harley. "Where's your Indian *companero*?"

"He's here," Wes said. "We're on our way to Dodge, and we're not alone. There's plenty to tell you, but first, I reckon I'd better make some arrangements with the railroad. We'll need a boxcar for our horses."

"I already have a boxcar," said Harley. "Your horses can travel with mine. There'll be a train east in about two hours. Just enough time for us to eat and talk."

Wes wasted no time introducing Harley to his companions.

"I've heard a lot about you," Silver said, taking Harley's hand.

"I've heard considerable about you," said Harley, "but most of it from Nathan. Wes and El Lobo have told me nothing, except that a bunch of *hombres* were out to kill them. I could damn near have figured that out for myself, since the last time they were in Dodge they'd been shot full of holes."

"You know more than Renita and me," Tamara said, her eyes on Harley. "We not told they be shot in Dodge."

"Sorry, ladies," said Harley. "I didn't mean to give

away any secrets. They were shot before they reached Dodge. Foster Hagerman and me weren't told anything, except that the trail they were riding might be their last. If all of you are returning to Dodge, I hope you can tell me somethin' about this bunch with killing on their minds. If somebody's shootin' in my direction, I aim to shoot back."

"Wes and Palo had been sworn to silence," Silver said, "but things have changed to the extent that you can be told probably more than you'll want to know. We have some talkin' to do."

Gandy Franks wasted no time getting to the telegraph office. He sent coded messages to contacts in Cheyenne, Boulder, Kansas City, and Dodge. Only then did he call on Drade Hogan with his admission of failure and what he had done to counter it.

"So they've given us the slip again," said Hogan. "At least you had the presence of mind to use the telegraph. As long as we know where they're going, they haven't escaped."

"I didn't telegraph west or south," Franks said. "I could think of no reason for them going back to California, or south to Santa Fe or El Paso."

"There is one thing bothering me," said Hogan. "The Denver and Rio Grande has plans to go south all the way to El Paso. End of track is near Santa Fe now. I've learned that Silver, Stone, and Elfego rode to Durango—a hundred miles—and from there took a train to Denver. Why?"

"Hell, I don't know," Franks said. "You think they had a reason?"

"Of course they had a reason," said Hogan irritably. "We chose Durango because of its virtual isolation and the railroad connecting it to Denver. Now I don't intend to see all those plans shot to hell because of Silver and his gun-throwers. We must warn Hawk and Denbow. I want security doubled, and I want them made aware of the penalty for failure."

"There's the telegraph," Franks said.

"Too risky," said Hogan. "I intend to send a messenger."

"You want me to go?"

"I want you right here, keeping track of Silver and his men," Hogan said. "What do you think of Turk Pardue and Dent Shankler from our operation in Carson City, and Emo Hanks from New Orleans?"

"I haven't seen any of 'em in action since they come here," said Franks. "I reckon one is good as the other. Only thing I have against any of them is that they've all had a shot at these two gunslingers ridin' with Silver, and they've all failed."

"That's sound thinking," Hogan said. "I should have considered that before Stringfield rode to El Paso. I'll send somebody else to Durango."

Sighing with relief, Franks departed, closing the door behind him.

Harley Stafford listened in amazement as Bryan Silver told him as much as he needed to know about the Golden Dragon, and of their need to ensure the safety of Renita, Tamara, and Molly.

"I reckon they'll be safe enough in Dodge," Harley said, "but arming them is the smart thing to do. I saw what those varmints did to Wes and Palo after stopping the train on its way to Dodge. Hagerman's a member of the town council, and I'm sure he'll do anything that he can."

"Who's the sheriff in Dodge?" Silver asked.

"Jack Dumery," said Harley. "They don't last long, and he's the latest. Good man, far as I know."

"Seems like the trail towns would settle down, now that the cattle drives are done," Silver said.

"They have, to some extent," said Harley, "and

now that they can't blame all the hell-raising on Texas cowboys, they're havin' to face up to the *real* problem. All the killers and renegades are still holed up in Indian Territory, and following their bank, train, and stage robberies, they return there. The federals should send a company of soldiers in there and clean up the territory."

"Maybe when it becomes a state," Silver said.[2]

"I reckon that's one possibility we didn't consider when we thought of Dodge," said Wes. "The kind of money the Golden Dragon throws around—even if it is phony—could recruit an army of killers just a day's ride away."

"Maybe after we reach Dodge, we'd better allow them a few days to come after us," Silver said. "Since our only lead was in Denver, and it didn't pan out, we really don't have any sense of direction."

"If you lost them before leaving Denver," said Harley, "how are they going to know *where* you are?"

"They'll know," Silver said. "By the time we're ready to board the train for Dodge, I suspect they'll be watching us."

"My God," said Harley, "they might stop or derail the train."

"I doubt it," Silver said. "They know Renita and Tamara are with us, and that we'll be taking them to a place of safety. They'll telegraph ahead to Dodge and Kansas City, having somebody waiting at both railroad depots. I think we'll check in at the Dodge House and wait for them to make their move."

"You're *that* sure they'll be coming?" Harley asked.

"I'm sure," said Silver. "They want us dead."

"*Sí,*" El Lobo said. "They come."

[2] Not until 1907 did Indian Territory finally become the state of Oklahoma.

Chapter 4

Boulder, Colorado, March 28, 1885

While the locomotive got up steam, Silver, Wes, and El Lobo led their five horses into the boxcar Harley Stafford had provided. Silver, Wes, El Lobo, Renita, and Tamara then joined Harley in one of the passenger coaches. Unseen eyes watched, and when the train pulled out, a stranger was aboard in the coach directly behind Silver and his party.

In Denver, Gandy Franks read with satisfaction the telegram he had sent to Boulder, and a second one that had gone to Dodge. Hutsinger and his deadly Winchester would be aboard the eastbound train, with instructions to kill. If, for any reason, Hutsinger failed, yet another trusted member of the legion of outlaws, Gannon, would be waiting in Dodge. He would immediately telegraph Denver, so that Franks would know if Silver and his party left the train at Dodge, or continued on to Kansas City.

Aboard the eastbound, Hutsinger got up and made his way to the end of the coach, to the glass-paneled door that opened to the observation deck. He opened the door and went out, coughing as smoke from the locomotive's stack swirled about him. When the smoke cleared, he stepped across to the deck of the coach that was coupled behind his own. He removed his hat and knelt down, so that he could see through the door's glass panel with little chance of his being seen. He noted with satisfaction that Silver, Harley Stafford, Wes, and El Lobo sat in seats facing the opposite end of the coach. Their backs were to him, with only the two women facing him. He would be returning to Boulder afoot, so he could not afford to stay aboard the train much longer. Swiftly he drew the Winchester from its canvas pouch, jacking a shell into the chamber. He got to his knees, prepared to shoot through the glass panel of the door. Wes Stone and Bryan Silver, the backs of their heads to him, were perfect targets. There were no other passengers in the way. Only Renita and Tamara were facing him. Slowly his finger tightened on the trigger. . . .

"*Asesino!*" Tamara shouted.

She had earlier belted the .31-caliber Colt around her slender waist, and with a swiftness that her companions would later recall with wonder, she drew the weapon and fired. While the slug missed Hutsinger, it shattered the glass in the door, and the slug from the bushwhacker's Winchester ripped into the ceiling of the coach. In an instant, Silver, Wes, El Lobo, and Harley had their Colts out, and answering lead screamed through the shattered door. Hutsinger dropped the Winchester, seeking only to escape with his life. But one of the slugs sang off the iron railing of the adjoining coach, and the deadly ricochet ripped into the unfortunate gunman. With a scream, Hutsinger slipped between the coaches and fell to the track below.

"*Sangre de Christo,*" said El Lobo, struggling into the aisle.

In the coach ahead, the conductor pulled the emergency signal, and the train lurched to a shuddering, grinding halt. Wes, Silver, and El Lobo were thrown to their knees in the aisle, their Colts in their hands. Empty crept fearfully from beneath a seat, not quite sure the world hadn't come to an end. Tamara, her teeth clenched and her face pale as death, still gripped her Colt.

"*Por Dios*," El Lobo said. "You save us."

Glass from the shattered door panel rattled to the floor as the conductor came in. He looked from one to the other, before riveting his eyes on Silver.

"What in the world happened back here?"

"Somebody was hunkered outside that door with a Winchester, trying to kill us," said Silver. "We returned the fire. I think one of us got lucky."

"There's blood outside the door," the conductor said. "Some of the crew is searching the tracks and the right-of-way."

Only then did they discover Harley Stafford was gone. When he returned, he came in through the undamaged door at the other end of the coach.

"A ricochet got him," Harley said. "If that wasn't enough, he fell beneath the wheels of the train. We gathered up what's left of him in a piece of canvas. He's in the caboose."

"God almighty," said the conductor, gripping the back of a seat. "You'll report this to the law, won't you?"

"When we get to Dodge," Harley said. "Sheriff Jack Dumery will love this."

The passengers took their seats again and the train lurched into motion. The others sat across the aisle, as far as they could get from Silver's party. Silver and Wes sat facing one end of the car, while El Lobo and Harley faced the other end, having changed seats with Tamara and Renita.

"That's the kind of varmints we're up against, Harley," said Wes. "Before this is over, you may be sorry we came to Dodge."

"No," Harley said. "If there's to be a showdown, let it be where you have friends to watch your back."

"You're a *bueno hombre* to ride the river with," said Silver, "but I don't believe the end will come in Dodge. Evidently, the plan for taking Renita and Tamara from El Paso came together in Denver, and the *hombre* responsible for it returned there. I can't get the possibility out of my head that for some reason, the Dragon has moved inland."

"All we know for sure is that Stringfield returned there, after hiring those killers," Wes said. "It's hard to believe they've pulled out of San Francisco and New Orleans. They were depending on sailing ships to bring in their copper, silver, and gold from outside the United States for the counterfeiting of double eagles, and then for shipping the stolen genuine coins to other countries."

"Unless they no longer intend to import materials for making counterfeit, and have no need to ship the genuine coins out of the country," said Harley. "That does away with the need for a convenient harbor."

"You've just put my thoughts into words," Silver said. "They saw the writing on the wall when we boarded that sailing ship and recovered millions in stolen double eagles, and then found crates of imported metals when we invaded their headquarters. They knew, with that kind of hard evidence, I could have justified the searching of any incoming or outgoing vessel in any U.S. port."[1]

"So they don't aim to ship in foreign metals or ship stolen gold out of the country," said Harley.

"No," Silver said. "That tells me they'll have a stronghold for the stolen gold here in the West, and that they have a source of gold, silver, and copper without importing it."

[1] *Sixguns and Double Eagles*

"There's silver and gold being mined all over Colorado," said Wes, "but no legitimate mine would sell gold or silver ore that might be used for a questionable purpose."

"There must be some government regulation, too," Harley added.

"You're both right, to some degree," said Silver, "but there's always a few who are more than willing to operate outside the law and in the face of government regulation. The names Hawk, Denbow, and Durango come to mind."

"Elias Hawk and Hobie Denbow could likely account for the necessary silver and gold," Wes said, "but what about the copper?"

"Some copper is mined in eastern Arizona," said Silver, "and it's not quite as regulated as silver and gold."

"That sounds like the leads you're looking for," Harley said.

"Maybe," said Silver, "but we'll have to consider them secondary. We've tried rounding up lesser criminals who might have led us to bigger fish, but they're very expendable. The Golden Dragon kills quickly and without mercy when one of its own is caught up in some circumstance in which he might talk to the law."

"That's the gospel truth," Wes said. "The varmints blew up a railroad coach in San Francisco, killing your federal men, just to silence two of their own."[2]

"You're goin' back to Colorado, then," said Harley.

"I'm leaning in that direction," Silver said, "but after what just happened, I'm inclined to wait a spell and see if they intend to continue this vendetta. They're not goin' to have the edge they had in El Paso."

[2] *Sixguns and Double Eagles*

Harley laughed. "I'm inclined to believe you, the way this young lady pulls a Colt."

"They both have one," said Silver, "and I have a third one for Molly when she gets to Dodge. How often is there a stage from Santa Fe?"

"Once a week," Harley said. "We'll be in Dodge well before it arrives."

"Harley," said Wes, "I have a big favor to ask of Foster Hagerman."

"And you want to run it by me first, I reckon," Harley said.

"Yeah," said Wes. "I may need your help convincing him. I want to see all telegrams sent to or from Dodge. Is there a law against that?"

"I don't know," Harley said.

"There is," said Silver, "but we can get around it. I'll take full responsibility."

"Then you'd better talk to him," Harley said. "Tell him what you've told me about this conspiracy, and I'll back you up when you tell him about this attempted ambush aboard the train. It's bad publicity for the railroad, and I'm thinking he'll back your play."

"I think we'd better start by looking at the telegrams that came in today," said Wes. "The Dragon never puts all his eggs in one basket, and if they don't have a man in Dodge today, I'd bet my saddle there'll be one arriving sometime tomorrow."

"This could be a means of getting our hands on some of them," Silver said, "if we can intercept their messages without their knowing it. There's not much use in any of us goin' back to Denver until there's a need for it. They'll not find it so easy, comin' after us in Dodge."

"You don't know that they will," said Harley, "since their bushwhacker on the train didn't pan out."

"They won't be satisfied as long as Wes, Palo, and me are alive, no matter where we are," Silver said. "Before we whipped them in California, they might have backed off, but not now. They're a vengeance-minded bunch of bastards, and they'll kill us for the damage we've already done."

"*Sí*," said El Lobo, "but we kill them first."

"He's right," Wes said. "We got to shoot our way to the tall dog in the brass collar—the leader of the pack—and then put a slug between his eyes. Only then will we be free of the varmints."

"Then I'm glad Tamara and me have guns," said Renita, "and I'm glad there'll be one for Molly when she arrives."

"This is not a woman's fight," Silver said, "and I'm sorry the three of you are being dragged into it, but there's no other way. Wes and Palo tried to leave you out of it, and the two of you could easily have been murdered. We won't risk there being a next time."

"*Sí*," Tamara said, "and let there be no regrets. In Mexico they sell us like the *mulo*, and these *bastardos* who would murder us here are *perros* from the same evil empire. We relish the right to kill them as they would kill us."

"She's right," said Renita, "and I'll stand behind every damn word she said."

"*Bueno*," Silver said. "That's what it will take to finish them."

With a blast of its whistle, the locomotive signaled their pending arrival in Dodge. The train slowed, and with some hope of escaping the monster, Empty crept out from beneath a seat.

"One of you lead my horse from one boxcar," said Harley, getting to his feet. "I want to talk to Hagerman before he gets any secondhand information from the train's crew."

"We'll stay out of the way until we hear from

you," Silver said. "Don't tell Hagerman any more than you have to. He may not be impressed with me, but I have the office of the attorney general and the federal government to back my play."

When the train shuddered to a halt, Empty was first out, bounding down the coach's iron steps. Renita and Tamara remained on board until Silver, Wes, and El Lobo had led the six horses from the boxcar. Renita and Tamara then left the passenger coach, and the five of them waited for Harley Stafford. The conductor stood beside one of the passenger coaches, waiting. The train wouldn't depart until the grisly remains of the dead gunman had been removed from the caboose. When Harley and the division chief left Hagerman's office, his first words were to the driver of one of the hacks awaiting passengers from the train.

"There's a dead man in the caboose. Take him to Sheriff Dumery's office and tell the sheriff he's needed here. Here's your fare."

As the hack rattled away toward the caboose, Hagerman spoke to the conductor.

"Have a couple of your crew remove the body from the caboose and put it in the hack. You'll have to wait until Sheriff Dumery gets here. He'll want a statement from you."

The conductor climbed the steps to the passenger coach, and Hagerman then allowed himself to be introduced to Silver, Wes, El Lobo, Renita, and Tamara.

"There's still a lot you need to know," Harley told Hagerman, "and you'll need to hear it from Silver. I don't know how much of it you'll want the sheriff to hear. I reckon we'd better satisfy him first, if we can."

"All he needs to know immediately is that there was an attempted bushwhacking," said Silver. "If there's any difficulty, Mr. Hagerman, you have me and the office of the attorney general to take full responsibility."

"Thank you," said Hagerman. "Sheriff Dumery is a reasonable man, and since this took place well out of his jurisdiction, I doubt that he'll pursue it beyond the filing of a report. Before we involve him further, if we must, I would appreciate knowing as much as you can tell me. I know Wes and El Lobo, and Harley is a trusted employee, so you are in good company. Tie your horses here where you can see them, and come on in to my office."

Seated in Hagerman's office, Silver spoke rapidly. The division chief must be briefed before the arrival of the sheriff.

"You're expecting a showdown here, then," said Hagerman, when Silver had finished.

"Maybe," Silver said. "They tried to dry-gulch us on the train, and that tells me they don't intend to forgive and forget. I'd bet the farm that if we don't make any immediate moves, they'll come after us here. With that in mind, there's something I must ask of you."

Hagerman nodded, and Silver told him of the need to know the content of telegrams sent to or from Dodge.

"You know the law," said Hagerman, "so I won't lecture you on the legality of what you are suggesting."

"I'm obliged," Silver said. "Legal or not, it's a necessary move, and the responsibility is mine. Naturally we'll keep it as quiet as we can."

There was a thump of hooves, and a rider reined up outside. The sheriff had arrived.

"Sheriff Jack Dumery," said Hagerman, when the lawman entered the office.

As Hagerman introduced Silver, Wes, and El Lobo, Dumery extended his hand to each of them. When introduced to Renita and Tamara, he tipped his hat, his eyes lingering on their belted Colts. Silver handed

Dumery his credentials, and after looking at them briefly, the sheriff returned them.

"Talk," Dumery said, his eyes on Silver.

"Scrape the surface of them with your knife," said Silver, handing Dumery several of the Golden Dragon double eagles.

Dumery scraped away the thin coating of gold from one of the coins. He dropped the second coin on the floor, retrieved it, and scraped its surface with his knife.

"My God," Dumery said, "they look and sound real. I reckon there's lots more."

"Untold millions of dollars worth," said Silver. "Now listen carefully to what I'm about to tell you."

Silver spoke for half an hour, and had barely finished when there was a knock on the door. It was the locomotive's engineer.

"I hope you wired the Kansas City dispatcher," said the engineer. "Otherwise, we'll be meetin' the westbound train head-on."

"I wired them, first thing," Hagerman said. "They'll be waiting for you on the siding at Wichita. Sheriff, if you need a statement from anyone on the train, you'd better get it. They must be on their way."

"I can't see that I'll need any statements," said the sheriff. "It all took place outside my jurisdiction, and Mr. Silver, a federal lawman, was there. Send them on their way."

"You heard him," Hagerman said. "You're free to go."

The engineer nodded, closing the door.

"Mr. Silver," said Sheriff Dumery, "I can appreciate your position, and I don't envy you. If I were to deputize every available man in town, I'm not sure I could protect any of you against such odds. What would you have me do?"

"Nothing," Silver said. "We have no idea from

what direction the next attack is likely to come. You've been brought into this because you represent the law on a local level. I'm telling you here and now that we intend to protect ourselves, and if they shoot at us, we intend to return the fire. You could end up with some dead men on your hands, and if you do, then we don't want any misunderstanding. It's a favorite tactic of this bunch to force a man to fight for his life, and then leave him in a bad position with local lawmen."

"You'll find yourselves at no such disadvantage with me," Dumery said, "and I'm much obliged for your having explained the situation. The jail's at your disposal, and I'll help you in any way that I can. It's not often a small-town sheriff has the privilege of working with a federal man."

"We're obliged, Sheriff," said Silver. "We'll be staying at the Dodge House for a while, should you need to reach us."

Sheriff Dumery departed, closing the door behind him.

"You handled that well," Hagerman said. "What's next?"

"I want you to review any telegrams sent today," said Silver. "If these outlaws have a contact here, he'll be telegraphing Denver. The message would have been sent after we got off the train, probably while we've been here in your office."

"I'll talk to the telegrapher," Hagerman said.

He returned almost immediately. The yellow slip of paper in his hand brought a look of amazement to his face.

"You called it perfectly," said Hagerman, passing the message to Silver.

Silver read it quickly and passed it to his companions. Unsigned, it was addressed to Franks, in Denver, and consisted of a single word: *Dodge*.

"The telegrapher said a courier from the Dodge House brought the message and paid for the telegram," Hagerman said.

"That figures," said Silver. "The varmint wouldn't want to be seen near the depot while we're here. It'll be more difficult identifying him."

"Maybe you shouldn't be in any hurry to identify him," Hagerman said. "He may send or receive other messages if he thinks he hasn't been detected."

"My God, yes," said Harley. "If they communicate by telegraph, you may know ahead of time what they're planning to do."

"Maybe," Silver said, "but I doubt there'll be any more telegrams sent from here or any answer from Denver. They know we're here. All we're likely to learn is the name of the *hombre* who received this message in Denver, and that may not be his real name."

"Let's get settled in at the Dodge House," said Wes. "I reckon we'll know soon enough what they intend to do next."

"I'll let you know if any more telegrams are sent to or received from Denver," Foster Hagerman said.

"I'll go with you to the Dodge House," said Harley. "I'll be in town for the next two days."

Silver, Wes, and El Lobo were able to get three adjoining rooms on the first floor, just across the hall from Harley's room.

"Let's take a rest until suppertime," Silver suggested.

Harley laughed. "You'd better rest while you can. The stage from Santa Fe will be here tomorrow."

Closing the door and locking it behind him, Wes hung his hat and gunbelts on a bedpost. He then sat down on the bed, tugging off his boots. Renita stood watching him.

"Well," said Wes, "aren't you going to join me?"

"I don't have anything to wear that's nice enough for me to stand before a preacher," Renita said.

"You can buy some new clothes," said Wes, "but you don't have to have them now, do you?"

"No," Renita said, "but when?"

"Maybe tomorrow," said Wes. "Tamara and Molly may want to go with you."

"And you don't," Renita said.

"No," said Wes. "I don't. I'd feel like a bull in a sheep corral, surrounded by all that female finery. I'll see it when you're wearin' it."

"So you'd leave me at the mercy of those outlaws? I wonder if Silver and El Lobo will feel that way about Molly and Tamara."

"Damn it, if that's what's bitin' you, I'll go with you," Wes said. "Now let's rest."

Removing only her hat and gunbelt, she stretched out on the bed beside him. But she was restless, and when Wes opened his eyes, she was looking at him.

"I'm afraid," she said.

"So am I," said Wes, "but you must learn to face your fears one at a time, as they become real. Hell, if I let everything that's botherin' me jump on me at one time, I reckon I'd dig me a hole, crawl in, and pull it all in over me."

She laughed nervously. "I am taking one thing at a time. On the train, I was facing the door, just as Tamara was, but I didn't see the gunman. I'm afraid I won't see him the next time, either."

"There may not be a next time," Wes said. "That was an unusual situation, and there's no way of knowing that Tamara could pull off the same thing twice. Neither of you was armed for such a shoot-out. But to defend yourselves against men like those who took you away in El Paso, just having a gun may be enough. You may never have to use it. Tamara didn't shoot the gunman on the train, but her shot startled him, and his went wild. It was enough to buy some time, until Silver, El Lob, Harley, and me could take a hand."

"I didn't mean to burden you with my fears," said Renita. "I just want to help you in your fight, and I'm just not sure I'm capable."

"Put it out of your mind," Wes said. "You don't know what you can do until you're in a position of have to."

Empty growled, and suddenly there was a knock on the door. Wes came off the bed with a Colt in his hand. The knock came again, accompanied by a voice.

"It's Harley."

Wes unlocked the door, opening it just enough for Harley to enter.

"I'm goin' back to the depot for a while," Harley said. "You need anything while I'm out?"

"The westbound should be bringing newspapers," said Wes. "Get me one of each."

Wes let him out, locked the door behind him, and again stretched out on the bed. He had no idea how long he had slept when Empty awakened him with a growl.

"Your newspapers," said Harley, outside the door.

Renita was awake, so Wes threw the newspapers on the bed. There was the current paper from Kansas City, with day-old editions from St. Louis, Cheyenne, and Denver.

"Take one of them and see if you can find anything of interest to us," Wes said.

Wes had gone through the Kansas City paper and was almost through with the St. Louis edition when Renita spoke.

"Here's something."

There were only six lines. A man had been stabbed to death near the Plains Hotel in Cheyenne. The motive was unknown, for his wallet, with money and identification, had not been taken. His name was Rance Stringfield, and his last known address had been Denver.

"That confirms what we suspected," said Wes. "The bastards don't always pay off in counterfeit double eagles."

Wes tore out the brief article, and at suppertime allowed his companions to read it.

"Not in the least surprising," Silver said. "That's why we've had such a hell of a time tracking them down. By the time we have word of a possible witness, he's already dead."

Foster Hagerman joined them for supper, and Wes passed him the article from the Cheyenne newspaper.

"That won't mean much," said Wes, "until you know a little about Stringfield."

Wes looked at Silver, and Silver nodded. Wes then told Hagerman of the attempted ambush Stringfield had arranged, using Renita and Tamara as bait.

"They are ruthless, then," Hagerman said.

"That, and worse," said Wes. "That's why Renita and Tamara are here, and why Silver has Molly Horrel coming here."

"I wish we could assure you they'll be safe here," Hagerman said, "but the more I hear of this conspiracy, the less certain I am."

"*Sí,*" said El Lobo. "We leave them here, go Dragon hunting. We be damn fools."

"Let me remind you that you and Wes don't *have* to do any such thing," Silver said.

"The hell we don't," said Wes. "They don't aim to leave us be, whether we're looking for them or not. We've hurt them enough to get ourselves lined up against a wall and shot ten times over. We can save ourselves only by getting them before they get us."

"You have given your word to Señor Silver," Tamara said, her eyes on El Lobo. "You do not go back on your word, or I hate you."

El Lobo laughed. "We kill *bastardo* Dragon before it kill us."

Renita's face was pale, and it cost her, but she took her stand with Tamara.

"Wes will do what he feels he must do," said Renita, "and I will stand beside him."

With admiration in his eyes, Bryan Silver looked from one of them to the other. Molly Horrel would be arriving on tomorrow's stage from Santa Fe. He could only hope the girl would have the courage of these two who had already been to hell and back, and were more than willing to go again, if they had to.

Chapter 5

Boulder, Colorado, March 29, 1885

Just minutes before the eastbound train would depart for Kansas City, Gandy Franks spoke to the baggage man who was loading sacks of mail.

"I didn't get this letter posted in time, and it must reach Kansas City today."

"That ain't my responsibility," said the baggage man. "I just load and unload sacks of mail."

"I realize that," Franks said. "I'm making it worth your while."

With the sealed envelope, he handed the baggage man a double eagle.

"There's nothin' on this envelope but a name," said the baggage man. "I never heard of no Morton Tindall."

"The name's all you'll need," Franks said. "Just leave the letter with the telegrapher. I'll telegraph Tindall that it's coming, and he'll pick it up, just like a telegram."

"If that's all I got to do, then I'll do it," said the baggage man.

Franks quickly left the depot, satisfied that Drade Hogan could find no fault with his handling of the situation in Dodge. He had dared not telegraph Gannon in Dodge, for he well knew that Wes Stone had friends there. His instructions to Tindall in Kansas City he was sending by letter, for its very nature forbade use of the telegraph. The letter itself could be deadly evidence if it fell into the wrong hands. Franks immediately sent a telegram to Tindall.

Morton Tindall was waiting when the eastbound train reached Kansas City, and he watched as the baggage man delivered the letter to the telegrapher. He waited a few minutes before going to the telegraph office to claim it. The unsigned letter was two pages long, and when Tindall had read it, he read it a second time. One paragraph stood out.

There is a reward of twenty-five thousand dollars on the heads of each of these three men: Bryan Silver, Wes Stone, and Palo Elfego.

Within the envelope was a second sealed envelope, and within it, drawn on a Kansas City bank, was a draft for fifty thousand dollars. With it was a note that read: *Hire as many men as you must, for as long as may be necessary. You know the penalty for failure.*

Tindall swallowed hard, again referring to information provided in the letter. Just how difficult could it be, killing three men in Dodge?

Dodge City, Kansas, March 29, 1885

The stage from Santa Fe arrived in the late afternoon. Molly Horrel was the last of the dusty, weary passengers to emerge.

"Molly," said Silver, "this is Harley Stafford and Foster Hagerman. You remember the rest of this bunch, I reckon."

"I feel like every bone is my body is broken, or at

least fractured," Molly said. "If I had it to do over, I think I'd just walk."

She made it a point to go immediately to Renita and Tamara, for she hadn't seen them since they had been taken by the outlaws in El Paso.

"You and Tamara are wearing guns," said Molly. "Are you still in danger?"

"Yes," Renita said, "and so are you. Silver has a lot to tell you."

"She's right," said Silver. "The situation is far more dangerous than when I sent for you to join me here. Let's get back to the Dodge House, where we can talk."

"I need a bath," Molly said. "I have dust in places I can't talk about."

"We'll join the rest of you for supper," said Silver.

When they reached the Dodge House, Silver arranged for a tub and bathwater to be brought to his room. Harley had returned to the depot with Foster Hagerman, leaving El Lobo, Wes, Renita, and Tamara on their own.

"The Dodge House is nice," Renita said, "but can't we do something between now and supper besides sleep?"

El Lobo laughed.

"She does not mean *that*," Tamara said, glaring at him.

"I am in need of some new clothes," said Renita. "Can we afford them?"

"I reckon," Wes said.

"I need clothes, too," said Tamara. "Palo do not notice if I am stark naked."

"Come on, Palo," Wes said. "Give her some money. If they're together, we won't have to wander around through all that female finery."

"You wouldn't send us to town alone?" said Renita.

"No," Wes said. "We'll be somewhere in the store. We just don't aim to get trapped in among the corsets and that other female stuff."

Being a railroad town, and with Fort Dodge only eight miles distant, Dodge boasted a varied array of shops and stores. One of them had devoted an entire upper floor to female apparel. Wes and El Lobo occupied themselves on the first floor, admiring an assortment of new Winchester and Remington rifles in a gun rack. When a stranger stepped out from behind a display, Wes caught the movement off to the side. He whirled, a Colt cocked and in his hand. Though the stranger was armed he made no move toward his holstered weapon. He laughed.

"You're mighty sudden with that iron, and mighty jumpy."

"I don't like *hombres* cat-footin' up behind me," said Wes shortly. "What do you want of me?"

"Nothin', at the moment," the stranger said. "You're Wes Stone, the gunslinger, ain't you?"

"I'm Wes Stone," Wes said coldly. "Who are you?"

The stranger laughed again. "Nobody you'd know. I ain't famous like you."

Hitching his thumbs in his gunbelt, he wandered away. Following a few paces behind, Wes followed, watching him out the front door.

"*Malo?*" El Lobo asked.

"Maybe," said Wes. "While I was with the railroad, I made a name for myself with a gun. Now it looks like as long as I'm alive, I'll never overcome the need to prove myself."

El Lobo said nothing. It was yet another danger for which Wes must be prepared. For the better part of two hours they waited, and when Renita and Tamara came down the stairs, they were radiant. Each wore a long dress.

"Madre mia," El Lobo groaned. "It take so long just for one dress?"

"There are others," said Tamara. "I can wear but one at a time."

When the rest of their purchases were delivered to the cash register on the first floor, there was a formidable load.

"Tarnation," Wes said, "we'll have to make three trips."

"If it's not too far," said the saleslady, "it can be delivered."

"The Dodge House," Wes said.

Wes and El Lobo paid the bill.

"I'm goin' out first," said Wes, when they reached the door.

"I follow," El Lobo said.

"It's daylight and we're in town," said Renita. "What's wrong?"

"Maybe nothing," Wes said. "Both of you stay inside for a minute."

Half a block away, across the street, a man leaned against an awning post. Seeing Wes, he stepped off the boardwalk into the dusty street.

"You got a reputation, Stone. I want it."

"I don't know you," said Wes, "and I have nothing against you. I won't fight."

"You got to," the stranger said. "It's the way things is done."

His sandy hair licked out from beneath his used-up old black hat, and he didn't look old enough to shave. His Levi's and denim shirt had seen many washings, and his rough-out boots were runover. Only his gunbelt and the Colt with the polished walnut grips looked new.

"That's far enough," said Wes.

"Draw, damn you," the kid shouted, his hand hovering near the butt of his Colt.

"No," said Wes, his hands on his hips. "If there's a hand to be played out, the first draw is yours."

The kid went for his gun, but just as his Colt cleared leather, a slug crashed into it. The weapon went flying, and the kid stood there, wringing his bloody hand. Wes Stone had already holstered his smoking Colt, and several who had witnessed the event hadn't seen him draw.

"Damn you," the kid bawled, "you've shamed me. For God's sake, shoot me and put me out of my misery."

"I'm not goin' to shoot you," Wes said, "unless you come after me again. Then I'll kill you. Now vamoose."

His young face filled with hate, he turned away, walking down the dusty street. Doors had suddenly opened, and men stood on the boardwalk. Reining up his horse, Sheriff Jack Dumery dismounted.

"He forced the fight, Sheriff," said Wes. "I didn't want to fight him."

"Curly Dismukes," Sheriff Dumery said. "His daddy drank himself to death, and Curly wants almighty bad to be somebody. He thinks he can make a name for himself with a gun. You'd better be mighty careful."

"I aim to," said Wes. "He'll have a sore hand, and he's without a gun. Maybe that will be enough to change his mind."

"I doubt it," Dumery said. "Somebody will have to kill him. He's the kind who won't have it any other way."

Renita and Tamara had left the store as soon as the echo of the shot had died away. Without a word, they followed Wes and El Lobo back to the Dodge House. Empty had been left in the room, and Wes let him out. El Lobo followed Tamara into their room and then locked the door behind them. Somewhere in the distance, the westbound train whistled for the stop in Dodge.

"What was the shooting about?" Renita asked, after Wes had locked their door.

"A kid looking for a reputation as a fast draw," said Wes. "He knew me from my railroad days, I reckon."

"He wasn't one of the outlaws, then."

"No," Wes said.

"It's worse than I thought," said Renita. "Besides the outlaws, you could be shot by someone you don't even know."

"A fast gun is a blessing and a curse," Wes said. "It's a blessing because it can keep a man alive, but a curse because of his continual need to depend on it."

"Don't send Tamara and me off alone anymore," said Renita. "I have a gun, and if I have to watch your back to keep you alive, I will."

In El Lobo's room, he had just endured a similar argument with Tamara.

"Do not send Renita and me away again," Tamara said. "We have guns, and we will use them when we must."

Silver had removed his boots, hat, and gunbelt, and had stretched out on the bed while Molly had lounged in the tub of hot, soapy water. He awoke to find her out of the tub, drying herself with a towel.

"This is the first time a man ever fell asleep while I was naked, taking a bath," said Molly. "I must be losing it."

Silver laughed. "So there have been other men."

"I've lost count," Molly said. "You want references?"

"I reckon not," said Silver. "If you were good enough for Nathan Stone, then you're good enough for me."

"If another man said that to me, I'd show him the door and give him hell," Molly said.

"If I was fillin' anybody's boots but Nathan's, you wouldn't be here," said Silver.

"Then I suppose I'd better not tell you about my days with King Fisher," Molly said. "I'd never been with a man, when he took me to south Texas, promising to marry me. But he never gave up his drinking, gambling, and hell-raising."[1]

"So you left him and went to Nathan," said Silver.

"I didn't go to Nathan in the way that you think," Molly said. "I knew he was there in El Paso, but I went there because that's all the stage fare I had, not because I expected anything from him. He saw me get off the stage and took me to a cafe, where I ate like a pig. I was half starved and hadn't eaten for three days. Then he took me to the boardinghouse, and Granny Boudleaux made me welcome. After that, Nathan and me just seemed to come together. I felt guilty when I learned that Wes was Nathan's son. Wes had a very old photograph of his mother as a young girl. Her name was Molly, and I always believed I reminded Nathan of her. But he was a good man, a kind man, and he never seemed to feel bad toward me about my days with King Fisher."

"Nor do I," said Silver. "Not for those days with King Fisher, or for those days that followed, with Nathan. I didn't tell you in the letter I sent from Santa Fe, but this will be my last assignment. I'm resigning my position with the government and goin' back to good old Texas. I'm thinking of a horse ranch."

She dropped the towel and threw herself on the bed beside him.

"I'm so glad," Molly said. "I've been afraid for you, ever since you left El Paso."

"I wish I could tell you that you no longer have

[1] *The Autumn of the Gun*

to be afraid," said Silver, "but there's some hard trails ahead. In Denver we bought three .31-caliber Colt revolvers, each with a gunbelt and a supply of ammunition. Renita and Tamara are armed, and I have one of the weapons for you."

"Then I'll carry it and learn to use it," Molly said. "Perhaps I can help you, where I was unable to help Nathan."

"You'd better get dressed," said Silver. "Wes and Palo will be ready to put on the feed bag pretty soon. Tomorrow we'll buy you some new clothes."

Harley and Foster Hagerman were already at Delmonico's when Silver and his party arrived. When all the meals had been ordered, Harley produced a Kansas City newspaper.

"Anything in there of interest to us?" Wes asked.

"Yes," said Harley, "but you won't like it. It's on the second page."

Wes folded the paper and spread it on the table. He couldn't believe his eyes. In large bold type, the headline read: *Wes Stone, noted gunfighter, returns to Dodge City.*

"Who in tarnation is responsible for this?" Wes shouted.

Silver took the paper and began reading the article aloud. Whoever had written it went to great lengths reporting the various gunfights in which Wes had been forced to defend himself. There was some reference to the violent gunfight in El Paso, when Nathan Stone had died, and the bloody venture into old Mexico after the killers were referred to as a "murdering spree." The devilish piece of journalism concluded by stating that Wes Stone had begun keeping company with an evil, bloodthirsty Indian.

"*Bastardos,*" El Lobo snarled. "I show them."

"Why?" Molly asked. "Who could have done such a terrible thing? Someone's trying to force Wes into the same kind of life Nathan tried so hard to escape. There'll be gunmen coming from everywhere, forcing him to fight."

"There's already been one," said Renita. "He was waiting for Wes when we left the store."

"I didn't hear about that," Foster Hagerman said.

"Neither did Molly and me," said Silver. "We were at the Dodge House."

"Just a kid," Wes said. "He left with a broken Colt and a bloody hand."

"You should have killed him," said Hagerman. "Now he'll likely ambush you if he gets the chance."

"I didn't want to kill him," Wes said. "Somehow he and others like him have to learn that how tall a man stands has nothing to do with how quick he can pull a gun."

"Unfortunately, that's the standard for measuring a man on the frontier," said Silver. "The time is coming when we'll become a nation of laws, and men can hang up their guns, but there'll be a few more hard years. I have no doubt this story was planted in the newspaper by the very bunch of outlaws we're after. It will suit their purpose if the town's full of would-be gunslingers trying to force Wes into a gunfight."

"I think you've come up with the answer," Harley said. "While Wes is being forced to defend himself against some young coyote hungry for a reputation, what better time for a bushwhacker to gun him down?"

"We watch," said El Lobo. "Kill."

"*Sí*," Tamara said.

"I'm obliged to all of you," said Wes, "but this creates a whole new set of problems. I had hoped, by staying here a few days, we could force the Golden Dragon into the open. Now I suspect every damn pistol-packer west of the Mississippi will be comin' here, looking to beat me with his fast draw. Like Harley says, it's likely the reason for the story in the newspaper. I reckon I'll have to go back to Denver. If I'm goin' to become a target, I might as well lure out some of the varmints we're after."

"I'm not staying in Dodge while you go to Denver to be shot," Renita said.

"I go with you, *amigo*," said El Lobo.

"*Sí*," Tamara said. "I go."

"Nobody's going to Denver just yet," said Silver. "I'm satisfied Wes can defend himself against any gun-throwers looking for a reputation. Our chances of rooting out the Dragon in a city the size of Denver are slim. In Dodge, we have the edge. We'll return to Denver when we have a reason to. Right now, we don't."

"It makes sense to me," said Foster Hagerman. "Here, you have access to telegrams into and out of Dodge, and you have Harley and me keeping a watch on incoming trains. It won't be easy for them, getting gunmen into town without them being seen."

"That's true," Silver said, "but their killers won't be coming on the train. Dodge isn't more than fifty miles from Indian Territory, and it's loaded with thieves and killers."

"My God, yes," said Foster Hagerman, "we're overlooking the obvious. When Nathan was riding security for the railroad, he chased a gang of thieves into Indian Territory. They were almost the death of him."[2]

"That explains why there were no telegrams sent to Dodge," Harley said. "They'll have a contact in Wichita or Kansas City."

"Yes," said Silver. "They'll send a man from there into Indian Territory."

[2] *The Dawn of Fury*

"Killers," Renita said. "What are we going to do?"

"We'll have to keep watch," said Silver. "They'll ride in, one or two at a time. In fact, some of them may pose as fast guns, looking for a fight with Wes."

"If they come looking for me, it's my fight," Wes said.

"Not if we can identify them as killers hired by the Golden Dragon," said Silver.

"That may not be possible if they ride in one at a time," Wes said. "If they show up after dark, we won't know where they're from. I don't like the way this is shapin' up."

"Neither do I," said Silver, "but we came here with a plan. Since we don't have anything better, we're going to give this one a chance. I aim to talk to Sheriff Dumery. He needs to know of this story somebody planted in the Kansas City newspaper, and that Wes may be forced to defend himself at any time."

"If he's like most lawmen, he'll suggest that I get out of town," Wes said.

"I expect he'll think of that," said Silver, "but I can override him if I have to. I have a plan that will destroy their efforts to send hired killers after us from Indian Territory."

"Indian Territory is a disgrace," Foster Hagerman said. "Washington should long since have sent in soldiers to rid it of renegades and killers."

"Precisely my thoughts," said Silver. "How many shipments of gold has the railroad lost to renegades from the territory?"

"Entirely too many," Hagerman said gloomily. "The most recent one was a twenty-five-thousand-dollar army payroll."

"I tracked them all the way across the Cimarron," said Harley. "When they rode into Indian Territory, the posse turned back, leaving me out-gunned twelve-to-one."

"What does any of this have to do with your plan?" Wes asked Silver.

"Like I've said, we'll have to keep watch for a while," said Silver, "but I have an idea that may pull the fangs of Indian Territory for all time. It should also put a crimp in the Dragon's tail by drying up their source of hired killers."

"The West would be eternally grateful to you," Hagerman said, "but hired killers can be brought in from Texas, New Mexico, Colorado, or Missouri."

"I agree," said Silver, "but as it now stands, they're an hour away from losing themselves in Indian Territory. Without that sanctuary, a posse could ride them down."

"Since we're virtually certain that the Golden Dragon's hired killers will be comin' from Indian Territory," Wes said, "tell us what you have in mind. What can you do, and what would you have El Lobo and me do?"

"We'll need to buy some time," said Silver. "That means there may be killers gunning for us as soon as tomorrow. Starting tonight, in four-hour watches, you, El Lobo, or me will be outside the Dodge House from dusk until dawn. Tomorrow, when the eastbound train arrives, I'll have letters going to Washington. I will be requesting that a company of soldiers be deployed to Wichita and a second company to Dodge, for the express purpose of invading and cleaning up Indian Territory."

"You can't do that without the approval of Congress," said Foster Hagerman.

"The president of the United States can," Silver replied.

"Tarnation," said Wes. "You can get through to the president?"

"I can," Silver said. "President Grover Cleveland has few friends in Washington, and the Congress is hostile to his every move. He's sorely in need of a popular issue that will appeal to the people. This bunch of thieves and killers in Indian Territory, with their constant plundering of railroad shipments and banks, might be exactly what he needs to show the country he's a man with a mind of his own."

"*Bueno*," said El Lobo. "He sends *soldados*."

"I always thought Congress had to approve the money for any kind of conflict," Harley said. "Especially for the declaration of war, and that's what it'll be in Indian Territory."

"They do," said Silver, "but once the soldiers are in Wichita and Dodge, and their purpose for being there is known, there's not a politician in Washington with guts enough to say no to the funds to continue the mission. As for planting stories in the newspapers, these Golden Dragon varmints are about to learn something. As soon as the president decides to deploy soldiers, there'll be a news release sent to every major newspaper in the country."

Harley laughed. "You play rough, Silver."

"*Sí*," El Lobo said. "*Bueno*."

"It'll be one hell of a hand if you can play it out to the finish," said Wes.

"I aim to try," Silver said. "It's time we were getting back to the Dodge House. I'll take the first four-hour watch. Harley, will you tell Sheriff Dumery I want to see him?"

"I'll tell him," said Harley, "and any time I'm in town, feel free to call on me."

The friends parted company. When Silver and his party reached the Dodge House, Silver, Wes, and El Lobo unlocked the doors and entered their rooms first. Silver took his Winchester from a corner and jacked a shell into the chamber.

"Oh, do be careful," Molly said.

"I aim to," said Silver. "This is the easy part, makin' them come to us."

When Silver stepped outside, Wes and El Lobo were waiting for him.

"Palo will take the second watch, leavin' me the third," Wes said. "We'll be sleeping light, with our guns handy."

"*Gracias*," said Silver. "I don't look for any trouble before tomorrow night, but we're in no position to risk it."

Silver had been on watch only a few minutes when Sheriff Dumery arrived.

"You're expecting trouble, I reckon," Dumery said.

"We're not inviting it," said Silver, "but if it comes, we're ready. Do you read the newspapers?"

"If you mean the latest one from Kansas City, I saw the story on Stone. What do you make of it?"

"Like you've been told, there's a bunch of outlaws wantin' us dead, and they're not too picky about who does the killing," Silver said. "I hope you'll keep that in mind, and that if you chance to meet a gun-thrower looking for a reputation, you'll encourage him to ride on."

"I'll do that," said Dumery.

"A lawman's inclined to frown on shooting, justifiable or not," Silver said, "so I want you to keep one thing in mind. We won't start anything, but we'll defend ourselves. If we are shot at, we'll shoot back."

"I wouldn't expect any man to do any less," said Dumery. "Good luck."

He rode away, and but for the comings and goings of Dodge House patrons, Silver saw nobody else until El Lobo relieved him. Silver knocked on the door, identified himself, and Molly let him in. She was fully dressed, except for her hat. The gunbelt with the Colt was buckled around her waist.

"You should have gone to bed," said Silver.

"If there's trouble, what good would I be to you in bed?"

"If there's trouble, I don't expect you to be slinging lead in the street," Silver said. "The gun is for you to protect yourself when I'm not there."

Silver leaned his Winchester up beside the bed, hung his hat and gunbelt on the bedpost, and pulled off his boots. Molly removed her gunbelt and boots.

"Go on to bed," said Silver. "I have some letters to write."

"I've spent too many nights in bed alone," Molly said. "I'll wait for you."

Wichita, Kansas, March 30, 1885

Morton Tindall left the train at Wichita. Renting a horse at the livery, he rode south, toward Indian Territory. His saddlebags were heavy with double eagles.

Chapter 6

In the office of the treasury, Simpkins and Taylor were reading Bryan Silver's letter for the second time.

"I hope there is some method to this madness," Simpkins said, shaking his head. "I can see where the renegades hiding out in Indian Territory have become a problem, but I fail to see any connection between them and this Golden Dragon conspiracy."

"Nor do I," said Taylor, "but the attorney general's office has the utmost confidence in Silver. Through his efforts, we have recovered millions in stolen gold in San Francisco.[1] I am inclined to go along with any plan he proposes. God knows, we certainly do not have anything better."

"I agree," Simpkins replied. "If our position in this matter is questioned, I propose we back Silver and allow him to play out his hand."

"So be it," said Taylor.

Elsewhere in Washington, President Grover Cleveland had just read a lengthy proposal from Silver. He passed it to Willoughby, his trusted aide.

"Read it, Willoughby, and tell me how it strikes you."

Willoughby read it twice and returned it.

[1] *Sixguns and Double Eagles*

"He strikes me as a man who's not afraid to rock the boat, or to sink it, if need be," Willoughby said. "Certainly he has an axe to grind, but no more so than you, sir."

"Precisely my thoughts," said Cleveland. "By God, it just might work, and if it does not, can my official position be any more precarious than it is already? Cut the necessary orders dispatching two hundred soldiers to Kansas. A hundred to Wichita and a hundred to Dodge City. Once they're on the way, telegraph all the major newspapers, telling them only what Silver has suggested."

"I will not mention him, then."

"You will not," Cleveland said. "Should this endeavor fail, I will not have it said that I did not accept full responsibility. Win or lose, when Mr. Silver returns to Washington, see that he is told I wish to meet him. Do you know where he's originally from?"

"Texas, I believe, sir."

"He would be," said Cleveland. "I seem to recall that when Texas wanted only to join the Union, our Congress gave them hell. I suspect there are better men riding the range than most of those sitting on their duffs in the United States Senate."

"Undoubtedly, sir," Willoughby said.

"Now get cracking," said Cleveland. "I want those orders cut and implemented immediately."

Dodge City, Kansas, April 1, 1885

When El Lobo awakened Wes for the third watch, Renita sat up.

"Get back to sleep," Wes said. "I'm goin' to relieve Palo."

"I can't sleep, with you out there," said Renita. "I'm going with you."

"No," Wes said. "I can better protect myself when I'm alone."

But Renita insisted on going with him, and Wes eventually gave in. With the small hours of the morning, the moon had set and the stars were meager pinpoints of light, as they seemed to be retreating to that realm where they spent their daylight hours. There was no light except for a single bracket lamp at the main entrance to the Dodge House. As dawn neared, the darkness seemed all the more intense. Suddenly there was the *clop-clop-clop* of a horse coming at them from the left.

"Back off," Wes hissed, for Renita was behind him.

Wes cocked his Winchester, straining his eyes, and when at last he could see the dim outline of the horse, the animal was riderless. Barely in time, Wes dropped to the ground and rolled, as off to his right, a rifle roared twice. Slugs ripped through the air just above him, but before he could return the fire, Renita's .31-caliber Colt spoke once, twice, three times. The decoy horse had been spooked, and nickering, ran back the way it had come. No lights were showing, but doors opened swiftly. Silver and El Lobo were there.

"Renita," Wes whispered, "where are you?"

"I . . . I'm here," said Renita.

In an instant, Wes was beside her. She still lay belly-down, gripping the Colt with both hands. Suddenly a lamp was lighted within the Dodge House, and there was the sound of a galloping horse.

"Rein up and identify yourself," Silver demanded.

"Sheriff Jack Dumery," said a voice from the darkness.

"Come on," Silver said.

The Dodge House night manager was approaching with a lantern.

"I heard shooting," said Sheriff Dumery. "Explanations, anybody?"

"The oldest trick in the book," Wes said. "A decoy horse, and when I was able to see it was riderless, it was almost too late. There were two shots, and Renita returned fire."

"I shot at the flash from his gun," said Renita. "I didn't know what else to do."

"You did exactly the right thing," Wes said, "but you might have been killed. There was a muzzle flash from your gun, too."

Other lamps were lighted and other doors opened, as Dodge House patrons sought to learn what had happened.

"This is terrible, and could give the establishment a bad name," said the manager. "I'd appreciate it, Sheriff, if you'd investigate this in daylight."

"I'll investigate it now," Dumery said. "Let me have that lantern."

Reluctantly the night manager handed the lantern to the sheriff.

"Now," said Sheriff Dumery, "one of you show me where those shots came from."

"Come on," Wes said.

Drumery immediately found two empty shell casings, but there was something more.

"Blood," Wes said. "There on the ground."

"I see it," said Dumery. "Maybe there's enough of it to leave a trail."

But the blood spots were not numerous enough, and with only the dim lantern light to guide them, they soon gave it up.

"Renita," Wes said, "at least one of your shots drew blood, but whatever trail there is, we can't follow by lantern light."

"At first light I'll try again," said Sheriff Dumery, "and I'll keep watch here until then. All of you get back to bed."

They all returned to their rooms, locking their doors. Only then did Renita surrender to her terror. Wordlessly, she clung to Wes, trembling. It was a while before she was able to speak.

"I saw you fall to the ground, and I did the same. I started shooting before I thought of what I should do. I . . . I don't know why. . . ."

"You have the instincts of a gunfighter," said Wes. "When a bushwhacker cuts down on you, there's not much time to think. You took the risk of being killed, and in spite of that, I must say I'm proud of you."

"That means a lot to me," Renita said. "It was worth the risk."

Dawn came, and when Silver and his party reached Delmonico's for breakfast, Harley Stafford and Foster Hagerman were already there.

"I heard the shooting," said Harley, "but it was over by the time I got to the door."

"I didn't get off a shot," Wes said. "Renita returned fire and got at least one hit."

"Ma'am," said Harley, "in the dark, that's good shootin' for anybody. I have just two ambitions in life. One is to have me a woman that can shoot like hell wouldn't have it, and the other is to always stay on the good side of her."

"I'll accept that as a compliment," Renita said. "Wes has told me a lot about you."

"Any idea who might have fired those shots?" Hagerman asked.

"I figure it was the kid who forced me to draw against him," said Wes. "He had no real grudge against me before. Now he may be after revenge, because I didn't kill him."

"Dear God," Renita said, "how can a man be so

foolish? He should be grateful to you for sparing him."

"They never are," said Wes. "Foolish pride has killed more men than bad whiskey. But those aiming to prove themselves by ventilating me will have to get in line. By now, the varmints behind the Golden Dragon will be gathering a legion of killers."

"But not from Indian Territory, if your plan works," Harley said. "How will you know if the president favors it?"

"There'll be no messages, because he can't risk word of it leaking out," said Silver. "I think we'll know by tomorrow, and the newspapers will tell us."

Indian Territory, April 1, 1885

The outlaw stronghold with which Morton Tindall was familiar was closer to Wichita than Dodge. Tindall was welcome there, for he had successfully hired killers from among their ranks before. He paid well, paid in gold, and paid in advance, and for those reasons, the outlaws went to great lengths to please him. Illivane, the renegade leader, spoke.

"Hell, for thirty thousand dollars, we'll gun down everybody in Dodge, women and kids included, but we don't like sneakin' in, one or two of us at a time. We're used to all of us ridin' in a bunch, doin' what's to be done, and then ridin' on. Why is these three peckerwoods so different from anybody else?"

"For one thing, they're hard as hell to kill," said Tindall. "You ain't doin' this for me. I represent an outfit that don't pay for failure. Foul this up, and it'll be the finish of me, but they won't stop there. They'll come after you. All of you."

Some of the outlaws laughed nervously, looking

around as though they feared Tindall might have led demons into their midst.

"We ain't superstitious," Illivane said. "Anybody comin' after us will have to unravel all of Indian Territory."

"That's why I'm here," said Tindall. "You can get within fifty miles of Dodge, but when you ride across the Cimarron, no sheriff's posse will follow you. I'm not the kind to pay a man to do a job and then tell him how to do it, but you'd better not ride into town, all of you in a bunch. One of the three *hombres* I'm payin' you to salt down is a federal man, Bryan Silver."

"A well-placed slug, and he'll bleed like anybody else," Illivane said.

"Maybe," said Tindall, "but he knows there's a price on his head. He may have alerted the local law, and there may be a reception committee waiting. That's why I'm sayin' it's a risk, all of you ridin' in at once. They'll expect that. The other two *hombres*— Palo Elfego and Wes Stone—have their women with them."

Illivane laughed. "All the better. We'll take the women alive and bring them back with us to the territory."

"Don't count on it," Tindall said. "These women have been taken before. Now they're armed, just like the men. Stone has a hound that follows him, and Elfego is a highfalutin Indian. Silver's a federal man, but he's also a Texan. He's hell on wheels with a Colt or a Winchester."

"Hell, these varmints that's nine feet tall don't scare us," said Illivane. "They're all just bigger targets. Show us your money, and we'll ride today."

"It's in my saddlebags," Tindall said. "Have somebody fetch them."

"Hampton," said Illivane, "bring them saddlebags and a blanket."

Tindall sat with his back to a tree, all the outlaws where he could see them. A tied-down Colt rode his right hip. Knowing the gold was a temptation, that any one of the men before him would kill for a handful of double eagles, he had made it his policy to always pay them in advance. While they might kill him and take the gold, that would be the end of their bonanza, as far as he was concerned. He was gambling they wouldn't be that foolish, and so far, he had won. Hampton returned with the saddlebags, and Illivane dumped their golden contents on the blanket.

"Count it," Tindall invited.

Illivane laughed. "You never shorted us before. We just like to see the color of the money before we ride. I reckon you could say it inspires us."

"Fail this time, and there won't be any more," said Tindall. "At least, not from me."

"We don't aim to fail," Illivane said. "Do we, boys?"

"Hell no," they shouted.

For some unaccountable reason, Tindall was ill at ease as he rode back to Wichita. He had the feeling that something was about to go wrong. He wouldn't fully understand the meaning of his premonitions until he read the next day's edition of the Kansas City newspaper.

Dodge City, Kansas, April 1, 1885

"Molly and me are going to buy her some new clothes," Silver said, when they had finished breakfast at Delmonico's. "All of you are welcome to go with us."

"I don't think so," said Wes. "I reckon Palo and me have had enough of that. At least, I have."

"*Sí*," El Lobo said.

"But there may be trouble," said Renita.

"None that I can't handle," Silver said. "I think we'll be safe enough, until tomorrow."

Wes, Renita, El Lob, and Tamara returned to the Dodge House.

"I do hope they'll be all right," said Renita. "After last night, I'm jumpy."

"We could have insisted on going with them," Wes said, "but I had the feeling Silver didn't want us along."

"I think he's been a very lonely man," said Renita. "He's never had a woman to think of, to buy for, and he wants the experience all to himself."

El Lobo laughed.

"You are insensitive brute, like the *mulos*," Tamara said. "*Silencio*."

"*Sangre de Christo*," said El Lobo mournfully. "For this I bring her from Mexico?"

Bryan Silver was enjoying what for him was a first-time experience. The more he saw of Molly Horrel—this woman who had once belonged to at least two other men—the more certain he was that he had made the right decision. Silver was by no means a poor man, and he was amused by Molly's reluctance to spend money.

"Sooner or later," Silver said, "you'll have to return to Washington with me, and I'll not have it appear that I'm too cheap to dress you properly."

"You're spoiling me," said Molly. "Before King Fisher took me in, I was still walking around barefooted. A grown woman, with just one old dress and not a stitch of underwear to call my own. We Horrels were what better folks called trash."

"Don't ever let me hear you refer to yourself like that again," Silver said.

Silver waited while Molly took some dresses into a fitting room.

"They're all so nice," she said, when she emerged. "I can't decide which one I like the most."

"Take them all," said Silver.

Silver paid for all the clothing that Molly had selected, and they left the store.

"You'll never have to buy me anything else," Molly said.

"That's what you think," said Silver. "Someday you're going to be the belle of south Texas. Now let's go to the mercantile. I need some more shells."

There were several men in the mercantile, and they watched with interest when Silver and Molly entered. Silver wasted no time, but went immediately to the counter to make his purchase. One of the men boldly eyed Molly from head to toe, and when she blushed, he grinned and spoke.

"Ma'am, lemme introduce myself. I'm Jake Turko, and I reckon I'm more an *hombre* than the varmint you come in with."

Molly was speechless, and before she could move, Turko had a hand on her arm. But Silver had heard. He turned, bringing a right all the way from his knees, and when his fist exploded against the big man's chin, Turko went down with a crash that shook the building. He didn't get up.

"Here, now," the storekeeper shouted, "I'll have none of that in here."

"Then you'd better be more watchful as to what comes in that door," said Silver, "and you'd better drag this coyote out before he comes to. If he so much as looks at her again, I'll kill him."

Two men, apparently Turko's companions, helped him to his feet and hustled him out the door.

"I'm sure he was drunk, or nearly so," the store-keeper mumbled.

Silver said nothing. When he had paid for his purchase, he led Molly out of the store. "I'm sorry," said Molly. "I didn't even look at him."

"No fault of yours," Silver said. "Some varmints take a drink or two, and they forget the few manners they had."

A second night at the Dodge House was spent quietly. Silver, Wes, and El Lobo again stood watch by turns, but there was no disturbance. When they went to Delmonico's for breakfast, Harley Stafford and Foster Hagerman were already there. Within a few minutes, Sheriff Jack Dumery joined them.

"A quiet night," said Dumery.

"Yes," Silver agreed.

"Maybe something you should know, Silver," said Dumery. "That little disagreement in the store yesterday may turn ugly. Turko fancies himself a gun-slick, and he's spreadin' the word in the saloons he aims to kill you."

"I reckon he'll have to get in line," Silver said.

"He was bothering me," said Molly.

"So I heard," Sheriff Dumery said. "Men have been killed for that. I'll try to talk some sense into him, if I can find him sober enough."

Nothing more was said. The little Wes and El Lobo had heard had been enough. Renita and Tamara eyed Silver with respect. Dumery had only coffee and soon left. Molly looked at Silver's grim face, worry in her eyes. As had become their custom, when breakfast was over, Silver, Wes, and El Lobo were first out the door. Harley Stafford and Foster Hagerman followed, with Molly, Renita, and Tamara. Seeing a rider coming, they all waited.

"Silver," said Sheriff Dumery, "Turko's waiting for

you in front of the Dodge House. I tried to talk some sense into him."

"Can't you arrest him?" Molly cried.

"I could," said Dumery, "but I can't hold him."

"Don't bother, Sheriff," Silver said. "If he won't have it any other way, then we might as well be done with it. The rest of you wait here."

"No," said Molly. "He had other men with him. You can't face them all."

"She's right," Wes said. "We'll stay out of the line of fire, but we'll buy in if it looks like this varmint's settin' you up for somebody else to back-shoot you."

"I'll be there too," said Sheriff Dumery, "and I'll take care of any coyote that even looks like he's got back-shootin' on his mind."

Turko stood well away from the Dodge House, watching them approach. Nobody else was near. Silver nodded to his companions. From here he would go on alone. From his saddle boot, Sheriff Dumery took his Winchester.

"I'm so afraid for him," Molly said, her voice trembling.

"Don't be," said Wes. "He's a man with the bark on."

Silver walked on, his hands at his sides. Turko waited, his thumbs hooked under his gunbelt. His Colt, like Silver's, was tied down on his right hip. Forty feet from Turko, Silver halted.

"I have nothing against you, Turko," Silver said. "It's not too late to resolve this without shooting."

Turko laughed. "There'll be shootin', bucko. You'll shoot or be shot."

"When you're ready, then," said Silver.

Molly tried not to watch, but she was unable to take her frightened eyes off the scene about to be played out to its deadly conclusion. Turko's hand fell first, and Molly cried out, for Silver seemed not to have moved. But suddenly Silver's Colt was in his hand, and it spoke once. An instant later, the sound of Turko's shot might have been an echo. But his weapon had not been leveled, and the lead kicked up dust at his feet. His knees buckled, and he collapsed on his back, his hat tumbling away in the early morning breeze. Silver thumbed out the empty shell casing and reloaded his weapon. Holstering it, he waited, for Molly was running to him, weeping.

"Great God," Sheriff Dumery said, "for a federal man, he's chain lightning with a gun."

"He's a Texan," said Wes.

"Small wonder he and Nathan Stone were friends," Harley said. "Silver's as sudden with a Colt as Nathan was."

Wes, El Lobo, Renita, and Tamara joined Silver and Molly. Harley Stafford and Foster Hagerman went with Sheriff Dumery to meet the curious who had come to investigate the shooting.

"Let's get back to our rooms," said Silver. "This will only attract more unwelcome attention."

They remained at the Dodge House until they heard the whistle of the westbound train as it approached Dodge.

"There'll be today's newspapers from Kansas City," Silver said. "I'm going after them."

"Harley will bring us one at suppertime," said Molly.

"Harley will be leaving on the westbound for the run to Colorado," Wes said. "I'll go for the papers. We can't hide out here forever."

"You shouldn't go alone," said Renita. "You've already been ambushed once."

"Maybe she's right, Wes," Silver said. "One of us should go with you."

"I go," said El Lobo.

Silver said nothing, only too much aware of the

relief in Molly's eyes. The westbound had gone on
its way when Wes and El Lobo reached the depot.
They entered Hagerman's office and found him reading one of the Kansas City newspapers.

"Silver's struck pay dirt," Hagerman said. "Front
page."

*By presidential order, soldiers bound for Indian Terri-
tory,* the big black headline read. Hagerman read the
story aloud.

"That'll play hell with the outlaws and renegades
in Indian Territory," said Wes, "but it may have
come too late to stop them from comin' after us. This
bunch of killers lookin' to salt us down don't waste
any time. I won't be surprised if there's a pack of
coyotes across the Cimarron, just waiting for dark."

Kansas City, Missouri, April 2, 1885

Not believing his eyes, Morton Tindall read the
story a second time, cursing under his breath. While
the outlaws in Indian Territory generally kept up
with the Kansas City newspapers, there was little
chance that Illivane and his bunch would learn of
this development before they rode into Dodge. Any
hell-raising they did in Dodge would further under-
score the need to eliminate the thieves and killers
that infested the frontier. Not just in Indian Territory,
but throughout the Southwest. Now Tindall faced the
unwelcome task of breaking the news to the Golden
Dragon's upper echelons in Denver. The only small
factor in his favor was that Gandy Franks had suggested he hire a band of killers from the wilds of
Indian Territory.

Denver, Colorado, April 2, 1885

Gandy Franks stared grimly at the telegram he had just received from Morton Tindall. He had only the bare facts, with an assurance a letter would follow. The loss of the wild bunch that inhabited Indian Territory would be a serious blow, for its thieves and killers had been employed profitably in Kansas, Missouri, Texas, Arkansas, and Louisiana. Now the Golden Dragon would be forced to import hired killers from elsewhere, at greater expense, and the increased possibility of unwelcome public attention.

Indian Territory, on the Cimarron, April 3, 1885

"I reckon we better pay some attention to what Tindall told us," said Illivane. "There's three *hombres* we got to gun down, and we can't be sure of gettin' 'em all in one visit. I'd say three of us should ride in at a time. If anything goes wrong, it'll be a hell of a lot easier for three to lose themselves, than if there's a dozen of us."

"Yeah," Hampton said, "but who goes first? If the first three gets their string cut, it'll be hell on the rest of us."

"We'll cut the cards," said Illivane. "The three drawin' the lowest cards will be ridin' to Dodge."

Each man drew a card, dropping it faceup.

"You can all see how it is," Illivane said. "Hampton's low, with a deuce, Lawton with a four, and Damark with a six."

"So we ride in at night," said Damark. "We don't know where to start lookin' for the three *hombres* we're supposed to ventilate. How long you aim for us to nose around?"

"Hell, you'll have to be the judge of that," Illivane

said. "Don't foller one another like sheep. Split up, damn it. Visit the saloons and cafes, and keep an eye on the depot. Stone, the *hombre* with the dog, used to work for the railroad. Pay for a round of drinks, if you have to, go watch the train come in, and don't drink nothin' stronger than beer. There's a chance you might force one of these varmints into what looks like a fair fight, and if you do, just be sure you ain't blinded with booze."

Hampton laughed. "You seem to of forgot that Tindall said these three are just plain hell on wheels with a gun. You want a fair fight, then you ride in and draw agin 'em. I ain't about to."

"Me, neither," said Lawton.

"Not me, either," Damark said. "Some things I won't do for money, and gettin' gunned down in a fair fight is one of 'em."

"When you come back—if you come back—you'd all better have somethin' to your credit," said Illivane. "You don't, then maybe we'll be splittin' that money nine ways, instead of twelve."

They all eyed each other with distrust as they waited for darkness to fall.

Chapter 7

Upon their arrival in Dodge, Hampton, Lawton, and Damark had split up. Now it was two o'clock in the morning, and by prior agreement, they came together in the shadow of the water tank, beside the tracks.

"We flat ain't gonna learn a lot in the saloons," Hampton said. "I lost twenty dollars at the poker table, and all I heard was that this Silver *hombre* was in a gunfight over a woman."

"That's what I heard," said Lawton, "and the varmint he gunned down was Jake Turko. Turko was almighty good with a pistol. Had five notches on his gun."

"Yeah," Damark said, "and I reckon we can learn from that. Turko pulled iron first, and then Silver bored him clean, with just one shot. I'd say we got some bushwhackin' to do."

"I'd say you're right," said Hampton, "but when and how? Nobody seems to know why Silver, Elfego, and Stone are holed up at the Dodge House, but they are, and they all got a woman with 'em."

"They're takin' all their meals at Delmonico's," Damark said, "and the three of 'em take turns standin' watch after dark outside the Dodge House. Should be one of 'em out there right now. Hell, if three of us can't bushwhack one *hombre*, then we better hang up our guns and take up somethin' less dangerous. Like sod bustin'. Come on."

There was only the usual bracket lamp outside the main entrance to the Dodge House, and there was no sign of life in the surrounding shadows. The three bushwhackers crept up from behind the Dodge House, having left their horses a good distance away.

"Damn a man that don't roll himself a quirly," said Hampton. "One draw, and we'd get some idea as to where he is."

"You don't shut your mouth," Damark hissed, "you'll *know* where he is."

"Let him talk," said Lawton. "The *hombre* needs somethin' to shoot at, so's we got us a muzzle flash target."

"We're downwind and within rifle range," Damark said. "I got a couple of stones, and when I throw 'em, he'll shoot if he's the least bit jumpy. Get ready."

In the shadows of the Dodge House, Wes Stone waited, his Winchester cocked. Empty had growled softly, his warning that someone was out there. Then, seeming loud in the stillness, there was a soft thump, as if somebody had kicked a stone—or thrown one. But Empty ignored the sound, growling softly. The sound came again, from another direction, and again Empty ignored it. The hound growled again, louder this time, and Wes answered as he so often had.

"Get them, Empty," he said quietly.

In an instant, Empty was gone, and the next sound Wes heard was a screech from the darkness.

"A damn wolf's got me," Hampton bawled. "Shoot him."

But there was no shooting, only another cry of pain, and then the thumping of running feet. Finally there was rustling of grass and leaves. Empty had returned.

"Bueno, Empty," said Wes softly. "Let the varmints come after us in daylight, if they got the sand."

"Sí," El Lobo said, from the darkness.

Silver laughed. "We couldn't help hearin' him sing out. That means they're here."

"It means we'll have to be damn careful every time we step out the door," said Wes. "With Empty's help, we can stop them in the dark, but we'll be fair game in daylight."

In silence, the three would-be bushwhackers returned to their horses.

"So much for that," Damark growled. "You squalled loud enough to wake the dead."

"You'd beller too, damn it, if somethin' was chawin' your leg off," said Hampton with a snarl.

"Just Sone's dog," Lawton said. "That means we'll have trouble bushwhackin' them in the dark."

Damark laughed. "So we got to face three gun-throwers because we been buffaloed by a damn dog."

"It wasn't your leg he was rippin' apart," said Hampton. "I can feel the blood runnin' down in my boot. Fine pair of *hombres* you are. One of you could of shot the varmint."

"Use your head for somethin' besides a hat rack," Lawton said. "One shot at the dog, and Stone would of cut down on us, shootin' at the muzzle flash. Better a dog bite than a slug in your gizzard."

"We'll find us some cover within range, and gun them down when they leave there in daylight," said Damark. "We'll be laughed out of town, if word gets out that the three of us was scared off by a dog."

"You varmints do whatever you want," Hampton said. "Come daylight, I aim to find a doc and have him patch up my leg."

"No," Lawton said. "Stone knows one of us got

bloodied. All he's gotta do is talk to the local saw-
bones, and the law will be lookin' for you."

"Come on," said Damark. "We'll find a creek,
wash the wound, and bandage it with a bandanna,
until we can do better."

At the Dodge House, Silver and El Lobo had returned to their rooms. Although Wes tried to talk
her out of it, Renita insisted on remaining outside
with him.

"Thank God for Empty," Renita said. "At least
they can't get close enough to ambush you in the
dark."

"No," said Wes, "but if they can't come after us
in the dark, it'll be all the more of a risk in daylight.
They'll come gunning for Silver, Palo, and me while
Molly, Tamara, and you are with us."

"So let them come," Renita said. "Molly, Tamara,
and me have guns."

"They'll be out of range, using Winchesters," said
Wes. "All we have in our favor is that they'll be
gunning mostly for Silver, Palo, and me."

Renita said no more, but when they went up the
street to Delmonico's for breakfast, Silver, Wes, and
El Lobo each carried a Winchester. Heads turned
when they entered the cafe. Sheriff Dumery was
there, and when they were seated, he brought his
coffee cup and joined them for breakfast.

"Expecting trouble?" Dumery asked, his eyes on
the Winchesters.

"We are," said Silver. "It showed up early this
morning."

"I didn't hear any shots," Dumery said.

"My dog got to one of them before they could
figure out where I was," said Wes. "By the time he
sampled a leg or two, they just all changed their
minds and vamoosed."

Sheriff Dumery laughed. "Nothin' like a good dog to keep varmints away. Last night, I noticed three new *hombres* in town, but they was just havin' some drinks and losin' money at poker. They hung around till the saloons closed, and I didn't see 'em again."

"If they're still here tonight, one of them will be limping," Wes said.

Indian Territory, on the Cimarron, April 5, 1885

Illivane and his comrades were hunkered around their breakfast fire when they saw the riders coming, riding in from the east. The fifteen reined up, and the lead rider raised his hand, for he recognized Illivane and some of his men.

"Hardesty," said Illivane, "you and your boys step down and have some coffee."

"Ain't got time," Hardesty said. "You and your bunch better saddle up and ride along with us."

"For what reason?" Illivane asked.

"You can see for yourself," said Hardesty. "I got something for you tor read."

Standing in his stirrups, the outlaw wrestled a much folded page of a newspaper from his back pocket. He passed it to Illivane, and when he unfolded it, all the outlaws crowded around, trying to see. The big black headline was sufficient to get their attention, but it was impossible for them all to read at the same time. Swiftly, Illivane read the entire story aloud. When he had finished, there was a shocked silence. Illivane finally spoke.

"Where you *hombres* goin'?"

"New Mexico," said Hardesty. "Maybe Arizona."

"Maybe you're bein' a mite hasty," Illivane said. "This could be a trick. You seen any soldiers?"

"No," said Hardesty, "but I seen it in the St. Louis

and New Orleans papers, so it'll be in all the others. The territory won't never be the same."

"Hell, they ain't gonna keep soldiers here forever," Illivane said. "When they're gone, ever'thing will be just like it was."

"Don't you believe it," said Hardesty. "There's been talk about this for a long time. I reckon it'll cost a bundle. Folks will raise hell if they don't see some results after the federals have spent so much money."

The bunch rode on, Hardesty's companions having said nothing.

"Damn," Giddings said, "we're ruint."

"Maybe not," said Illivane. "We'll wait and see. We got some money to earn before we do anything else."

They eyed one another grimly, uncertainly.

In Dodge, Hampton, Lawton, and Damark had watched from a distance as their quarry had entered Delmonico's for breakfast. The trio then crept down an alley until they were behind a vacant building. Its doors and windows had been boarded up, but vandals had ripped away enough of the barrier to get in through one of the windows. Inside, Hampton, Lawton, and Damark climbed the rickety stairs that led to a second floor. Once there, they found an open door leading to a balcony facing the street.

"Perfect," Damark said.

"But not a damn bit of cover, except that rail," said Hampton. "When they went into that cafe, all three of 'em had Winchesters."

"We got to make first shots count," Lawton said. "We miss just one of 'em, and we'll have to run for it. We get trapped up here, and no amount of cover will be enough."

"The sheriff's in there," said Hampton. "I don't

like that. He comes out with them, and that's an extra gun."

"Forget about the sheriff,' Damark said. "He'll be lookin' for a hidin' place, once we gun down them three *hombres* with Winchesters."

"I hope nobody finds our horses in that alley," said Hampton. "My leg's sore as hell, and I ain't in no shape for runnin'."

"Then get in position with that Winchester, and don't miss," Lawton said.

"I'll take Stone," said Hampton. "I owe him somethin' for that damn bitin' dog."

"Let me have the Indian," Damark said. "I ain't never liked the varmints."

"That leaves Silver for me, then," said Lawton.

The three of them hunkered down behind the rail, their Winchesters ready and their eyes on the cafe's entrance.

Inside Delmonico's, Sheriff Dumery had finished his breakfast.

"I'll go out and mosey around a while," Dumery said. "Maybe I'll spot some *hombre* that's walkin' with a limp."

A few minutes later, Silver, Wes, and El Lobo shoved back their chairs.

"You ladies stay put," said Silver. "We're goin' out first, and if it's safe, one of us will open the door for you."

Empty was not allowed in the cafe, but the establishment had agreed to feed him outside on the boardwalk. Wes always returned the empty pan to the kitchen, and with that in mind, he was first out the door. Silver and El Lobo were a step behind. Wes leaned over to retrieve the empty pan, and a slug thunked into the wall behind him. The roar of a distant Winchester seemed loud in the early morning stillness. Wes rolled off the boardwalk, cocking his Winchester. Silver and El Lobo went belly-down as slugs smashed into the heavy door where they had been standing. Like Wes, they had their Winchesters ready when they rolled off into the dusty street. Powder smoke still hung over the balcony from where the shots had come, and the trio in the street laid down a withering return fire.

"Damn you, Hampton," Lawton snarled, as a slug ripped off his hat.

Damark was already past the door, pounding toward the stairs. Hampton and Lawton wasted no time following him.

"Coyotes run," El Lobo cried.

Silver, Wes, and El Lobo were off and running—not toward the vacant building itself, but toward the alley that ran behind it. They were in time to see Hampton, Lawton, and Damark emerge from the open window and run for their horses. The pursuers drew their Colts, for they were within range. The outlaws were mounting their horses when a slug struck Hampton in the thigh. His boot slipped out of the stirrup, and spooked, his horse trotted away.

"I'm hit," Hampton cried, struggling to his knees. "Don't leave me."

But his pleas were ignored. Lawton and Damark, their heads down, were madly spurring their horses. The firing from behind them had ceased, and they quickly discovered the reason. Two slugs slammed into the ground ahead of them, and their horses reared. Forty yards away, Sheriff Dumery had stepped out into the alley, a Colt steady in his hand.

"Drop those weapons," Dumery ordered, "and then get down. Do it slow."

El Lobo had caught up Hampton's horse, and after the outlaw had been disarmed, Wes helped him mount. El Lobo led the horse.

"Damn good piece of work," Sheriff Dumery said, as Silver and his companions strode along behind the wounded outlaw. "Let's lead these varmints to the jail. I won't be a bit surprised if we find 'em looking back at us from some wanted posters."

"Palo and Silver can go with you," said Wes. "I'd better get back to Delmonico's. Our ladies won't know if we're alive or dead."

"By all means," Silver said. "Escort them back to the Dodge House and remain there with them. There may be more of these coyotes around."

Sheriff Dumery, Silver, and El Lobo remained with the three captives, while Wes lost no time getting back to Delmonico's. Several men stood outside on the boardwalk, but there was no sign of Molly, Renita, and Tamara. Wes opened the door and found them still inside, silent and scared.

"Come on," said Wes. "None of us were hurt, and we took some prisoners. Silver and Palo are with Sheriff Dumery."

Renita clung to him as they left the cafe, Molly and Tamara following. Not until they were crossing the street to the Dodge House did any one of them speak.

"After the first shot, I opened the door just enough to see you tumble into the street," Renita said. "I thought you had been shot."

"None of us got a scratch," said Wes, "and I reckon we owe Empty for that. When I leaned over to get the pan in which he'd been fed, the slug went high. That shot warned Silver and Palo, and we caught up to the three bushwhackers in the alley while they were mounting their horses. We wounded one, and Sheriff Dumery got the drop on the others."

"You all *bueno hombres*," Tamara said.

"Molly," said Wes, "are you all right?"

"I suppose I will be," Molly said. "I respect all of

you for having us wait inside. I'm afraid I wouldn't have been much help when the shooting started."

"We had our reasons," said Wes. "When lead begins to fly, a man has trouble enough, just keepin' himself alive. If any one of you had been out there with us, our concern for you might have gotten a couple of us killed. It's one of those times when the most helpful thing you can do is stay in a safe place, out of the line of fire."

"I understand," Molly said.

"So do I," said Renita. "When someone's shooting at you, that's problem enough. You don't need a frightened female to look after."

"I wasn't going to be quite that blunt," said Wes, "but that's exactly what it amounts to. You know now that our concern for you is not only very real, but justified as well."

"*Sí,*" Tamara said. "You care."

"Now," said Sheriff Dumery, when the three outlaws were locked in a cell, "what are your names?"

"I want a doc," Hampton said.

"He's been sent for," said Dumery. "Now tell me your names."

"Go to hell," Damark said.

"Then don't talk," said Sheriff Dumery. "I'll book all of you on John Doe warrants if I have to. More than one bushwhacker's got the rope without anybody knowin' or carin' who he was."

"Let's look at those wanted posters," Silver said. "A varmint who'll hire out to kill has probably killed before. Maybe we can tighten the noose some."

"Good idea," said Sheriff Dumery.

The trio had been locked in the first cell. When Dumery opened the door that led into the office, Empty could see the prisoners. He began barking furiously.

El Lobo laughed. *"Perro,* he know."

"I'd bet a horse and saddle one of those coyotes has teeth marks on his leg," Silver said.

Sheriff Dumery brought a stack of dog-eared wanted posters from his desk drawer and began to separate them on his desk, one at a time.

"Whoa," said Silver. "There's the one with a slug in his leg."

"He's got a jugful of names," Sheriff Dumery said. "Wonder which one of 'em he's usin' now?"

"It won't matter," said Silver. "According to this, he's wanted in Texas and Missouri, for robbery and murder."

"A thousand dollars reward," Sheriff Dumery said. "He ain't changed his habits none. Damn bushwhacker."

A further search through the wanted posters revealed that the remaining two outlaws were wanted in Missouri. There was a five-hundred-dollar reward for each of them, and the charge was attempted murder.

"These are old wanted dodgers," said Silver. "These varmints have been hidin' out for a while."

"Won't matter," Sheriff Dumery said. "I'll get telegrams off to whoever's after them. You gents will get your rewards."

"We're not nearly as interested in rewards as we are in getting these coyotes locked up," said Silver. "Give it another couple of days, and I won't be surprised if there's a new bunch of them in town, with bushwhacking on their minds."

"If they show up," Sheriff Dumery said, "just handle 'em the way you handled these. I got plenty of room here in the jail if you can take 'em alive."

*   *   *

Silver and El Lobo returned to the Dodge House with the news that the three outlaws were all wanted men.

"That pretty well stacks up to what you suspected," Wes told Silver. "These varmints must have been holed up in Indian Territory. When these don't ride back, I reckon there'll be another bunch coming."

"That's what I expect," said Silver. "At least until the threat of soldiers gets through to them. Give it another week, and I suspect Indian Territory will have more Indians than outlaws."

Dodge City, Kansas, April 5, 1885

The capture and jailing of the three outlaws hadn't gone unnoticed. After the sheriff had led the prisoners away, one of the observers hurried to his room at the Dodge House. After sending the telegram to Franks in Denver, Gannon had kept out of sight. Now he could see his usefulness in Dodge coming to an end. Quickly he packed his few belongings, and when the eastbound train arrived, Gannon went aboard, bound for Kansas City.

"What the hell are you doin' here?" Morton Tindall demanded, when he answered the knock on his door.

"I'm on my way east," said Gannon. "Thought I'd bring you some news."

"You was told to stay in Dodge," Tindall said.

"I don't like the way the cards are fallin'," said Gannon. "I'm foldin' while I can still walk away forked-end down. Them three *hombres* that Franks wanted me to watch just took the bit in their teeth and captured some coyotes that tried to bushwhack 'em. I just figured they was some of your boys, and

I reckoned you'd want to know they're locked up in Dodge. Word is they're facin' the rope."

"You're lying," Tindall snarled. "You're just looking for an excuse to run."

Gannon laughed. "I don't care a damn what you think. These killers you're sendin' to Dodge are in over their heads. You're about to lose big time, and I don't aim to be close enough for any of it to boil over on me."

With that, Gannon turned and walked away. Tindall was about to shout an angry reply when he discovered other doors were open along the hall. Ignoring the curious looks of his neighbors, Tindall closed the door and threw himself on the bed.

Dodge City, Kansas, April 5, 1885

"Silver," said Wes, "why don't we telegraph Franks in Denver?"

"Give me a good reason," Silver said.

"We know the Golden Dragon is behind these killers that tried to bushwhack us," said Wes. "Don't you reckon Franks and the rest would like to know their killers are alive and well in jail?"

"*Sí*," El Lobo said. "We use the talking wire, like we do in Mexico."[1]

Silver laughed. "Why not? We'll tell them in great detail about the failed ambush, and that the bushwhackers are in jail. We won't sign it, of course."

They spent the better part of an hour composing a telegram. When it was ready, Wes took it to Foster Hagerman at the railroad depot. Harley Stafford was there, having come in on the eastbound train.

---

[1] *The Border Empire*

"I heard about the ambush," Hagerman said. "Congratulations."

"Just my luck," said Harley. "I always miss out on the fun."

"There's more to come," Wes said. "We think the bunch that's paid these coyotes to come gunnin' for us should know they're in jail. Send this telegram to Denver."

With Harley looking over Hagerman's shoulder, the two of them read the message.

Harley laughed. "You gents know how to rub it in. But how do you know Franks isn't just a code name? They may not get this."

"They'll get it," said Wes. "They'll have their own telegraph instrument. Whether Franks exists or not, they'll still intercept this."

"If they do," Hagerman said, "what do you expect to happen?"

"If they still have a contact here in Dodge, he'll be in big trouble," said Wes. "I think we've violated all their rules for use of the telegraph. At least we tried to."

"Take over the instrument and do the honors yourself," Foster Hagerman said.

Wes sat down before the instrument, and when given permission to send, rapidly sent the telegram.

"He knows Morse as well as any man alive," said Harley proudly. "I taught him."

"I know," Hagerman said. "After what he pulled off in Mexico, he's practically a legend among telegraphers."

Denver, Colorado, April 5, 1885

Drade Hogan answered a knock on his door.

"Sorry to bother you, sir," the telegrapher said,

"but I have no idea where Mr. Franks is. The nature of this message is such that I . . . I thought you should see it immediately."

Hogan took the scribbled message, and without a word, closed the door in the face of the telegrapher. He sat down at his desk, stubbing out his cigar in his coffee cup. Having read the message once, he quickly read it again. Angrily, he pounded the desk with his fist, shoved the telegram into his pocket, and seized his hat. He slammed the door behind him, and his secretary looked up in alarm.

"If Franks shows up," Hogan growled, "send him into my office and tell him I said wait there until I return."

"Yes, sir," said the secretary.

Gandy Franks had been on the second floor of the Pretty Girl Saloon all day, sitting in on a high-stakes poker game. He kicked back his chair, three hundred dollars ahead. One of the pretty girls, wearing only red slippers, a short, open-fronted red jacket, and a big red ribbon in her hair smiled at him.

"You're not leaving, are you?" she chided.

"Yes," said Franks. "This has been my lucky day."

He thought about returning to the office, but changed his mind. Instead, he stopped at a fashionable restaurant, where he ordered a steak and an expensive cigar.

Dodge City, Kansas, April 5, 1885

"There shouldn't be any trouble for a couple more days," Silver said. "It'll be a while before that bunch in Indian Territory suspects something went wrong with their planned ambush."

"There's the telegram you sent to Denver,"' said

Molly. "Perhaps there'll be trouble coming from there."

"Not for us," Silver said. "I figure if the varmints still have a contact in Dodge and they believe he sent this telegram, they'll want his head on a platter, just as much or more than they want ours. We'll wait and see what happens."

Chapter 8

Indian Territory, on the Cimarron, April 6, 1885

"Somethin' must of gone wrong," Easterly said. "It ain't that far from here to Dodge. Hampton, Lawton, and Damark should of been back by now."

"I reckon you're right," said Illivane. "If they're not back by suppertime, I'll ride in and find out what's happened to 'em."

"I don't like the way this is stackin' up," Concho said. "With a showdown comin' here in the territory, there won't be no more gold from Tindall. Why don't we just take what we got and ride out?"

"Because I don't run out on a job after I been paid to do it," said Illivane. "Ain't you got no honor?"

Not one of the outlaws agreed with him, and some of them laughed. Illivane swallowed hard. Time was running out.

Denver, Colorado, April 6, 1885

When Gandy Franks reached the outwardly respectable offices of the Golden Dragon, he was confronted with some disturbing news.

"Mr. Hogan left word for you to wait for him in his office," the secretary said.

"It's still early," said Franks. "Has he already been in?"

"No. That's the message he left yesterday," the girl replied.

"What's happened?" Franks asked.

"I have no idea," said the secretary. "From what the telegrapher said, he was given a telegram intended for you. He seemed very angry."

Franks hurried down the hall to the telegrapher's office. When he entered, Harper, the telegrapher, looked up.

"Why didn't you hold that telegram for me?" Franks demanded.

"It seemed important," said Harper. "I didn't know where you were, or when you'd be back."

Harper didn't like Franks, and made no pretense of it.

"I reckon you didn't keep a copy," Franks said sarcastically.

"You know damn well I have orders not to keep copies of anything sent or received," said Harper. "However," he said with some satisfaction, "I can remember most of it."

"Then tell me," Franks growled, swallowing his pride.

Harper recited the message almost word for word, enjoying the shocked expression on Franks's face as he proceeded. At the conclusion, it took a moment for Franks to recover. When he finally spoke, he choked out the words as though he were strangling.

"It wasn't signed?"

"Of course it wasn't," said Harper in disgust. "Are our messages *ever* signed?"

Franks said nothing. He closed the door behind him and started down the hall. In his anger and confusion, he almost collided with Drade Hogan, who had just entered the building.

"Well, bless my soul," Hogan said in mock surprise. "You're just the fellow I've been wanting to see. Come on in to my office."

Franks said nothing. Having no choice, he followed. They entered the outer office, and Hogan only nodded to the secretary. Taking one look at Franks, she quickly found something to do, for the look in his eyes reminded her of a trapped animal seeking to escape. Feeling like a condemned man, Franks closed the door behind him. Hogan wasted no time, and when he spoke, his voice was like ice.

"For starters, where the hell were you all day yesterday?"

"I . . . I had business to attend to," said Franks lamely.

"When you work for me, my business comes first," Hogan roared. "Do you understand that?"

"Yes."

"Yes, what?"

"Yes, sir," said Franks, almost in a whisper.

"Read this, and tell me what it means," Hogan said, taking the crumpled telegram from his pocket.

Franks took it, scarcely looking at it. But Hogan wasn't finished. From his coat pocket he took an envelope, which he passed to Franks. Fearfully, suspecting what he was about to find, Franks took the contents from the envelope. There was a two-page letter, along with the front page from the Kansas City newspaper. Franks ignored the newspaper story, scanning the letter Morton Tindall had written. Finished, he didn't bother returning any of it to the envelope. Without a word, he handed it all back to Hogan.

"There's nothin' more I can tell you," said Franks weakly. "It's all there."

"How much?" Hogan demanded. "How much money has he sunk into this . . . this bunch of bungling misfits from Indian Territory?"

"I sent him fifty thousand," said Franks.

"Good money or counterfeit?"

"I sent a check on our Kansas City account," Franks said. "I thought—"

"You *didn't* think, damn you," said Hogan. "Now we're out fifty thousand, three men who are supposed to be dead are very much alive, and that fool in Dodge has violated all the rules I laid down concerning use of the telegraph."

"By God, you don't know *everything*," Franks exploded. "Gannon didn't send that telegram from Dodge."

"Then who did?" Hogan asked in a near whisper. "It had your name on it."

"That telegram came from Stone or Silver," said Franks. "They likely got my name from the telegram Gannon sent me, telling me they had stopped in Dodge. This telegram is their way of stirring up trouble among us."

"I am indebted to them," Hogan said. "Otherwise, I wouldn't have known of this fool blunder of yours, hiring unreliable scum from Indian Territory."

"Let me remind you," said Franks, mustering what dignity he could, "that it was you who suggested hiring bushwhackers from Indian Territory. You've sent money to Tindall, just like I did, and he's hired men to do your dirty work more than once. Now, as for soldiers bein' sent to the territory, I knew nothing of that."

"Get out," snarled Hogan. "I have some thinking and some planning to do."

"Don't you go writin' me out of the play," Franks shouted. "Not after all I've done for this outfit."

"Believe me," said Hogan, his voice dangerously low, "you will be rewarded for all you have done. Now stay out until I call for you."

Franks stumbled blindly down the hall, only too much aware that Rance Stringfield had disappeared only a week ago. Now Hogan was tallying up Gandy Franks's faults, and while the situation in Dodge had been beyond his control, he would be held responsible. Franks racked his brain for some means of redeeming himself, then finally gave it up. His only hope was to run far enough and fast enough that the vindictive conspiracy that was the Golden Dragon could not reach him.

Dodge City, Kansas, April 6, 1885

Illivane rode into town just at dusk. The saloons being the best sources of information, he entered the Long Branch. It was near the supper hour, and there were few patrons. One table was occupied, where a poker game was in progress.

"Beer," said Illivane, leaning on the bar.

The mug was slid down the bar to him, and Illivane paid with a two-bit piece. When he drained the mug and ordered another, the barkeep still hadn't spoken.

"You don't say much, do you?" Illivane said in what could have been a joking manner.

"I get paid for serving drinks, and you got yours," said the barkeep gruffly. "What else you want?"

"I just rode in from Texas," Illivane lied, "and wondered if there's anything goin' on around here. Any excitement?"

"Depends on what you find excitin'," said the barkeep. "Three damn fools was caught when their bushwhackin' failed. Now they're in jail, facin' the rope, I hear. Dodge ain't a trail town no more, and Sheriff Dumery keeps the lid on. If there's anything else you got to know, it'll cost you another beer."

Illivane was tempted to draw his Colt and slug the insolent barkeep. Instead, he slid his empty mug along the bar, turned, and left the saloon. He now knew what he had come to Dodge to learn, and found himself in a quandary. Hampton, Lawton, and Damark were all killers, yet they had failed. Now Silver, Stone, and Elfego were aware of their danger, and further attempts to bushwhack them might result in similar failure. Illivane was standing on the boardwalk, undecided as to his next move. Suddenly he stiffened. Three men had just stepped out of the Dodge House. After a moment, one of them turned back and opened the door. Three women came out, and the six of them started across the street. Beside them trotted a hound.

"By God," said Illivane under his breath, "it's them."

Illivane waited until the six entered Delmonico's. Then he made his way along the boardwalk to the corner, where he paused. The dog was watching him warily, and lost interest only when one of the cooks brought him a pan of food. Illivane then crossed the street and entered Delmonico's. Silver and his party were at a table that would seat twelve, and with them was Sheriff Dumery, Foster Hagerman, and Harley Stafford. Illivane seated himself at a table where he could watch them. He quickly averted his eyes when he found the three men in whom he was interested were watching *him*.

"Coyote," said El Lobo quietly.

"Stranger, with a tied-down Colt," Wes said.

"I've been watching him since he came in," said Silver. "He was watching us from the other side of the street when we left the Dodge House. It's just about time that bunch in Indian Territory started to wonder what's happened to their *companeros*."

"You think there's more than the three that's in jail, then?" Molly asked.

"I'm sure there are more," said Silver. "They'd at-

tract too much attention if they were to all ride in
together. The three who are in jail is just the
beginning."

"What are we going to do?" Renita asked.

"We're going to watch him as long as he's in
here," said Silver, "and if he leaves here ahead of
us, one of us will follow. If he's come to find out
what's happened to the others, he may be alone, but
we can't risk that. All of you—Renita, Tamara, and
Molly—will stay here at this table until we're sure
it's safe for you to leave."

Illivane ordered a meal, and when it arrived, he
seemed interested in nothing else. He ate hurriedly,
and when he had finished, he left money on the table.
Silver nodded to El Lobo, and when Illivane had
closed the door behind him, the Indian got up and
followed.

"Lord," Renita said, "I hope they're not out there
with rifles again."

"It's unlikely," said Silver. "Except for the time it
takes to step past the door, it'll be dark out there. If
the *hombre* that's been watching us is one of them, I
doubt he'll try anything alone."

"Maybe I should have followed him," Sheriff
Dumery said.

"No," said Wes. "Palo moves like a shadow in the
dark, and Empty will go with him."

Quickly El Lobo stepped through the door. Empty
had finished eating and was waiting patiently.

"Come, *perro*," said El Lobo.

Palo Elfego had made friends with Empty almost
immediately, and they had since gone man hunting
together enough for the dog to know what was expected of him. Illivane was already lost in darkness,
but Empty set out after him. Illivane had left his
horse in the alley near where his three companions
had been captured. Pausing before entering the alley,

he looked around. He thought he had seen a shadow on the boardwalk across the street, but he couldn't be sure. There were a few distant lights, but the mouth of the alley loomed dark before him. Again he paused, drawing his Colt. He *had* seen something move. Just for an instant, he saw it again. *Stone's damn dog was following him!*

"Ho, *perro*," said El Lobo, as Empty returned to him. "He waits for me, eh?"

El Lobo, keeping to the shadows, crept along the boardwalk until he was well beyond where Empty had crossed the street. Again the dog vanished in the darkness, and this time the Indian followed.

"Come on, damn you," Illivane gritted through clenched teeth. But he heard and saw nothing. As he stepped into the blackness of the alley, his horse snorted, stamping its feet. Fearing he was about to be left afoot, Illivane managed to grab the reins before the animal could run. He thrust his foot into the stirrup, but before he could mount, Empty seized his other leg. Feeling the flesh tear, he ripped his leg free. Already spooked, the horse broke into a fast gallop down the alley. With no proof of their suspicions of the stranger, El Lobo holstered his Colt and remained in the shadows, watching the stranger race away.

"*Bueno perro*," El Lobo said.

Empty following, El Lobo returned to Delmonico's, where he joined his companions.

"It's good you didn't shoot the varmint," said Sheriff Dumery. "He wasn't breakin' the law, comin' in and lookin' around."

"If he's who we think he is, we gained one advantage," Wes said. "He'll know better than to try bushwhacking us in the dark, with Empty around."

"Get horse, take *perro*, and follow," said El Lobo.

"No," Silver said. "He'll be worth more to us,

goin' back and taking the word to his *compadres* that we're not easy to kill."

"Good thinking," said Sheriff Dumery. "If he comes back, we'll recognize him. I'll keep my eyes open in case there's other strangers ridin' in. I ought to be gettin' answers to the telegrams I sent about them three that's in jail."

"I'll let you know when you get answers," Hagerman said.

Illivane reined up to rest his sweating horse. His leg throbbed like a sore tooth, and he cursed all dogs in general and Empty in particular. Having been to Dodge before, he knew where the jail was. With some vague hope of freeing his comrades, he started there. There was no light before the jail, and at first, Illivane saw nothing. But as he drew near and the sound of his coming could be heard, two men stepped out of the surrounding shadows. In the dim light of stars, there was no mistaking who they were, or their intentions. Each of them was armed with a long gun. Illivane swallowed hard, and not looking in their direction again, rode on. As soon as the lights of town were behind, he circled around, crossed the railroad tracks, and started in a fast gallop toward Indian Territory.

"Rein up and sing out," a voice challenged.

"Illivane," the outlaw replied.

His remaining eight men hunkered around a burned-out fire, waiting. Illivane got down and began unsaddling his weary horse. He was in no hurry to break the unwelcome news.

"I'll take care of the horse," said Hawser. "You tell us what you found out in Dodge."

There was no help for it, and Illivane told them, concluding with his narrow escape and the armed men before the jail. When he had finished, there was a long silence. Concho finally spoke.

"How in hell did Hampton, Damark, and Lawton end up in jail?"

"I wasn't able to find out," Illivane said.

"I reckon you're gonna leave 'em there to hang," said Easterly.

"Hell, no," Illivane shouted angrily. "We'll ride in and bust 'em out, if every one of us is gunned down to the last man."

It had the desired effect—an uproar of shouting, cursing protests. Illivane said nothing until it all dribbled down to an uneasy silence. Then he spoke.

"A man with a price on his head has two choices. He can hide where he hopes the law won't never find him, keepin' his nose clean, or he can keep pushin' his luck till it's run out. You think if any one of us was in the *juzgado*, that them three would risk their necks tryin' to bust us loose?"

"Hell, no," they growled in a single voice.

"Then we'll split the gold nine ways, and it's every man for himself," said Illivane.

"So much for honor," Bender said.

They all laughed uproariously. Illivane said nothing. His leg hurt like hell.

Dodge City, Kansas, April 7, 1885

There was no disturbance during the night, and by the time Silver and his companions reached Delmonico's for breakfast, Foster Hagerman, Harley Stafford, and Sheriff Dumery were already there.

"I got some telegrams," Sheriff Dumery said, "but not them I was looking for. There's one from a newspaper in St. Louis, another newspaper in Kansas City, and a third from a paper in San Antonio."

"They intercepted his telegrams regarding those three killers," said Hagerman. "They're wantin' a confirmation before they print anything."

Silver laughed. "Send them one. That ought to put the fear of God into the varmint in Kansas City who hired this pack of killers. The Golden Dragon is quick to reward those who fail, whether they're at fault or not."

"Maybe they won't find it so easy, hiring a new bunch of killers," Harley said.

"I wish we could be sure of that," said Wes. "Gold has some strange effects on men, shooting their judgment all to hell."

"I'll get telegrams off to them newspapers today," Sheriff Dumery said. "I'm for doing whatever it takes to keep killers out of Dodge. I got to admit this has turned around in a way I didn't expect."

Hagerman laughed. "He thought this conspiracy was going to draw killers from everywhere, and I was afraid he might be right. Now, with three of them facing the rope, I'd say it's having the opposite effect."

"Don't crow too loud, too soon," Silver warned. "The Dragon always hires killers outside its own ranks, when it can, because there's little danger to the organization if they're killed or captured. Our move in Indian Territory, our use of the telegraph, and especially our use of the press has crimped their tail feathers, but it won't stop them."

"*El Diablo de oro,*" said El Lobo.

Sheriff Dumery had taken some paper and a pencil from his pocket, and was writing.

"Here," he said, passing what he had written to Foster Hagerman. "These are answers to them three newspapers. Get 'em off as soon as you can."

"I'll send them when I return to the depot," Hagerman promised.

"I reckon some of us ought to keep a close watch on the eastbounds," said Harley. "If these Dragon *hombres* is all gathered in Colorado, the next trouble may come from there."

"You watch the trains when you're in town," Hagerman said, "and when you're away, I'll be watching."

"*Bueno*," said Silver. "We're obliged."

Warily, they all left Delmonico's together. Harley Stafford and Foster Hagerman headed for the depot, and after a moment's hesitation, Sheriff Dumery went with them.

"I like Dodge," Molly said, when she and Silver were in their room, "but I'm getting awful tired of just doing nothing. How much longer?"

"I don't know," said Silver. "I'm counting on those hired killers from Indian Territory pulling up stakes and riding on, now that they know their *amigos* are locked up. If they do, the Dragon will be forced to back off and try again. Once they pull out all the stops and turn their big guns on us, we won't be able to hole up here in Dodge. Eventually we'll have to take the offensive, and hit them hard, where it hurts."

When the westbound train rolled into Dodge, Harley Stafford was there. Only one man got off, and as he stood looking around, Harley was watching him. He carried two tied-down Colts, and his dress was not that of a cowboy. His Stetson hat was tipped forward so that the brim shaded his eyes, and he wore a ruffled white shirt beneath a fancy red tie. His dark trousers were tight and tailor-made, and his highly polished black boots reflected bright in the morning sun. Since there was nobody else around, he fixed his cold blue eyes on Harley, a half smile on his lips.

"You lookin' for somebody?" Harley asked.

"Matter of fact, I am," said the stranger. "Is Wes Stone still in these parts?"

"He is," Harley said.

"You see him, tell him Gabe Wilkins has got business with him."

"I'll tell him," said Harley. "And you'll be where?"

"Around," Wilkins said.

He turned away, and ignoring Harley, started toward town.

"He looks like trouble," said Foster Hagerman, who had joined Harley.

"He is," Harley said. "Another gun-thrower looking for a reputation at Wes Stone's expense. I might as well tell Wes he's here."

It was still early, and the saloons hadn't opened. Sheriff Jack Dumery, recognizing the newcomer for what he was, stopped Wilkins on the boardwalk.

"You aim to be in town a while?" Sheriff Dumery asked.

"Until I'm ready to leave," said Wilkins. "What business is it of yours?"

"It's always my business, when an *hombre* shows up with a tied-down brace of Colts," Sheriff Dumery said.

'You got a gun law in Dodge?"

"No," said Sheriff Dumery.

"Then back off," Wilkins said.

Dumery stepped aside, allowing the haughty gunman to proceed. Harley Stafford was on the opposite side of the street, and the sheriff waited for him.

"That two-gun varmint's looking for Wes," said Harley. "I'm goin' to warn him."

"You might as well," Sheriff Dumery said. "I reckon he won't be surprised."

Reaching the Dodge House, Harley knocked on the door of the room Wes and Renita occupied. It was opened almost immediately. Wes was dressed, except for his hat. Harley entered, and Wes closed the door.

Renita sat on the bed, a worried look in her eyes, but there was no way of sparing her. Harley relayed the bad news.

"You should have told him Wes wasn't here," said Renita angrily.

"Renita," Wes said, "Harley did exactly what he should have done. A man can run, but he can't hide from this kind of thing. It's better I face him and be done with it."

Wes checked both his Colts, thumbing a sixth load into each of them. He reached for his hat.

"I'm going with you," Renita cried.

"You're staying right here," said Wes, "and until I return, don't you open the door."

"Wes can take care of himself," Harley said reassuringly. "I'll be goin' with him."

Harley and Wes went out, and Wes locked the door.

"I'd better tell Silver," said Wes.

But Silver had been aware of Harley's arrival, and when Wes closed and locked the door, Silver opened his.

"Trouble?" Silver asked.

"No more than I've been expecting," said Wes. "I'm bein' called out again."

"Palo and me will go with you," Silver said.

"Harley's going," said Wes.

"Fine," Silver said, "but Palo and me are going too."

Another door opened, and El Lobo stepped out. Wes said no more, and when he began his walk, Harley, Silver, and El Lobo were two paces behind. Sheriff Dumery waited across the street. The few citizens who were up and about quickly ducked through doorways into the shops, nearby. Wilkins had reached the end of the boardwalk, and when he saw the four men approaching, he grinned in anticipation.

So there would be no obstruction, he stepped into the dusty street. A block away, Wes left the boardwalk and entered the street. Harley stepped off the boardwalk into the street and remained there. Silver and El Lobo crossed to the other side and avoiding the boardwalk, waited in the street. His three friends were out of the line of fire, but were positioned to side Wes if there was any sign of treachery. Wes walked on, his hands swinging at his sides. When he was sixty yards from his antagonist, he halted.

"You're Stone, are you?" Wilkins inquired.

"I am," said Wes. "What business do you have with me?"

"Gun business," Wilkins said. "My draw against yours."

"You're a fool," said Wes.

Wilkins laughed. "You ain't gettin' out of it. Pull your iron."

"I don't need the advantage," Wes said. "When you're ready, make your play."

"Draw, damn you!" Wilkins shouted. His trembling hands hovered near the butts of his twin Colts.

Wes Stone said nothing, waiting. Suddenly Wilkins moved with blinding speed, drawing both Colts. He fired, the roar of his first shot blending into the thunder of the other. But he was about to learn—as so many had learned before him—speed without accuracy only got a man killed. Both Wilkins's shots were wide, and he stood there unbelievingly, his eyes on Wes Stone. Wes drew his right-hand Colt, and it seemed he did so reluctantly. He fired once, with deadly accuracy, and Wilkins stumbled backward. Blood welled out of the hole in his chest, soaking the front of his boiled shirt. As his grip weakened, the twin Colts fell into the dusty street. Then his knees buckled, and Wilkins collapsed, his cold, sightless eyes turned to the blue of the morning sky. Wes started back along the boardwalk. Sheriff Jack Dumery still leaned against an awning post.

"Sorry, Sheriff," Wes said. "It wasn't of my choosing, and I can't promise there won't be more."

"You did what you had to do," said Sheriff Dumery. "It couldn't have been any more fair. A two-gun man that draws 'em both at once is a damn fool."

Wes went on, bound for the Dodge House. He was aware that El Lobo, Silver, and Harley followed. They said nothing, nor did they need to. Reaching the Dodge House, Wes knocked on the door and identified himself. Renita opened the door and ran to him, tears of relief streaking her cheeks. Wes sat her down on the bed. He then removed his hat, his gunbelts, and finally, his boots.

"Come on," Wes said. "It's over and done."

"Until the next time," said Renita.

"You know I had no choice, just as I'll have no choice the next time," Wes said. "I'm learning the same deadly lesson my father, Nathan Stone, learned before me. He tried to hang up his guns, but he couldn't. Come the end, he died as he had lived. By the gun."

"Then let's go somewhere else," Renita begged. "Somewhere where nobody knows you."

"We'll go when it's time," said Wes, "but not so that I can hide. I believe God allows some of us to shape our own destiny, and if my trail comes to an early end, I'll have none to blame but myself."

"I'll be with you until the end," Renita said, "whenever and wherever it comes."

It was just as well she didn't know that more would-be gunslingers would soon be coming, and that Wes Stone's life-and-death drama would be played out again and again.

Chapter 9

In the aftermath of the shooting, Wes was in a somber mood. Silver and El Lobo, respecting his feelings, left him and Renita alone. A letter to Silver had arrived on the westbound train, but Foster Hagerman had decided not to deliver it until after Wes had faced Gabe Wilkins. Even though there was no return address and the letter was unsigned, Silver knew who had sent it. Quickly he read the contents, Molly beside him.

"Oh, hell's bells," said Silver angrily.

"When are you going to tell the others?" Molly asked.

"Suppertime will be soon enough," said Silver. "There's not a blessed thing we can do about it."

Silver waited until supper was over. For a change, Harley Stafford, Foster Hagerman, and Sheriff Dumery were absent. When he produced the letter, Wes and El Lobo looked at it without enthusiasm. When Silver received written messages from Washington, it rarely was good news.

"I can tell you in just a few words what this is about," Silver said. "President Grover Cleveland's plans for sending soldiers to Indian Territory leaked out, and some powerful enemies in the Senate have blocked the move. The only saving grace is that these varmints who killed the proposal are using their influence to silence the newspapers."

"While there won't be any soldiers coming," said Wes, "the outlaws in the territory won't know that, with the newspapers keepin' quiet."

"Probably not for a while," Silver said, "but it won't matter to us. After that first bushwhacking failed and three men went to jail, I doubt the Golden Dragon will be sending more killers from Indian Territory. The next bunch will be more professional."

"You try," said El Lobo.

"It was a good move," Wes agreed, "but all the killers aren't in Indian Territory. From now on, I doubt the forces behind the Golden Dragon will do anything so obvious."

"You're probably right," said Silver. "We'll have to be more cautious than ever."

Denver, Colorado, April 8, 1885

Dent Shankler, who had once been in charge of the Dragon's forces in Carson City, knocked on Drade Hogan's door. Hogan bid him enter, and he did so, closing the door behind him. Hogan nodded to a chair and Shankler sat down.

"You served us well in Carson City, and I'm about to ask you to perform an even greater service," Hogan said.

"I'll do the best I can," said Shankler cautiously.

"Splendid," Hogan said. "Do you know of one other within our ranks with whom you'd prefer to work?"

"Turk Pardue," said Shankler. "He was with me in Carson City."

"Get him," Hogan said, "and both of you report back to me."

*　　*　　*

Gandy Franks sat on his sagging bed in the room he had rented in a rundown rooming house. He reached for the bottle on the floor, found it empty, and cursed under his breath. Nervously he counted his money. There was a little more than five hundred dollars. Since his fall from grace, he had forsaken all his dreams. Now he was obsessed with the will to live, and the killers he had so often hired and sent after others would soon be coming for him. He couldn't afford to run and hide with the little money in his pocket, and suddenly, as though by inspiration, he thought of something. Frantically he searched through all the assorted papers in his wallet, coming up with a blank check. The bank was in Kansas City, so he would have to travel there first. He swallowed hard. If he wasn't doomed already, he would seal his fate when he took unauthorized funds from the Golden Dragon's account. He took a traveling case with his few clothes and went in search of a livery. He must have a horse and saddle. While the nearest railroad was in Boulder, it was also the most obvious. He would ride to Cheyenne, and from there, take the Union Pacific.

Shankler and Pardue returned to Drade Hogan's office within the hour.

"I suppose you recall the troublesome gunmen who helped to spoil our operation in Mexico, New Orleans, Carson City, and San Francisco," Hogan said.

"Only too well," said Shankler. "Wes Stone and Palo Elfego. They're still on the loose, are they?"

"Worse than that," Hogan said. "They now have Bryan Silver with them, and he's their equal with a Colt revolver or a Winchester."

"So you want us to find and dispose of them," said Pardue.

"Finding them won't be difficult," Hogan replied. "They're in Dodge. Disposing of them may be another matter entirely, and it seems they're daring us to come after them. They have considerable influence there, including a friendly sheriff. We hired a dozen man-killers from Indian Territory. Three of them were captured during a failed ambush, and they're in the jail at Dodge, facing the rope. The rest of them have ridden to parts unknown."

"Before we jump in over our heads," said Shankler, "do you have any advice for us?"

"Yes," Hogan said. "Avoid use of the telegraph. Stone sends and receives Morse as well or better than any man alive. The only other thing that might be helpful to you is the fact that Stone's likely the fastest gun west of the Mississippi. He's become a target for all the would-be gun-slicks who are ready to kill him and assume his reputation. His latest victim was Gabe Wilkins."

Shankler whistled. "I knew Wilkins. He killed his share of men."

"Stone buffaloed him, somehow," said Hogan. "Wilkins fired twice, missing both times, and only then did Stone fire. He didn't miss."

"If that's the caliber of varmints challenging Stone," Shankler said, "I can't see them being of much use to us."

"They might be useful in drawing attention from you," said Hogan. "When Stone gets called out, Silver and Elfego are in the street with him. Siding him, but out of the line of fire. Does that suggest anything to you?"

"It does, for a fact," Shankler said, "if we can track down some of these gunslingers and head 'em toward Dodge."

"You know where Mobeetie, Texas, is?" Hogan asked.

"Just barely in north Texas," said Shankler. "A wide place in the trail."

"The young man you'll be looking for is Curly Dismukes," said Hogan. "He has the rare distinction of having called out Wes Stone and lived to talk about it."

"Then he ain't gonna be anxious to try it again," Pardue said.

Hogan laughed. "Word has it that Dismukes is ready to ride back to Dodge right now, even before his wound has healed. He'll be interested in anything you can suggest that might give him an edge. Use him any way you see fit, and if he's reluctant, sweeten the pot with five hundred dollars. It'll be worth twenty times that, if he kills Stone. But if it goes the other way, and Stone guns him down, we haven't lost a thing. In this bag is your expense money. Ten thousand, in double eagles."

"Our double eagles, or real ones?" Shankler asked.

"The real ones," said Hogan, not in the least disturbed. "From now on, we're going to be much more careful."

Taking the canvas sack, Shankler and Pardue left Hogan's office. When they had gone. Hogan took stationery and envelopes from a desk drawer and began writing. There were two thorns in his side that were becoming more painful by the day. Gandy Franks had, he was sure, decided to run for it. He had little doubt that Morton Tindall, in Kansas City, would be of like mind. In the letters he was writing, he placed a ten-thousand-dollar reward—dead or alive—on the heads of Franks and Tindall. Hogan had been toying with the idea of sending Franks to Durango, to confer with Elias Hawk and Hobie Denbow. Now he could think of nobody in whom he could trust for so important a mission. He would go himself, for much depended on what Hawk and Denbow had accomplished.

Mobeetie, Texas, April 10, 1885

Shankler and Pardue could have taken the train from Boulder to Dodge, and from there ridden horseback to Mobeetie, but they did not. Instead, they saddled their horses, placed a Winchester in their saddle boots, and rode directly from Denver to Mobeetie.

"So what if we'd of got off the train in Dodge?" Pardue complained. "Stone and none of his friends know us."

"Maybe not," said Shankler, "but they'll be watching the trains. You can be damn sure they'd be suspicious of us. We got to handle this so we got Dismukes facin' Stone without Stone or none of his *compadres* knowin' we're around."

Pardue laughed. "While Stone's shootin' Dismukes full of holes, you and me can be cuttin' down Silver and Elfego."

"You're gettin' the idea," said Shankler. "All we got to do is convince Dismukes that he can't lose."

Mobeetie consisted of a rundown hotel, a livery and blacksmith shop, a mercantile, a cafe, and an enormous building with PANHANDLE SALOON in foot-high red letters across the front.

"We'll try the saloon first," Shankler said.

It was early afternoon, and except for a barkeep the establishment was deserted.

"Couple of beers," said Shankler.

The drinks came, and Shankler downed half of his before he spoke again.

"We're lookin' for a young gent name of Curly Dismukes," Shankler said. "Know him?"

"He's nursin' a gunshot wound," said the barkeep cautiously. "You here to finish the job?"

Shankler laughed. "We're here to pay him some money, unless you figure he don't need it."

"He needs it," the barkeep said. "His bar tab ain't goin' no higher till he pays. You'll find him at the hotel."

Shankler pounded on the door, and curses from inside told them Dismukes had likely been awakened from drunken sleep. But he was sober enough to stand away from the door, his Colt drawn and cocked, until Shankler and Pardue were inside. Dismukes wore only his trousers, and his hair curled in unruly tufts all over his head.

"What do you want of me?" Dismukes growled. "You the law?"

"No," said Shankler. "I'm Shankler, and he's Pardue. We got three reasons for us bein' here. We want you to do yourself a favor and us a favor. We don't expect a man to work for nothin'. We'll pay you five hundred dollars to do what you're plannin' to do anyway."

"Tell me," Dismukes said sourly.

"You aim to gun down Wes Stone," said Shankler.

"Yes," Dismukes said, "and I won't take money for that. It's a personal thing."

Shankler laughed. "Sure it is, just like the five hundred we're offering you. Nobody will know of it except you and us, and you'll still get the credit for gunnin' down Stone."

"You want him dead, why don't you bushwhack him?" Dismukes asked. "It won't cost you nothin' except a couple of slugs."

"Because we're wanted in Kansas, and we can't afford a run-in with the law," Shankler said, "but there ain't a law that stands in the way of you callin' him out and gunnin' him down."

"Just like there ain't no law agin Stone gunnin' *me* down," said Dismukes. "Why don't one of you call him out and do your own killin'?"

"Neither of us is his equal with a gun," Pardue said. "You're a real gun-thrower, and nothin' less will be enough to salt down this *hombre*."

Dismukes laughed. "Scairt of him, huh?"

"Damn right," said Shankler. "The gun-thrower that drops Stone will have some big boots to fill. There's others like you, so we'll track down some of them, since you ain't interested in our deal."

"I didn't say I wasn't interested," Dismukes said. "I just can't figure why you're payin' me to gun down a man I plan to kill anyway. If you ain't picky about how he dies, why don't you set up an ambush and shoot him in the back?"

Shankler laughed. "Stone ain't an easy man to bushwhack. He just walked away from one without a scratch, and the three varmints that cut down on him are in jail, facing the rope."

"Stone has a dog with him, and the varmint won't let you get close enough for bushwhacking," Pardue added. "That damn hound will hunt you down in the dark and sink his fangs into you like a lobo wolf."

"Show me the color of your money," said Dismukes.

From his pocket, Shankler withdrew a canvas bag. He dropped it on the floor, between Dismukes's bare feet.

Dismukes's eyes slitted, his hands twitched, and greed got the better of him. Seizing the bag, he dumped its golden contents on the bed.

"Count it," Shankler ordered.

"I aim to," said Dismukes.

He counted out the double eagles in stacks of five. Satisfied that the five hundred was there, he shoved it all back into the bag.

"Keep it," Shankler said. "It's yours."

"You'd trust me to ride to Dodge and keep my end of the bargain?" Dismukes asked.

"When it comes to money or women, I don't trust any man," said Shankler. "We'll be ridin' to Dodge with you, but keepin' out of sight. When you decide where you aim to face Stone, we want to know. We want to see him get his."

"Have it your way," Dismukes said. "I don't care. When do we start for Dodge?"

"Soon as you can clean yourself up and get mounted," said Shankler. "We leave now, we'll reach Dodge after dark. You can call out Stone in the morning."

"The barkeep at the saloon says you got a right hefty bar tab," Pardue said. "That is, if you aim to pay it."

"I don't," said Dismukes. "After I gun down Stone, I reckon I'll be gettin' drinks on the house, wherever I go."

"That and more," Shankler said. "You'll be famous."

Dismukes reached for his shirt, buttoned it, and then drew on his boots. He buckled his gunbelt around his lean middle, thonging down the holster on his right hip. He then drew the Colt and stood there border-shifting it from one hand to the other. Shankler and Pardue said nothing. The ego-smitten young fool was playing right into their hands.

Omaha, Nebraska, April 10, 1885

Morton Tindall had taken a steamboat from Kansas City to Omaha. There he could take the Union Pacific all the way to California, or he could travel eastward. He still had twenty thousand dollars of the fifty thousand he had received from Gandy Franks, and he thanked his lucky stars he hadn't given Illivane and his outlaws all the money. After learning that three of their comrades had been captured, he had no doubt that Illivane and the others had scattered like quail. Now he must decide if he was to travel by train or steamboat. Vivid in his mind was the time a train was stopped near Dodge, and a dozen gunmen had shot down Wes Stone and Palo Elfego.[1] He would remain in Omaha another day, admitting to himself that he hadn't the faintest idea as to how he could outsmart or outrun the evil forces of the Golden Dragon.

Cheynne, Wyoming, April 10, 1885

When he was in sight of the town, Gandy Franks dismounted. Looping the reins over the saddle horn, he slapped the horse on the rump, sending it running back the way they had come. The animal could find its way back to the livery in Denver. By then, Franks would be aboard the Union Pacific, and long gone. He would go to Omaha and from there to Kansas City. He would get the money, if Drade Hogan hadn't cut him off at the bank, and then travel eastward. Warily, Franks boarded the eastbound, taking a seat at one end of the coach so he could watch the other passengers. He viewed them all with a suspicion that soon became evident, and they returned his stares, adding to his unease. When the eastbound reached Omaha, Gandy Franks was standing by the coach door, waiting to be the first off. To his total surprise, among the people waiting to board the train stood Morton Tindall, looking for the world like a

[1] *Sixguns and Double Eagles*

stray dog expecting to be kicked. As soon as the train had slowed enough, Franks hit the ground running. But Tindall saw him coming and took refuge inside the depot waiting room.

"Don't come any closer, damn you," said Tindall, a cocked Colt in his hand. "I know why you're here."

Franks laughed. "Do you? I'm running, just like you. That whole sorry mess there in Indian Territory was laid to me. I sent you fifty thousand. Was there any left?"

"None," Tindall lied. "I'm tryin' to figure a way to get some coin. Got any ideas?"

"Maybe," said Franks. "I still have a check on that bank in Kansas City."

"Let's go there and clean it out," Tindall said. "You might as well be shot for a sheep as a lamb."

"I *will* be shot dead if I'm caught," said Franks, "and I can't see you gettin' a share when I'll be taking all the risk."

Tindall laughed. "We're both in the same leaky boat, *amigo*. If you can mine some of the Dragon's gold, go ahead. I won't expect a thing, and I'll stay out of the line of fire."

None of those who were part of the Dragon's evil empire were known for their compassion and generosity. Franks stared at Tindall, and when he spoke, his voice was cold, his words not so much a question as a statement of fact.

"You got some of that fifty thousand, ain't you."

"That's none of your damn business," Tindall said. "When Hogan brought me in, I was told to use my own judgment, and I done that. Now, if they catch up to me, my life won't be worth a plugged *peso*. You go on to Kansas City and raid that bank. I'll never stand in your way. I'll be busy enough, just trying to stay alive."

The eastbound signaled its departure with a shrill

blast of the locomotive's whistle. Without turning his back on Franks, Tindall stepped out of the depot waiting room. The train was already moving when he swung aboard. Franks watched the departing train until it was lost to distance, and the smoke from the locomotive's stack had been swallowed up in the blue of the sky. With a sigh he left the depot, bound for the steamboat landing. If his plans fell through in Kansas City, he wouldn't have money enough to run much farther.

Dodge City, Kansas, April 11, 1885

Dismukes, Shankler, and Pardue reached Dodge at dusk, as Shankler and Pardue had planned. Shankler spoke.

"Pardue and me will stay out here on the prairie until sometime before first light. You got any idea where you and Stone will face one another?"

"Near the Dodge House, I reckon," said Dismukes. "There's plenty of flat roofs and empty buildings where you can see without bein' seen."

"We'll be watching," Shankler said. "What do you aim to do now?"

"I'll be spreadin' the word that I'm back, that I'm expecting Stone to face me at first light," said Dismukes.

"See that you don't get too loud," Shankler warned. "Stone's the kind that might come looking for you tonight, forcing a shoot-out."

"I know what I'm doin', damn it," said Dismukes.

"I hope the little fool's still alive, come morning," Pardue said, as Dismukes rode away.

"I hope he doesn't lose his nerve," said Shankler. "Stone's just pure chain lightning with a pistol, and he never misses."

*   *   *

With an eye for trouble, Sheriff Dumery approached Curly Dismukes as he dismounted near the Long Branch.

"I reckon I was expectin' too much, hopin' you'd ride out and keep going," the sheriff said. "You here to cause trouble?"

"Not for you," said Dismukes.

"You're a damn fool if you aim to face Stone again," Sheriff Dumery said. "He won't let you out of it alive this time, and I don't blame him."

"I ain't lookin' for no quarter from him," said Dismukes. "All I'm expectin' of him is that he meet me on the street outside the Dodge House at first light. See that he gets the message."

He went on into the Long Branch, and Sheriff Dumery started for the Dodge House. The supper hour was past, and when he knocked on the door, Wes asked him to identify himself. When Dumery did so, Wes opened the door and the sheriff entered.

"You have that bad-news look," Wes said. "What is it?"

"Curly Dismukes rode in a while ago. He aims to call you out at first light, right here before the Dodge House."

"Can't you arrest him, Sheriff?" Renita begged.

"Got nothin' to charge him with, ma'am," said Sheriff Dumery. "I'd just have to turn him loose, and he'd start the whole thing all over again."

"The sheriff's right," Wes said. "I'll have to face him in the morning."

"You spared him once," said Renita. "Why won't he leave you alone?"

"Because I outdrew him and allowed him to live," Wes said. "He'll keep hounding me as long as he's alive."

Durango, Colorado, April 11, 1885

Drade Hogan stepped down from the train, impressed with the way the narrow gauge locomotive had taken the mountain grades and formidable curves. All his meetings with Elias Hawk and Hobie Denbow had taken place in Denver, and Hogan was in Durango for the first time. Hawk and Denbow didn't know he was coming, and that was just as he had planned. He would be the judge of their progress, or the lack of it. He was afoot, for the little town had no livery. He started for the combination saloon and cafe. He would order a meal and go from there. The cafe was deserted, but a poker game was in progress in the saloon. Five men at the table all looked up as Hogan stepped into the restaurant.

"I'm folding," said Hawk, shoving back his chair.

"Me too," Denbow said, swallowing hard.

"You ain't goin' nowhere until we've had a shot at winnin' back our money," said one of the remaining men. A Colt was in his hand, practically under Hawk's nose.

"I don't take money from sore losers," Hawk said. "Here's my winnings. Now all of you root for them like the swine you are."

The three of them looked at him sullenly, and the man with the drawn Colt holstered it. Having been a loser, Denbow was unchallenged. He quickly left the table, heading for the saloon's door. Hawk backed away from the table, his eyes on the remaining three men who were watching him. Quickly he stepped out, closing the door behind him.

"My God," said Denbow, "did you see who come into the cafe?"

"Of course I did," Hawk snarled. "Why do you suppose I folded when I was better than a hundred dollars ahead? Come on."

There was a hitching rail at each end of the building, and five horses at the rail next to the saloon. But that wasn't all. Drade Hogan leaned on the rail, waiting.

"We came to the cafe for dinner," said Hawks, "and stayed for a few hands of poker."

"Yeah," Denbow said. "We was just about to start back."

"Good," said Hogan, his hard eyes on them. "I'm going with you."

"There's no livery here, and we got no extra horse," Denbow said nervously.

"Of course you do," said Hogan. "You and the good judge will share one, and I'll take the other."

Denbow bit his tongue, stifling a stinging response. He loosed the reins of his horse from the hitching rail and handed the reins to Hogan. Quickly Hogan mounted, watching with some amusement as Denbow scrambled up behind Hawk. Hawk and Denbow rode ahead, Hogan following. The ride was a lengthy one. Hawk finally reined up before an unimposing hole that had been blasted out of the stone face of a mountain.

"This is it," said Hawk. "*Caballito del diablo*. In English that means 'the dragonfly.' "

"I know what it means," Hogan snapped, "and I am not amused. I trust you've made progress enough to justify the two of you being draped over a poker table in the middle of the day."

"See for yourself," said Hawk, regaining some of his confidence.

"I intend to," Hogan said. "Lead the way."

Hogan followed Hawk and Denbow into the gloomy interior of the mine.

"We picked this one because, in addition to the gold, it also yields a little silver," said Hawk.

"Splendid," Hogan said. "Who works the mine?"

"Denbow and me," said Hawk. "You told us to keep the lid on, and we couldn't do it with hired help."

"The place don't yield enough to pay day wages," Denbow added. "Low-grade ore."

"That shouldn't concern either of you," said Hogan. "I believe you are being paid well for your labor."

"We are," said Hawk hastily. "Now we'll show you what you came to see."

Denbow lit a lantern, leading the way, while Hawk and Hogan followed. Shafts angled off to the right and left of the main tunnel.

"We still work those shafts," Hawk said. "Not much ore, but more than enough to supply your needs."

Finally there was a bend in the tunnel, and rounding it, they came face-to-face with a stone wall. Denbow approached what appeared to be solid rock. Suddenly, at his touch, the wall of stone swung silently back out of the way. Quickly the trio entered, and Denbow closed the stone door as silently as he had opened it.

"I expected nothing as sophisticated as this," said Hogan. "It's the most unusual device I've ever seen."

"Thank you," Hawk said. "It's something I learned from an old Aztec Indian. Now are you satisfied that Denbow and me can live up to your plans in Durango?"

"I am," said Hogan. "The first shipment will be ready by the time I return to Denver, and will be shipped by train. The bill of lading will list the contents as mining machinery."

"We'll be looking for it," Hawk said. "Now take a look at the rest of our diggings."

Kansas City, Missouri, April 11, 1885

"This account has been closed," said the bank teller.

"You're sure?" Gandy Franks asked, almost in a whisper.

"Absolutely," said the teller.

Franks said nothing, making his way slowly toward the door. The teller watched him go, and when the door had closed behind him, there was a distant sound of gunfire, then a crash, as the heavy Winchester slugs slammed Gandy Franks through the bank's big glass door. He lay there on his back, the life pumping out of him through two holes in his chest.

Chapter 10

Dodge City, Kansas, April 12, 1885

Dent Shankler and Turk Pardue spent most of an uncomfortable night on the plains, waiting until an hour before first light to ride into Dodge.

"We'll position ourselves as near the Dodge House as we can, without being seen," said Shankler. "You'll be on one side of the street, and I'll be on the other. The instant Stone or Dismukes fires, we'll cut loose on Elfego and Silver. We got to take them by surprise. If we miss the first two or three shots, we'll be in big trouble."

"I just hope Dismukes ain't figured out that he's bein' used as a diversion for a bushwhackin'," Pardue said.

"He won't live long enough to figure it out," said Shankler. "He can't see beyond his own ego."

Reaching town, Shankler and Pardue concealed their horses as best they could. Before the Dodge House was a single bracket lamp. The street was dark and deserted. Shankler crossed the street, seeking a good position, leaving Pardue to do the same. Pardue slipped between two store buildings, back into the alley where they had left their horses. What he had in mind was a flat-roofed building with a false front, behind which he could conceal himself. Instead, he found something better. The two-story building was vacant, and while it had once been boarded up, the rear of it—facing the alley—was open to marauders and the elements. Slowly, careful where he stepped, Pardue made his way up the stairs to the second floor. A door hung drunkenly on one hinge, and beyond it was a balcony overlooking the street. He sighed with satisfaction, hoping Shankler had found himself as good a position on the other side of the street. Pardue had no way of knowing that just a few days before, a trio of killers had fired from this same deserted balcony.

Wes Stone sat up in bed, aware that Renita was no longer beside him. In the darkness he could see the shape of her, sitting in the room's only chair, facing the door.

"How long have you been sitting there?"

"Since you fell asleep," Renita said. "I can't sleep, and my thrashing around would only have kept you awake."

"It wouldn't have mattered," said Wes. "I don't want you sitting there alone, brooding about me. Three more hours, and it'll all be over."

"This time," Renita said. "What about the next time, and the times after that?"

"I've cured myself of thinkin' that far ahead," said Wes.

"That's how you manage to sleep, knowing you have to face a killer at dawn?"

"That's it," said Wes.

She said no more. Slipping back into bed beside him, she lay there with her troubled mind in a whirl until she fell into exhausted sleep. She was still sleeping when Wes got up, for first light was only minutes away. There was a knock on the door, and Wes reached for one of his Colts. Anticipating his move, a voice spoke softly through the door.

"Twenty-one."

Buckling on his gunbelts, Wes eased the door open enough to slip through. Quickly he closed it behind him.

"I'd invite you in," Wes said, "but Renita's still sleeping. She's been awake most of the night."

"I reckon I know why," said Silver. "After Sheriff Dumery brought the news to you, he told Palo and me. He has a feeling there's more to this than just a grudge on the part of Curly Dismukes."

"He may be right," Wes said. "I can take Dismukes. Maybe you and Palo shouldn't be in the street behind me."

"Maybe not," said Silver, "but we'll be there. If this develops into anything more than a shoot-or-be-shot fight between you and Dismukes, you may need us."

A door opened, and like a shadow, El Lobo was with them.

All three men tensed as they heard the clop-clop-clop of a horse's hooves.

"Sheriff Dumery ridin' in," said a quiet voice.

"Come on," said Wes.

Dumery dismounted, looping the reins about a hitch rail. Nobody said anything, for they expected him to speak, and he did.

"Stone, I got me an uneasy feeling about this thing between you and Dismukes. It's all just too damn pat. Is there any way he could be part of this conspiracy that's tryin' to get the three of you killed?"

"I don't see how," said Wes. "He's just looking for a reputation at my expense, and if it wasn't him, it would be somebody else."

"I think what the sheriff is considering is the possibility that Curly Dismukes could be a diversion," Silver said. "Maybe he's being used without his being aware of it."

"You got a handle on it," said Sheriff Dumery, "but I got no proof."

"You don't always need proof," Wes said. "Sometimes, a good dose of intuition will be enough. With this bunch gunning for us, we can't afford to overlook anything."

"All the more reason for Palo and me to be there siding you," said Silver. "Fighting for your life, you shouldn't have anything else on your mind."

"I'm going to spend a little time with Renita," Wes said. "If Dismukes shows before I return, knock on the door."

He found Renita sitting on the edge of the bed, her eyes fixed on the oval rug beneath her bare feet. She looked at him, and trying to smile, failed miserably.

"I thought you had slipped away to . . . to do this without me knowing," she said. "I'm so glad you didn't."

"You've been up most of the night," said Wes. "I slipped out, hoping you could sleep. I needed to talk to Silver and Palo. Sheriff Dumery's out there too."

"I'm not going with you," Renita said. "I'm a coward. In that last split second before you draw, my heart just stands still. You have enough on your mind without being further burdened with a swooning female."

Wes laughed. "I don't think of you as a swooning female. Not after those outlaws took you away and sold you to a Mexican whorehouse."[1]

"You won't ever forget that, will you?"

"No," said Wes, "and I hope you don't. When you've been to hell and back once, you know you can face it again if you must."

"I never thought of it that way," Renita said, "but I'm going to try, starting now."

"Stone," said Sheriff Dumery through the closed door, "Dismukes is waiting."

Wes helped Renita to her feet, holding her close. Neither spoke, for there was nothing more to be said. Wes loaded the empty chamber in both Colts and reached for his hat. It was time.

Durango, Colorado, April 12, 1885

The huge vault appeared to have been hewn out of solid rock, and in one corner, fresh water bubbled out of a cleft in the rock and disappeared at its base. There were four bunks, a table and chairs, utensils for cooking and eating, and a supply of food and provisions. The rest of the interior was bare.

"We left enough room, I think, for those shipments of machinery you'll be sending us," said Hawk. "Nobody but Denbow and me knows this place exists."

"I'm pleased to hear that," Hogan said. "If anything falls through at this end, I'll only have to track down one or both of you."

Hobie Denbow laughed, but it trailed off into a nervous titter when he looked into the cold, murderous eyes of Drade Hogan.

"There won't be a train to Denver until tomorrow," said Elias Hawk. "We have plenty of room and bunks, so you're welcome to stay with us tonight."

"I think not," Hogan said. "I saw a rooming house within walking distance of the railroad depot, and I may have need of the telegraph."

"Take my horse, then," said Hawk. "Hobie can ride with you and return him."

"I'll saddle the horses," Denbow said.

Not until Denbow and Hogan had gone did Hawk

sigh with relief. He was waiting outside when Denbow returned, leading Hawk's horse.

"Damnation," said Denbow, "I'm glad he's gone. He looks at you like he knows every thought passin' through your head."

Hawk laughed. "It's his way. He's big only because he makes others feel small."

"It just spooks the hell out of me, thinking about double-crossin' him," Denbow said.

"Don't go gettin' cold feet on me," said Hawk. "Why settle for a sack of corn when you can take the whole crop?"

"You didn't tell him about none of the trip wires?" Denbow said. "Scatterguns at close range could spread a man's innards all over that cavern wall."

Hawk laughed. "I can't get over the possibility that when the dust settles and it's time to pay you and me, that the payoff may not be quite what we expect. Our three scatterguns, with trip wires attached to the triggers, will make it almighty expensive for anybody besides us to reach that room where the gold will be."

"It takes a damn good thief to steal from other thieves," said Denbow. "It makes me feel like we might pull off this double-cross and live to tell about it."

Hawk eyed him coldly. "I resent being referred to as a thief. Watch your mouth."

In his rented room, Drade Hogan slept very little. The more he thought of Elias Hawk and Hobie Denbow, the more certain he became that the two were playing out a devious hand that was going to cost him dearly. He would need them for a while, until his wealth had accumulated to the extent that he could leave for South America. By then, Elias Hawk and Hobie Denbow would have outlived their usefulness.

Dodge City, Kansas, April 12, 1885

A hundred yards down the dusty street Curly Dismukes waited. His hands hung at his sides, and he appeared not to have a care in the world. Wes stepped out into the street and began his slow walk toward the little gunman.

"Dismukes," said Wes, "the last time you came after me, I let you live. I won't make that mistake again. It's still not too late to back off."

"I ain't backin' off," Dismukes shouted, "and I ain't needin' your damn charity."

He began walking slowly toward Wes, and Wes waited. He was aware that El Lobo and Silver were a few paces behind him, Silver to his left and El Lobo to his right. The town seemed uninterested in the drama that was about to take place. Only Sheriff Dumery stood on the boardwalk, watching Wes Stone.

On the second-floor balcony of an old store building, Turk Pardue had the sights of his Winchester dead-center on Palo Elfego. He was well within range, and Pardue waited only for Dismukes or Stone to draw.

Across the street, Shankler had taken his position atop a flat-roofed building, using its false front to conceal himself. He had removed his hat so that he might see without being seen. He had the Winchester fully loaded, waiting only for one of the men in the street to draw and fire. But suddenly everything went wrong.

In the street, Curly Dismukes was still walking toward Wes, but Wes Stone scarcely looked at him.

He thought he had seen something—or somebody—
on the balcony from which the last bushwhacking
had been attempted. There it was again, in the early
morning sunlight! Like chain lightning, Wes drew his
left-hand Colt and fired three times, all the shots
coming together like rolling thunder. Turk Pardue
fell from the second-story balcony from which he had
been about to fire, and the suddenness of it took
Shankler by surprise. Hurriedly he fired at Silver, but
Silver had his Colt out, returning the fire. Then Silver
was running along the boardwalk, while El Lobo had
taken to the boardwalk across the street, with the
same idea. Shankler saw his chances of escape dimin-
ishing rapidly. Taking his Winchester, he slid off the
roof of the building into an alley behind it.

In the street, nobody had been more surprised than
Curly Dismukes. He stood there looking at the grim
muzzle of Wes Stone's Colt, frozen by the chilling
realization that he could and should be dead. When
he made no move toward his revolver, Wes holstered
his Colt and spoke.

"I ought to gut-shoot you," said Wes coldly. "You
set me and my *amigos* up for a bushwhacking."

"You lie," Dismukes snarled. "A man don't get a
gun reputation like that."

"It won't matter to you, one way or the other,"
said Wes. "It's your play. You can turn around and
walk, or you can pull iron."

"I'll walk," Dismukes said sullenly.

But after he turned his back, the treacherous little
gunman whirled and drew. But Wes Stone was
ready. Drawing his right-hand Colt, he fired once.
The slug struck Curly Dismukes in the chest just as
his finger tightened on the trigger. His shot splin-
tered one end of a hitch rail. The Colt slipped from
his fingers, and he stumbled backward. His knees
buckling, he sat down in the street as though very

tired. As his blood drenched the front of his shirt, he collapsed on his back, his sightless eyes looking into the morning sun. Aware that Silver and El Lobo were pursuing the would-be killers, Sheriff Dumery had watched the drama unfold between Stone and Dismukes. Wes had punched out the empty casings and proceeded to reload his weapons. Only then did he walk back toward the Dodge House. By the time he reached the boardwalk, Renita was running to meet him.

Silver and El Lobo reached the building from which Shankler had fired, only to find no sign of the gunman.

"He was shooting from the roof," said Silver. "Now he's trying to work his way back to his horse. I'll continue searching this alley, and you take the one across the street."

Drawn by the gunfire, there were men on the street, but they scattered quickly when they saw El Lobo and Silver coming with Colts in their hands. Silver ducked between a cafe and a barbershop, neither of which was open. Coming into the alley, Silver's eyes were on the roofs of several buildings from which the shots might have come. Some fifty yards away, Dent Shankler found himself in trouble. He and Pardue had left their horses in the alley behind the deserted building where Pardue had concealed himself. Shankler was about to run for it, when he saw El Lobo disappear into that very alley. The damn Indian was sure to discover his and Pardue's mounts! But there was a more immediate danger. Bryan Silver was coming down the alley on the run. Shaken by his unbelievably bad luck, Shankler fired at Silver, but the hurried shot went wild. Silver fired twice, the slugs tearing splinters from a building's wall just above Shankler's head. Knowing he was lost without his horse, Shankler made a run for it into the street

where Curly Dismukes had died only moments before. Silver fired again. The slug slammed into the
stock of Shankler's Winchester, ripping the weapon
from his hand. Drawing his Colt, he turned and fired,
only to have the shot go wild. Silver was still coming!
Terrified, breathing hard, Shankler made it into the
alley where he and Pardue had left the horses, and
he couldn't believe his eyes. The horses were gone,
and just ahead of him, El Lobo waited.

"Damn you," Shankler sobbed.

He fired, and the slug whipped through the sleeve
of El Lobo's shirt. Seemingly in no hurry, El Lobo
drew and fired once. Shankler was struck high in the
right shoulder, near the collarbone, and the force of
it turned him around. He fell to his knees, dropping
his Colt. He started to reach for the weapon, only to
have Silver fire and send it skittering out of his reach.

"That's enough," said Silver. "Get up."

"I . . . I can't," Shankler mumbled.

El Lobo had hidden the horses belonging to Shankler and Pardue. Now he led them down the alley.
Saying nothing, the Indian nodded toward the
wounded Shankler.

"In the saddle," Silver ordered, "unless you'd
rather be tied across it belly-down."

Sheriff Dumery arrived just as the wounded
would-be killer was mounting his horse.

"I searched the varmint Stone shot off the balcony," said the sheriff. "Wasn't nothin' on him but
four hundred dollars in gold coin, and I found five
hundred on Dismukes. Glad you took this coyote
alive. Maybe he can tell us what the connection is."

"I'm tellin' you nothin'," the wounded Shankler
growled.

"I think you will," Silver said. "It's that, or we'll
send you back to Denver and drop you in the midst
of the bastards that sent you."

"*Bueno*," said El Lobo.

"Wes wasn't hit, I reckon," Silver said.

"Not a scratch," said Sheriff Dumery. "I never seen such shootin' in my life. I believe, after he shot that *hombre* off the balcony, he could *still* have gunned down Curly Dismukes before the kid got off a shot. How old is Stone?"

"In gun years, about thirty," Silver replied. "You need some help gettin' this *bastardo* to jail?"

"I can manage," said Sheriff Dumery. "I'll have the doc patch him up. When do you want to question him?"

"Later today," Silver said. "Keep him under armed guard until then."

"All of you can go to hell," said Shankler defiantly.

"That's where you'd be right now, if we didn't need some answers," Silver said. "Palo, I want to congratulate you on taking him alive. Dirty bushwhacker that he is, I'm tempted to gut-shoot him myself."

Sheriff Dumery mounted one of the horses, and with the wounded, unarmed Shankler on the other, started for the jail. Silver and El Lobo crossed the street, bound for the Dodge House. The bodies of the two dead men had been removed, and men stood about in awed silence, their curious eyes on those about whom they had heard so much, yet knew so little. Silver and El Lobo looked neither to the left or right. Reaching the Dodge House, they found Wes, Renita, Tamara, and Molly outside, waiting for them.

"I wasn't going to wait for you much longer," said Wes. "I'm hungry."

"You ungrateful coyote," Silver said in feigned anger, "where were you when Palo and me were tracking down that other bushwhacker?"

"I had a gunfight on my hands," said Wes. "Besides, there are two of you, and I had no idea you needed help. Did you?"

"*Madre mia,*" El Lobo said.

It was a perfectly ridiculous conversation, but in the aftermath of what might have been a tragedy, they needed to laugh. And they did, making their way to Delmonico's for breakfast. Not until they had eaten were the events of the morning mentioned.

"Later this afternoon," said Silver, "we're going to have a serious talk with the varmint Sheriff Dumery's taken to jail. Palo could have killed him, but only wounded him. Injun, you have the makings of a lawman."

El Lobo laughed, and Tamara beamed.

"I hope you cautioned the sheriff not to lock him in an open cell," Wes said. "They'll get to him just as they got to our captives in California."[2]

"I think Sheriff Dumery is aware of the danger of that," said Silver, "but I'll make it a point to talk to him before I return to the Dodge House. We'll wait about questioning the captive until the doc's tended his wound."

"That'll be interesting," Wes said. "You really expect him to talk?"

"Not until he's more afraid of us than he is of the Golden Dragon," said Silver. "We'll wait and see. Whether he does or doesn't, I have plans for him."

"Then you'd better make your move before word of this gets back to Denver," Wes said. "Dodge used to have a weekly newspaper. I wonder what became of it?"

"I have no idea," said Silver.

At that point, Foster Hagerman joined them.

"Everybody's talking about what happened," Hagerman said, "and the town council's got a mad on.

Dodge hasn't had two dead men in the street since the days of the Texas cowboys and the trail drives."

"Sorry," said Wes. "Would the town council have felt better if I had just stood there and allowed Curly Dismukes to shoot me dead?"

"You had every right to defend yourself," Hagerman said, "and I pointed that out. But some feel that Dismukes wouldn't have come here—"

"If I hadn't been here," Wes finished.

"That's the talk goin' around," said Hagerman, "and some believe there'll be others like Dismukes, with thoughts of gunnin' you down."

"Hell's fire," Silver said, "a man shouldn't have to become an outcast over something not of his doing. Does the town council have anything to say about the two-legged coyotes that tried to bushwhack us?"

"Unfortunately, yes," said Hagerman. "There's speculation that the bushwhackers were friends of Curly Dismukes."

"That ties it all up with a big red ribbon," Silver said. "The next gun-thrower showin' up may have his *amigos* staked out with Winchesters, like the two varmints that seemed to be sidin' Dismukes."

Sheriff Dumery sighed. "That's about how it stacks up. Some folks has got the idea that Dismukes had the bushwhackers backin' him, because you and Elfego were there in the street with Wes."

"I don't think Dismukes had anything to do with the bushwhackers being there," said Wes. "I accused him of that, and he denied it. I think they used him, without him realizing it. Sheriff Dumery found five hundred dollars in gold on him."

"It's all too deep for me," Hagerman said. "I just wanted all of you to know that the town council's got its hackles up. To make matters worse, Ashe Wexler will be comin' in from Kansas City on the east bound."

"I reckon that should mean somethin' to us," said Silver. "What?"

"Wexler bought out the weekly newspaper here in Dodge," Hagerman said, "and before he could publish his first issue, he was injured. His horse spooked, and when his buckboard crashed, he was partly paralyzed. He's been in the hospital in Kansas City, and there was some doubt that he'd ever walk again. I'm tellin' you this because Ashe Wexler not only owns the paper here, he's a stringer for one of the daily papers in Kansas City."

"I see what you mean," said Silver. "Maybe I can talk some sense to him before the town council gets on his back."

"Good luck," Hagerman said. "Wexler's a Yankee, more prone to the giving of advice than he is at taking it. If his tongue's loose, and he can hold a pencil in his teeth, I look for him to become the conscience of Dodge."

"Thanks for the warning," said Silver. "Before Wexler hits town, I'd better have a talk with Sheriff Dumery."

"You definitely should," Hagerman said. "The town council is giving him hell, and when Ashe Wexler gets here, he'll side with them. Jack Dumery is an old boomtown sheriff, and I don't expect him to win another election."

Leaving money on the table, Silver, Wes, and El Lobo stepped out the front door of the cafe. When they were sure it was safe, Wes opened the door for Molly, Renita, and Tamara.

"Why must the newspapers make it hard on us?" Molly asked. "Is there nothing we can do to stop them?"

"Not much," said Silver. "They see it as their duty to publish the news, and there is virtually nothing I can tell Wexler about the Golden Dragon without revealing the nature of the conspiracy. I regret that I must swear Sheriff Dumery to silence. He's a good man, and instead of kicking him out, the West should be looking for more like him."

"Palo and me can go with you if you think there's any advantage," Wes said.

"I don't see any," said Silver. "Sheriff Dumery knows both of you, and he's well aware that there may be more gun-throwers looking for you. The trouble is, some long-nosed newspaper editor like Ashe Wexler can suggest that, since Palo and me are always with you, that we're three of a kind. That would more or less justify Curly Dismukes setting us up with the pair of killers."

"Perhaps it would be better, having it thought the three of you are gunfighters," said Renita. "That might be enough to satisfy the newspapers, without them knowing of the Golden Dragon conspiracy."

"By God, that's an idea," Wes said. "If we're gonna catch hell every time we have to pull a gun to stay alive, then let everybody—including Ashe Wexler—think the three of us are cut from the same cloth. We protect each other."

"*Bueno*," said El Lobo. "It be true."

"That's generous of you both," Silver said, "but you should consider the consequences. With some prodding from Wexler, the town council may order us to get the hell out and stay out."

"*Infierno*," said El Lobo. "We don't go."

"That's our only chance of keeping the lid on the conspiracy that could destroy the nation," Wes said. "I just hope the damn town won't come up with an ordinance and lay it on Sheriff Dumery before we can skin the Golden Dragon."

"It's all the more important that I talk to Sheriff Dumery before Wexler arrives and begins baying with the rest of the dogs," said Silver. "The eastbound train will be arriving soon. The rest of you return to the Dodge House.''

"I'm going with you," Molly said.

"I don't know if you should," said Silver. "Our whole purpose in coming to Dodge was to keep you, Renita, and Tamara out of sight, and so out of mind."

"Well, I don't intend to run and hide while you're being shot at," Molly said.

"That's how I feel," said Renita. "If it comes to another fight, I'll be right there on the street with my Colt."

"*Sí,*" Tamara said. "*Matar.*"

Looking into their grim, determined faces, Silver laughed, taking Molly's arm.

"Come on, woman. If we have to shoot our way out, I'll expect you to see that none of 'em shoots me in the back."

Wes, Renita, El Lobo, and Tamara went on to the Dodge House, while Silver and Molly started for the sheriff's office.

Chapter 11

When Silver and Molly reached the jail, the doctor had already been there. The would-be bushwhacker sat on a bunk in the first cell, and he regarded Silver with contempt.

"Close that door to the cell block, Sheriff," Silver said. "I'd as soon that coyote can't hear what I have to say."

"From what you said, I reckoned I'd better keep an eye on him," said Sheriff Dumery.

Silver nodded, and Dumery closed the door. Only then did Silver speak.

"I reckon you've heard the town council's got a burr under its tail."

"I have," Sheriff Dumery said, "and it's no more than I expected. But nobody's broken any law except the damn bushwhackers. Dodge is halfway between what it used to be, and what it wants to become, I reckon. Too many second generation folks here that don't know how it was when Dodge was a trail town, full of brawling Texas cowboys. Do you have any ideas that might let the steam out of folks that's all riled up?"

"Maybe," said Silver.

He then told Sheriff Dumery what he, Wes, and El Lobo had discussed, ending it with Renita's suggestion.

"You're willing to have it look like you and Elfego are friends of Wes Stone, that the three of you work together for no better reason than wantin' to stay alive," the sheriff said.

"That's exactly what we want," Silver replied. "If any more killers come gunning for us, let the town think they're gun-throwers looking for a reputation. I'm in no position to justify these bushwhackers by revealing their true purpose. To do that would force me to make known the nature of the conspiracy that's about to ruin the nation."

"I won't say nothin' about that part of it," said Sheriff Dumery.

"We're obliged, Sheriff," Silver said. "When all this is done, when we've whipped the Dragon, I'll see that you are credited with assisting the federal government."

Sheriff Dumery laughed. "I expect I'll need all the help I can get. I'm obliged."

"We just had breakfast with Foster Hagerman," said Silver, "and according to him, the editor of the local newspaper is returning from Kansas City."

Sheriff Dumery sighed. "That means he's well enough to start printin' the paper, and I reckon he'll be looking for some big news to get him started. First thing he's likely to do is meet with the town council."

"Yes," Silver agreed, "and before he shows up at the jail, I need time to question that bushwhacker in the first cell. If he has anything to say, the last thing we need is for him to say it to a newspaper editor."

"Then you'd better do your talkin' now," said Sheriff Dumery, "before Ashe Wexler gets here. If he's able to crawl on his hands and knees, he'll be comin'."

"I promised Palo and Wes that we'd do the questioning together," Silver said. "They're neck-deep in this conspiracy."

"You don't have much time," said Sheriff Dumery. "You'd better question the varmint yourself. But I doubt it will do any good. While we know he was one of the killers, we don't have a shred of proof. Any jackleg lawyer in the country could force me to charge him or turn him loose. Whatever hand you got in mind, you'd better play it before our sainted editor gets here."

"I suppose you're right," Silver said. "I'll question him now."

"Leave your Colt out here," said Sheriff Dumery.

Silver removed his Colt from the holster, flipped it, and handed it to Sheriff Dumery butt first. Silver started for the door that opened to the cell block, Molly following.

"Molly," Silver said, "I wish you'd wait here. Besides the varmint I'll be talking to, those three killers waiting to be extradited are back there. They might do or say something to embarrass you."

"I'm not easily embarrassed," said Molly. "I'm going with you."

Hampton, Lawton, and Damark lay on their bunks in various stages of undress. While Lawton and Damark wore only their trousers, Hampton wore nothing at all. The three of them laughed when Silver and Molly entered the cell block, and Hampton stood up close to the bars, grinning.

"A she-male," said Hampton. "I reckon you can see I'm ready, gal."

"You crude son of a bitch, get dressed. You're insulting a lady," Silver said.

"Haw, haw," said Hampton. "How can she be a lady, when she's sharin' your bed? You ain't embarrassed, are you, gal?"

"No," said Molly, looking Hampton in the eye. "I'm not so much a lady that I haven't seen my share of foolish naked men, and any one of them had more to his credit than you have."

Silver could hear Sheriff Dumery laughing in the

outer office. Then, to his surprise, Hampton walked back to his bunk and sat down, his face flaming red. His comrades began bully-ragging him, and he started cursing them. In a cell on the other side of the cell block, Dent Shankler sat on his bunk.

"Molly," Silver said, "I want you to stay out here in the corridor. You can see and hear through the bars."

"I'll wait," said Molly, "but I'll be watching that other cell. I'd like to know if either of the other two are any better off than the one I've seen. Come on," she taunted. "Embarrass me."

Hampton's cursing had dribbled away to nothing, and the trio sat there in silence. They watched Silver use the key Sheriff Dumery had given him. When he was inside Shankler's cell, he locked the door and passed the key through the bars to Molly. Shankler sat on his bunk, saying nothing. Wasting no time, Silver spoke.

"What's your name?"

"None of your damn business," said Shankler.

He sat in silence as Silver asked him one question after another, none of which he took the trouble to answer. Only when Silver became silent did Shankler speak.

"You can't hold me without me being charged, and you got no evidence. I'm entitled to a lawyer."

"You're entitled to nothing," Silver said, "unless you're willing to talk. Since you don't seem so inclined, that makes you a hostile witness. As of now, you may consider yourself charged with attempted murder. I have a federal John Doe warrant for you."

"Charge and be damned," said Shankler. "You can't prove I've done anything wrong, and I ain't tellin' you nothin'. Whatever you aim to do, then do it."

"I will," Silver said. "Molly, let me out."

Molly unlocked the cell door, and when Silver stepped out, he took the key and locked the door. The three outlaws watched, saying nothing, as Silver and Molly went into the outer office. Silver closed the door behind them.

"Did you learn anything?" Sheriff Dumery asked.

"Only that he thinks we can't hold him without charges," said Silver, "so I am charging him with attempted murder on a federal John Doe warrant."

"Good, far as it goes," Sheriff Dumery said, "but this town's got more than its share of lawyers. I reckon it won't surprise you when I tell you Ashe Wexler keeps the biggest shyster in the bunch on retainer. By this time tomorrow, Wexler will know as much as anybody can tell him about what's happened here. Then he'll have his pet law dog barking at my door."

"Tomorrow won't be soon enough," said Silver. "I aim to leave here on the eastbound train later today, and this closemouthed bushwhacker goes with me. I'll see that he gets a nice quiet cell at Fort Leavenworth, for the time being."

"Good thinking," Sheriff Dumery said. "Before I forget, there's somethin' that may interest you. This bushwhacker had more than nine thousand dollars in gold in his saddlebag. What should I do with it?"

"Did you test it to see if it's real?" Silver asked.

"I did," said Sheriff Dumery. "It's the real stuff."

"Then don't tell anybody you have it," Silver said. "When we're done, there won't be anybody to claim it, and it'll belong to you, as far as I'm concerned."

Suddenly there came the distant wail of a locomotive as it whistled for the stop at Dodge. Time was running out.

"I'm obliged," said Sheriff Dumery. "When the dust settles, I may be out of a job."

"Not if I have anything to say about it," Silver

said. "I'll return here a few minutes before train time."

Molly said nothing until they had left the sheriff's office. Then she spoke.

"You didn't tell me you were taking him to Fort Leavenworth."

"I didn't know it myself, until a few minutes ago," said Silver. "It's our only chance to move him before his bunch in Denver learns what's happened. Then they'll kill him, just as they murdered all the captives we took in California."

"I'm going with you," Molly said.

"Good," said Silver. "I wish I didn't have to let you out of my sight until we've skinned the Dragon and staked his hide out to dry."

When Silver and Molly reached the Dodge House, Silver knocked on the doors of Wes and El Lobo. Three short knocks, followed by a delayed fourth, was the signal calling them together. Almost immediately, doors opened. Wes and El Lobo had questions in their eyes.

"Come on to my room," Silver said, "and bring Renita and Tamara with you."

Once they were all inside, Silver locked the door. Then he told them first of the return of Ashe Wexler and the probable difficulties arising from the man's crusading.

"Damn," said Wes, "the westbound's at the depot now."

"I know," Silver said, "and I can't take that bushwhacker from the jail until it's near time for the eastbound. It'll be just my rotten luck for Wexler to show up at the jail long before I can get our captive aboard."

"If you're turning him over to the military," said Renita, "Fort Dodge is close. Why not take him there?"

"Because I know the post commander at Fort Leavenworth," Silver replied. "At Dodge, I'd have to explain my position from square one, and they might be reluctant to accept my John Doe warrant. Leavenworth has a company of military police, and a stockade so well secured that nobody's ever broken out."

"I like the idea of the stockade," said Wes. "We need this varmint alive and talking."

"I went ahead and questioned him, since Wexler's coming," Silver said, "and I learned no more than Sheriff Dumery had. We don't even know the man's name."

"Per'ap he talk to newspaper," said El Lobo.

"That's precisely what we don't want," Silver said, "and odds are that he'll keep his mouth shut about his connection with the Golden Dragon. When he finally talks, I think he will try to convince the law that he and his dead partner were only siding their friend, Curly Dismukes. He knows what happens to those who betray the Dragon."

"I'm not sure the rest of us shouldn't be going with you," said Wes. "I feel like we've played out our string, here in Dodge."

"I don't think so," Silver said. "I know it seems like we're on the defensive, but they know where we are. They're being forced to come after us, so it amounts to us having chosen our own battlefield. All of you keep your eyes open and your guns handy. Molly and me will return on tomorrow's westbound. Now let's go to Delmonico's and eat. We'll be on the train during the supper hour."

At the depot, Foster Hagerman watched as the conductor helped a partially crippled Ashe Wexler down the steps from the passenger coach. He hailed one of the hacks that were always there for the arrival of the trains, and on crutches he made his painful way to the buckboard. The driver helped him over the big front wheel, to the broad seat.

"The Dodge House," Wexler said.

Their arrival at the Dodge House didn't go unnoticed, and that was exactly as Wexler had planned. Having the power of the press behind him, he thoroughly enjoyed intimidating others. Given time, he thought with satisfaction, he could rid the town of its troublesome old sheriff and pack the town council with men he could control. His suite at the Dodge House included a parlor, and he sent word for Elmo Giddings, president of the town council, to meet him there.

"I'd have come to you," said Wexler with false humility, "if I had two good legs. The doc says it's unlikely I'll ever walk again."

"Sorry to hear that," Giddings mumbled.

"Thanks," said Wexler, "but that's not why you're here. Tell me what's been going on while I've been away. There must have been *something* newsworthy."

"Oh, there was, and is," Giddings said.

He spoke for almost an hour, Wexler listening without comment. Wexler spoke only when he was certain that Giddings had finished.

"So there's four men in jail here in Dodge," said Wexler, "and all of them victims of a failed ambush. They—and others who will probably follow—are here for the specific purpose of gunning down Silver, Stone, and Elfego. Why hasn't the town council demanded, through the sheriff's office, that the three leave town immediately?"

"That possibility has been suggested to Sheriff Dumery," Giddings said, "and he refuses to consider it. Dodge has no gun ordinance. Stone, Elfego, and Silver have only defended themselves, and there's no law against that."

"Perhaps it's time Dodge *had* a gun ordinance,"

said Wexler. "Can you steer the council toward such a measure?"

"No," Giddings said. "These are businessmen, and they're all armed. Not a man of them is willing to give up his own weapon."

"I find this all quite interesting," said Wexler. "What began as a gunfight between Wes Stone and another of his kind has now become a series of ambushes involving Silver and Elfego. That's damned strange, and there's a lot more to it than meets the eye. I'm going to the jail and demand some answers from Sheriff Dumery. While I'm there, I'll question some of those would-be killers. Giddings, go to the livery and rent a buckboard in my name."

"I must get back to the store," Giddings said uncomfortably. "I'm a businessman too, you know."

"You're also president of the town council, at least for the time being," said Wexler. "Now fetch me that buckboard."

Giddings enjoyed the prestige that went with being president of the town council, and he was convinced that if Wexler wished, he could head the council with a man of his own choosing. Giddings, swallowing his anger and his pride, mounted his horse and rode to the livery.

"I need a buckboard," Giddings told the hostler, old man Belkin. "Charge it to Ashe Wexler."

Belkin laughed. "I wondered how he could poke his nose in everybody's business, him on crutches. So you're gonna be drivin' him where he wants to go."

"Hell, no," said Giddings. "I'm taking him to the jail and back to the Dodge House, and that's all. He aims to give the sheriff hell, and to maybe question them bushwhackers that's locked up."

Having just returned from Kansas City, Harley Stafford had gone to the livery for his horse. He listened with interest to the conversation between Belkin and Giddings. Quickly he saddled his mount and rode to the Dodge House. He knocked on the door to Silver's room, identified himself, and the door was quickly opened.

"I heard something at the livery that might interest you," Harley said. "Giddings, the president of the town council, was rentin' a buckboard. He's taking Ashe Wexler to the jail to give Sheriff Dumery a headache. While he's there, he aims to question those coyotes who were involved in bushwhacking."

"I'm obliged, Harley," Silver said. "I knew Wexler was coming in on the westbound, but I didn't expect him to go immediately to the jail. I'll be there when he arrives, so the sheriff won't have to face him alone."

Aware of Harley's arrival, Wes and El Lobo had been listening at their doors. Quietly they stepped out.

"We're goin' with you," said Wes. "We can raise some hell of our own if need be."

"Come on, then," Silver said, "but don't make any moves you don't have to. Just keep in mind that Wexler is a newspaper man, and he'll pry as much out of us as he can. Let me do the talking, as much as possible."

"What about us?" Molly asked.

"Unless he speaks directly to you, stay out of it," said Silver, "and don't answer any questions that make you uncomfortable. We've broken no laws, and I don't intend for any of us to be intimidated. Harley, since you're mounted, ride on ahead. Tell Sheriff Dumery that Wexler's coming, and so are we."

"Too far," El Lobo said. "No walk."

"Stay here, then," said Silver. "Wes and me can handle it."

"I walk," Tamara said, her dark eyes boring into his. "You walk with me."

"*Sí*," said El Lobo. "I walk with you."

El Lobo glared at them all, to see if anyone was about to laugh. They all managed to keep a straight face, and the moment passed. Harley mounted his horse and rode away.

"Come on," Silver said. "We need to get there ahead of Wexler."

"I have an idea he'll raise hell when he learns you're takin' one of those bushwhackers off to Leavenworth," said Wes. "If nothing else, it'll fire up his suspicions, and he'll just about know there's more to this than friends siding with friends during a gunfight."

"That's a chance we'll have to take," Silver said. "The only thing he can print that will hurt us is an account of the capture of one of the bushwhackers. He can't prove that this whole thing isn't just gun-throwers looking for a reputation. I don't want him knowing I'll be leaving on the eastbound for Kansas City. Before he can print anything, our prisoner should be under tight security at Fort Leavenworth."

When Silver and his party reached the jail, Harley had already warned the sheriff, and he looked grim.

"I didn't expect him today," said Sheriff Dumery.

"No matter," Silver replied. "We might as well face him and get it behind us."

"I've stood up to him, and he hates my guts," said Sheriff Dumery. "Just don't say any more than you have to, and let him unload on me."

"No," Silver said. "If I have to, I can tell him you're cooperating in a federal case, without telling him the nature of it. There'll be no keeping it from him when I board the eastbound with a captured bushwhacker."

"If you tell him who you are, and that you're involved in a federal case," said Sheriff Dumery, "why don't you tell him these bushwhackers were after *you*? That will account for Wes and Palo traveling with you, and for Wes having to defend himself in gunfights."

"Maybe I'll just do that," Silver said. "It would be reason enough for me taking one of the bushwhackers to Fort Leavenworth's stockade."

There was the rattle of an approaching buckboard.

"Here he comes," said Sheriff Dumery, "and Elmo Giddings is with him. You want me to keep Giddings outside?"

"No," Silver said. "Invite him in. Being president of the town council, he needs to see Ashe Wexler cut down to size."

Sheriff Dumery stepped out, closing the door behind him. Giddings reined up the team, stepped down, and assisted Ashe Wexler. Supporting himself by holding to the buckboard's front wheel, Wexler reached for his crutches.

"Giddings," said Wexler, "wait here."

"As president of the town council, Mr. Giddings is entitled to attend this meeting," Sheriff Dumery said. "Come on, Giddings."

Giddings paused, aware of the storm brewing in Wexler's eyes. But Sheriff Dumery was unyielding, and Giddings looped the reins of the team about a hitch rail. The sheriff held the door open until Wexler and Giddings had entered. Dumery came in behind them and closed the door. Wexler eased himself into a chair near the door, while Giddings took up a position beside him, leaning against the wall.

"I suppose you can justify the presence of these people, Sheriff," said Wexler.

"I can," Dumery replied.

Taking his time, Sheriff Dumery introduced them all, saving Wes and Renita for last.

"So you're the young hellion responsible for luring killers to Dodge City," said the newspaper editor.

"Sheriff, why have you permitted him to remain here?"

"He's broken no law, Mr. Wexler," Sheriff Dumery said. "He defended himself. I was a witness, and it was a fair fight."

"Giddings," said Wexler, "perhaps it's time Dodge had a gun ordinance."

"I . . . we . . ." Giddings stammered.

But he was silenced when Bryan Silver spoke.

"Mr. Wexler, I represent the office of the attorney general of the United States. I am involved in an investigation the nature of which I cannot reveal at this time. I cannot—will not—allow you to blame these attempted bushwhackings on Wes Stone. These killers were after me, and they've used these gunmen who would kill Stone for his reputation. Today I am taking one of these would-be killers east, to Fort Leavenworth. There he will be held in federal custody."

"Have you finished, Mr. Silver?" Wexler asked, his voice dripping sarcasm.

"For the moment," said Silver. "I'm sure I'll have more to say, after you've revealed your purpose for being here. Go on."

"I'm here to learn the truth behind these legalized murders, and the true purpose of the attempted bushwhackings," Wexler said. "When I know those truths, I'll print them."

"Mr. Wexler," said Wes, "these men who have been calling me out, testing my draw, are nothing more than they seem. They're after a reputation for killing me, and you can't make anything else of it. None of the bushwhackers has fired on me, while I stood there waiting for my opponent to draw. When you demand a gun law for Dodge, do you plan to disarm the bushwhackers?"

"I am not the law," Wexler said stiffly. "Guns are

silenced by removing them from the hands of men who live by them. Men such as you, Stone."

"Mr. Wexler," said Silver, "I'm asking you, man-to-man, to back off until such a time as I can reveal the nature of my investigation."

"And if I don't," Wexler said, "can you stop me?"

"I can and will counter any move you make," said Silver. "As for your gun law, I have friendly newspapers that will testify to the truth Wes Stone has told you. You'll become the laughingstock of the West, attempting to sentence a man to death by taking away his guns. Your gun law certainly won't disarm the bushwhackers who are determined to see me dead, and when this investigation is finished, I'll finish you."

Wexler laughed. "Silver, you're a man after my own heart. I can see that you will be a worthy adversary. You have convinced me Wes Stone is no more than a gunslinger on his way to a grave on Boot Hill. You, Silver, are the man to watch, and I'll be watching."

"You'd better confine yourself to watching," Silver said, "until this case is closed. And I won't have you persecuting my friends, including Sheriff Dumery. One sneaky, lowdown trick from you, and I'll personally cut your string."

Wexler said nothing. Rising, he reached for his crutches, and Giddings opened the door for him to exit. Giddings virtually lifted Wexler to the seat of the buckboard. Untying the reins of the team, Giddings mounted the box and drove away.

Sheriff Dumery sighed. "Mr. Silver, I never seen nothin' like it. Can you *really* do all you promised?"

Silver laughed. "I'm not entirely sure, Sheriff," said Silver, "but Wexler won't know that. I'm counting on him not having the sand to find out."

"He as much as admitted he won't demand a gun law," Wes said.

"That part wasn't a threat, but a promise," said Silver. "Someday there'll be enough law to protect us. Until then, only a fool disarms the honest man, while allowing the bushwhackers and fast-draw killers to intimidate and kill."

"The Kansas City papers will be the ones to watch," Sheriff Dumery said. "If Wexler is telling the truth—if he *is* only interested in this federal case—he may run everything he writes through the better-known papers. I suspect he'll see this as the biggest crusade he's ever been close to. He'll bear watching."

"None of us will take him for granted," said Silver. "I'll want you to accompany me and the bushwhacker to the depot a few minutes before train time."

"I'll be ready," Sheriff Dumery said. "His horse is behind the jail."

"We'll be going, then," said Silver, "and I'll meet you here half an hour before the eastbound is due."

"*Bueno,*" Sheriff Dumery said, "and I'm obliged for you comin' down on Wexler."

Silver, Wes, El Lobo, Molly, Renita, and Tamara walked back to the Dodge House.

"You *bueno hombre,*" said El Lobo, slapping Silver on the back.

Silver laughed. "Coming from you, I'll take that as a compliment."

"He said it all," Wes said, "and I learned something. Wexler and men like him are only as big as they're allowed to be. They force their ideas and ideals on the rest of us to the extent that we're willing to swallow them."

"And you don't always have to use a gun," said Renita.

"I'll talk to all of you again," Silver said, when

they reached the Dodge House. "When I return from Kansas City, we're going Dragon hunting. In Colorado."

Three-quarters of an hour before train time, Silver knocked on the door to the rooms of Wes and El Lobo.

"I'll need one of you to go with us, to return our horses to the livery after Molly and me have boarded the train with our bushwhacker," said Silver. "I brought a livery horse."

"I go," El Lobo said.

El Lobo mounted the third horse, while Silver helped Molly into her saddle. The three of them then started for the jail.

"Oh, Lord," Renita said, "I hope nothing goes wrong before Silver can get that man to Fort Leavenworth."

"I don't see how it could," said Wes. "News of the killing and capture can't possibly have gotten back to the Dragon so soon."

Denver, Colorado, April 13, 1885

Emo Hanks entered Drade Hogan's office, waiting nervously until Hogan nodded to a chair. Hanks sat down, saying nothing.

"You know Dent Shankler and Turk Pardue?" Hogan asked.

"Yeah," said Hanks, "I know 'em."

"Good," Hogan said. "I want you to go to Dodge and find out what's become of them. I fear they've bungled a situation I sent them there to handle, and I suspect they've been killed or captured. The eastbound will be pulling out in an hour. Be on it."

"I'll be on it," said Hanks. "Any specific orders?"

"Just one," Hogan said. "If either or both have been captured, eliminate them."

Chapter 12

When Silver, Molly, and El Lobo reached the jail, Sheriff Dumery had already saddled his own horse, as well as the animal Shankler would ride to the depot.

"I aim to handcuff him and tie a lead rope around his middle," Sheriff Dumery said. "You reckon that'll be enough?"

"I think so," said Silver.

Shankler's hands were cuffed behind his back, and Sheriff Dumery helped him mount the horse. Dumery then knotted a lead rope around Shankler's middle. The lawman and the captive went first. Sheriff Dumery in control of the lead rope. Silver, Molly, and El Lobo followed. They had barely reached the depot when the eastbound's whistle blew, preparing for the stop at Dodge.

"Good luck, Silver," said Sheriff Dumery.

"I'm obliged," Silver said. "This will be the first time we've been able to capture one of these coyotes and lock him up where they can't kill him."

"I've never seen such a crowd waitin' for the train to come in," said Sheriff Dumery.

"They're not concerned with the arrival of the train," Silver said. "Maybe it was a big mistake on my part, telling Ashe Wexler what I aimed to do, for he seems to have told everybody else. While he probably can't hurt us in print, his big mouth could turn public opinion against us."

With clanging bell, the train rolled in, the locomotive coming to a stop near the water tank. Aboard one of the passenger coaches, Emo Hanks looked out the window. His heart skipped a beat when he saw Dent Shankler in handcuffs, obviously waiting to board the train. The conductor was coming down the aisle, and Hanks spoke to him.

"I've decided not to stop in Dodge, conductor. I'll be going on to Kansas City. Might not have time to buy another ticket. Will you take the money?"

Hanks dropped two double eagles—more than twice the cost of the fare—into the conductor's hand.

"You're cleared to Kansas City," the railroad man said.

Hanks retreated to the far end of the coach, because the handcuffed Shankler would know him. It was a dangerous situation, for if Shankler believed Hanks had been sent to silence him, Shankler might talk to save his own hide. Choosing a seat with its back to the far end of the coach, Hanks sat down. He sighed with relief when Shankler and his captor took seats near the opposite end of the coach. Turning his head slightly, he could see them from the corner of his eye. For the first time, he noticed a bandage just above Shankler's collar. Shankler had been taken alive, and Hanks immediately wrote off Pardue as dead. All he must do is learn where Shankler was being taken, and eliminate him, as Drade Hogan had ordered. He tipped his hat over his eyes and was about to doze, when the conductor came down the aisle, taking tickets. While the conductor ignored Hanks, his elbow struck the tilted hat, dropping it over the back of the seat. He went on, not aware of the fallen hat.

"Damn," Hanks mumbled. Leaning out into the

aisle, he reached behind the seat for his hat. Seizing it, he straightened up, only to find himself staring into the frightened eyes of Dent Shankler.

Shankler caught himself, and all recognition vanished from his face, but not before Silver had seen and understood. The surprise and fear in his captive's eyes told Silver the man was well aware of the Dragon's policy of just eliminating those who might talk to save themselves.

"What did you see?" Molly whispered, having seen Silver's reaction.

"I'll tell you later," said Silver.

Emo Hanks silently cursed himself for having allowed Dent Shankler to see his face. In Shankler's desperate mind, he would believe his and Pardue's failure was known, and that he, Emo Hanks, had been sent to kill Shankler. Vainly Hanks listened for Shankler's voice, but Shankler remained silent. When he eventually spoke, it was in a whisper.

"When we get to Leavenworth, what's it worth to you if I talk?"

"It'll be worth a hell of a lot more to you than to me," Silver said. "It's the difference between doing some time, and the rope."

"I'll do what I have to do," said Shankler. "Just don't let them get to me."

"I reckon they've made a good start," Silver said. "Who is the *hombre* that dropped his hat and scared the bejabbers out of you?"

"Emo Hanks," Shankler whispered. "He come to us from New Orleans."

"I've heard of him," said Silver. "Now who are *you*?"

"Dent Shankler."

"That's a start," Silver said. "Who was your partner?"

"Turk Pardue."

While the whispered conversation was taking place, Molly observed the back of Hanks's head. It moved from side to side, just short of turning, but Hanks didn't allow them to see his face again. He tilted the hat over his eyes, appearing to sleep, rousing when there was a blast of the locomotive's whistle or when the train passed over a rough section of track. Finally there were three quick blasts of the whistle announcing their arrival in Kansas City.

"Shankler," said Silver, "we're nearest the door, so we'll get off first. I want you to have a good look at that *hombre* ahead of us."

Shankler said nothing, but as the train shuddered and began to slow, Hanks wasted no time in getting to his feet.

"Molly, stay behind me," Silver said.

Silver removed the handcuff from his own wrist, coupling Shankler's wrists together. He started down the aisle, Shankler in front of him, Molly behind. But Emo Hanks had been out the door before the train stopped. He dropped off the car's iron steps and hit the ground running. Drawing his Colt, he took refuge between the tender and the first of the passenger coaches. Just as Shankler stepped to the ground, Hanks fired. The slug burned a fiery path across Shankler's chest. But there were no more shots, for in an instant, Silver had a Colt in his hand, returning fire. Lead whanged off the tender's iron shell, and Emo Hanks grunted when part of a ricochet tore a bloody gash across his arm. The situation had taken a deadly turn. Holstering his Colt, he hurried to the other end of the passenger coach. When he looked up, a woman within the coach was staring in horrified fascination at the blood on the sleeve of Hanks's shirt. Quickly he rolled up the sleeve, and using his teeth, knotted his bandanna around the bleeding wound. He knew his hasty shot had missed Shankler.

Now he must learn where Shankler was being taken, or all would be lost.

"I'm hit," Shankler cried.

"You were creased," said Silver. "We'll go to the depot waiting room and send for a doctor to patch you up."

"The man who did the shooting may still be around," Molly said.

"I'm sure he is," said Silver. "He'll want to know where we're taking Shankler. Keep your eyes open and your pistol handy."

Several railroad men—one of them the conductor—were coming to investigate the gunfire.

"What's going on?" the conductor demanded. "What's the shootin' about?"

"This man is in federal custody," said Silver. "Somebody from the train just tried to kill him. We're going to the depot. Get him a doctor, *pronto*."

Hanks had hidden behind some boxcars on a side track, and from there he was able to see Silver, Shankler, and Molly enter the depot. While he hadn't killed Shankler, he had drawn blood, and that might be his undoing. Aware that he was marked for death, Dent Shankler might be all the more willing to talk. Hanks had but one choice, and that was to silence Shankler with lead.

"Cleanse the wound again tomorrow," the doctor said, "and apply a fresh bandage."

With clanging bell and shrieking whistle, the train departed. Just as the doctor stepped out the door, the sheriff arrived. He was dressed like a cowboy, in Levi's, denim shirt, and rough-out boots. A gray Stetson and a lawman's badge completed his attire.

"I'm Sheriff Benteen," he said. "I'm here because of the shooting."

"I'm not at liberty to tell you a lot, Sheriff," said Silver. "Here are my credentials."

Sheriff Benteen studied Silver's identification and returned it.

"This man is to become a witness in a federal case," Silver said, "and I'm taking him to Fort Leavenworth. The outfit we're after will kill him if they can. One of them fired at us as we stepped off the train. I returned his fire, but he was shooting from cover, and I have no doubt he escaped."

"Mister," said Sheriff Benteen, his eyes on Shankler, "you got anything to say?"

"He told you the truth," Shankler said. "They aim to kill me. Emo Hanks will follow us wherever we go."

"Maybe not," said Sheriff Benteen. "The town's full of soldiers, and most of them will be returning to Leavenworth today. I know some of the officers. All of you remain where you are, and I may be able to fix you up with a military escort."

"We'd be obliged," Silver said. "I'll need to rent a buckboard at the livery."

"Let that wait until I see if I can find you an escort," said Benteen.

Then he was gone, and Molly sighed with relief.

Durango, Colorado, April 13, 1885

Using an old wagon they had purchased for that purpose, Elias Hawk and Hobie Denbow had picked up a heavy crate at the depot, and were on their way back to the mine. Once there, they wrestled the crate inside. After resting a moment, they managed to take it through the hidden door.

"Unhitch the horses," Hawk ordered, "and then we'll have a look at all this expensive machinery."

When Denbow returned, Hawk was using a

hatchet to break away the heavy wooden crate. He finally succeeded in prying off the top.

"Damn," said Denbow, "it's locked."

Hawk laughed. "Just Hogan's way of delivering us from temptation, my boy."

Drawing his Colt, Hawk blasted away the lock. He then opened the heavy case, revealing its golden contents.

"Great gallopin' horn toads," Denbow cried, "we're rich. But how're you gonna account for bustin' the lock?"

"I don't intend to account for anything," said Hawk. "Soon as we get a few more shipments of machinery, we'll board a sailing ship for parts unknown."

"I like the sound of that," Denbow said, "but we're one hell of a long ways from any water deep enough to float a sailin' ship."

"You know as much as you need to, for now," said Hawk. "You'll know more before we make our move."

"By God, you don't trust me," Denbow snarled.

"I don't trust any man, when there's gold involved," said Hawk.

Kansas City, Missouri, April 13, 1885

Emo Hanks had found an empty boxcar on the siding, and from within the car, he was able to observe the depot. He sighed with relief when Sheriff Benteen eventually left, but grew increasingly impatient because there was no sign of Shankler or his captor. Hanks was about to try working his way to the depot, when he heard horses coming. The four soldiers dismounted before the depot, and the evening sun flashed off the officer's brass on the collar of one of the men. Hanks cursed under his breath, and within seconds, five more of the bluecoats reined up before the depot.

"Damn the rotten luck," said Hanks aloud. "They're takin' him to Fort Leavenworth."

Captain Bidler, among the first four soldiers to reach the depot, introduced himself and the men with him.

"All we've been told is that you're taking a federal prisoner to Fort Leavenworth," Bidler said, "and there's a possibility that he'll be killed before you get him there."

"That's what it amounts to," said Silver. "I can't go into detail about the nature of this case. Sheriff Benteen suggested that some of you might escort us to Fort Leavenworth. I can tell you very little, but I can satisfy you as to my credentials."

He passed his federal identification to Captain Bidler.

"Mr. Silver," Captain Bidler said, "we almost never see anybody of importance, except visiting brass from Washington. There must be something God-awful important, to bring you here."

"There is," said Silver, "and I regret that I can't tell you more. But I can tell you this much. There's a threat to the well-being of this nation, unless it's stopped, and this man in handcuffs is a federal witness. I must get him to Fort Leavenworth alive."

"We'll be glad to escort you, sir," Captain Bidler said. "Some more of our outfit will be along shortly. How do you intend to travel?"

"I'll rent a buckboard from the livery," said Silver.

"I'll send a man for it," Captain Bidler said. "Corporal Ulmer, take care of it."

"Yes, sir," said Ulmer.

As Ulmer was leaving, five more soldiers arrived. Captain Bidler introduced them, and Silver told them as much as he'd told Bidler. There seemed little more to be said, and they waited in silence until they heard the rattle of the approaching buckboard. There were seats front and back, and Shankler climbed into the back. One end of his handcuff was secured to his right wrist, while the other was locked to the iron frame of the buckboard's seat. Silver helped Molly up to the front seat and mounted the box beside her. Captain Bidler led out, with four soldiers riding behind the buckboard and two on either side.

"I feel safe with them escorting us," Molly said.

"So do I," said Silver. "We owe Sheriff Benteen one."

Emo Hanks hurried to a livery, where he rented a horse. There was only a slim chance he could accomplish what he had set out to do, for Fort Leavenworth was less than an hour's ride. Silver would have Shankler there well before it was dark enough for Hanks to make his move. Still, he had to try, knowing Drade Hogan would give him hell if this bid to silence Dent Shankler failed. The soldier escort kept to the open as much as possible, and there was no cover. Not once was Emo Hanks able to get within gun range. He sat on his rented horse and watched helplessly as the buckboard bearing Shankler entered the military reservation. Captain Bidler dropped back, riding beside the buckboard.

"We'll take you directly to the post commander," said Bidler.

"If it's Colonel Pendleton, I know him," Silver said.

"It's Colonel Pendleton," said Bidler. "It's getting late, and he may have left his office, but I can track him down."

The rest of the soldiers remained with the buckboard until Captain Bidler returned.

"I hope we didn't interrupt anything important," Silver said.

Bidler laughed. "I found him in the bathhouse. I told him only who you were, and that you wanted to see him."

"Thanks," said Silver.

Colonel Pendleton arrived, and Silver introduced Molly. He then quickly told Pendleton as much as he could, requesting sanctuary for Dent Shankler, with tight security around the clock.

"We'll take him to the guardhouse," Pendleton said. "Nobody's ever escaped from there, and unless you can fly, it's impossible to get in."

"Bueno," said Silver. "Let's take him there. He's already been shot at and wounded. If you will, have your post doctor look at the wound in the morning."

"I'll do that," Captain Pendleton said. "If there's a killer loose out there, you have no business returning to Kansas City in the dark. We'll put you and Molly up for the night, and if you haven't eaten, the officers' mess is still serving."

"We're obliged," said Silver, "but if you don't mind, I want to personally see this man locked in the guardhouse. I may want to question him before I leave tomorrow."

As three of the soldiers led Shankler away, Silver and Molly followed. Reaching the guardhouse, one of the soldiers unlocked the heavy door. Shankler looked back at Silver, naked fear in his eyes.

"Remember," Silver said, "you made a promise. I'll talk to you tomorrow."

The soldiers escorted Shankler into the guardhouse, while Silver and Molly made their way to the officers' mess. There was a rumble of thunder and the distant flare of lightning in the west. Emo Hanks had dismounted, and from where he stood, he could see the high walls of Fort Leavenworth. He had no legitimate business at Leavenworth, and even if he were able to scale the massive walls, he would be captured or killed before he could find and eliminate Shankler.

"You got Shankler, Mr. Federal Man," said Hanks

aloud, "but you still got to return to Kansas City. I'll
be out here waiting for you."

Hanks hunched down to wait, without food, without a bed, cursing the elements as the rain drenched
him to the hide.

Denver, Colorado, April 14, 1885

"Any mail or telegrams?" Drade Hogan asked, as
he entered the outer office.

"No telegrams," said the receptionist, "but there's
a letter on your desk."

Hogan sat down in his swivel chair and examined
the letter. It bore no return address, and when he
opened the envelope, there was a single sheet of
paper. The message was brief and to the point.

*Your proposal is accepted, señor. The fee is twenty-five
thousand in gold. In advance.*

While there was no signature, Hogan knew only
too well it had come from Antonio Diaz, captain of
a Mexican freighter. Hogan had lost millions in gold,
when the Diaz vessel had been searched and its
golden cargo seized in San Francisco Bay.[1]

"You'll get your gold in advance, you bastard,"
said Hogan aloud, "but you'll live only as long as it
takes to get me out of the country."

Dodge City, Kansas, April 14, 1885

"It's been awful quiet," Renita said, as she and
Wes prepared to go to Delmonico's for breakfast.
"What's going to happen next?"

[1] *Sixguns and Double Eagles*

"I wish I knew," said Wes. "If Silver gets that bushwhacker into federal hands and he talks, it'll be a brand-new game."

There were three rapid knocks on the door, a pause and then a fourth knock. El Lobo and Tamara were ready.

"*Silencioso*," El Lobo said, when Wes opened the door.

"Enjoy the quiet while you can," said Wes. "If Silver gets that bushwhacker to Leavenworth alive, and he talks, all hell's goin' to bust loose."

"You don't know that he'll talk," Renita said. "Suppose he doesn't?"

"He will, when he learns what his choices are," said Wes. "I doubt there's a man alive who would sacrifice himself to the rope, protecting outlaws who want only to silence him with lead."

When they reached Delmonico's, Harley Stafford and Foster Hagerman were already there, having coffee.

"Telegram," Hagerman said, handing Wes a folded sheet of paper. The unsigned message consisted of two words: *Returning tomorrow.*

"Good news," said Harley. "We asked the sender for verification and location. It came from Fort Leavenworth."

"*Bueno,*" Wes said. "That means Silver made it, and the federals have their first live witness against the Golden Dragon."

"*Sí,*" said El Lobo. "Silver say we go to Colorado."

"We can," Wes said, "if that *hombre* Silver took to Leavenworth talks. We've all been fighting a conspiracy without the foggiest notion of who's behind it. We need names."

"I think you'll have them when Silver returns," said Renita.

Fort Leavenworth, Kansas, April 14, 1885

Silver and Molly arose early. Leaving the cabin Colonel Pendleton had assigned them, they went to the officers' mess for breakfast. Pendleton was there, and getting to his feet, met Silver and Molly at the door.

"The post doctor's been to see Shankler," said Colonel Pendleton. "His wound will heal without complications. How long do you suppose he'll be here?"

"I honestly don't know," Silver said, "except to say that he must be protected until we get our hands on the bunch trying to silence him."

"He's still afraid of them, even in the guardhouse," said Colonel Pendleton. "When do you want to talk to him?"

"Shortly," Silver said. "I appreciate your sending that telegram for me last night. I want to send another to Washington, and it may be lengthy."

"Write it, and I'll see that it's sent," said Colonel Pendleton. "You're aware, of course, that it may be intercepted by the band of outlaws you're after, provided they have access to the telegraph."

"I'm fully aware of it, and they *do* have access to the telegraph," Silver said. "But this is one telegram I want them to intercept. I want them to know we have a potential witness in federal custody. It'll force them to make a move, if it's only to run."

After breakfast, Silver and Molly returned with Colonel Pendleton to his office. There, Silver carefully composed the telegram to Washington.

"I'm obliged," said Silver, handing the message to Colonel Pendleton.

"Edwards," Pendleton said to one of his aides, "take this to the telegrapher and tell him he is to send it immediately.

"Now," said Colonel Pendleton, when Edwards

had departed with the message, "are you ready to question your witness?"

"Yes," Silver said.

"Shall I have him brought here, or will you go to the guardhouse?"

"I'll go to the guardhouse," said Silver. "I'm taking no chances. Molly, I want you to remain here in Colonel Pendleton's office, until we return."

While Molly wanted very much to go, she remained silent, for she well understood the importance of what Silver was about to do. The presence of a female in a military guardhouse might become a distraction.

"This is the interrogation room," Colonel Pendleton said, when he and Silver entered the guardhouse. "Wait here, and I'll have your witness brought to you."

Silver waited, and when a pair of soldiers brought Shankler in, he seemed considerably less distraught than he had the day before.

"Sit down," said Silver. "We have some talking to do."

"I'll tell you what I know," Shankler said, "on the condition you go easy on me. I want somethin' in writing, so you don't double-cross me."

"Nothing in writing," said Silver. "I wouldn't double-cross even a coyote like you, but you'll have to take my word."

Silver said no more, and after a prolonged silence, Shankler spoke.

"I ain't used to *hombres* treatin' me square," Shankler said grudgingly. "Where d'you want me to start?"

"You can begin by telling me who is behind this Dragon empire," said Silver, taking from his coat pocket a notebook and a pencil.

Haltingly, fearfully, Shankler began. There were

long intervals of silence, but swallowing hard, he continued. After half an hour, Silver interrupted.

"You haven't told me where the stronghold is, where the gold is kept."

"Because I don't know," Shankler cried. "All I know is, it ain't in California no more."

"What about the gold, silver, and copper? It was once shipped in from abroad. Where is it coming from now?"

"I don't know," said Shankler. "None of us was told anything we didn't have to know."

"I want as many names as you can remember," Silver said, "and I don't care whether they mean anything to you or not."

Shankler talked until his voice was little more than a whisper, while Silver continued to take rapid notes. Finally he closed the notebook.

"That's enough for now, Shankler."

"Where do I go from here?" Shankler asked. "I just signed my own death warrant."

"I don't think so," said Silver. "Eventually you'll be taken to Washington, but I intend to see that you remain here until there's nobody left to come gunning for you. There'll be a trial later on, and I'll be there to speak up for you."

Silver knocked on the door through which the soldiers had brought Shankler, and they returned to take him away. Silver went back to Colonel Pendleton's office and knocked on the door. He was bid enter, and did so. Molly said nothing, and Colonel Pendleton spoke.

"I hope you learned what you needed to know."

"Not everything," said Silver, "but enough to give me a sense of direction. We need to get back to Kansas City in time to catch the westbound."

"You want an escort back to town, to the depot?"

"No," Silver said. "I doubt we'll be in any real danger from here to Kansas City."

Colonel Pendleton ordered the buckboard's team harnessed and the rig brought out.

"I'm obliged, sir, for everything," said Silver.

"Glad I could help you," Colonel Pendleton said, taking Silver's hand.

Silver helped Molly up to the front seat, climbed up beside her, and took the reins. He raised his hand to the sentry at the gate as they passed through.

"I hope nobody's waiting to ambush us," said Molly.

"I can't promise there won't be," Silver said, "but I aim to keep to open ground. It's doubtful there'll be anybody laying for us, unless it's Emo Hanks, the varmint that tried to kill Shankler as we got off the train."

Emo Hanks followed at a considerable distance, cursing Silver as he kept to the open. There was absolutely no cover for an ambush. Hanks knew he must reach Kansas City in time to catch the westbound to Denver but found himself on the horns of a dilemma. Had Silver seen his face on the train? If Silver returned to Dodge—and Hanks believed he would—would Silver recognize him aboard the train?

"Damn him," said Hanks. "He's likely milked Shankler dry. I got to get to Denver."

With little or no possibility of ambushing Silver, Hanks gave it up. He rode wide, so as not to be seen, and got ahead of the slower buckboard. He would reach Kansas City first, get his ticket, and wait until Silver and his woman were aboard the westbound train. Then Hanks would board a different coach. He might yet ambush Silver, he thought, for much could happen on a moving train.

Chapter 13

The buckboard and team had been rented at a livery nearest the railroad, and after returning the rig, it was but a short walk to the depot. There was nobody in sight as Silver and Molly approached, but Silver paused, looking carefully around.

"What or who are you expecting?" Molly asked.

"Emo Hanks," said Silver. "I don't know how the varmints found out so quickly that we had Shankler, but Emo Hanks came here to kill him. He'll catch hell, returning to Denver with Shankler still alive, but he might still be within the good graces of the Golden Dragon if he can gun me down."

"He's nowhere in sight," Molly said. "We already have our tickets, so we can board the train from this side of the track, keeping it between us and the depot."

"That's what we'll do," said Silver.

Molly eyed him critically. She knew him well enough to realize he had thought of something he wasn't ready to tell her. Her hands felt cold and stiff as she loosened the Colt in its holster. In the distance, there was the blast of a locomotive whistle, as the westbound signaled for the stop at Dodge. When the train rolled in, there were three passenger coaches.

Ahead of them were two boxcars and a baggage coach. A caboose trailed the third passenger coach.

"Let's take the last coach," Molly suggested.

"We can do better than that," said Silver. "We have tickets. I'm going to see if I have enough influence to get us into the caboose."

The brakeman was just stepping down from the caboose when he saw Silver and Molly approaching. He waited, and Silver spoke.

"Pardner, we have our tickets, but we'd like to ride with you in the caboose from here to Dodge. I'm Bryan Silver, and this is Molly."

"I'm O. L. Whiteside," said the brakeman, "and it's against railroad regulations for you to ride in the caboose. Why are you wantin' to do that, if you have tickets?"

"Because I suspect there'll be an *hombre* on board who plans to kill me, if he can," Silver replied, "and if we're in one of the passenger coaches, others could be in the line of fire. With all due respect to railroad regulations, don't refuse us the caboose until you've had a look at my credentials."

Whiteside looked at the identification Silver had presented and returned it. His voice, when he spoke, was more kindly.

"That's enough to override railroad regulations if anybody gets curious. Go ahead and climb aboard. I'll be back shortly."

Silver and Molly entered the caboose, finding it less roomy than it had appeared. There was an iron rung ladder extending from the floor to the glassed-in cupola atop the caboose.

"From up there," said Silver, "I can see the entire train ahead of us."

"You're expecting Hanks to come gunning for you back here?"

"I don't know *what* I expect," Silver said. "In fairness to Whiteside, I'll have to talk to him when he returns."

Emo Hanks had been in the depot waiting room. He had seen Silver and Molly pause as they neared the tracks, and when the westbound train pulled in between them and the depot, he lost sight of them. When the train stopped, he believed they would enter the third coach, so he quickly made his way to the first. The passengers on the first coach remained in their seats, bound for points west. When the conductor put down the step, Hanks climbed up to the railed landing, where he could see through the glass in the door. He breathed a sigh of relief when he saw no sign of Silver and the woman. Looking back toward the depot, he saw nobody except a trainman in overalls on his way to the caboose. Feeling more confident, Hanks then entered the passenger coach and took a seat. There were no other passengers near. He broke his Colt and made sure a sixth shell was in an empty chamber where the hammer rested. He then returned the weapon to its holster, knowing he would likely need all six loads in his desperate bid to gun down Bryan Silver. The train lurched into motion. With clanging bell and a blast of the locomotive's whistle, it headed west, to Dodge City and finally to Colorado. When they were well under way, Kansas City more than an hour behind, Emo Hanks got up and walked to the far end of the coach, where it was coupled to a second coach. He slipped through the door, and stepping across the couplings, reached the landing before the door of the second coach. Peering cautiously into the coach through the glass in the door, he saw no sign of Silver and the woman. Boldly Hanks entered the second coach, certain that he would find Silver and Molly in the third. He cursed under his breath, when looking into the third coach he saw no sign of his intended quarry.

"Damn him," Hanks grunted, "where *is* he?" Then realization hit him like a lightning bolt. Silver and the woman were in the caboose!

From the landing of the third passenger coach, Hanks studied the caboose. While there was a door, there was no glass, and Hanks couldn't see inside. But on that end of the caboose, there was an iron rung ladder to the roof, and Hanks climbed it. Raising his head just above the roof, he could see the glassed-in hump atop the caboose. Inside, Silver was talking to Whiteside, the brakeman.

"I can't promise you the *hombre* that's after me won't try to get to me here. Take that bench farthest away, by the front wall. Whatever happens, don't get involved."

"Like hell," said Whiteside. "The Winchester there under the bench is loaded. If some varmints start slinging lead, I'll sling a double dose right back at him."

"Bueno," Silver said, "but don't get yourself hurt. If this *hombre* stalking me plays out his hand, I may have to do some tall talking to satisfy the railroad."

Atop the caboose, Emo Hanks inched his way along a catwalk toward the glassed-in cupola. If Silver was there, Hanks had made up his mind to try for the kill. With anything less to his credit, he dared not enter Drade Hogan's office.

"Molly," said Silver, "move to that bench in the front of the car. It's time I went up this ladder."

"The cupola's hinged at the front and swings open," the brakeman said.

"I reckon I can see through the glass," said Silver.

But just ahead of the caboose, Emo Hanks hunkered atop the third passenger coach and pondered his next move. Startled when Silver's face appeared behind the glass of the cupola, Hanks fired hurriedly. The slug shattered the glass of the cupola and slammed part of the wooden frame into Silver's head. Stunned, he fell to the floor of the caboose, aware that Whiteside had seized his Winchester and had started up the iron ladder. Her frightened eyes on Silver, Molly had drawn her Colt.

"Hold it," said Silver, getting unsteadily to his feet. "I'm going after him."

"You're hurt," Molly cried, her eyes on the bloody gash extending from Silver's left temple to the point of his chin.

Heeding Silver's command, Whiteside had stepped out of the way. Silver sleeved the blood from his face, and without a word, mounted the ladder. Keeping his head down, he cautiously raised what remained of the shattered cupola. There were no more shots, and Silver climbed out onto the roof of the caboose. He had no idea where Hanks was, but he suspected the man would take refuge in one of the passenger coaches. There Silver would be at a great disadvantage, for he couldn't risk wounding or killing another passenger in his eagerness to get at Hanks. But Hanks had not entered a passenger coach. He clung to the iron rung ladder at the forward end of the second coach, his Colt in his hand.

"Come on, damn you," said Hanks, as Silver balanced himself atop the caboose.

In daylight, the westbound traveled at top speed. Silver moved slowly forward along the catwalk, finding it difficult to keep his balance with the swaying of the train. He had just bridged the gap between the roof of the caboose and that of the third passenger coach when, from his position between the first and second coaches, Hanks fired. The slug struck Silver in the upper left arm. Stumbling backward, he fell to his knees, causing the second slug to pass over his head. Through it all, he had clung to his Colt, and raising the weapon, he fired. His lead slammed into the iron shell of the second passenger coach, just below the roofline. There was a deadly ricochet, and a fragment of lead found Emo Hanks where he crouched between the two coaches. For a few horrified seconds, he stared at his bloody left thigh. Now afraid for his life, he forgot the remaining three loads in his Colt and sought only to escape. There was no feeling in his left leg as he mounted the ladder to the roof of the second passenger coach. Silver had been hit, but it hadn't in the least hurt his accuracy. Hanks had barely reached the roof of the coach when a slug tore splinters from the catwalk beneath his feet. He stumbled, regained his balance, and stumbled on. His fear of Drade Hogan had given way to fear of Silver, and his mind searched frantically for a way out of what had become a life-or-death situation. He dared not leap from the train, for he had no horse, and he could feel his boot filling with blood from his wound. He must escape this devil pursuing him, reach a place of safety, and have a doctor tend his wound. Then, as though by inspiration, he realized what he must do. He stumbled on, as lead from Silver's Colt came painfully close. He must reach the locomotive's cab and take control of the train, but first he would rid himself of Silver.

Silver's Colt was empty, and rather than try to reload atop the swaying, fast-moving train, he holstered the weapon. He thought he knew what Hanks had in mind, and when Hanks reached the forward end of the baggage coach, he was sure of it. Hanks disappeared between the baggage coach and the tender, but hearing the shooting, the engineer and fireman had witnessed the deadly chase. When Hanks dropped between the baggage coach and the tender, the fireman bought in. Climbing over the piled-high wood, he found Hanks between the tender and baggage coach, desperately trying to loose the coupling.

"Hey, you," the railroad man shouted.

Hanks responded by drawing his Colt, but the fireman flung a heavy stick of wood. It struck Hanks in the head, blunt end first, and he was flung to the ballast beside the track. There was a scream of brakes and a jolt as the engineer sought to stop the train. Silver was thrown belly-down atop the baggage coach, and he lay there until the train shuddered to a stop. Silver sat up, aware of running footsteps, and there was Molly coming along the catwalk from the caboose. She reached Silver just as the fireman did, and this time, the railroad man had a Winchester.

"What the hell was you tryin' to do?" the fireman shouted.

"Can't you see he's wounded?" cried Molly.

"I'll live," Silver said. "The *hombre* I was after is wanted by the federal government. Where is he?"

"Alongside the track," said the fireman. "The damn fool was uncouplin' the tender from the rest of the train. I slugged him with a chunk of wood. Now just who are you?"

"I have proper identification," Silver said, "but before we get into that let's find that *hombre* who fell from the train."

The fireman swung down a ladder to the ground, Silver and Molly following. Far down the track, well beyond the caboose, some passengers from aboard the train had gathered. The train's engineer and conductor were there, and they turned inquiring eyes on Silver. It was the fireman who spoke.

"This gent was chasin' the feller that was tryin' to uncouple the engine and tender from the rest of the train. He's a federal man of some kind. Claims he got identification."

"We'll have to see it," said the engineer. "The man he was chasin'—the one you hit with a chunk of wood—is stone dead. Busted neck."

"Stand aside," Silver said. "I'll have to confirm it."

Reluctantly they moved away, allowing Silver to view what remained of Emo Hanks. He then took his identification from his coat pocket and passed it to the engineer.

"Silver and his woman were in the caboose with me," the brakeman volunteered. "It was the dead man that started the shootin'."

"Untanglin' all this is a job for the law," the fireman said. "Let's load this dead gent in the baggage car and get on to Dodge."

"All you passengers get aboard," ordered the conductor.

The fireman and brakeman carried the dead Emo Hanks to the baggage coach. Silver and Molly entered the third passenger coach and took their seats.

"Does it hurt much?" Molly asked, eyeing the blood-soaked sleeve of Silver's shirt.

"I've had more pleasant experiences," said Silver. "Here, take my bandanna and tie it as tight as you can, just above the wound. I'll last until we reach Dodge and a doctor. I wish I'd insisted on searching Hanks, before he was put into the baggage coach."

"You know who he was and what he was," Molly said, "and he tried to kill you. What more do you need to know?"

"Nothing, I reckon," said Silver. "What I'd like to know is how the hell they knew we had Shankler. They had to know, almost the minute we took him, for Hanks to get on our trail so quickly."

"You don't suppose Wexler . . ."

"No," Silver said. "We left Dodge with Shankler the same day Wexler arrived. Hanks had to arrive from Denver on the same train we took to Kansas City. It makes no sense him gettin' here so fast."

"Perhaps it does," said Molly, "if you forget about Hanks. Turk Pardue was dead, and Dent Shankler was in jail. Hanks could have been sent to Dodge to find out what had become of Shankler and Pardue."

Silver laughed. "I thought I was pretty good, but you're better than I am. When the trail pulled in from Denver, Hanks must have seen us waiting to board the train, with Shankler in handcuffs. Instead of getting off at Dodge, he followed us on to Kansas City. When he was unable to kill Shankler, he decided to come after me."

When the westbound train reached Dodge, Silver and Molly found Wes, El Lobo, Renita, and Tamara waiting. Foster Hagerman and Harley Stafford were there as well, and while the locomotive took on water the engineer approached Hagerman. He quickly explained the shooting, mentioning the dead man in the baggage coach.

"I'll get you a blanket to cover the dead man," said Hagerman. "A couple of you take him into the waiting room, until the sheriff gets here."

"We're already behind schedule," the engineer said.

"Then go on when you're ready," Hagerman replied. "Sheriff Dumery knows Silver, and a report from him should be sufficient."

"Let it wait until I've seen a doctor," said Silver. "I've lost a lot of blood."

"I'll get you a hack," Wes said.

He whistled, and one of the hacks drew up beside them. Silver and Molly climbed into the back.

"To the nearest doctor," Wes ordered.

"We'll see you at the Dodge House," cried Molly.

"We might as well start back," Renita said.

"*Sí,*" said El Lobo. "Silver have much to say."

An hour later, a hack drew up before the Dodge House. Silver and Molly stepped down, and Silver paid the driver. Molly carried Silver's bloody shirt, and his left arm had a bandage from shoulder to elbow.

"Why don't you rest until suppertime?" Molly suggested.

"Because there's some talking to be done," said Silver. "I'll rest after supper. Go get Wes and Palo."

"Renita and Tamara too?"

"If they want to come," Silver said.

Wes, El Lobo, Renita, and Tamara came in. Molly closed and locked the door behind them. Wes and El Lobo hunkered on the floor, their backs to the wall. The others sat on the bed. Molly had gotten Silver a clean shirt.

"We got the captive to Fort Leavenworth alive," said Silver. "His name is Shankler, and his partner— the varmint that was killed—was Turk Pardue. The *hombre* that came after me aboard the train was Emo Hanks, from what Shankler told me."

"We've heard of Hanks," Wes said. "He's the bastard that tried to use a pair of New Orleans whores to lure Palo and me into a trap in Kansas City."[1]

"You do not tell me of that," said Tamara, looking accusingly at El Lobo.

"Madre mia," said El Lobo, shaking his head.

"Hanks tried to bushwhack Shankler," Silver continued, "but the sheriff in Kansas City rounded up some soldiers bound for the fort, and we had a military escort."

"Shankler talked then?" asked Wes.

"He did," Silver said. "When Hanks tried to kill Shankler, he wanted my promise that if he talked, we'd guarantee his safety and that the law would go easy on him. He's locked in the post guardhouse at Fort Leavenworth, and I have the post commander's

[1] *Sixguns and Double Eagles*

promise that he'll remain there until we're ready for him."

"My hat's off to you," said Wes. "This is the first one of the varmints that was taken alive and made to talk."

"Now I'm going to read you my notes," Silver said. "Stop me if you hear anything that sounds familiar."

They were silent as Silver read from the notebook.

"One important fact is missing," said Wes, when Silver had finished. "We don't have any idea where the Golden Dragon is hoarding the gold."

"I fought as hard for that as I could," Silver said, "but Shankler didn't know. He said there's a lot that he and others like him are never told. I questioned him at length as to where their supplies of silver, gold, and copper were coming from, and again Shankler just didn't know."

"That, or he was afraid to tell," said Wes.

"I don't think he knows," Silver said. "He told me enough to get himself shot dead at least ten times, if the Golden Dragon could get its claws into him."

"We go to Denver," El Lobo said.

"Yes," said Silver.

"But not until your wound heals," Molly said.

"We don't have that much time," said Silver. "This Drade Hogan that Shankler swears is the brains behind the Golden Dragon is nobody's fool. He's heard nothing from Pardue and Shankler, and when he gets no report from Hanks, he'll expect the worst. I think it's time Wes, Palo, and me take tomorrow's westbound to Colorado."

"Not without me," Molly cried.

"Nor me," said Renita and Tamara in a single voice.

"You're all making it difficult for us," Silver said. "When all hell busts loose, it's hard for a man to just keep himself alive. The whole idea of coming to Dodge was to leave the three of you safe in a friendly town."

"I don't think of it as a friendly town anymore," said Molly.

"It will be safer than it has been," Silver said, "because we're going on the offensive. We'll be going after them, instead of them coming after us. You can have an extra bed brought in, and the three of you can stay in the same room until we return. Remember, all of you are armed."

Renita and Tamara looked at Wes and El Lobo, but found no compromise. Molly said nothing more, and when they reached Delmonico's for supper, it was a somber occasion. Renita finally spoke.

"When . . . will you be going?"

"On tomorrow's westbound," said Silver. "I'll be talking to Sheriff Dumery before we go, asking him to look out for you while we're away."

As though on cue, Sheriff Dumery entered the cafe, and not waiting for an invitation, he took a seat at Silver's table. Wasting no time, Dumery spoke.

"I reckon I ought to talk to you about the dead man that come in on the westbound, Silver. Just for the record, of course."

"Of course," Silver said.

Sheriff Dumery had only a few questions, which Silver answered readily.

"Thanks," said Sheriff Dumery. "I reckon I don't have to tell you that Ashe Wexler is raisin' hell over the dead *hombre.* He's demanding that the three of you leave town and not come back."

"We'll be able to meet half that demand, Sheriff," Silver said. "Tomorrow the three of us will be taking the westbound to Colorado. Molly, Renita, and Tamara will remain here at the Dodge House. We'll appreciate your looking out for them while we're away."

"I will," said Sheriff Dumery, "and I'll ask Harley Stafford to help me. He'll be in town for the next two weeks."

"*Bueno*," Wes said. "I've never had a better friend than Harley, and with a pistol, he's almighty sudden."

Denver, Colorado, April 15, 1885

Drade Hogan sat at his desk, puffing a cigar and drinking coffee. Though there had been no word, Hogan believed Shankler and Pardue were dead, or worse, that they had been taken alive. Hogan then turned his thoughts to Emo Hanks. While Hogan had warned them all against careless use of the telegraph, he had given Hanks a coded message to report the success of his mission. Yet he had heard nothing. Not until one of his men, Abel Hamlet, rode in from Boulder was there any news, and it was all bad.

"I thought you ought to know about this," Hamlet said. "It come in this morning on the westbound."

Hogan took the Kansas City newspaper, and a big black headline leaped out at him.

A bushwhacking and a shoot-out in Dodge. Two men dead in the street.

Ashe Wexler had written the piece, and Hogan read it with growing anger. He ground his teeth as he learned that not only had Wes Stone gunned down Curly Dismukes, he had killed one of two bushwhackers who had been siding Dismukes. One of the bushwhackers had been taken alive, and Bryan Silver had taken him to Fort Leavenworth. There he was to be held as a witness for the federal government.

"Damn it," Hogan bawled aloud, "where *is* Emo Hanks?"

The receptionist thought Hogan was shouting at her, and opened the door.

"I just read something in the paper that made me angry," said Hogan. "Get on back to your desk, and if anybody wants me, I'm not here."

Drade Hogan had prepared for just such an occasion. He quickly addressed half a dozen envelopes and then wrote a brief message for each of them. These he took to the girl in the front office.

"Take these downstairs to the courier's," Hogan said. "It's important that they be delivered immediately."

"Yes, sir," said the receptionist.

Hogan returned to his office to await the expected responses.

Dodge City, Kansas, April 16, 1885

"I wish I was going with you," Renita said, as Wes prepared to leave for the depot.

"But you can't," said Wes. "We're going to make it so hot for them, they won't have the chance to even think of you in Dodge."

Silver and El Lobo were having an equally hard time leaving Molly and Tamara behind.

"I'm going to the depot with you," Molly said.

"No," said Silver. "That's an unnecessary risk."

"I have a gun," Molly said.

"Damn it," said Silver, "I didn't buy you the Colt so you could go looking for trouble. I don't want the three of you leaving the Dodge House, except to eat at Delmonico's, and that rule's in effect until we return. I'm depending on you to keep Renita and Tamara in line. They've been through hell in Mexico, and they're just reckless enough to follow us on the next train."

"And you think I'm not?"

"I hope you're not," Silver said.

There was a coded knock on the door. Silver opened it to find Wes and El Lobo there.

"We'd better go," said Wes, "or I'll have to hog-tie Renita."

"*Sangre de Christo*," El Lobo said, "per'ap Tamara hog-tie *me*."

Silver kissed Molly long and hard. He then stepped out the door and closed it behind him. Carrying their Winchesters, Silver, Wes, and El Lobo set out for the livery, where they had left their horses. Reaching the depot, Silver went to Foster Hagerman's office.

"Wes, Palo, and me are leaving for Colorado," said Silver. "We'll need the use of a boxcar for our horses."

"You're in luck," Hagerman said. "Harley's coming in from Kansas City, and he made arrangements for a boxcar there. I'll consign it to continue on to Boulder. You're not taking the ladies with you?"

"No," said Silver. "Don't hesitate to join them for meals at Delmonico's when you can. They've been warned against going anywhere else."

"I'll assist them any way that I can," Hagerman said. "In case Harley hasn't told you, he's been planning for this. I've arranged for him to remain in Dodge for the next two weeks."

"I'm obliged," said Silver. "I appreciate you and Harley more than you'll ever know. It is a tribute to Wes Stone, that honorable men call him friend."

"Wes and his father before him," Hagerman said.

There was the distant wail of a whistle as the westbound train approached Dodge. Harley Stafford swung to the ground while the train was still moving. He didn't seem surprised to see Silver, Wes, and El Lobo.

"Here," said Harley, handing Silver the Kansas City paper.

Silver, with Wes and El Lobo listening, read the story that had angered Drade Hogan.

"I thought you might find that interesting," Harley said, when Silver finished reading the story. "Our friend Wexler didn't waste any time."

"This will likely play hell with the information we got out of Shankler," said Silver. "We're leaving for Colorado, taking the fight to them, instead of waiting for them to come to us."

"Wish I was goin' with you," Harley said, "but I reckoned I could be more help if I stuck around Dodge for a while. Anybody comes lookin' for your women, they'll have to climb over me."

"*Bueno*," said El Lobo.

"You're an *hombre* to ride the river with, Harley," Wes said. "We're obliged."

"We certainly are," said Silver. "Now we'd better get our horses aboard that boxcar."

Chapter 14

At the Dodge House, Renita, Tamara, and Molly had all moved into a single room. They heard the screech of the whistle as the westbound train approached Dodge, and Renita sprawled facedown on the bed.

"Come on," said Molly. "We'll be all right. Wes left Empty here with us."

"It's not us I'm worried about," Renita said with a muffled sob.

"They *bueno hombres*," said Tamara.

Renita rolled over and sat up, rubbing her eyes. When she finally spoke, her voice was steady.

"Don't mind me; I'm just selfish. I keep remembering that Wes said as soon as we got to Dodge, we'd stand before a preacher. But we didn't, and he hasn't spoke of it since."

"Palo no speak of it either," said Tamara. "Silver per'ap?"

"No," Molly said, "he hasn't spoken of it, but there's no doubt in my mind. One day it will happen."

"Silver didn't rescue you from a Mexican whorehouse," said Renita. "By the time Wes found me, I'd been pawed and manhandled by every damn Mexican with a few extra *pesos* in his pocket. I feel used up, like parts of me are gone forever."[1]

"You forget Palo take me from Mexican whore-

[1] *The Border Empire*

house," Tamara said. "All my parts still be there. Ask Palo."

Renita blushed furiously, and Molly laughed.

"I *will* ask him, when they return," said Renita. "You think I won't?"

"No give a damn," Tamara said.

She and Molly laughed, and Renita swapped her frown for a smile. They all waited for the whistle of the departing westbound, and when it came, they grew serious.

"The sooner they go, the sooner all this shoot-or-be-shot will be over," said Molly.

At the depot, Silver, Wes, and El Lobo had loaded their horses and saddles into the boxcar. As they entered one of the passenger coaches, the train shuddered. Then came a departing blast from the locomotive's whistle. Dodge was soon left behind, and there was nothing before them but the flat plains of western Kansas.

Denver, Colorado, April 16, 1885

Drade Hogan looked at his now empty suite with some regret. It had served him well, but circumstances had forced him to vacate. He locked the door for the last time. He had no way of knowing if the federals had identified him by name, but he wasn't taking any chances. He had taken a six-month lease at a new location, using a fictitious name. In less than six months, he would be safely out of the country.

Durango, Colorado, April 16, 1885

Elias Hawk and Hobie Denbow had just returned to the mine with two heavy wooden boxes that the bill of lading said contained machinery.

"With the one we already got, and these two, there must be near a million dollars," Denbow said. "How much we got to have before we make a run for it?"

"As much as we can safely take," said Hawk. "This has got to be playin' hell with the Treasury, and it's just a matter of time until the federals put a stop to it. I figure when the law comes down hard enough on Hogan, he'll be so busy tryin' to save his own hide, he won't have time for us."

"Trouble is," Denbow said, "we got no way of knowin' when Hogan may decide to run for it. Suppose he shows up, wantin' the gold before we've had a chance to take it and get out of the country?"

Hawk laughed. "Hobie, my boy, the kind of riches we're talkin' about, I'd gut-shoot Drade Hogan and a dozen like him."

Reaching the mine, they wrestled the heavy crates inside. Hawk attacked them with the hatchet until he could remove the wooden top. Each of the metal containers were locked, as the first one had been.

"Why are you openin' these?" Denbow asked. "They're just like the first one."

"Because I won't believe there's gold in there until I see it with my own eyes," said Hawk. "A thief will steal from his friends as quick as he'll steal from anybody else."

"Like we're doin'," Denbow said.

"Yeah," said Hawk, "like we're doing."

Hawk smashed the lock on both strongboxes. But only one of them contained the gold double eagles. The second was full of rocks.

"Damn," Denbow said. "He cheated us. We oughta raise hell."

"The Señor Hogan is testing us," said Hawk. "These strongboxes are locked. Should we complain that one of them contains only rocks, it's an admission that we opened them. We'll say nothing, and when we go, we'll leave Hogan the boxes filled with rocks."

"These boxes is mighty heavy," Denbow said. "You ain't told me where we're takin' 'em or where we're goin'."

"You'll know when the time comes," said Hawk. "There's still some loose ends that must be tied. I'll have to ride to Santa Fe."

"Leavin' me here?" Denbow shouted. "What if Hogan comes for the gold while you're gone? He'll kill me when he finds them locks has been blown off the strongboxes."

"Hogan was just here," said Hawk, "and we have only two shipments of actual gold. I must take care of business in Santa Fe if we're to get out of here alive. One of us must stay here. Even if nobody can get to the gold, we don't want them snooping around our diggings."

"I reckon not," Denbow said doubtfully. "But we never even come close to this kind of money before, and I just can't help feelin' this whole thing is gonna blow up in our faces."

"You're a poor gambler, Hobie. Only the long shots pay off big."

Denver, Colorado, April 17, 1885

Cautiously, Silver, Wes, and El Lobo stepped down from the train. They immediately claimed their horses, and saddling them, rode away. While still a considerable distance from Denver, they reined up to rest the horses.

"This Drade Hogan may not exist," Wes said. "It sounds like a made-up name."

"We don't care what he calls himself," said Silver, "just as long as we know he's the brains behind the

Golden Dragon. I'm not as concerned with his true identity as I am with the possibility that he'll be gone. That story in the Kansas City paper told him all he needs to know."

"We owe Ashe Wexler one for that," Wes said.

"He's broken no law," said Silver. "You ever heard of freedom of the press?"

"I've heard of it," Wes said, "and it always seems to work in favor of renegades and outlaws. I've heard how this same damn newspaper almost destroyed my father. Or have you forgotten that?"

"I'll never forget that," said Silver. "I defended Nathan Stone in court, and only by the grace of God did he go free on a plea of self-defense."[2]

"*Bueno*," El Lobo said. "You win."

"I had to," said Silver. "Anything less would have gotten Nathan Stone the rope."

Mounting their horses, they rode on, growing silent as they reached the outskirts of Denver. The address they sought was in a fashionable section of town. The building, when they found it, had a law office, a real estate office, and a courier and delivery service on the first floor.

"Upstairs," said Silver. "Wes, you and El Lobo wait here on the street. I'll check out the upstairs."

Wes and El Lobo said nothing. Not knowing what awaited them upstairs, Silver chose not to endanger them all. He started up the steps while Wes and El Lobo looked for anything or anybody that seemed the least suspicious. Reaching the second floor, Silver found every door locked. On one of them was a FOR RENT sign, with instructions to apply to the real estate office on the first floor. Silver started down the stairs, and had no sooner reached the street when all hell broke loose. The first slug narrowly missed Silver,

[2] *The Killing Season*

tearing into one of the wooden steps behind him. Lead slammed into the brick wall, shrieking off in deadly ricochets. The nearest sanctuary was the real estate office. Wes and El Lobo ran for it, Silver on their heels. But the bushwhackers were expecting that. Lead whanged off the sidewalk at their feet, and when Wes swung open the door, they literally fell into the real estate office. Next to the door, a plate glass window shattered, while another shot took the glass panel out of the door. A man cursed, a woman screamed, and then there was only silence. Silver, Wes, and El Lobo got to their feet. It seemed a miracle that none of them had been hit. But their trouble wasn't over. A big man in town clothes glared at them, so furious he was unable to speak. Finding his voice, he began cursing them.

"Shut your mouth, or I'll shut it for you," Silver said in a dangerously calm voice.

"Don't you threaten me," the real estate man shouted. "You've destroyed my office, and somebody's going to pay. I'm calling the law."

"Go ahead," said Silver. "I'm sure they'll want to talk to you. I have a federal warrant for the arrest of the *hombre* that was rentin' the upstairs. Just how involved are you?"

"I am Sam Middleton, a reputable man," the real estate man snarled. "I know nothing of the party who rented the upstairs. He moved out yesterday."

"Mr. Hogan was always so nice," said a woman peering out from behind a desk.

"Who *are* you?" Middleton demanded.

Silver handed Middleton his identification, and the real estate man's face went white as he studied it. In silence, he returned it, waiting for Silver to speak.

"The men firing at us were sent by your Mr. Hogan," said Silver. "I'll contact the law before I leave Denver, and see that they're aware of this incident. You're welcome to ask for damages from the government."

"I don't need the publicity," Middleton said. "All I ask is that you take your friends and go. Don't come near me again."

Silver said nothing. He opened the bullet-riddled door and stepped out, Wes and El Lobo following. When El Lobo closed the door, the remainder of the shattered glass fell tinkling to the floor.

"I still don't know where the varmints were hiding," said Wes. "Everything within gun range has peaked roofs."

"They were at street level," Silver said, "because they didn't start shooting until I was off the stairs. I'd say they were shooting from the windows of that low-slung building over there."

"Then maybe we'd better have a look at it, whatever it is," said Wes.

When they reached the mysterious building, they found it locked. Across the glassed-in front were foot-high red-and-gold letters, reading: PRETTY GIRL SALOON AND GENTLEMAN'S EMPORIUM.

"They're likely open until three in the morning," Silver said. "That would account for them being closed now."

"Those bushwhackers had to get in there somehow, and they had to get out," said Wes. "That means this place is in cahoots with this bunch behind the Golden Dragon."

"There's some connection," Silver said, "and I'd like to search the place before they open for business. There may be some evidence we can use. This would be a good time to tell the sheriff about Middleton's office bein' shot up. We'll ask the sheriff for a search warrant, and bring him back with us."

"*Bueno,*" said El Lobo.

Returning to their horses, they went in search of the sheriff's office.

"Interesting," said Sheriff Jennings, as he studied Silver's identification, "but all this seems a little far-fetched to me. I've had no report of any shooting."

"That much you can see with your own eyes," Silver said, trying to hold his temper. "As for my mission here, I can tell you nothing more than I already have. When this case is closed, I'll see that you have all the details. Now, will you issue that search warrant and come with us?"

"I'll do it against my better judgment," said Jennings, "on the condition that you can show me evidence of this attempted ambush."

"Come on," Silver said.

Jennings saddled his horse and rode with them. They dismounted across the street from the two-story brick building, leaving their horses there. When they entered the bullet-riddled office, a woman with a push broom was sweeping up broken glass.

"Oh," she cried, "they're back!"

"Damn it," Middleton bawled from his small office. "I told you—"

"Hold it," said the lawman. "This is Sheriff Jennings, and I want to talk to you."

Middleton came out, glaring at Silver, Wes, and El Lobo as though he could cheerfully murder them. He stood there with his doubled fists on his hips, waiting for the sheriff to speak. Jennings did.

"I am told an attempted bushwhacking took place here, and from the look of things, I can believe it. What can you tell me?"

"Not much," said Middleton. "When the shootin' started, it was like a war goin' on. There was glass breaking, and when these three come bustin' in, the shootin' got worse."

"I've been told the truth of it, then," Sheriff Jennings said.

"Yeah," said Middleton wearily. "Now get them three out of my sight."

When Sheriff Jennings, Silver, Wes, and El Lobo had left the office, Silver pointed to the distant saloon, the only cover within Winchester range.

"The shooting had to come from there," Silver said. "There's no other cover that's close enough."

"The Pretty Girl Saloon is owned by Madame Renae," said Sheriff Jennings, "and in all the years I've been sheriff, I've had no trouble with her or any of the women she employs. Now you're wanting me to present her with a search warrant."

"I am," Silver said. "With all due respect to the lady and your relationship with her, I believe those bushwhackers were firing from that building. One way or another, I intend to search every room on the side of that building facing the ambush site."

"We may have to wait," said Jennings. "The place doesn't open for another hour."

"Madame Renae doesn't live here, then?" Silver asked.

"Not as far as I know," said Jennings. "The office is in the back. Come on."

When they reached the back of the buildling, the office door was standing wide open.

"Something's bad wrong here," Sheriff Jennings said. "Looks like a break-in."

"Not quite," said Silver, examining the door. "None of the glass panels is broken, and the lock's still intact. Whoever entered this saloon did so with a key."

"I'll have to agree with you," Jennings said. "When Madame Renae arrives, we'll find out who else has a key. This fully justifies our searching the place."

They waited, and Madame Renae eventually drove up in a buckboard. Dressed in the most fashionable

clothing of the time, she looked like anything but
what she was. She had green eyes and red hair, and
from every finger diamonds flashed in the sun.
Climbing out of the buckboard like a man, she left
the team standing, turning her full attention to the
sheriff.

"Whatever is going on here, Sheriff Jennings?
Who's been in my office?"

"We're hoping you can shed some light on it,"
said Jennings.

Quickly he introduced Silver, Wes, and El Lobo.
He then told her of the shooting that had taken place,
and that it had to have come from the Pretty Girl
Saloon.

"Besides you," said Silver, "who else has a key to
your office?"

"Nobody that I know of," Madame Renae said. "I
own this place, and I can prove it."

"But you can't deny that somebody opened this
door with a key," said the sheriff. "It's as much to
your benefit to search the place as it is to ours. You
need to find out if you've been robbed."

"I suppose you're right," Madame Renae said. "Go
ahead and search. There's never any money left
loose, so thieves would have to go to the safe. I'll
see if anybody's tampered with it."

Sheriff Jennings, Silver, Wes, and El Lobo followed
her into the office. An old safe stood in the corner,
and it appeared undisturbed.

"Open the safe," said Sheriff Jennings.

"Nobody knows the combination but me," Madame Renae protested.

"Nobody has a key to the door but you, and it
was standing open," said Jennings. "Go on and open
the safe."

"All right," she said angrily. "Stand back."

She knelt before the safe in such a way that they

couldn't read the pattern of numbers in the combination. Silver eyed Sheriff Jennings, but Jennings said nothing. The heavy door of the old safe swung noiselessly open. After a few seconds, Madame Renae closed the safe's door and spun the dial.

"The safe is just as I left it," said Madame Renae, getting to her feet. "Now please conclude your search and get out of here. I don't want any of you wandering around after I open for business."

"I can't make any promises," Sheriff Jennings said. "It all depends on what we find."

"You're treating me like a common criminal," she said, pouting.

Her green eyes spoke volumes, but Sheriff Jennings seemed not to notice.

"Ma'am," said Silver, "if you have nothing to hide, you have nothing to fear. It'll be to your advantage for us to search the place."

"Do it, then," Madame Renae said.

She was all business again, her eyes flashing green fire. Sheriff Jennings pushed open a door that led into the saloon. Silver, Wes, and El Lobo followed. A long hall extended two-thirds of the distance to the front of the building. The front was open, with a long mahogany bar, a billiard table, a roulette wheel, and an array of solid oak tables with matching chairs.

"I think we'll save the front for last, Sheriff," said Silver. "I'm concerned with those windows that are within Winchester range of that brick office building where we had to take cover."

"With all that gambling space up front," Wes said, "why all these private rooms? This looks more like a whorehouse than a saloon."

"The individual rooms are for high-stakes games," said Sheriff Jennings. "Pretty girls are near naked, and they're provided to take the minds of the high rollers off how much money they've lost."

"There's a dozen rooms that could concern us," Silver said. "Suppose we each take one of them? We should be finished well before it's time for her to open."

"Good thinking," said Sheriff Jennings. "The woman's kept a decent place, never causing me any trouble. I don't want to be any harder on her than I have to."

Silver took the first room, Wes the second, El Lobo the third, and Sheriff Jennings the fourth. It was Jennings who found a broken windowpane.

"I'd say there were at least three bushwhackers," Silver said, "and I suspect they were grouped fairly close together. Let's look at the two adjoining rooms."

In each of the adjoining rooms, a single windowpane had been broken, and on the frame of one of the windows, there were powder burns.

"Damn," said Sheriff Jennings. "You called it, Silver, but what am I gonna do with this woman? The bushwhackers were holed up in here, but there's no real evidence against her, unless we consider the possibility she gave somebody else a key."

"She's already denied that, and we have no proof," Silver said. "If you will, Sheriff, do me a favor. Tell Madame Renae that, beyond a doubt, the bushwhackers fired through the broken windowpanes in three of her rooms."

"It's the truth, as near as I can tell," said Sheriff Jennings. "I'll tell her, and I'll show her the broken windows. I suppose you have some plan in mind."

"I have," Silver admitted, "but it won't involve you."

"I'm obliged," said Sheriff Jennings. "You and your friends go on. I'll stay behind and tell Madame what she won't like to hear."

"You've been a big help to us, Sheriff," Silver said.

"Once this case is wrapped up, I'll see you before I leave Denver, and eventually you'll receive an official commendation from Washington."

Silver, Wes, and El Lobo had reached their horses before Silver spoke.

"What do you gents think of Madame Renae and her open door?"

"I think she's pretty much what she seems," said Wes. "If she had let those varmints in, knowing they were killers, I don't think she'd have left the door standing open. She got a rotten deal, and I'd say somebody will catch hell."

Silver laughed. "I'm counting on that. We're going to follow Madame wherever she goes for the next several days."

"Find *bastardo* with key," said El Lobo.

"Exactly," Silver replied. "As Sheriff Jennings said, she's kept her nose clean, as far as the law's concerned. Now there's conclusive evidence that at least three bushwhackers tried to commit murder after entering her place with a key. Somebody *else* has a key, by God, and she can deny it till hell freezes. My suspicious mind tells me that sooner or later she'll go looking for the *hombre* who has that key. But we have to play it close. The attempted bushwhacking was only the start. When Madame gets her claws into the *hombre* who has that key, he's going to know that we know of him. He'll suspect that we backed off only so that we could trail Madame, which will make it all the more important to him that all of us are graveyard dead."

"Not if we find out who he is and put a crimp in his tail first," said Wes. "There's a good chance that when we get our hands on that coyote with the key, he'll be Drade Hogan, or somebody close to him."

"I'm remembering some of the things Shankler told me when I questioned him at Fort Leavenworth," Silver said. "Hogan keeps a tight rein on his outfit, revealing nothing to his men that they don't have to know. Any kind of relationship he may have had with Madame Renae would have been kept under wraps. It's almost a sure bet that if Madame gave that key to Drade Hogan, he passed it on to the bushwhackers who tried to gun us down."

"It's the best lead we've had so far," said Wes. "Who's going to trail Madame Renae first?"

"I will," Silver said. "We'll stay with it in eight-hour shifts until she either leads us to the varmint we're looking for, or until we decide we're barking up the wrong tree. Do you know where the Denver House is?"

"Yes," said Wes. "It's a boardinghouse."

"Go there and take a room," Silver said, "but don't use your own name."

"I'll sign us in under my first and middle names," said Wes. "Does John Wesley sound right?"

"Yes," Silver said. "I expect Madame to raise some hell this afternoon, before any of the high rollers show up. Wherever she goes, I'll follow. Give me seven hours. Then one of you can relieve me here and stay until closing."

"We'll both relieve you," said Wes. "If something really breaks big, one of us can get word to you, while the other keeps an eye on Madame."

"I like that better," Silver said. "Once she leaves the saloon, we can't afford to lose her. If I'm not somewhere near when you return, you'll know she's gone and I'm following her."

"*Bueno*," said Wes, "but don't take any chances. I don't relish the thought of explaining to Molly why we allowed you to get shot full of holes."

Silver laughed. "Your compassion is touching. You're sounding more and more like my old *amigo*, Nathan Stone. Now get going."

Wes and El Lobo rode to the Denver House. There Wes took a room for the three of them. Leaving their horses at a nearby livery, they returned to their room at the boardinghouse.

"I miss Empty," said Wes. "It might have been a mistake, not bringing him with us."

"*Perro* no like trains," El Lobo said.

There being little else to do, they removed their hats, gunbelts, and boots and stretched out on the bed to wait.

Drade Hogan was furious. Partly because Kent, Hollis, and Bidamer had failed to kill their intended victims, and partly because his fit of temper hadn't intimidated them in the least.

"We done the best we could," said Bidamer, "but they didn't stay put and shoot back. They took cover in that real estate office on the first floor, and we shot it all to hell, but somehow they escaped. Before we left that saloon, I saw the three of 'em on their feet."

Drade Hogan swallowed his anger. These three had killed before, and if the money was right, they would kill again. Hogan spoke as calmly as he could.

"I told you these three aren't easy to kill. For that reason, I'm going to sweeten the pot. Starting now, there's a fifty-thousand-dollar price on the head of each of them. Just remember that I don't pay without proof."

"For that kind of money, we'll bring you their heads on a platter," said Hollis.

"Damn right," Kent agreed.

"Hold it," said Hogan, as the trio started to leave. "Where's that key I gave you?"

"Here," Bidamer said, tossing the key to Hogan.

After the three of them had gone, Hogan lit a cigar, hoping to calm his nerves. He regretted having suggested the Pretty Girl Saloon as cover for the bush-whacking, but its location had been perfect. Now he was beset with nagging doubts. Had the would-be killers left some evidence—some sign—that would point to Drade Hogan? Suddenly there came a knock on the door, and Hogan drew a loaded Colt from a desk drawer.

"Identify yourself," said Hogan.

"Blanton Hood," a voice replied.

"Come on," said Hogan, concealing the Colt behind the desk.

Hood had a three-day beard and scraggly black hair down over his shirt collar. Denim shirt, Levi's, run-over boots, and a nearly used-up black Stetson completed his attire. He carried a tied-down Colt on his left hip, and without being invited, flopped down in a chair beside Hogan's desk.

"I didn't invite you to sit," Hogan said coldly.

"So you didn't," said Hood, remaining where he was. "What do you want?"

"There are three men I want eliminated," Hogan said. "There's a fifty-thousand-dollar price on the head of each of them. Hire as many men as you need. What you agree to pay them is your business, and the rest of the money is yours."

"Hell, I'll gun them all down myself," said Hood. "Git the money ready."

"It's been tried by better men than you," Hogan said with thinly veiled contempt. "I pay nothing for failure, and I'll demand proof. You're a damn fool to go after these three with less than a dozen gun-quick men."

"Just tell me who these dead men are, and how I can find 'em," Hood said.

Chapter 15

Denver, Colorado, April 16, 1885

For lack of cover, Silver was forced to conceal his horse a considerable distance from the Pretty Girl Saloon. The problem of concealing himself was even more difficult, for he had to be within sight of the back door. He managed, however, and he waited almost two hours before some of the girls arrived. Within minutes, Madame Renae emerged and began harnessing her team to the buckboard. That was Silver's cue to fetch his horse, and he did so. He was able to remain far behind the buckboard and still keep it in sight. He followed it to a residential area of expensive homes. Madame Renae reined up before a two-story mansion surrounded by trees and shrubbery, and then she did a curious thing. Instead of knocking or ringing the bell, she slipped a piece of paper under the door and returned to her buckboard. Mounting the box, she drove off. Silver waited until she was well away from the house. He then rode by the house and made note of the number and the street on which it was located. When he eventually came within sight of the buckboard, he followed at a safe distance. Madame Renae drove directly back to the saloon, and Silver again concealed his horse. He waited another two hours, and when Madame Renae failed to appear again, he reached a decision.

Mounting his horse, he rode to the Denver House and asked where he might find John Wesley.

"Identify yourself," said Wes, when Silver knocked.

"Twenty-one," Silver said.

Wes let Silver in, then locked the door behind him.

"I reckon there's been a change in plans," said Wes. "Has Madame tipped her hand?"

"We won't waste any more time trailing her," Silver said. "We have a better prospect."

He told them what he had learned.

"You think she left a message for the *hombre* who has a key to her place, then," Wes said.

"Yes," said Silver. "Hogan—if that's his name—vacated that building in a hurry, and it's unlikely she knows where he went. But if he's close enough to her to have a key to the Pretty Girl Saloon, I think there's a good possibility that she knows where he lives."

"We watch, follow Dragon," El Lobo said.

"We're stakin' out that house and following whoever enters or leaves it," said Silver, "and we'll all stay with it until we successfully draw to an inside straight or fold with a busted flush. Saddle your horses and let's ride."

Reaching the street they rode past the house, seeking cover for themselves and their horses.

"In a highfalutin' neighborhood like this, there should be a livery," Wes said. "If there is, we can leave the horses there."

"Depends on how far away the livery is," said Silver.

They found a livery barn on the next street, facing the house and a block behind it.

"Damn shame it's not facing the front of the place," Wes said. "We could maybe pay the hostler to let us sleep in the hay loft and watch from there."

"It may be a problem finding a place to conceal ourselves and still watch the place," said Silver. "Let's leave the horses here and get at it."

They had just led their horses into stalls and were about to leave, when a buckboard came rattling down the street. The two women perched on the seat looked vaguely familiar.

"*Sangre de Christo*," El Lobo said. "It be Monique and Louise. We go."

"Whoa," said Wes. "Maybe they live around here close. They owe us."

"How much am I entitled to know about this?" Silver asked.

"Not much to know," said Wes. "Monique and Louise are just a pair of New Orleans whores Emo Hanks paid to set us up for an ambush in a Kansas City hotel. Scared hell out of them when they learned they were to be gunned down with us. They were supposed to go on to California. Come on, Palo. Let's greet them."[1]

"Go ahead," said Silver. "I'll stay out of sight and see what develops."

Wes and El Lobo waited within one of the stalls until the women had turned the buckboard and team over to the hostler. When they stepped out, Monique and Louise were speechless, but not for long. To El Lobo's disgust, Monique threw her arms around him, while Louise went after Wes in similar fashion.

"You're a long ways from California," Wes said.

"We didn't go," said Louise. "We have something better here."

"I may be sorry I asked," Wes said, "but what are you doing?"

"We have a house of our own," said Louise.

"Right here in this fancied-up part of town. We have other girls working for us."

"We don't entertain anymore," Monique said, "except on special occasions." She clung to El Lobo in a manner that suggested one of those occasions might be fast approaching.

"We may need your help," said Wes, freeing himself from Louise.

"Whatever we can do, we will," said Louise.

"You remember what happened in Kansas City, then," Wes said.

"My God, yes," said Louise. "How could we ever forget?"

"It might interest you to know that Emo Hanks, the varmint that sent you, is dead," Wes said. "We have yet to get our hands on the leader of the gang. We have reason to believe he's here in Denver."

"Damn," said Monique. "Why didn't we go on to California when we had the chance?"

"I'm glad you didn't," Wes said. "We need a place to conceal ourselves while we watch a certain *hombre* enter or leave his place. Take us to this house of yours."

"They'll kill us if they find you there," said Monique.

"They won't find us there," Wes said, "because we won't be there long enough. Now I want you to meet the gent that's goin' to blow this gang of thieves and killers wide open."

Silver had been listening, and he stepped out of the livery barn.

"This is Bryan Silver," said Wes. "Silver, this is Monique and Louise."

"My pleasure," Silver said, tipping his hat.

He then passed his identification to Louise. Monique moved in close, and they studied the impressive credentials.

"You look like you could bust up anything you're of a mind to," Louise said.

"Yeah," said Monique. "I'd like to see you in action."

"I can't make any promises," Silver said. "Right now, we need a place where we can see without being seen. Look at this address and tell us where your house is in relation to it."

Monique and Louise looked at the page from the notebook on which Silver had written an address and a street name.

"That's across the street from us," said Louise.

"*Bueno*," Silver said. "We'll pay you for the use of a room facing that street."

"You don't have to pay," said Louise. "There's an upstairs room that we never use, and it has a window facing the street."

"Wes and Palo helped us get out of Kansas City alive, after we set them up to be shot down," Monique said. "They've more than paid for anything we have to offer, and that includes our—"

"If you don't mind," Wes interrupted, "we need to go on to your place and stake out that house across the street."

"Yes," said Silver. "Somebody's likely to wonder what's going on outside this livery."

The house, when they reached it, was two-story, like most of the others in the neighborhood. The interior could only be described as plush, with deep-pile carpets, matching floor-length drapes, and an array of expensive furniture. Silver, Wes, and El Lobo followed Monique and Louise up a winding staircase to the second floor. They had started down the hall when a girl stepped out of one of the rooms, clad only in a towel. So surprised was she that she dropped the towel.

"Priscilla," said Louise, trying not to laugh, "we're

going to have visitors in the front room for a while. It could be embarrassing, you wandering in the hall stark naked."

"I don't embarrass easily," Priscilla said, "and these visitors all look like they've had a roll in the hay. If they ain't, they're in need of one. I'm in room ten, gents."

She left the dropped towel where it had fallen and went on down the hall.

"Damn it," said Monique, "if she wasn't the best draw in the house, I'd kick her and her sharp tongue out into the street."

"There's a tub for bathing in the last room on the left at the end of the hall," Louise said. "That's where Priscilla's going."

Silver and Wes looked after the naked girl, and even El Lobo showed some interest.

"Come on," said Monique impatiently, obviously piqued at their interest in Priscilla.

The last room at the front end of the hall proved to be ideal. While there was but a single window, it afforded a view of the house across the street, where Madame Renae had slipped a message under the door.

"I'll bring up an extra cot," Louise said, "and the three of you can remain here just as long as you need to. You'll eat with Monique and me in our quarters."

When the two women had gone, Silver sighed with relief, and Wes laughed.

"*Desnudo señorita*," said El Lobo.

"*Sí*," Silver said. "Just don't ever get on the bad side of me, or I'll tell Tamara you're hiding out in whorehouses, getting an eyeful."

"We have business here," said Wes. "When this is all behind us, the less said about whorehouses, the better. Especially where Renita and Tamara are concerned."

"There's no use in all of us hunkerin' before this window," Silver said. "I'll watch for a while. Both of you kick off your boots and catch a few winks. We don't know how long we'll be watching, and you'd better sleep a little while you can."

Wes and El Lobo took Silver's advice, and soon they were snoring. It was late afternoon when a lone horseman approached the house in question.

"You *hombres* better pull on your boots," Silver said. "A rider just rode in behind the house. He must have a stable there for his horse."

Drade Hogan set about unsaddling the horse. He was in a foul mood, for he had heard nothing from the killers he had hired. Despite the fact there was a back door, Hogan went around to the front of the house and unlocked the front door. Immediately his eyes fell on the sheet of paper Madame Renae had slipped under the door. He quickly read the brief message: *I don't know how else to get to you. We need to talk. If you don't come to my place, then I'll be at yours before dawn.*

It was signed "Renae."

"Damn that woman," said Hogan.

He purposely waited until dusk before saddling his horse, and when he went around behind the house, Silver, Wes, and El Lobo were watching.

"I don't know what his relationship with Madame Renae is," Silver said, "but I'd bet the farm she aims to give him hell over the use of that key. Come on. We'd better get to the livery and get our horses. We could lose him in the dark."

"Followin' him shouldn't be a problem," said Wes, "if he heads for the Pretty Girl Saloon."

"We don't know that he will," Silver said, "but I'm hoping he will. That will confirm what we only suspect, that he sent those bushwhackers after us, and the shooting all took place from within Madame Renae's place."

Silver, Wes, and El Lobo went down the back stairs and from there made their way to the livery.

"Palo," Silver said, "it's dark enough that you can't be seen. Walk down there to the corner and watch that house. Wes and me will saddle our horses."

El Lobo did as bidden. Wes and Silver led out all three horses and began saddling them. Quickly they mounted, Wes leading El Lobo's horse. When they got to the corner, El Lobo swung into the saddle.

"Coyote run," said El Lobo.

"Lead out," Silver said. "Take us the way he went."

El Lobo took the lead. To their advantage, lamplight streamed out of many windows, and they soon sighted the distant rider. It became more and more obvious that he was bound for the part of town where Madame Renae's place was. Hogan rode in behind the Pretty Girl Saloon, and from the shadows on the other side of the street, Silver, Wes, and El Lobo watched him dismount. He stood looking for a moment before entering the saloon.

"What I wouldn't give to hear that conversation," said Wes.

"That won't be necessary," Silver replied. "His coming here proves our suspicions are no longer just bare bones. He's added some meat to them. When he leaves here, I expect him to return to the house. We'll follow him home and keep watch until he rides out in the morning. We know he once had a suite of offices, and that's reason enough to believe he's rented similar quarters elsewhere. Once we know where, we can consider breaking in and looking for evidence."

"Consider, hell," said Wes. "There's no place on

the face of the earth that can't be busted into if there's a good enough reason, and we have one."

"*Sí,*" El Lobo said.

Drade Hogan waited within Madame Renae's office, while a servant went to fetch her. Theirs had been an ongoing affair, but she had never come to his house or to his office. He had some disturbing thoughts, the foremost of which suggested this wasn't going to be a romantic rendezvous. When Madame Renae entered the office and closed the door behind her, the stormy look in her green eyes confirmed his suspicions.

"I've told you never to come to the house," said Hogan.

"Since you moved your office without telling me, I had no other way of reaching you," she snapped. "How the hell was I to know you hadn't skipped town?"

"You know I'd never go without you," said Hogan soothingly. "Are you needing more money?"

"You think money's the answer to everything, don't you? All I want from you is the key to this building, and I want it now."

"You're forgetting something," Hogan said. "I brought you from California and bought this place for you. Now you owe me."

"So sue me, and when you leave here, I don't want to see you ever again."

"I'll go," said Hogan, "and you can forget anything I said about South America."

"Then give me the key and get out."

Hogan laughed. "I'll go, but the key goes with me. My lawyer drew up the contract in a manner that, if anything happens to you, this place reverts back to me. It would be quite embarrassing for you to meet an untimely end, leaving me without a key to my own saloon. It's all one hundred percent legal, I might add."

"You're a fine one to speak of legalities. It was one of your underhanded schemes that brought the law down on me. You brought in a bunch of killers, and when they failed to kill as you'd paid them to, they ran out of here, leaving the door standing open. It was like that when the sheriff showed up to investigate the shooting."

"The law's been here?" Hogan asked, alarmed.

"Sheriff Jennings," said Madame Renae, and then she twisted the knife. "With him were the three men you tried to ambush. The sheriff had a search warrant, and they found the broken glass in the three rooms where your killers were hidden."

"They can't prove a damn thing," Hogan shouted.

It was Madame Renae's turn to laugh. "Legally, perhaps not, but there's a lot more to it than just an overly nosy sheriff. He was here only because the three men you tried to kill needed a search warrant."

"They were here?" Hogan cried.

"They were," said Madame Renae with some satisfaction.

Drade Hogan just stood there cursing under his breath until Madame Renae interrupted his tirade.

"Damn you, I want that key, and then I want you out of here."

"I'll see that you get everything that's coming to you," Hogan snarled, "but I think I'll just keep the key to remember you by."

"It won't be of any use to you in hell," said Madame Renae.

As though by magic, a double barrel .41-caliber Derringer had appeared in her hand, and its ugly snout was pointed unwaveringly at Drade Hogan's middle.

"You wouldn't dare," Hogan said.

"Try me," said Madame Renae. "I'll shoot you dead, and then I'll go free. All I'll have to do is tell the law it was you who hired those killers, and that you came here threatening me. Now hand me that key, and don't try anything foolish."

Hogan looked again into her green, hate-filled eyes and surrendered the key. He turned and left the office, his mind racing frantically, like a doomed mouse seeking to escape a determined cat. Mounting his horse, he rode as fast as he dared without attracting undue attention. He looked back, and just for a moment, he fancied he had seen riders following, keeping to the shadows of the tree-lined street. He rode on, cursing Kent, Hollis, and Bidamer for having left the door open after the failed ambush . . .

"He rides like he expects to be followed," said Wes, as they kept to the shadows. "I'd say she told him we were there, with the sheriff and a search warrant."

"Exactly what I wanted her to tell him," Silver said. "As things now stand, we haven't a shred of real evidence against him. A slick lawyer could free him in twenty-four hours."

"He suspects he's being followed," said Wes. "He keeps looking back."

"I'm counting on him *knowing* he's being followed," Silver said. "He'll hire his killing done, and when it's do or die—time for him to stand up on his hind legs and be a man—he'll run like a frightened rat. But he won't go without his ill-gotten treasure, and that's when we'll get him."

"Shankler talk," said El Lobo. "That not be evidence?"

"In the long run, it will be," Silver said, "but until we build a stronger case, it would only be Shankler's word against Hogan's."

Silver, Wes, and El Lobo reined up in the shadows,

well before reaching the big Hogan house. They could see Hogan in the starlight as he dismounted. He seemed to be watching, listening. Finally he led the horse around the house to the stable.

"The real test comes tomorrow," said Silver, "when we'll have to trail him in daylight."

"We don't know for *certain* that he has rented a place somewhere," Wes said. "Could be that he pulls all the strings from where he lives."

"That's generally not the way of criminals," said Silver, "and almost certainly not the way of this varmint. If you'd hired as many killers as Hogan probably has, would you be satisfied having them know where you live?"

"No," Wes said, "I reckon I wouldn't. We'd better be gettin' back to the house if we aim to get any supper."

Silver laughed. "The kind of reception you *hombres* got, I wouldn't be surprised if Monique and Louise fed you anytime of the day or night."

"They gave up on El Lobo and me," said Wes. "That's why they've had their eyes on you."

"Maybe I'll sleep in the barn with the horses," Silver said. "One of you can holler at me if Hogan decides to ride out."

They went in behind the house, going to the back door as Monique and Louise had suggested. Silver knocked, and after peering out around the curtain, Monique unlocked the door and allowed them to enter. The cooking and dining area were combined. Louise sat at the dining table, sipping coffee.

"I reckon we're too late for supper," Wes said.

"Of course not," said Louise. "It isn't often we have guests, so we waited for you. Do all of you like fried chicken?"

"Southern fried?" Wes asked.

"Southern fried," said Monique. "Folks in New

Orleans have to eat too. They don't spend all their time . . . ah . . . pursuing the ladies. Whatever else a woman becomes, she first learns to cook."

When the meal was over, and they were down to final cups of coffee, Louise spoke.

"You haven't told us anything about how your investigation is going. That is, if we're allowed to know."

"We kind of feel like we have a stake in this," Monique said, "since the bunch you're after used us for bait in that ambush in Kansas City. I won't feel safe until they're shot, hanged, or locked up."

"Neither will I," said Louise.

"I don't know how we'd have managed to keep a close watch on this *hombre*, without the use of your front room," Silver said. "Not to mention the excellent food. While it will be strictly confidential, I think you're entitled to know what progress we've made."

Silver then told them of their visit to Madame Renae's, and of their suspicion there was a second key, possibly in the possession of Drade Hogan.

"And when you followed him," said Louise, "he went straight to her place, didn't he?"

"That he did," Silver said.

"This is so exciting," said Monique. "I'm glad we're able to help. When this is all over, the three of you can stay here as long as you like. There must be *something* you enjoy besides chasing thieves and killers."

"Oh, there is," Silver said with a straight face. "We can eat Southern fried chicken any time of the day or night."

When Silver, Wes, and El Lobo returned to their upstairs front room, they could see lamps through several windows of the Hogan house.

"Looks normal enough," said Wes. "Maybe he's not as skittish as we think he is."

"He's spooked, all right," Silver said, "but not to the extent he won't get his hands on as much loot as he can before he runs."

Drade Hogan kept well away from the windows. A single lamp, turned low, left most of the parlor in shadow. Hogan sat in a ladder-back chair, a loaded Winchester within his reach. On a small table beside him was a shot glass and a whiskey decanter two-thirds full. He waited impatiently for the dawn, so that he might set in motion his escape, but even the thought of that didn't raise his spirits. His only consolation was that he had personally shipped another four crates of "machinery" south, to Durango. His goal had been to escape to South America with five million dollars in gold. Now he had less than half that, thanks to their setback in California and the persistence of Bryan Silver and his gun-slinging friends.[2]

Durango, Colorado, April 17, 1885

Elias Hawk, mindful that he was leaving Hobie Denbow alone with almost a million in gold, took the train to Santa Fe one day and returned the next.

"I made arrangements for us to leave the country," Hawk said. "Captain Antonio Diaz will do anything if the price is right. The old pirate's charging us twenty-five thousand."

"Not bad," said Denbow, "as long as he's floatin' that ship up here to get the gold."

"He'll anchor in the Gulf of California," Hawk said. "It'll be up to us to get the gold to his ship."

[2] *Sixguns and Double Eagles*

"Tarnation," said Denbow, "that must be five hunnert miles."

"More like four hundred, travelin' across country," Hawk said.

"I ain't trustin' nobody to haul all this gold four hunnert miles," said Denbow.

"Neither am I," Hawk said. "I bought us a heavy freight wagon in Santa Fe. It'll come by train, on a flat car. Then you and me will take the gold and head south."

"I got a feeling we'd better not wait much longer," said Denbow. "There's four more crates of machinery at the depot, waitin' for us."

"You may be right," Hawk said. "There's something damned suspicious about him sending four cases at a time. If these crates have gold instead of rocks, we'll have enough gold to make our move. Let's find out."

Reaching the depot, they wrestled the four heavy cases aboard the wagon. Getting them into the hidden cavern within the mine was a frustrating, exhausting task, and it took them a while before they had the strength to attack the crates. Using the hatchet, Denbow tore the lid off the first crate, and with the hatchet's flat head, smashed the lock.

"This one's pure gold," said Denbow, raising the lid.

Excited now, Denbow attacked the rest of the heavy wooden crates, ripping off the top of each so that he might get to the metal containers inside. Quickly he smashed all three locks and raised the lids. All three boxes contained gold double eagles.

"With these and the two that was already here," Denbow said, "there's millions."

"Between two and three million," said Hawk. "Our wagon should be arriving tomorrow on the train. We'll load up and leave late at night when everybody's asleep. With luck, nobody will know we're gone until it's too late to stop us."

Denbow laughed. "Not a bad deal for us, considerin' that all we contributed is the little gold and silver we've been able to dig."

Denver, Colorado, April 17, 1885

Silver, Wes, and El Lobo were up before first light.

"Breakfast," said Monique, knocking on their door.

Reaching the dining room, they found the table already set.

"Usually Monique and me don't get up for a couple more hours," Louise said, "but we made an exception. Now when it gets light enough to see, you'll be ready to go."

"We appreciate your sacrifice," said Silver. "It's important that we don't lose sight of our man. If he's as spooked as I think he is, he's about ready to run. There's one more important step, and that's to follow him to his headquarters."

"But if he suspects he's being followed," Louise said, "will he go there?"

"He'll likely have no choice if he's to get his affairs in order," said Silver.

Silver, Wes, and El Lobo didn't delay at the breakfast table, but returned to the room from which they could observe the Hogan house.

"One of us should go to the stable, saddle the horses, and bring them in behind this house," Wes said. "If we wait for him to saddle up and ride, we may lose him."

"I go," said El Lobo.

"*Bueno,*" Silver said. "Get the horses back here as quickly as you can. I have an idea we'll be needing them *pronto.*"

Chapter 16

Denver, Colorado, April 18, 1885

Drade Hogan had spent a sleepless night, thinking, planning, and cursing the woman who had led his enemies to him. While he had seen nobody the night before, he was now virtually certain he had been followed from Madame Renae's to his own house. Now they would trail him to his newly rented suite, and there was absolutely nothing he could do to prevent it.

"Come on, damn you," he growled aloud.

Hogan had no doubt that Silver and his men would be coming, but he consoled himself with the thought that it mattered not how much they knew about him, as long as they did not leave Denver alive. Today, Kent, Hollis, and Bidamer were to report to him, as was Blanton Hood. While Hogan couldn't stop Silver and his friends from following, he could surround himself with killers for hire. He finished his coffee and reached for his hat. Then he did something he hadn't done since leaving California. He buckled on a gunbelt, thonging down the holster on his right hip. Drawing the Colt, he broke it and thumbed in a sixth shell. From a closet, he took a Winchester and made sure it was fully loaded. He then stepped out the door and started around the house to saddle his horse.

"There he goes," said Silver, watching Hogan from the upstairs window, "and he's fully armed. Where the hell is Palo with our horses?"

"He hasn't had time," Wes said. "He'll be here by the time Hogan's ready to ride. We can wait for him out back, and it'll save him having to come up here."

"Good thinking," said Silver. "Come on."

In the hall, they met Priscilla, her wet hair evidence that she had been bathing. Again she wore not a stitch, nor did she have a towel.

"None of you have come to see me," she said. "I'm not accustomed to being ignored by men."

"Sorry," said Silver, "but we have women of our own, and any one of them is as well endowed as you. I reckon we can enjoy the view, but that's as far as we go."

They left her standing naked in the hall. Reaching the back stairs they could still hear her saying some very unladylike things about men in general and a certain trio in particular. Reaching the alley behind the house, they waited. A short time later, El Lobo rode in, leading the other two horses.

"Get down," Silver said. "We can't ride out until Hogan does."

They peered around the corner until Drade Hogan rode out into the street. Reining up and standing in his stirrups, he looked all around before riding on.

"He knows," said Wes.

"I want him to," Silver replied. "I want him feeling like a trapped rat, with nothing on his mind but escape. Then he'll take us to the gold, wherever it is."

They waited until Hogan was far down the street before following. Twice he turned and looked back.

"He see us," said El Lobo.

"It won't matter," Silver said. "He knew last night he was being followed. Unless he's a fool, he knows by now that we used Madame Renae and that extra key to get to him. I won't be surprised if his head-quarters is surrounded by gunmen."

"But when he leaves there, we can follow him wherever he goes," said Wes. "When he goes after the gold, he won't feel easy with too many killers around. Tempt a gun-thrower with enough gold, and he'll forget who his friends are."

They continued following Hogan, remaining as far behind as they dared. Eventually he reined up, dismounted, and led his horse around a brick office building.

"We won't go any closer," Silver said. "There's bound to be a back door and a stairway. Palo, take your horse with you and watch the back door, but be careful not to allow anybody within this office building to see you."

El Lobo rode up the street well beyond the building in question. He circled in behind, coming down an alley from the far end of the block. Dismounting, he led his horse until he was in a position to see the back of the building. There he waited, just out of sight, until Kent, Hollis, and Bidamer reined up behind the place. Each man removed from his saddle boot a Winchester, and thus armed, they entered the building by the back stairs.

"Who are you?" Hogan asked in response to the knock on his door.

"Bidamer, Hollis, and Kent," said a voice.

Hogan unlocked the door, allowed them to enter, and then locked it behind them.

"Well, ain't we jumpy this mornin'," Kent said. "The hobgoblins been after you?"

"I am in no mood for your perverted sense of humor," said Hogan. "The three men in question have been following me since last night. Where the hell were the three of you?"

"Checking out all the saloons," Bidamer said. "If

you expect us to become your bodyguards, it's fifty dollars a day for each of us."

"All I want of any of you is to rid me of the three men following me," said Hogan. "That is, if you can. Don't expect to find them lurking in the halls or in broom closets."

"Then we'll wait until you're ready to leave here," Bidamer said, "and we'll follow anybody that follows you."

"I'm here for the day, and I have work to do," said Hogan. "I strongly suspect this building is being watched. If I'm not expecting too much, will the three of you get out of here and start earning that bounty? I'll be here until five o'clock."

"We'll look around some," Bidamer said, "but we ain't protectin' your carcass for free. When and where we earn that bounty is our business."

Without another word, the three departed, leaving Hogan alone with his thoughts. He looked for them to return at five but suspected until then they would spend their time in a saloon. Quickly, Hogan composed a telegram to his contact in Santa Fe. While its content would be meaningless to anyone else, a prearranged code would relay a message starting a chain of events that would allow Hogan to escape with the gold. When the heavy wagon reached Durango, a coded telegram would be sent to Hogan. Then only Hawk and Denbow stood in his way. But they could be eliminated.

Durango, Colorado, April 18, 1885

The canvas-topped wagon Elias Hawk had bought in Santa Fe arrived on a railroad flat car. Hawk and Denbow were there to take it away the minute it was unloaded.

"When certain people discover we're gone," said Hawk, "somebody will remember this wagon showing up and us driving it away. We must get it away from here and out of sight as quickly as we can."

"When Hogan gets the word, he'll know damn well we didn't need it to haul personal goods," Denbow said. "Let's load all the stuff and get away from here tonight."

"I think we'd better do just that," said Hawk. "The shortest distance to the Gulf of California is crosscountry to Yuma, Arizona, but we don't know the territory, and there may be some trouble getting a wagon through. We have an extra wheel and a spare rear axle."

"My God," Denbow said, "if we make twenty miles a day, it'll still take us almost a month. Ain't there some faster way we can go?"

"Not to get us out of the country," said Hawk. "One month from today, Captain Diaz will anchor his sailing ship in the Gulf of California. While I was away, did you arrange to buy two more horses?"

"Yeah," Denbow said. "Couple of miners decided they wanted mules to work their gold claims, so I arranged to buy their horses. Two hundred dollars apiece. I didn't get 'em because I ain't paid for 'em yet."

"Soon as we return to the mine, take enough double eagles to get the horses," said Hawk. "Tonight we'll load the wagon and head for Yuma."

"What about grub for us and grain for the horses?"

"I bought adequate supplies and grain in Santa Fe," said Hawk. "What do you think is under that wagon canvas?"

"By God, you think of everything," Denbow said admiringly.

"I try," said Hawk. "If we had bought supplies here in Durango, it would be something else for somebody to tell Hogan when he comes looking for us."

When they reached the mine, Denbow took one of the horses and four hundred dollars in gold to pay for a second team. When he returned with the newly purchased horses, it was only an hour shy of sundown.

"We'd better rearrange everything in this wagon and load the gold while it's still light enough to see," Hawk said.

"We ought to take an extra wheel off our old wagon," said Denbow. "Just in case."

"I doubt there'll be room," Hawk said, "and it would add to the weight of the load. The spare that came with the new wagon will have to do."

Hawk removed the wagon canvas, and all the supplies and sacks of grain were moved to the rear. One by one, the heavy metal containers of gold double eagles were lifted into the wagon box, near the front. When the task was finished, Hawk and Denbow were exhausted from the effort. When they had rested, they again secured the wagon canvas as tight as they could over the load. It was near midnight when they harnessed the teams to the new wagon. They returned to the tunnel for one last look around.

"Leave that door to the inner room standing partially open," Hawk said. "When Hogan comes looking for us, I don't want him to have trouble getting in there."

"What about them trip wires and scatterguns?" Denbow asked.

"Leave them armed," said Hawk. "Remember the old code: Do unto others as they'd do unto you, but do it first."

Mounting the wagon box, they left the claim in which they had labored for the metal to make Drade Hogan a wealthy man. Nothing dampened their spirits except realization of sudden death if Hogan discovered his loss and caught up to them.

Denver, Colorado, April 17, 1885

Shortly after Drade Hogan had sent the coded telegram to Santa Fe, there was a knock at the door.

"Who are you?" Hogan demanded, his Colt in his hand.

"Blanton Hood," came the response. "I got to talk to you."

Again without invitation, Hood seated himself beside Hogan's desk.

"Well," said Hogan, eyeing him distastefully, "have you accomplished anything?"

"Yeah," Hood replied, "I took your advice and lined up eleven gun-throwing *hombres*. Trouble is, they want some money in advance, and I ain't got it."

"And you're expecting to get it from me," said Hogan.

"It's that, or tell this bunch the manhunt's off, and turn 'em loose," Hood said.

"How much?" Hogan asked.

"I'm payin' 'em fifty dollars a day and grub," said Hood. "They want three days' pay in advance."

"I'll advance you two thousand dollars," Hogan said. "Just don't forget it comes out of any bounty money due you."

"I ain't the forgetful kind," said Hood. "Now tell me somethin' about these three you're wantin' salted down."

"I've never seen them up close enough to give you a description," Hogan said, "but the three of them have been following me since last night. I'll leave here at five, and I have no doubt they'll follow. I'm sure they're watching this building right now."

"We'll wait until they follow you home," said Hood. "It's too damn busy around here. Shooting would bring the law down on us *pronto*."

Hood returned to the old deserted warehouse on Cherry Creek, where his assortment of killers waited. They eyed him expectantly, saying nothing.

"A hundred and fifty dollars for each of you," Hood said, "and when we gun down the *hombres* in question, each of you will get another thousand dollars, no matter who fires the shot. Our work begins at five o'clock, and I'll expect all of you here no later than half past three."

They trooped out, mounted their horses, and rode toward town, leaving Hood to wonder if they might just keep on riding. Except for Ginsler and Arrington, the gang consisted of the nine men remaining after Hampton, Lawton, and Damark had been locked up in the jail at Dodge.

"Well, don't look so damn whipped," said Illivane to his disgruntled companions. "This ain't Indian Territory, but fifty dollars a day's better than nothing."

"This is just one hell of a long day," Wes said, as he and Silver continued to watch the front of the office building.

"It is, for a fact," said Silver, "and I doubt Hogan will go anywhere until he's ready to call it a day. Why don't you find a mercantile, buy a jug, and fill it with water? Palo must be almighty thirsty, and I know I am."

"I'll do it," Wes said, "and I'll give Palo a slug of it before coming back here."

Wes brought the water, spent a few minutes with

El Lobo, and then joined Silver. The boring, seemingly fruitless vigil continued.

"Four o'clock," said Silver, looking at his watch.
"He should be leaving pretty soon, if only to go
home."

"Something's startin' to bother me," Wes said.
"Suppose this coyote's not as spooked as we think
he is? He could wear us out without doing one damn
thing illegal."

"He could," said Silver, "but he won't. I have a
hunch he had a serious falling out with Madame
Renae, and testimony from her could drop that failed
ambush right into Hogan's lap. Even if nothing else
goes wrong, you don't ignore a woman with a serious mad on."

Somewhere in the distance, a tower clock struck
five times, and as the tones faded and died away,
Drade Hogan left the office building. His horse had
been picketed in the shade of a tree, and he began
saddling the animal.

"I'd better get the word to Palo," said Wes. "I'll
stay with him until Hogan rides out, and we'll join
you on the back trail."

Hogan rode out, keeping his horse at a trot and
not looking back. Silver didn't follow immediately,
and when he did, it was with caution.

"What did you see?" Wes asked, when he and El
Lobo caught up to Silver.

"Nothing," said Silver, "but I think the hunters
may be about to become the hunted. I suspect, from
Hogan's actions, we're about to be followed."

"We won't be doing Monique and Louise any favors, having a bunch of killers follow us back to the
house," Wes said. "They could set the place afire and
shoot anybody trying to escape."

"That's precisely why we aren't going to follow
Hogan home. We'll go another way, leave our horses

at the livery, and enter the house by the back stairs," said Silver. "If his hired killers can't find us, it'll worry the hell out of Hogan, wondering where we are and what we'll do next."

"*Bueno,*" El Lobo said. "*El Diablo modo.*"

Reaching the livery, they led their horses inside and unsaddled them. They took their Winchesters from saddle boots and made their way the several blocks to an alley that would allow them to reach the back of the house without being seen from the street. They entered the house through the kitchen and dining area.

"We're just getting supper started," Louise said. "It'll be ready in less than an hour."

"Good enough," said Silver. "Is Priscilla in the hall, or is it safe for us to go up?"

Louise and Monique thought that hilariously funny. Silver, Wes, and El Lobo mounted the stairs and hurried to the room at the end of the hall.

"I hope we got here ahead of Hogan," Silver said. "I want to see his reaction when he discovers we didn't follow him."

"Well, hell, we know where he lives and where his office is," said Wes. "We don't have to follow him, unless we think he's about to skip town."

"That won't come until he's made some arrangements to escape with the gold," Silver said. "Even if it's in Denver, he'll be careful not to lead us to it."

"I don't know why," said Wes, "but I don't believe it's in Denver. If it's not, then he's having to rely on somebody else to secure it for him. I'm wondering whom he can trust to hide millions in gold, without the possibility of a double cross."

"Maybe nobody," Silver said. "From what I've seen of the Golden Dragon, Hogan's the kind who will use others as long as he can, killing them when their usefulness is done."

Their attention was drawn to the window, for Hogan had reined up before the house. He dismounted, and still looking back, led his horse around the house to the stable.

"He can't believe he wasn't followed," said Silver.

"He may get the horse laugh if he's got a bunch of bushwhackers following him," Wes said. "There won't be a sign of us or our horses."

"*Comico*," said El Lobo. "Now what we do?"

"Useless as it seems," Silver said, "we'll keep watching, waiting for Hogan to make his move toward the gold. We know he will. What we don't know is the when and where of it. I think we can be sure of one thing, and that's that he doesn't plan to share it with his hired killers."

"It might be interesting to get into that office of his and look around," said Wes.

"We'll save that for a last resort," Silver said. "I doubt any of the gold is kept there. Whatever we think of him, he's not foolish enough to leave evidence lying around that can incriminate him."

There was unexpected activity on the street below as three horsemen reined up before the Hogan house. After a few moments they rode away, not looking back.

Wes laughed. "After a few more days like this, he may have trouble hiring gunmen to do his killing. For the first time, we know who the bastard is, and it's him that's on the run."

"One thing bothers me," said Silver. "We may never learn who's been supplying the quantities of gold and silver the Golden Dragon's been using to cast those counterfeit double eagles."

"Don't be too sure of that," Wes said. "Remember after we rescued Renita and Tamara near Santa Fe, we rode to Durango and took the train to Denver?"

"Yes," said Silver. "Go on."

"We saw Elias Hawk and Hobie Denbow in a saloon there," Wes said.

"*Bastardos*," said El Lobo.

"Just because you had a bad experience with them before," said Silver, "doesn't mean they're crooked now. If they're in any way associated with the Golden Dragon—if they have anything to do with the gold—Hogan will lead us to them."

"That's one thing I don't like about your federal position," Wes replied. "Knowin' some varmint is guilty as hell is never enough. You have to have evidence to please the court."

"It's necessary if we're ever to have law," said Silver. "The days when one man can pull a gun and become judge and jury must come to an end."

"Supper," Monique said, knocking on the door.

Silver, Wes, and El Lobo made it to the stairs at the end of the hall without meeting Priscilla. Supper was a quiet meal, and not until it was over did Louise speak.

"Have you made any progress?"

"Yes," said Silver. "For the next few days we'll be playing a waiting game, until the rat decides to run."

"You have to catch him," Monique said. "We barely escaped from Kansas City with our lives. Now we find the leader of the gang living across the street from us."

"Hogan wouldn't bother you if he knew who you are," said Silver. "His vindictive days are over. From here on, he'll be trying to save his own hide."

"Oh, I hope you're right," Louise said, "but how do you know he won't slip away in the night?"

"We don't know that he won't," said Silver, "but there is at least one good reason why we don't expect him to."

"Just to be sure he doesn't escape in the night, one of us will always be watching the house," Wes said.

"After all we've been through at his hands, I'd follow him to hell and go in after him."

Drade Hogan sat in the darkness of his parlor, a half-full whiskey decanter his only companion. He was at a loss as to what had gone wrong. While he wasn't all that sure of Blanton Hood and his gunmen, he had seen Kent, Hollis, and Bidamer rein up in the street. They had followed him, but obviously nobody else had. He had no doubt they would confront him the next day, and he had no answers. His only consolation was that he had received an immediate response to his telegram. His contact in Santa Fe had shipped a new freight wagon to Durango by train. But as he thought about it, it further complicated things. How was he going to take the train to Durango without Silver and his comrades following?

"Damn it," Hogan said aloud, "I'll go if I have to hire fifty gunslingers to go along to protect me."

Dodge City, Kansas, April 19, 1885

Harley Stafford had made it a point to escort Molly, Renita, and Tamara to Delmonico's for their meals. When Harley met them for supper, he had a recent edition of one of the Kansas City newspapers.

"Our friend Ashe Wexler's at it again," said Harley. "Look."

The story, under Wexler's byline, was on page two. It began by stating, "Gunslingers Silver, Elfego, and Stone have left Dodge City." It went to great length in placing the blame for all the recent violence in Dodge. It ended with a question and a plea: "How long will Dodge City continue to be a mecca for outlaws and killers? True, three of them are gone, but their women are still here. Is there any doubt they'll return?"

"Damn him," said Molly. "I hate him almost as much as those Golden Dragon outlaws."

"Silver can do nothing now," Harley said, "but when he has the lid on this case, he'll be in a position to burn Wexler's tail feathers. When newspapers are given the full story, Ashe Wexler will be known for the meddling old fool that he is."

"Foster Hagerman said Wexler's been giving Sheriff Dumery a hard time over those three killers who are in jail," said Renita.

"He has," Harley said, "but the sheriff has stood his ground. The two killers wanted in Missouri will be leaving on today's eastbound, under armed guard. The third man, wanted in Texas for murder, is waiting for a deputy U.S. marshal from Fort Worth."

"I'm glad," said Molly. "The sheriff should be rewarded."

"I'm sure he will be," Harley said. "Bryan Silver never forgets his friends. I've seen him stand by Nathan Stone when it seemed like Nathan didn't have another friend in all the world."

Durango, Colorado, April 19, 1885

Despite their desire to be gone, Elias Hawk and Hobie Denbow were only three or four miles south of Durango when they had to give it up for the night.

"Damn it," said Denbow, "I was hopin' we could be twenty miles away by first light."

"So was I," Hawk said, "but starlight's not good enough to see all the chuck holes and drop-offs. It's not worth risking a shattered wheel or busted axle. We'll just have to make good use of the daylight."

They got an early start, but the heavily loaded

wagon worked against them. With Denbow at the reins, the left rear wheel slid into a stump hole. The horses strained in their harness until they were exhausted, and the bogged-down wagon didn't move.

"We'll have to unload it," Hawk said.

They set about unloading the wagon, and the chests of gold seemed twice as heavy as before. Finally, with the wagon freed of its load, the team was able to pull it free. Denbow and Hawk then began reloading.

"Two damn hours," said Denbow, when the job was finally done. "Take the reins for a while. I ain't done so good."

Hawk took the reins, and they continued keeping to the high ground, heading toward the southwest.

Denver, Colorado, April 19, 1885

After a virtually sleepless night, Drade Hogan made a pot of black coffee and slumped down at his dining room table. He felt like he'd fallen from the top of the world and it had rolled over on him. What was wrong?

"That damned saloon woman," he said aloud, bitterly.

There seemed little he could do. While there had been no trouble with the law, the incident at the Pretty Girl Saloon had been sufficient to get Bryan Silver on his trail. He gritted his teeth, more determined than ever that Silver was going to pay. He got up from the table, dressed, and buckled on his gunbelt. He then stepped out the door and went around the house to saddle his horse.

"There he goes," said Silver. "He's likely going to his office, but we're going to follow him. I want him so damned spooked he can't sleep at night."

By the time they had saddled their horses, Hogan had already ridden away, but they soon were within sight of him. Twice Hogan looked back, and the second time, Wes drew one of his Colts and held it up. El Lobo laughed.

"Careful," said Silver.

Hogan reached his office building, unsaddled his horse, and picketed it in the shade of a tree. He unlocked his door, and the place seemed especially desolate and lonely, for he had not bothered hiring another receptionist. He would spend his days behind locked doors with a loaded Colt in his hand, until he could escape with his wealth.

Wes, El Lobo, and Silver had taken up a position where they could see the front of the building, where Hogan had left his horse. They had been there for almost an hour when three horsemen reined up and picketed their horses. One of them pounded on the door, and when it was opened, they went inside.

"That looks like the three that followed Hogan home last night," Wes said.

"I expect they're here to give Mr. Hogan a hard time," said Silver. "I doubt they'll be following him home tonight."

The trio had entered Hogan's office, and ignoring his invitation to sit, they remained standing. It was Bidamer who spoke.

"We follered you all the way home and didn't see nobody but you. We ain't chasing ghosts. Take your bounty and stick it."

The door was locked, and before Hogan could make a move, Hollis drew his Colt and blasted the lock. The trio left, leaving the mutilated door standing open.

Chapter 17

Denver, Colorado, April 19, 1885

Drade Hogan's day had gotten off to a bad start. He had little hope of it getting any better, and it did not. Within an hour after Kent, Hollis, and Bidamer had stormed out of his office, Blanton Hood arrived. This time, Hood didn't bother to sit, but took a position directly before Hogan's desk.

"Put that Colt away," Hood ordered. "A wrong move, and I'd have to kill you."

Hogan opened a desk drawer and disposed of the weapon. When he said nothing, Hood continued.

"I reckon you know we come up dry yesterday. Wasn't nobody follerin' you but three other gunslicks of my acquaintance. By God, it's us or them. My boys has been paid for two more days. After that, we're done."

"Like hell," Hogan snarled, getting to his feet. "Kent, Hollis, and Bidamer are out of it. Where I made my mistake was allowing you to hog all the bounty money, while paying the rest of your outfit a daily pittance. Now we're going to change that. The bounty, if there is one, will be split equally among all of you."

"My boys has been promised fifty dollars a day, and they're gonna git it," said Hood.

"They'll get that, plus a possible bounty," Hogan growled, "but it'll be on my terms, not yours."

"Then talk, big man," said Hood. "What *are* your terms?"

"I want you to get me to Yuma, Arizona, alive," Hogan replied.

Hood laughed. "So instead of fighting back, you aim to run like a scared coyote."

"The federals are after me, damn it," said Hogan. "Now I want you to tell this gang of gun-throwers—"

"I'm tellin' 'em nothin'," Hood said, "except that you're payin' the money and dealin' the cards. The lot of 'em are waitin' on Cherry Creek for some word of what we're to do next. Now you're gonna tell 'em what you've told me, and you better hope they decide to stick, because if they ride out, I'm goin' with 'em. Now saddle your horse and let's ride."

Silver, Wes, and El Lobo had witnessed the arrival and departure of Kent, Hollis, and Bidamer, and the purpose of the single gunshot remained a mystery.

"Maybe there was a fallin' out, and they shot Hogan," said Wes. "Why in tarnation didn't somebody come to see what the shootin' was about?"

"It's too early," Silver said. "There's nobody in the building, other than Hogan."

"If Hogan be dead," said El Lobo, "why we wait?"

"Because I doubt that he's dead," Silver replied, "and I want to see what he'll do next. I suspect what we did last night put a crimp in his tail and got him in trouble with some of his hired guns. I predict there are others, that if they don't come to him, then he'll be going to them."

"You may be right," said Wes. "If we can avoid his gunmen long enough, he may give up the idea of having us gunned down. Every man has a breaking point, and there may soon come a time when

Hogan will be satisfied to take the gold and run for it."

"I'm counting on that," Silver said. "I think we've pulled the Dragon's teeth, that in no way can the outfit operate as it has in the past. From now on, they'll be running and we'll be chasing them."

"*Hombre* come," said El Lobo.

They watched Blanton Hood rein up, dismount, and enter Hogan's office suite.

"It might be interesting to know who he is, and how he fits in," Wes said. "When he leaves, why don't I follow him?"

"Do that," said Silver. "We're getting nowhere fast, trailing Hogan."

But when Blanton Hood left the building, Hogan was with him. Hood waited impatiently while Hogan saddled his horse.

"That settles it," Silver said. "We'll all follow them. Something's about to break."

Hogan and Hood rode away, Hood leading. Hogan kept looking back.

"What are you lookin' for?" Hood demanded.

"Those three damned gunslingers," said Hogan. "They'll be following us."

"*Bueno*," Hood replied. "It'll give us a chance at that bounty."

"Claim the bounty if you can," said Hogan, "but I'm primarily interested in going well beyond the reach of the federals. If I can't kill the bastards, then I'll have to escape them."

Hood laughed. "They're everywhere. Where do you aim to go?"

"As far as you're concerned, Yuma, Arizona," Hogan said shortly.

"Tarnation," said Hood, "we're touchy, ain't we?"

Nothing more was said. When they reached Cherry Creek, there was an abundance of abandoned claims and buildings in varying stages of disrepair. They reined up before one that still had most of its roof. Nearby, eleven horses were picketed.

"They're all here," Hood said. "You'd better not say nothin' about offerin' me a bounty while payin' them fifty dollars a day. They'll likely tell you to go to hell."

Once they were inside, Hood wasted no time.

"Gents, this here is Hogan. It's him we're workin' for, and he's got somethin' to say."

Hogan looked at the assortment of killers before him, as chills crept up his spine. He swallowed hard and spoke.

"I have put a bounty on the men pursuing me," said Hogan. "The head of each of them is worth fifty thousand dollars, and you can split it among you."

"That's all right, as far as it goes," Illivane said, "but suppose we can't find them three *hombres*? Fifty dollars a day ain't much when you're riskin' gettin' your string cut. Will we be losin' that if we go for the bounty?"

"No," said Hogan. "I'll continue paying each of you fifty dollars a day, plus food, but there's been a change in my plans. The federals are after me, and I see no sense in staying here, engaging in a fight I can't win. I want you all to accompany me to Yuma, Arizona, seeing that I get there alive."

"I don't like the sound of that," Ginsler said. "There goes our bounty."

"I don't think so," said Hogan. "The three men I want dead will be trailing us. If the entire lot of you can't bushwhack them, then I don't need you."

Some of the gunmen laughed, for it was the kind of macabre humor they understood.

"Come on," said Hood, "and give the man an answer. Are we goin' or not?"

They shouted their agreement, and Hogan breathed a little easier.

"Now that we got that settled," Hood said, "when do we start?"

"I want all of you to leave tomorrow," said Hogan. "Get a boxcar for your horses and take the train south to Durango. There's a hotel of sorts. I'll be there as soon as I can tie up the loose ends here. From Durango, we'll travel southwest to Yuma, Arizona."

"You're sure these *hombres* with prices on their heads will be following us?" Illivane asked.

"I know they will," said Hogan. "They followed Hood and me here."

"You don't know that," Hood said. "I didn't see nobody."

"Then you'd better open your eyes," said Hogan. "You think I'd be spending this kind of money if they wasn't breathing down my neck? Now I want all of you on that train to Durango tomorrow. Go there and wait for me."

With that, Hogan left them all hunkered there, looking at one another. A considerable distance away, Silver, Wes, and El Lobo were watching.

"Well," said Wes, "he's leaving alone. Do we continue following him, or do we wait and follow this bunch he went to meet?"

"We continue following Hogan," Silver said. "While I suspect these men Hogan came to meet are probably killers of the bushwhacking stripe, we have no proof he's sending them after us."

"They kill us dead, then we know for sure," said El Lobo.

"Yeah," Wes said. "That's what I don't like about the law. You know damned well the varmints are out to get you, but you can't lay a hand on them until they've bushwhacked you."

Silver laughed. "I know the law sometimes leaves us at a disadvantage, but we're not much better than the criminals themselves if we sink to their level. When you wrestle a pig, you only get muddy, while the pig loves it."

Once Hogan was well on his way, Silver, Wes, and El Lobo followed.

"Why don't we just go back to his office building and wait?" Wes suggested. "He'll be going back there."

"We can't be sure of that," said Silver. "He may be gettin' ready to run for it, and we know he won't leave without the gold."

It soon became obvious that Silver had been right. They followed Hogan at a great distance, and he headed for the busiest part of town. He reined up before one of the largest banks and went inside.

"I want to close this account," said Hogan to one of the tellers, "and I want it all in gold coin."

"It will be very heavy," the teller said.

"I know that," said Hogan impatiently. "Get it."

Hogan left the bank with a canvas bag in which were almost twenty-five thousand dollars in double eagles. He hoisted it up over the withers of his horse and climbed up behind it.

"Not much doubt why he went in there," Wes said.

"That may be only the start," said Silver. "He may have money in other banks, under different names."

Again Silver was proven right, as Hogan visited two more banks, returning to his horse each time with a bulging canvas bag.

"*Oro*," El Lobo said.

"Yes," said Silver. "There must be thousands in gold. He's getting ready to run. From here on, we don't dare let him out of our sight."

"Those bags are heavy," Wes said, "but not near

as heavy as those crates of double eagles we took away from the Dragon in California. Hogan will need at least one freight wagon. Maybe more."

"All the more important that we don't lose him," said Silver. "When the time comes to move the gold, I think Hogan will try to do it himself. He won't trust anybody else."

"For that reason, I can't understand why the Golden Dragon moved inland," Wes said. "Hogan could have boarded a sailing ship and been out of the country before he could have been stopped."

"I think not," said Silver. "After we boarded the ship captained by Antonio Diaz and found those four cases of gold, the United States Coast Guard began boarding incoming and outgoing ships at random. Not just in San Francisco harbor, but in all others. When the Golden Dragon moved inland—to Denver—they didn't expect things to unravel as they have. That defeat we dealt them in California, and the capture of Dent Shankler was the beginning of the end."

After leaving the third bank, Hogan did not return to his office, but went directly to his home. Silver, Wes, and El Lobo left their horses at the livery and made their way on foot to the alley that led behind the place Monique and Louise owned.

"You're early," said Monique, as they entered through the kitchen. "Supper's still two hours off."

"Sorry," Silver said. "The gent we're following came in earlier than we expected."

"Are you going to capture him?" Louise asked hopefully.

"Eventually," said Silver. "In any event, neither of you have anything to fear. He'll be leaving here pretty soon."

"And all of you will be following him," Louise said. "We're going to miss you."

"Oh, yes," said Monique. "Nothing exciting ever happens in a whorehouse."

"Nothing?" Wes said. "There's Priscilla."

Monique laughed. "There *was* that one time when Priscilla got drunk and we couldn't get her out of bed. We poured a bucket of cold water on her."

"Yes," said Louise. "Monique and me learned some new cuss words that day."

By the time Silver, Wes, and El Lobo reached their upstairs room with its convenient window, lamplight shone in several windows of the Hogan house.

"There must be a back door to that place," Wes said, "and he keeps his horse in the back. One of us should be watching that back entrance, in case he tries to slip out during the night."

"You could be right," said Silver, "and we can't afford to take any chances. You keep watch until midnight, and Palo or me will take it until dawn."

Denver, Colorado, April 22, 1885

For three days and nights, Silver, Wes, and El Lobo watched the Hogan house. At no time did Hogan leave the house, except to feed and water his horse.

"I reckon we didn't spook him as much as we thought," said Wes.

When Hogan finally did leave the house, he rode toward town, reining up behind an old building with a FREIGHTING AND HAULING sign painted on the front.

"Now we're getting somewhere," Silver said.

Inside the establishment, Drade Hogan was making some arrangements.

"Here's my address, and here's a key," said Hogan. "Go in the back way, and there'll be a heavy wooden crate in the kitchen. It's addressed and ready to go. I want it taken to the railroad depot, and I want it done today. It must go south on the morning train."

"Fill out this bill of lading," a clerk said. "We'll have to make a special trip, so it'll cost you five dollars."

"Fair enough," said Hogan. "Just dispose of the key. I have others."

Silver, Wes, and El Lobo watched Hogan mount his horse and ride away.

"Wes," Silver said, "I want you and Palo to follow him, wherever he goes."

"*Sí*," said Wes. "And you?"

"Call it a hunch, but I doubt Hogan's returning to the house. If he does, then we'll be back where we started. I'm going back to watch the house. Stay with Hogan until he heads for home."

Silver rode out. Wes and El Lobo kept a great distance behind Hogan, and it quickly became obvious that the man wasn't returning to his house.

"Silver *bueno hombre*," El Lobo said.

"He's all of that, and more," said Wes. "He thinks Hogan's luring us away from the house."

Silver, keeping to alleys and less-traveled streets, made his way to the back of the old house belonging to Monique and Louise. Both women were at the table, drinking coffee.

"Where are your friends?" Monique asked.

"Taking care of some important business," said Silver. "I'll be upstairs a while."

"Just a minute and you can take some coffee with you," Louise said.

"Thanks," Silver said, accepting the cup. He went on up the stairs, taking them two at a time. Silver took his place at the window, and there was no sign of Drade Hogan. Most of an hour passed before there was any activity at the Hogan house. Then a freight wagon with a wooden box body drew up in front of the house, as though a delivery man was seeking an address. A sign painted on the wooden side of the wagon read: FREIGHTING AND HAULING. Silver waited until the wagon turned, losing sight of it as it went behind Hogan's house. He left the room in a run, only to encounter the naked Priscilla in the hall.

"What's your hurry?" Priscilla asked, blocking his path. "It's just you and me."

Silver said nothing. He lifted her bodily and thrust her back past the doorway through which she had come. He then closed the door behind her and hurried down the hall. When he reached the rear of the Hogan house, a big man had lowered the tailgate of the wagon and was wrestling a heavy crate into it.

"Hold it," said Silver. "I want to see who that's going to, and where it's going."

"My name's Moynihan," the hefty teamster said. "I been told to pick up and deliver this piece of freight, and I'm doin' it. Just who the hell are you, and what business is it of yours?"

"My name's Silver, and here are my credentials," said Silver.

"Federal man, huh?" he said, looking Silver over critically.

"I'm not going to interfere with your pickup and delivery," said Silver. "I need to see to whom it's addressed and where it's going. Then you can be on your way."

"I reckon I can't get in trouble over that," Moynihan said doubtfully. "Do what you got to do."

Quickly Silver looked at the address. It read *D. Hogan, Durango, Colorado.*

"That's all, Moynihan," said Silver. "Thanks."

"You're welcome, I reckon," Moynihan said.

Going in the back way, Silver returned to the upstairs room and took up his position before the window. It was an hour before sundown when Hogan finally appeared. Within a few minutes, Wes and El Lobo arrived.

"It's almighty dull, looking at Hogan's office building for seven hours," said Wes, "and after all that, just followin' him back to here."

Silver laughed. "You and Palo did what Hogan expected all of us to do. He had to get us away from the house for a while, so he could dispose of the gold he withdrew from the banks this morning."

Silver then told them what he had learned.

"That means the stolen gold will be sent there," Wes said.

"Per'ap it already be there," said El Lobo.

"That's a possibility we have to consider," Silver said.

"Hawk and Denbow," said Wes. "Maybe that's where they fit in. Remember, we found their names written on a scrap of paper when we invaded the Dragon headquarters in San Francisco."[1]

"I haven't forgotten them," Silver said. "Instead of riding all over southern Colorado, looking for them and the stolen gold, we'll let Hogan lead us to them."

"That much makes sense," said Wes. "but how does Hogan plan to get to Durango without us following?"

"I think he's counting on that," Silver said. "Why do you reckon he was meeting with that bunch on Cherry Creek?"

"He'll have a dozen killers waiting for us," said Wes.

"That many, or more," Silver said. "The showdown's coming, *amigos*, and it may well be a fight to the death."

"When Hogan runs," said Wes, "do you aim for us to board the same train?"

[1] *Sixguns and Double Eagles*

"Definitely," Silver said, "but we won't be traveling in a passenger coach. I intend to talk to the railroad officials in the morning. If we can't ride the caboose, we'll ride with our horses, in a boxcar. We'll get aboard well ahead of Hogan, and let him wonder where we are."

"*Sí*," said El Lobo, weary of following Hogan.

"But Durango's just a few shacks alongside the track," Wes said. "Hogan can't stay there for any longer than it takes for us to catch up to him."

"He won't be staying there," said Silver.

"He'll need a wagon to move all that gold," Wes said. "Where do you reckon he'll try to take it?"

"Into Mexico, if I had to guess," said Silver. "If he goes south, after leaving Durango, it'll be hell with the lid off. It's the most treacherous country—with deep arroyos and drop-offs—I've ever seen. It would be rough going, with pack mules, and near impossible with a wagon."

"Then we can just wait until he recovers the gold and heads out for wherever he aims to go," Wes said, "and catch him red-handed."

"Sounds simple enough," said Silver, "but I think we're going to find ourselves facing an army of gunmen."

Durango, Colorado, April 23, 1885

Blanton Hood and his eleven companions had been in Durango a day and a night, and boredom had already overtaken them.

"Damn it," said Easterly, "one crummy saloon, and it ain't got any decent whiskey."

"Yeah," Bender said. "It's so dull here, I feel like goin' out and shootin' the first gent that I see. Nothin' to do but eat and sleep."

"Oh, cut out the whining," said Blanton Hood. "How often do you pocket fifty dollars a day for doin' nothing?"

"Maybe he's right," Illivane said. "If the federals want Hogan bad enough to chase him here, we may soon be earning our money. Who *is* this federal boogey man, anyhow?"

"Bryan Silver," said Hood. "He represents the U.S. attorney general's office, and he's hard as hell to kill. He's sided by a pair of gun-throwers—Wes Stone and Palo Elfego—who are as tough as he is, and fast as forked lightning with a pistol."

"I've heard of them all," Illivane said, remembering Hampton, Lawton, and Damark in jail in Dodge City.

The eight men who had been riding with Illivane kept their silence, realizing that the man they now worked for had sent them thirty thousand dollars, which they had failed to earn. Instead, they had fled Indian Territory when they believed the government was sending soldiers, leaving their three comrades in the Dodge City jail.

"Let's go over to the saloon and play a few hands of poker," said Ginsler. "Their brew ain't the best, but it's better than nothin'."

"Don't swig too much of that rotgut," Hood said. "We don't know when Hogan will be here, and when he comes, I don't want nobody hung over."

There being little else to do, most of Durango's citizens gathered for the coming of the morning train from Denver, and for its return from Santa Fe to Denver later in the day. This day, the evening train from Santa Fe backed a flat car off onto the side track. On the car, chained securely, was a brand-new freight wagon. The bows were in place, but the canvas was neatly folded in the wagon box. There was more than the wagon on the flat car, but it was covered with canvas and lashed down securely.

"I can't imagine who would want a freight wagon in a little place like this," Concho said. "They got a railroad straight through to Denver."

"Somebody that ain't goin' to Denver," said Illivane. "I'd bet a double eagle against a Mex *peso* that fancy rig belongs to Hogan."

"He aims to take a damn wagon across country, from here to Yuma? What's he takin' with him that needs a wagon?"

"Gold, maybe," Illivane said. "For sure, I aim to find out. Why go for a bounty that may or may not be there, when Hogan may be haulin' a hundred times as much in that wagon?"

Concho laughed. "So we shoot one *hombre* instead of three."

"Wrong," said Illivane. "Somehow, Hogan managed to steal a pile of gold from the federals, and they won't let it go. We double-cross Hogan, and we'll still be up against Silver and his gun-throwing pards."

"Well, hell," Concho said, "we got to kill them anyhow if we play square with Hogan. You goin' to talk to Hood about this?"

"No," said Illivane. "Why should I? The cheap bastard was payin' us fifty dollars a day when there's a fifty-thousand-dollar bounty on the heads of Silver and his gunslingers. I think we'll deal ourselves some cards and play out our own hand. If anybody sides Hood, it'll be Ginsler and Arrington, and there's nine of us against the three of them."

"Yeah," Concho said. "When you aim to tell the others?"

"Not for a while," said Illivane. "We'll play both ends against the middle. We'll wait for Hogan and see what he aims to haul in that wagon. If it's gold, like we think, we'll go from there. But not a word of this to anybody, until I'm ready for them to know."

Southeastern Arizona, April 25, 1885

"How far you reckon we are from Durango?" Hobie Denbow asked again.

"Not more than a hundred miles," said Elias Hawk. "As I recall from a territorial map I once saw, we'll be a little more than halfway to Yuma, after we've crossed the Little Colorado."

"I've heard some scary things about the rivers in this canyon country," Denbow said. "If the river's down in a deep gorge, we may have to hunt all over hell, lookin' for some place to get the wagon across."

"We'll worry about that when the time comes," said Hawk. "We'd better rest the teams for a while. Then you can take the reins."

Denver, Colorado, April 25, 1885

"He's about ready to run," Silver said, as they watched Hogan enter the railroad depot.

"He'll have to arrange for a wagon," said Wes. "There'll be no extra horses and no wagon in Durango."

"Tomorrow," said Hogan to the dispatcher, "I'll be leaving for Durango, and I'm taking four horses with me. I'll need a boxcar."

"You got it," the dispatcher said. "Be here at least half an hour before train time."

From the depot, Silver, Wes, and El Lobo followed Hogan to a livery.

"I need three horses capable of pulling a wagon," Hogan told the hostler.

"Three?" said the hoster. "You'll need four."

"I have one," Hogan said impatiently. "How much?"

"A hundred dollars apiece," said the hostler.

"Here's your money, along with a little extra," Hogan said. "I want them taken to the railroad depot in the morning, three-quarters of an hour before train time."

Leaving the livery, Hogan rode back to the house. Going through his dresser drawers and closet, he carefully chose only the clothing that would fit into his carpetbag. Silver, Wes, and El Lobo were about to enter the women's house from the alley, when Silver paused and spoke.

"You and Palo go on in. I'd better make some arrangements with the railroad for us and our horses. I have an idea we may be leaving on short notice."

Chapter 18

"We're ready to go on short notice," Silver said, when he returned. "We'll be riding in the caboose, and there'll be a boxcar for our horses. The station agent allowed something to slip that I found interesting. There'll be another boxcar with four horses aboard."

"Hogan," said Wes. "He must have a wagon somewhere in Durango."

"We'll continue watching his house," Silver said. "The moment he heads for the depot, we'll follow. But not close enough for him to see us."

"He'll see us when we load the horses," said Wes.

"We aren't going to be loading them," Silver said. "Hogan's horses will be loaded first. Ours won't be loaded until he's boarded the train, and one of the railroad men will take care of that. We'll climb aboard the caboose just as the train's pulling out. Let him search the passenger coaches and wonder where we are."

Denver, Colorado, April 26, 1885

Silver, Wes, and El Lobo had been watching the Hogan house all night, and not until an hour before train time did Hogan emerge.

"He has a carpetbag," said Silver. "This may be it."

Monique and Louise had breakfast on the table.

"Sorry," Silver said. "I wish we had time to eat, but it looks like our bird's ready to fly away on the morning train. In case we don't get back this way, your generosity is most appreciated."

Silver was out the door, Wes and El Lobo right behind him, before the two women could react. Taking their time getting to the livery, the men waited until they could hear the whistle of the approaching train before starting for the depot. From a distance, they could see Hogan standing beside his saddled horse. A hostler held three more horses on lead ropes. The horses were led up a ramp into the box-car, and the sliding door was closed. Hogan didn't board the train immediately, but stood there looking around. Finally, when the train blew a departing blast from its whistle, Hogan boarded one of the passenger coaches. Only then did Silver, Wes, and El Lobo ride in behind the caboose. A brakeman took their horses to a boxcar directly behind the one Hogan had ordered. Silver, Wes, and El Lobo then climbed into the caboose.

"My name's Shawnessy," said the brakeman, when he returned.

"I'm Bryan Silver. This is Wes Stone and Palo Elfego. We're obliged to the railroad for allowing us to travel in the caboose."

"Glad to have you," Shawnessy said. "Our orders are to help you any way we can."

Shawnessy asked no questions, and none of his three passengers volunteered any information, so there was no conversation. The train stopped at Silverton long enough to take on water and unload some freight. With a clanging of its bell and a shriek of its whistle, the train lurched into motion. The next stop would be Durango.

The Little Colorado River, April 26, 1885

Elias Hawk and Hobie Denbow had discovered that the Little Colorado was, indeed, a difficult river to cross with a loaded wagon.

"Damn such a river," said Denbow. "We must of come thirty miles out of our way, lookin' for a crossing. We should of gone on downstream a ways. These canyons are only gettin' deeper and wider."

"Use your head," Hawk said angrily. "Every mile we traveled downstream would take us that much farther from where we have to go. If all else fails, we can follow this river to where it forks off from the Colorado, and then follow the Colorado to Yuma."

"Ain't you forgettin' something? We got the gold, so Hogan won't need a wagon. Him and his killers can ride us down. We got no time to spare," said Denbow.

"Thanks," Hawk said with some sarcasm. "I could never have figured that out by myself. We have no choice but to go on the way we're headed."

Durango, Colorado, April 26, 1885

With clanging bell, the train rolled into Durango and shuddered to a stop.

"Shawnessy," said Silver, "we're going to remain in here as long as we can. We have three horses and our saddles in a boxcar. Will you see that they're unloaded just before the train pulls out?"

"I'll do it," Shawnessy said. "Good luck."

When Shawnessy had gone, Silver climbed an iron

ladder that led to the glassed-in cupola on top of the caboose.

"See anything?" Wes asked.

"Yes," said Silver. "On a side track, there's a flat car with a brand-new freight wagon. It must have been brought in from Santa Fe, and I'm betting it belongs to Hogan. There go some railroad men with a ramp."

"And here's Shawnessy with our horses," Wes said.

There was a warning bellow from the locomotive's whistle signaling departure.

"Let's go," said Silver. "If that's Hogan's wagon, he'll be occupied with it for a while."

Hogan was indeed busy, for the gunmen he had hired had met the train.

"I don't see nobody follerin' you," Blanton Hood said suspiciously.

"You didn't see that other boxcar, with their horses?" Hogan asked. "Damn it, they're somewhere on that train. I told you they'll be following me. Now help me harness the horses to this wagon."

"You didn't tell us you aim to take a wagon through canyon country," said Hood.

"That's no business of yours," Hogan snapped. "You're being paid to see that I reach Yuma alive."

"Hell," said Illivane, "it'll take forever to get there in a wagon. You'll be lucky to get across the Little Colorado on a horse."

"Let me worry about that," Hogan said. "Concern yourselves with the three who will be following us. That's where the bounty is."

When the team had been harnessed, Hogan drove to the depot, where he picked up the heavy crate with the gold he had withdrawn and sent ahead.

"Now what?" Hood demanded.

"I have something more to load," said Hogan. "All of you are welcome to wait for me here. Then we'll head south."

"Since we're riskin' our necks to get you to Yuma," Hood said, "we'll just stick with you. Lead out."

There was no help for it, so Hogan started for the mine. Not only did he have a band of suspicious killers following him, he soon would have to settle with Hawk and Denbow. Hogan reined up a good distance from the mine and climbed down from the wagon box.

"All of you wait here," said Hogan, drawing his Colt. "There may be trouble."

Hood laughed. "That's what you hired us for, bucko. We're goin' with you."

Hogan had dire misgivings, but there was little he could do. His Colt cocked, he stepped into the tunnel.

"Anybody here?" Hogan shouted.

Only the sound of the wind whispered through nearby trees. Hogan went deeper into the tunnel, unsure as to how he might open Hawk's hidden door. But to his surprise, the door stood partially open, and Hogan paused in what had been the living quarters for Hawk and Denbow.

"Well, go on, damn it," said Hood. "The door's open."

"Then you go first," Hogan said, stepping aside.

Hood seized one of the ladder-back chairs and flung it through the door. It skittered across the stone floor of the cavern, and there were almost simultaneous bellows from two shotguns. One load slammed into the partially open door, chest-high.

"Well," said Hood, "you aim to go in there and look around?"

"I don't need to," Hogan said. "I've been double-crossed. They had to use a wagon and it had to leave tracks. We'll follow it."

"Like hell," said Hood. "Our deal was to get you to Yuma alive."

"We're still going to Yuma," Hogan said desperately, "but not until I catch up to the scoundrels who robbed me."

Hood laughed. "Robbed you of what?"

"None of your damn business," said Hogan.

"Then maybe we'll just track it down and make it our business," Hood said. "Some of you look around and see if you can find wagon tracks."

"There's a wagon over yonder," said Illivane.

"Their old one," Hogan said.

"Wagon tracks headin' south," said Ginsler.

"In that case," Hood said, "we'll follow. Maybe they're bound for Yuma too."

Drade Hogan said nothing. He had a strong suspicion that Hawk and Denbow would be leaving the country if they reached Yuma ahead of him.

"I'll travel as fast as I can," said Hogan. "I want you *hombres* behind me, because the three that's after me will be coming."

"Let 'em come, and get that bounty ready," Hood said. "We'll do a little bushwhackin' and find out just how hard these varmints are to kill. Easterly, Bender, and Arrington, I want you to fall back and unlimber your Winchesters."

Silver, Wes, and El Lobo had been close enough to observe Hogan and his companions enter the mine. They also heard the two shotgun blasts. Then they watched, as some of the men studied the ground. Finally, with Hogan again on the wagon box, they all headed south.

"Trip wires," said Silver. "If I'm any judge, the Señor Hogan has been double-crossed, and Hogan's taking this bunch to go after the culprits."

"They're all headin' south," Wes said. "The Mexican border, you reckon?"

"I doubt it," said Silver. "Since you and Palo raised so much hell last year in Mexico, the Mexican government looks with suspicion on Yankees of any stripe."[1]

"Yuma close to water," El Lobo said. "Sailing ship, per'ap?"

"Palo, that may be the answer," said Silver. "From Yuma, it's practically a stone's throw to the Gulf of California. A sailing ship could anchor far enough off-shore, and be out of reach of American authorities, while being ignored by the Mexicans."

"So we don't know if Hogan was headed for Yuma," Wes said. "He could be in pursuit of whoever double-crossed him and lit out with the gold."

"That's about the only thing that makes sense, whether it's Hogan making tracks, or the gents who double-crossed him," said Silver.

As they continued following Hogan's wagon and the hoof prints left by a dozen riders, it became more obvious the trail was leading southwest.

"I think we'd better be prepared for an ambush," Wes said. "Just because somebody's done Hogan out of most of his gold, he likely won't forget about us."

"We no have the *perro* with us," said El Lobo.

"No," Wes said, "and I regret leaving him behind. Empty's saved my life more than once, sniffing out bushwhackers."

"We'll split up," said Silver. "I'll continue following the wagon. Wes, you'll ride maybe a mile to the east, and Palo, you'll ride a mile or so to the west. Look for tracks where riders may have doubled back."

"Why don't you let me take the ride down the middle?" Wes said. "If Palo or me fail to spot the bushwhackers in time, they could drill you dead-center."

[1] *The Border Empire*

"Because I know you and Palo won't fail," said Silver. "Now ride."

Wes and El Lobo kicked their horses into a lope, leaving in opposite directions, while Silver continued following the tracks of Hogan's wagon. It was Wes who found the fresh tracks of three horses, circling wide, heading back the way they had come. Bryan Silver was in grave danger, and Wes kicked his horse into a fast gallop. He had to spring the trap before Silver rode within Winchester range. The three bush-whackers heard the galloping horse and began firing at Wes. But he reined up, just out of reach. The firing had served as a warning to Silver, and El Lobo came in riding hard, Winchester in hand. The three bush-whackers gave it up and rode madly to catch up with their comrades.

"Well?" said Blanton Hood, when Easterly, Bender, and Arrington reined up.

"They was ready for us," Arrington said. "One of 'em stayed on the trail, while the other two flanked us."

"So you all turned tail like a bunch of scairt wolves," said Hood.

"Our cover wasn't that good," Easterly said. "Hell, I ain't gettin' myself ventilated for a bounty that's to be split twelve ways."

"That goes double for me," said Bender.

"I reckon I'll have to go along with that," Arrington said. "A surprise bushwhacking is one thing, but by God, when they're waitin' for me with Winchesters, that's where I draw the line."

"Damn the three of you," said Blanton Hood. "Now we'll have one hell of a time bushwhacking them, if we're able to at all."

"What was the shooting about?" Hogan asked, slowing his teams.

"Failed ambush," said Hood. "Get them teams moving."

A mile and a half behind, Wes and El Lobo came together with Silver.

"*Bueno*," Silver said. "We'll stay back behind them, well out of range for a while, and let them think about that failed bushwhacking. They'll try again, and when they do, we'll rush them from three sides and gun them down."

But the outlaws, while watching their back trail, made no further attempts to ambush their pursuers.

"I'm a mite tired of this," said Wes. "We could move in at night and give 'em hell with our Winchesters."

"We could," Silver said, "but Hogan's headed for a showdown with whoever's taken the gold. When all these coyotes are bloodied from fighting among themselves, we'll move in. Right now, we're out-gunned four to one. We'll follow along for a while, yet."

The Little Colorado River, May 2, 1885

"They had trouble finding a place to cross," Hogan said exultantly. "This is our chance to catch up to them."

Blanton Hood said nothing. He was well aware that Illivane had been talking quietly to the eight men who had long been riding with him. Nothing had been said to Arrington or Ginsler, friends of Blanton Hood, but Hood kept his silence. He had long heard rumors of Drade Hogan's wealth, and he was virtually certain they were in pursuit of those riches. When at last they caught up to that elusive wagon, Hood would make his move.

"They've had some trouble gettin' across the Little Colorado," said Silver.

"The original wagon tracks lead upstream, and Hogan's following," Wes said. "They'd have a better chance of finding a crossing downstream."

"But that would take them the way they don't want to go," said Silver. "The more I see of this, the more certain I am that whoever has the gold is headed for the Gulf of California and a sailing ship."

Southwestern Arizona, May 5, 1885

Elias Hawk and Hobie Denbow were less than a hundred miles from Yuma when their luck turned sour. The wagon's left rear wheel slammed into an unseen hole, splintering the axle where it passed through the hub.

"Good thing we have a spare axle," said Denbow.

"A mixed blessing," Hawk said. "Replacing it will take time we just don't have."

It was more difficult than they expected, for the ground was soft and the foot of the wagon jack kept sinking into the earth. It would not lift the heavy wagon.

"Damn it," said Hawk, "we'll have to unload it again."

They labored for an hour, unloading the wagon, most of an hour replacing the broken axle, and another hour reloading the wagon. By then it was sundown. They unharnessed the teams for the night and lit a small fire, unaware they were being watched. Hood, Illivane, and Ginsler had ridden far ahead of Hogan's wagon.

"Well," said Illivane, "are we goin' to piddle along with Hogan's wagon, or do we end this chase on our own?"

"We'll end it when I say," Hood replied. "Hogan's still five days behind with that damn wagon. I don't want nothin' said to him about us catchin' up with these coyotes. We'll plan a surprise for them, once they're a little closer to Yuma."

The trio rode back to Hogan's camp, reaching it shortly before midnight. Surprisingly, Drade Hogan was awake and furious.

"Where the hell have you three been?" Hogan demanded. "I'm not paying you to gallivant around at night. I could have been attacked."

"We had some business to take care of," said Hood calmly.

The three of them unsaddled their horses, ignoring Hogan's cursing.

"They're gettin' tired following Hogan's wagon," Wes said. "Where you reckon those three went that rode out tonight?"

"I'm guessing they rode ahead to catch up to the *hombres* that took Hogan's gold," said Silver. "If they have any idea the wagon Hogan's chasing is full of gold double eagles, his life won't be worth a plugged *peso*. Next time they ride out, we'll follow them."

"They could leave Hogan behind, take the other wagon, and be across the border before Hogan could catch up to them," Wes said.

"That's what I'm expecting," said Silver. "Hogan's about to be double-crossed again, and by the very bunch he's brought along to protect him. However all this ends, I think Hogan will get what's coming to him. I want to recover that stolen gold, if we can."

Southwestern Arizona, May 6, 1885

"Even with the trouble we've had," said Denbow, "we'll reach Yuma before that ship's there in the Gulf of California. Then what?"

"We'll cross the border and wait," Hawk replied.

But they were never to reach Yuma or the border. After supper they turned in for the night, and just before dawn, Blanton Hood and five of his followers rode in shooting. They dragged the bullet-riddled bodies of Hawk and Denbow away from the wagon and then tore into the metal containers filled with double eagles.

"Great God Almighty," Ginsler shouted, "we're rich."

"Not till we're rid of Hogan," said Arrington.

"We ought to tell Hogan what we've done, and let him take the gold on to Yuma, or maybe even across the border. Hogan must have some plan for getting past them."

"Maybe you've got something there," Hood said, "but when we tell Hogan we killed the two varmints that double-crossed him, is he gonna believe we don't know what's so damn valuable in this wagon?"

"He'll have no choice," said Illivane. "We'll use him if we can, but if he starts pawin' the ground and raisin' hell, we can always just shoot him."

Hood laughed. "Exactly what I was thinking. Ride back and tell Hogan we're waiting here with the wagon."

"I don't think so," said Illivane. "Send one of your own boys, 'cause I'm looking out for mine."

"Ginsler," Hood said, "ride back and tell Hogan we've captured the wagon, that we'll be waiting for him."

Ginsler rode out, leaving Hood, Arrington, Illivane, Concho, and Hawser. Illivane looked at Hood, and the outlaw laughed. They understood one another. From a distance, Silver, Wes, and El Lobo had witnessed the shooting. They watched with interest as Ginsler rode back the way they had come.

"They're going to use Hogan to get the gold across the border," said Silver. "I think it's time we got ahead of them and rode on to Fort Yuma. A company of soldiers should even up the odds."

"They could travel due south from here and cross the border somewhere to the east of Yuma," Wes said.

"I think Hogan has considerably more in mind than just crossing the border," said Silver. "As you know, Americans—even wealthy ones—are not all that welcome these days in Mexico."

"*Sí*," said El Lobo. "*El Diablo gringos.*"

"Let's ride," said Silver. "If we run into trouble in Yuma, we may need time to get some telegrams off to Washington."

Fort Yuma, Arizona, May 9, 1885

"I'm not doubting your word, Silver," said Major Gately, "but we're right here on the border, and we've had our troubles with Mexico. I will not permit gold belonging to the federal treasury to be taken out of this country."

"But this conspiracy we're trying to destroy may have confederates across the border," Silver argued, "and they'll go free, unless we allow these outlaws to make contact."

"Sorry," said Major Gately. "We'll assist you in capturing these men and recovering the stolen gold, but it will have to take place on American soil."

"The damned military and its rules," Wes said, when they had left Gately's office.

"We'll ride back north a ways," said Silver, "and when we see the wagon coming, we'll tell Gately to be prepared."

"*Sangre de Christo*," El Lobo said. "*Soldados* don't go to Mexico, then I go."

"I'm just thinkin' the same damned thing," said Wes.

"I'm reluctant to end my career with a court-martial," Silver said, "but if there's a real need for crossing the border, I won't stop either of you."

Riding at night, the three of them reached the outlaw camp not more than twenty-five miles north of Fort Yuma.

"Hogan's still alive, and they're headed for Yuma," said Silver. "Let's ride back and wait for them."

There were two wagons now, Hogan driving one taken from Hawk and Denbow, and Albion, one of Illivane's men, driving the other. Hood rode alongside Hogan's wagon.

"You aim to stop at the fort?" Hood asked.

"Certainly not," said Hogan. "We'll travel at night, passing several miles east of the town and the fort. None of you are to go there."

Hood said nothing. Just north of Yuma, they waited for darkness. When Hogan judged it was dark enough, he led out with the first wagon. Suddenly, from the darkness, came a shouted command.

"Halt and surrender your arms. You're all under arrest in the name of the government of the United States."

"Damn you," Hogan shouted, seizing his Winchester.

Three rifles roared, and Hogan fell off the wagon box, dead before he hit the ground.

"We're surrenderin'," one of the outlaws shouted. "Don't shoot."

Silver accompanied the soldiers with their captives, while Wes and El Lobo rode toward the distant border. When they reached the Gulf of California, the rising moon illuminated a sailing ship anchored off shore.

"So that's where they were bound," said Wes. "Let's dismount and go closer."

"Halt," a voice commanded. "*Quien es?*"

"Per'ap who you expect," said El Lobo in a guttural tone. "*Nombre?*"

"Captain Antonio Diaz," the voice said. "You are on Mexican soil. We must sail soon."

"*Bastardo*," El Lobo snarled, "you do not sail again, ever."

Guns roared. Wes and El Lobo fired at the muzzle flashes, and there were groans of anguish. But Diaz had not been hit. He lunged at Wes and El Lobo, the blade of his knife flashing silver in the moonlight. But El Lobo had holstered his Colt and gripped his Bowie in his right hand. He avoided two savage thrusts by Diaz, and with a mighty sweep of the big Bowie, he slashed the front of the Mexican's coat from one side to the other. When Diaz came at him again, knife raised, El Lobo seized the Mexican's wrist. Dragging Diaz to him, he thrust savagely with the Bowie. With a groan of anguish, Diaz went limp, and El Lobo allowed him to slump to the ground.

"You would drown us in California's big water," El Lobo grunted. "Now you pay."[2]

"Come on," said Wes. "All that shooting may bring the border patrol."

They returned to the fort, and Silver was at the gate to meet them.

"I thought I heard shooting," Silver said.

"You did," said Wes. "If there are any medals, see that Palo gets one. Captain Antonio Diaz jumped us with a knife, and Palo taught him a permanent lesson."

"His ship is out there, then," Silver said.

"It is," said Wes, "but it's shy a captain and at least two of its crew."

"*Bueno*," Silver said, "and if it's ever mentioned, I don't know a thing about it. All the captives are in the guardhouse, the gold is in federal custody, and

[2] *Sixguns and Double Eagles*

in the morning I'll get off a full report to Washington by telegraph."

"After that," said Wes, "do us all a big favor and send a telegram to Dodge. There's some folks who'll want to know we're alive."

"I'm ahead of you," Silver said. "I sent that telegram tonight. Tomorrow, after all our business here is done, let's light a shuck for Dodge City."

Dodge City, Kansas, May 15, 1885

"Thank God it's over," said Molly, speaking for them all.

"Molly and me will be in Washington for a month, tying up loose ends," Silver said. "As my last official act, I'm going to recommend for you, Wes, and for you, Palo, a reward of fifty thousand dollars."

"*Por Dios*," said Tamara. "*Por Dios*."

"You meant what you said about retiring to south Texas and startin' a horse ranch, then," Wes said.

"I did," said Silver. "This worn-out old cowboy's goin' home."

"Palo and me will be lookin' around for a few hundred acres with plenty of grass and water," Wes said, "but we won't do anything serious until you and Molly get there."

"We'll be coming," said Silver. "Get yourselves some rooms at the Cattleman's Hotel in San Antone. Then look up Bodie West at the Texas Ranger office and tell him all that I couldn't tell him, the last time we talked. When Molly and me get there, we'll go after some of those wild horses that Nathan Stone and King Fisher loved so much."

"*Bueno*," Wes said, "but before we do anything else, let's find a preacher. I promised Renita we'd tie the knot, and if we do, I don't think Molly and Tamara will let you and Palo out of it."

Empty, the blue tick hound, barked his joy at seeing them all together again.

There's plenty more exciting
Ralph Compton.
Read on for a sneak peek at
Whiskey River.

Waco, Texas, June 25, 1866

Mark Rogers and Bill Harder had a lot in common. While still young men, they had "learned cow" together in south Texas. Later, when they were of age, they had each "proved up" on a half section of land, just north of Waco, on opposite banks of the Brazos River. The combined half sections were an ideal spread, with the Brazos providing abundant water. But when the war came and Texas seceded, Mark and Bill answered the call of the Confederacy, each just a few days shy of twenty-five. Now, after four long years of war, they were going home. They were self-conscious nearing the town, for they were dressed in rags which had once been the proud uniforms of the Confederacy. Neither man was armed, and for lack of saddles, they rode mules bareback. Mark Rogers and Bill Harder were as gaunt as the animals they rode. Entering Waco, the town didn't *look* any different, but somehow, it felt all wrong. They reined up before Bradley's Mercantile. Ab Bradley had known them all their lives, and as they entered the store, he came limping to meet them.

"My soul and body," Ab said. "Mark Rogers and Bill Harder. I heard you was dead."

"There was times when we wished we were, Ab,"

said Mark. "Better that than rotting away in a Yankee prison."

"Yeah," Bill agreed. "All we have is these rags we're wearin', and two poor old mules as hungry as we are. The Yankees stomped the hell out of us, took our guns, and sent us back with our tails between our legs. We heard soldiers would be comin' to put us under martial law until the congress can decide what our punishment should be. Has any of 'em showed up?"

"They have," said Ab gravely. "There's already a full company of them in Austin. But that's not the problem. The problem is the newly appointed tax collectors. First thing they done was re-assess everybody's spread, and them that couldn't pay lost everything. They started out by takin' what belonged to those of you who went to war."

"The sons of bitches," Mark said, "we wasn't here. They've taken our spread?"

"Yours, and a dozen others, all up and down the Brazos," said Ab. "They're bein' held by men armed with scatterguns."

"By God," Bill said, "we'll organize the rest of the rightful owners and raise hell."

"I don't think so," said Ab. "Riley Wilkerson, Mike Duvall, and Ellis Van Horn tried to do exactly that. Without weapons, they attacked armed men and were shot down like stray dogs. The others that come back saw how it was, and left, traveling west. You can fight, but you can't win."

"Legalized murder, then," Mark said.

"That's what I'd call it," said Ab, "but I wouldn't say it too loud."

"Ab," said Bill, "we don't have a peso between us, and I don't know when we'll be able to pay you, but we need grub. Can you help us?"

"Some," Ab said cautiously. "The state's been up

against a blockade, and supply lines still ain't open. All I got is home-grown beef, beans, pork, and corn meal. No coffee, salt or sugar."

"We'll accept whatever you can spare, and be thankful," said Mark.

"You don't aim to back off, then, do you?" Ab asked.

"Hell, no," said Mark. "I don't know what we'll do, but by the Eternal, we'll be doing something."

"Just be careful, boys," Ab said.

"We're obliged to you for the warning," said Bill. "At least we won't be walking into it cold."

Ab filled two gunnysacks with supplies. Mark and Bill thanked the old man and left the store. Nobody paid any attention to the two riders as they rode south. Darkness was several hours away, and they rode into a stand of cottonwood where there was a spring they remembered.

"Whatever bronc we have to ride," Mark said, "I'll feel better jumpin' on it with a full belly."

There was lush graze near the river, and the half-starved mules took advantage of it. Mark and Bill built a small fire over which they broiled bacon. Their meager meal finished, the angry duo set about making plans to reclaim their holdings.

"From what Ab told us," said Bill, "there shouldn't be more than two of these varmints with scatterguns guardin' our spread, and we'll likely find one of 'em holed up in my shack and the other in yours. We can take 'em one at a time and get our hands on them scatterguns."

"That'll bring the soldiers," Mark said. "We can't stand off the damn army with a pair of scatterguns. Besides, we were granted amnesty by signing pledges not to take up arms against the Union."

"Soldiers and amnesty be damned," said Bill. "Just because they beat us don't give 'em the right to move in and rob us blind while we're not here to defend what's ours. Soon as it's dark enough, I'm movin' in. You comin' with me?"

"I reckon," Mark said. "We'll likely light more fires than we can put out, but we can't just let them pick us clean. Hell, we'll do what we have to."

When darkness had fallen, they could see a distant light in the window of each of their shacks. They first approached Bill's spread, and in the dim light from a window there was the dark shadow of a horse tied outside the shack.

"You spook the horse," said Bill, "and I'll get him as he comes out the door."

Taking a handful of rocks, Mark began pelting the horse. It nickered, reared, and then nickered again. It had the desired effect. The door swung open and the man with the scattergun started out. In an instant, Bill had an arm around his throat and a death grip on the muzzle of the shotgun. He drove a knee into the man's groin, and with a gasp of pain, he released the shotgun. As he doubled up in agony, Bill seized the shotgun's stock and slammed it under the unfortunate man's chin.

"One of 'em down," said Bill with satisfaction.

"God Almighty," Mark said, kneeling by the fallen man, "his neck's broke. He's dead."

"I didn't shoot him," said Bill, more shaken than he wanted to admit. "I promised that I wouldn't take up arms, and I didn't."

"We can't leave him here," Mark said. "What do you aim to do with him?"

"Leave him where he is for now," said Bill. "He ain't goin' nowhere. After we've took care of the varmint at your place, we'll dispose of the both of them where they'll never be found. Nobody can prove anything against us."

"Maybe you're right," Mark said. "We've gone too far to back out now."

Mark and Bill found a shallows and crossed the Brazos afoot, Mark carrying the confiscated shotgun.

"Give me the scattergun," said Bill. "If this one goes sour, I'll do the shootin'. So far, they got nothin' on you."

"No," Mark said. "This is my place. I won't have you takin' a rap for what I should have done. This time, you spook the horse and I'll get the drop when the varmint comes bustin' out."

Bill began antagonizing the picketed horse, and the animal reacted predictably. But the animal's owner didn't come busting through the front door. He came around the corner of the house, and Bill threw himself facedown just in time to avoid a lethal blast from the scattergun. Like an echo, Mark fired, and the deadly charge caught the guard in the chest. He collapsed like a crumpled sack in the yard.

"My God," Bill said, "now we're into it."

"So we are," said Mark. "Would you feel better if I'd let him cut you in two with that cannon?"

"This is no time for damned foolishness," Bill said. "There's still a chance we can get out of this, if we can stash this pair where they'll never be found, and do it fast. There'll be rain before morning, and it'll cover our trail. Get a blanket from inside. We don't want blood all over this hombre's saddle, when his horse shows up somewhere."

Riding their mules, they each led a horse with a dead man slung over the saddle. Far down the Brazos, they disposed of both dead men in a bog hole that overflowed from the river.

"A damned shame, lettin' these horses and saddles go, while we're ridin' a broke-down pair of old mules," said Mark.

"Hell of a lot easier than explaining to the law where we got the horses and saddles," Bill replied.

Just for a moment, the moon peeked from behind the gathering clouds, and turning, Mark looked back.

"What are you lookin' at?" Bill asked.

"Them horses," said Mark. "They're followin' us."

"Won't matter," Bill replied. "There'll be rain before daylight."

But the shotgun blasts had been heard at the old Duvall place, and by the time Mark and Bill returned to Bill's shack, they had unwanted company. While the pair still had the weapons they had taken from the dead men, they had no chance to use them. A cold voice from the darkness spoke.

"You're covered, and there's three of us. Drop the guns and step down."